TEMPT ME

Dark Odyssey Book 4

FAITH SUMMERS
KHARDINE GRAY

Copyright © 2020 by Khardine Gray Please note : Faith Summers is the Dark Romance pen name of USA Today Bestselling Author Khardine Gray

All rights reserved.

Tempt Me Book 4 of Dark Odyssey Copyright © 2020 by Khardine Gray

Cover design © 2020 by Book Cover Couture

No part of this book may be reproduced in any form or by any electronic or mechanical means, including information storage and retrieval systems, without written permission from the author, except for the use of brief quotations in a book review.

This work is copyrighted. Apart from any use as permitted under the Copyright Act 1968, no part may be reproduced, copied, scanned, stored in a retrieval system, recorded or transmitted, in any form or by any means, without the prior written permission of the author, except for the use of brief quotations in a book review.

This is a work of fiction. Names, characters, businesses, places, events and incidents are either the products of the author's imagination or used in a fictitious manner. Any resemblance to actual persons, living or dead, or actual events is purely coincidental.

The author asserts that all characters and situations depicted in this work of fiction are entirely imaginary and bear no relation to any real person.

No part of this book may be reproduced in any form or by any electronic or mechanical means, including information storage and retrieval systems, without written permission from the author, except for the use of brief quotations in a book review.

The following story contains mature themes, strong language and sexual situations.

It is intended for mature readers. All characters are 18+ years of age and all sexual acts are consensual.

Dark Odyssey Book 4
USA Today Bestselling Author
Khardine Gray
writing as
Faith Summers

DARK ROMANCE WARNING

WARNING: This book is a standalone **DARK ROMANCE.** This book contains scenes that may be triggering to some readers and should be read by those only 18+ or older. **

AUTHOR NOTE

Please note Faith Summers is the Dark romance pen name of USA Today Bestselling Author Khardine Gray

PLAYLIST

1. Black Lab - Weightless
2. John Legend - All of Me
3. Natalie Imbruglia – Torn
4. Aerosmith - Jaded
5. Goo Goo Dolls - Fearless
6. Taylor Swift - Wildest Dreams
7. Nickelback - How You Remind Me
8. Maroon 5 - She Will Be Loved
9. Katy Perry - The One That Got Away
10. SaberZ - Mandragora
11. Shawn Mendes, Camila Cabello – Señorita
12. Savage Garden - Truly Madly Deeply
13. Sia - Cheap Thrills Ft. Sean Paul
14. JABBAWOCKEEZ x Tiësto - BOOM with Gucci Mane & Sevenn
15. Will.i.am - Scream & Shout ft. Britney Spears
16. The Cranberries - When You're Gone
17. The Calling - Wherever You Will Go
18. Richard Marx - Right Here Waiting

WELCOME TO THE DARK ODYSSEY

We hope you enjoy our masquerade parties.
Our aim is to connect you with your wildest fantasies.
To thrill and excite you all at once in a place where you can just be you.
When the masks go on and the lights go out, you decide what happens next.

PROLOGUE

Vincent

I still remember. I can't forget...
There was so much blood everywhere.
All over her.
Running from her head, right down to her body. Redness and blue. Those were the colors I remember. The red blood, and the blueness of her lips.
Then cold... her body was so cold and limp. Lifeless. Like a doll.
My baby girl may have lain there dead like that for a good hour before I made it home. She lay there in the kitchen with our son crying behind her, enclosed in the safety of the safe room I made for them.
She never made it inside with our boy.
Today marks two years and ten days since it happened, and I still have the image of her playing in my mind. Her sitting there against the wall, slumped against it, the baby crying and the tension of death thick in the room.

I still try to guess what could have happened. Why she never made it in, why she never escaped with the baby. Every time I think of it, I come to the same conclusion: I should have been there.

It was my fault, and as I sit here trying to forget and move on like I'm supposed to, and like I should have, I can't.

I wasn't there when my family needed me the most. I was too busy saving everyone else and falling into the enemy's trap.

No matter how many I kill to get vengeance, it won't be enough. Even cutting off the head of her killer wasn't enough.

I can't avenge her death. And every time I remember what happened, I feel like I failed her and our son.

I brought her into the darkness of my world. The bad boy and the good girl. I did that knowing one day, I'd have to step up and take charge of the family business. I was already in too deep when I married her. Underboss following Frankie's death. I should have left her alone.

Warm fingers flutter over my chest, and I'm brought back to reality. I didn't realize I was staring out into the nothing of the night, not quite seeing anything.

I blink and return my focus to Aurora. She smiles and runs her fingers over my jaw.

"You're miles away," she states, moving a lock of her long brown hair over her shoulder.

It's the hair. That's why I'm with her.

I know I'm an asshole, but I don't care. I'll pick my own medicine to help me do what I have to.

This is what I do to try to ease the guilt from my mind.

Aurora slides up the bed and starts undoing the buttons on my shirt. I should go home, but I can't just yet. Today has been shit, and I need this. I need to escape. After all, isn't that one reason people come to The Dark Odyssey?

The escape.

The escape into fantasy.

I don't have any fantasies, but I'll take the escape. I'll take the respite and the freedom my brothers and cousins provided when they set up this place. A sex club where you can live out any fantasy and be with any woman you choose. With the wild masquerade lingerie parties they hold here, it's all kinds of wild. A mating ground and the playpen for the billionaires. They all come to seek out a play mate.

I don't have to try. I'm Vincent Giordano, and I've never had to try for anything. Never lacked for a woman at my side, and I never will. I come here, and there's always a never-ending supply of them eager to please me, and I take it.

Falling into pleasure is better than rage.

"What do you want me to do to you tonight?" Aurora asks, running her fingers over my chest. She circles over my tattoo of the Japanese character for fire, and her smile widens.

I look up at her and slide my arm behind my head. This woman is a beauty. I'll get lost in her tonight, and then I'll go back to reality and be the leader I'm supposed to be.

"How about I allow you to be creative?" I tell her.

She slides off the bed, and her little red negligee floats about her thighs. "You like when I strip for you... and give you a lap dance. We could start there and see how creative I can get." She runs her hands over her massive tits and grins.

Good... this is my distraction.

It was a good idea to come here tonight. I need to forget my current debacle because I'm like a time bomb waiting to explode.

It's a good thing I didn't find Mark. You don't screw with mobsters and not expect to get burned.

"Yes, you do that," I say to her, and she nods. She's a good girl —that's why I pick her when I come here. She follows instructions well and knows what I want.

And... she looks a little like her. Like my Sorcha. It's the hair. She used to wear her long brown hair down just the way Aurora has it, with the long graceful waves kissing her elbows.

Aurora makes a show of smoothing her hands up to her tits again and circles her nipples, which strain against the lacy fabric.

Her hands go up to the straps, and she pushes them down her slender, silky smooth arms.

I watch, and I'm aroused, but I don't have that intense desire to take her. Not the way I did with Sorcha.

It's always a fuck with these women.

After Sorcha's death, I reverted to the guy I used to be in many ways, changed in others. I fuck to forget, especially when I can't kill.

That's what I'm doing tonight.

Her massive tits bobble when she pushes her negligee down her body and allows it to float down her legs. She's wearing a thong, and her perfect mind works just the way I want it to, so she knows to turn slowly so I can see her ass. The red line of the thong running down the middle of her cheeks only enhances the vision of her.

She gives me a saucy grin and grabs her tits again, squeezing. I smile back.

"Come here," I say. Just then, the fucking phone rings.

She stops when I answer straightaway.

That's what I'm like now, and I'm not thinking about the job when I do that. It's my son I'm thinking of. Timothy.

"Yes," I say in a hurried voice.

"Boss, it's me." It's Tony, one of my men. I bare my teeth and seethe.

My prior rage rushes right back, and I straighten up knowing what his call means, especially when I told him hours ago not to call me unless he had good news for me. Good news as in he found Mark, that piece of shit who thought he could fucking get away with stealing from me.

I told them all that. My brothers included.

"What do you have for me?"

"We found Mark. Salvatore and Gabe found him, but ... there's a complication."

"What the fuck is it?" I ball my fist and tighten my grip on the phone. Mark is a simpleton, a fucking simpleton. He shouldn't have been this hard to find, yet we've spent the last three days looking for him.

"His daughter was there, and... she's seen too much."

"You fool," I snap.

"Boss, there was nothing we could do about it. We caught up with them at the docks. Near the warehouses."

Fuck... fucking Mark. What did he think he was going to do? Swim away from us? And with his daughter?

I didn't even fucking know he had a daughter. Men like him make me sick. You have family and behave the way he does...

Stupid fucktard. I'll teach him a lesson tonight he won't forget. I stand, and Aurora starts putting her clothes back on. I look away from her and gaze around the suite. I need to calm down. I don't want to do any killing tonight, but duty calls, and I won't allow this to drag into tomorrow.

I call Mark a simpleton, but he's actually managed to screw with me in a way no one has.

This is what happens when you trust too much. You get screwed over. This is what happens when you give a man a chance when he looks desperate.

The problem with giving people chances is you facilitate their behavior. You make them worse, and others suffer for it.

I suffered big time.

I reach for my biker jacket and check for my gun. Aurora tenses when she sees it.

"Boss, are you still there?" Tony asks nervously.

"I am. Take them to La Volpe Rossa." That's where we question people. Pa had the place set up just for that. It also makes a good torture chamber for the less cooperative. I think I may need to make full use of the place tonight.

"Okay, got it."

"I'm on my way." I hang up and shove the phone in my pocket.

I start doing up my buttons and shrug into my jacket.

"Will... you be coming back?" Aurora asks. She presses her lips together nervously and folds her hands.

She looks so different when her true nature comes out, what she truly wants. She wants me. She wants this to be more. I know she puts on that act of being sassy and confident, like she's okay with us just fucking around. But I know she's not.

"No," I answer. Disappointment clouds her bright baby blues.

"What about tomorrow? Can I see you then?" She reaches up and touches my jaw. It's supposed to be a tender gesture of affection, but I feel nothing, and she mustn't feel for me either.

"Maybe..." I step away from her, and her hand falls to her side.

This is the part where I should end this. It's nothing. Not for me, and it can't be. I don't feel what she wants me to feel for her, and I won't go down that road again.

I am danger. I am death.

Death is what follows me. I was born with death encoded in my DNA. It follows me, and I exact it.

"Vincent I like seeing you. We have fun together." She gives me a nervous smile and her eyes beg me for what I can't give her. "Please try to—"

I hold up my hand and stop her. "Don't. Don't fall for me sweetheart. I can't be with you that way."

The light of hope in her eyes goes out and a dimness takes its place.

A stab of guilt tugs at my dead heart but I push it away. It's something I can't entertain, definitely not right now.

I turn and leave without another word.

I jump on my bike full of rage when I think of Mark and what the fuck this night will bring.

Like a beast I ride with animalistic fury, death on my mind.

CHAPTER ONE

Ava

2 hours earlier...

I open the apartment door, and my heart lifts when I hear the shuffle coming from the living room.

Rushing inside, I see him. *Dad.*

He looks a mess, but he's here.

My poor, terrified heart leaps with joy and relief and at the same time it shudders when he grabs the gun from the table and tries to point it at me.

When he sees it's me though, a bewildered look floods his face and a tear runs down his cheek.

"Oh God, Ava... Jesus." He winces, his hands shaking so much he drops the gun, and it clanks against the wooden floor.

I'm too happy to see him to worry about the gun. I rush over to him and wrap my arms around him.

"Dad, where were you? God... where *were* you?" I cry. Three days. I've been looking for him for the last three days and cursing myself for leaving him on Sunday when we had dinner and argued.

When I couldn't find him, I thought the worst happened. I truly did.

"Ava, you have to leave me," he says, pulling away. His usually vibrant green eyes are brimming with panic, terror even.

Something's happened. Something more. And he's high.

"Dad, why? Where have you been?" I demand. "I've been worried sick. You're using again... aren't you?"

His pupils are dilated like the usual drug addict, and he reeks of alcohol.

Fuck... Who knows what the drugs must be doing to a man of his age. He's nearly sixty-seven. He used to be healthy and a man who would never turn to drugs, but life has been so cruel to us.

To him.

"Ava, please, you need to go. Leave me. I can't have you here, not now, sweet girl. Please, just listen to me. Please," he begs.

I shake my head, and he runs a hand through his thick graying hair. Bloodshot eyes stare back at me with the same plea for me to leave, but I'm not going anywhere. I shouldn't have left him in the first place.

I don't mean Sunday. No. I mean I shouldn't have moved out after Sasha was killed.

Dad didn't live here then. In this dank and dinky little apartment.

We had a house. A home he provided for us to live in as a family. Then he lost it when drugs infiltrated his life.

I shouldn't have listened to him and believed he would be okay by himself. How could he have been okay? With his last son dead and me gone. *How?*

I was a coward, and like everything, I blamed myself for it. Maybe I left because I could no longer face him. The pain was too much. It's hard to blame yourself for everything whether it happens as a direct result of your actions or not.

I'm not leaving this time. He's begging me to go, but he

needs me. What I need to do is get him off the drugs and take care of him the way he took care of me when I needed him.

"Dad, please. Listen, let's go back to the clinic. Dr. Cooper said we can come anytime you need him. Let's just go." It's eight now. After his last stint in rehab, the doctors were certain Dad would be back.

I tried to be positive, but I knew they were right. That was close to eight months ago. He looked like he was doing okay, but there were signs that he wasn't.

"Come, Dad, let's go. You and me. We can do this. We can, right?"

"No, Ava, I can't go to the clinic. He'll kill me. You too if he finds you, and I can't let that happen." His voice shakes, and tears roll down his cheeks.

My heart stills and fright sweeps through me. I don't know what he's talking about. Or *who* he's talking about. I wish I could blame the drugs and believe he's talking like that because he's high. The terrified look in his eyes tells me different though, as well as the cold pulsing knot that's formed in my stomach.

He's serious.

What has he gotten himself into this time?

"What's going on, Dad? Who are you talking about?"

He shakes his head and moves away from me, back to packing his duffel bag on the table.

I reach for his arm and wince when I feel how frail he is. This is a man who was built of solid muscle at one point. Tall like a giant and as strong as an ox. That's what Mom used to say.

He looks to me and shakes his head. "Please, Ava, leave me before it's too late. Go now."

"What have you done? Why would someone want to kill you?" My voice quivers, and tears sting the backs of my eyes. "What did you do?"

"Something terrible. Terrible things that I can't get out of. I did bad things. Gambling and shit... I borrowed some money. I can't pay it back. I ...can't pay it back, Ava. It's too much," he sputters, tripping over his words as he tries to get them out. "It's only a matter of time before he finds me. I can't keep running. I'm too tired and too weak. Too drained." He chokes back a cry and starts panting.

I can't believe what I'm hearing. My mind races along a thousand miles per hour thinking of what to do.

He said *pay back*. If this is about money, I'll pay it back. I don't have much. I'm still paying back the last loan he got, and that drained me.

"I'll pay it back, Dad," I offer.

"You can't... Not this time."

"How much is it?"

He starts crying harder and is shaking. I know then that it's more than the ten grand he got last time to pay his rent arrears. He borrowed that from some bookies, and I paid to keep us out of trouble. Who does he owe this time?

I feel worse when he brings his hand to his head and breaks down.

How did I not see this coming? I visit him three times a week. It was just that he seemed to be doing okay. He works as an accountant and is always busy. I thought that meant he was busy at work.

I would be an idiot if I didn't know it was the anniversary of Sasha's death that triggered him. It's been six years now, but the pain is the same. We went to the cemetery, and I remember he looked from me to the grave and said, "*I wish I could have saved him.*"

I couldn't have felt worse because he was so busy saving me, he didn't see that his own son was in trouble.

The last two months, things were neither here nor there. I sensed Dad was going through his own trouble and I didn't listen to those gut instincts.

I'm too late again.

God... I can't do this. I can't walk down memory lane and the path of guilt. Not tonight. First things first. I need to get him back to the rehab center, then we'll talk about the money later. I'll ask Freddie for an advance or get a loan. *I'll do something.*

"Dad, let's go to the clinic and sort this out tomorrow."

A loud knock pounds on the door, making us both jump.

Dad's eyes go wide. "Oh Jesus, no." He looks at the door I just came through then snaps his gaze to me. "They found me. You need to go."

My heart slams in my chest, and my lungs tighten painfully. He looks to the window when the pounding on the door comes again. He means for me to take the fire escape, but I'm not leaving without him.

Instinct takes over. Instinct, adrenaline, and the need to survive.

"You are coming with me. I will never forgive you if you stay and get yourself killed," I proclaim with balled fists.

The person is now kicking against the door. If I didn't believe Dad was in danger before, I believe it now.

"Ava—"

"Come." I grab his hand and drag him to the long French window.

I prize it open, and the crisp night air stings my cheeks. We get out onto the shaky metal steps and start our descent. It's unstable, but we don't waste time. We make good speed getting down them, and I'm glad Dad is cooperating.

I don't know what I'm doing. I can't believe what I'm doing. I just know we have to try.

We get to the bottom of the stairs, and I take his hand. My car is parked just around the corner by the convenience store. I run with him, practically pulling him along.

We manage to get to my car, and I get him inside, but before I can get in, a man runs around the corner by the tallest lamp post and starts calling to us to stop.

When another man jumps on his motorcycle, I jump in the car and gun the engine.

I drive top speed running a red light, panic fueling me.

I'm driving, but I don't know where the fuck to go. I glance in the rearview mirror and see I have two bikers on my ass, on bikes that look like they were pulled from the set of

The Terminator. Joining them in the chase is a midnight black Ferrari.

I'm screwed... fucked.

I glance at Dad, who has his eyes trained on the men chasing us, a muscle twitching in his jaw.

Where can we go?
Who are these people?
How much does Dad owe that this is happening to us?
How much is it?

We're driving, and I can't think straight.

It's almost like I'm coaxed into driving toward the docks. I hate going there at any time, let alone at this time of night. I absolutely hate it. The place is too enclosed and suffocating. I know mobsters hang out there too. I can feel it, and that's enough for me to stay away. Anyone with half a brain would do the same, yet here I am, driving straight to more danger.

I have no choice though—that's where the road curves. Other than driving through the apartment complex—and I mean literally driving through the walls of the place—I have to take this road.

I speed up, going a hundred miles an hour, and flip the car around the next corner, hoping to lose our friends. It works, but only because there's a truck passing.

I take the stroke of luck I was just handed and speed faster. *One fifty.* I've never even driven past the hundred mark. Now I know I'm sure to get more than a ticket. I'll probably be banned from driving for life.

I wonder if the judge will understand that we were fleeing for our lives, and fleeing is exactly what we are doing because we're still facing the problem of going to the docks, meaning eventually, we'll run out of roads. There'll be nothing but Lake Michigan all around us.

What will we do? Swim?

Fuck.

On that thought, I turn down another road. I think we need to get out and hide. If we can hide somewhere, then we may be okay. We could hide out until morning and go to the police.

I verge onto a road that's completely deserted. There are large warehouses all around that are probably used as storage facilities because there're no signs on them.

"Ava, there's nowhere else to go," Dad states.

"I know. We have to hide."

I park up by the corner of the furthest warehouse, and we get out. We're parked practically in an alleyway. It's dark enough to keep close to the shadows and not be seen. Someone can see us though if they're looking hard enough.

We keep close to the shadows and run. It's Dad who's pulling me now, holding my hand like that terrified girl I was so long ago who needed him.

It seems like the ride sobered him up. He doesn't seem so stoned. There's an air of the man he used to be taking over as he runs with me, protecting me.

We get to the end of the road, and my heart freezes when I hear it.

A motorcycle engine.

Dad tightens his grip on me. Holding my hand like he never wants to let me go.

We turn to the right then to the left looking for an escape, but we're stuck. The road is a dead end, and there's nowhere to go besides back where we came or climb up the side of the warehouse.

The sound of the motorcycle is getting closer.

Dad looks up at the side of the warehouse, flicks his gaze to me, and takes my shoulders.

"Ava, please go. It's me they want."

I'm shaking my head before he can even finish the words. "No. You want me to just leave you here so they can kill you?" Tears blind my eyes.

I don't know what to do and where to go. I don't know what the hell to do. How could I just leave? I can't.

"I promised her... your mother. I promised her I'd look after you." He nods, and my soul shivers at the mention of my mother.

I don't think he knew that promise was going to be his curse. Although I think he would have still made the promise, even after everything that's happened.

He would have still done everything the same.

"I loved her so much. Please, go. Let me keep my promise one last time," he begs.

"No, Dad—"

"Don't," he cuts me off. "Don't call me that. It's not true... and I hate it. I hate that it's not true, because you should have been mine."

My mouth falls open. I don't know what feels worse—his painfilled words or the situation.

It brings the past right back to the forefront of my mind, along with helplessness.

He's never said that to me before. I'm certain he wouldn't if he were himself. We don't talk about the truth, *ever*. Not ever. And we can't talk about it now.

He's my father, no matter what. No matter the truth. The truth of the past that I can't think of now. Neither of us can, so just like every time when the past attempts to haunt me, I push it away. I push it right to the back of my mind and focus on the present. The here and now, where we're in danger.

"Come with me, please," I beg, but he pushes me away.

Dred fills me when he starts walking back the way we came, toward the sound of the oncoming motorcycles. I rush after him, grabbing his arm.

"Dad, no," I wail.

His words are stolen when a motorcycle leaps over one of the warehouses and lands a few feet away from us. Whoever is on it is some daredevil. The other cyclist speeds around the corner along with the Ferrari.

We never stood any chance.

Maybe I did, though. I could have left him, but that's not a thought I'm going to entertain.

Dad puts his arms around me and holds me as the first biker whips off his helmet. He's a tall, muscular Italian man. The other biker does the same, and I can tell straightaway they're brothers.

Two other men file out of the car, then more come. They're carrying guns.

We can't escape. We can't even try...

What will happen now?

The first biker comes closer, and Dad holds me tighter.

"Salvatore, please. Salvatore, Gabe, please just let my girl go," Dad begs.

I'm shaking so much I can't think. I can't.

The first guy he referred to as Salvatore doesn't answer. He just pulls me from Dad's arms, and I scream. He's strong. Too strong.

The other guy called Gabe counters Dad.

"Please, Gabe," Dad says.

"Mark, you really stepped over the line," Gabe answers.

"I know—"

Gabe hits Dad, and he falls to the ground. I scream again, but my screams are muffled when something pungent hits me. It covers my face and strikes my mind.

My lids grow heavy, and it's like my mind is folding in on itself.

"Call the boss. Tell him we got Mark," I hear someone say. Then darkness surrounds me.

CHAPTER TWO

VINCENT

I already know I'm not going to like what's to come from the minute I pull up outside La Volpe Rossa.

The place looks like an ordinary Italian bistro. It's massive and could hold about two hundred people. The interior and exterior are stylishly decorated too, like the other restaurants that line Main Street, but what goes on behind those doors is anything but ordinary.

Pa bought the building and built it up over twenty years ago. Before that, it was a rundown dry cleaner with the signs falling off, and home to all kinds of vermin.

Now, it's a Michelin-starred restaurant listed as one of Chicago's finest. The top section is for the elite. For bosses in our alliance to hold meetings. Some of the most top-secret alliances and plans have taken place in here, and in true La Costa Nostra style, they've been secret as fuck.

The bottom, the basement, has seen me there far too often

over the last few months. I'm there almost as much as I am home or at The Dark Odyssey. Some dumb shit is always rubbing me the wrong way, or maybe it's just that I've gotten more vigilant and I'm not as tolerant as I used to be.

I'm older. I'm forty-four, and I'm not the lighthearted boss I was when I first got the title.

The men outside look tense, like they always do when they see me. It's respect and fear mixed together. Most of them are long-time patrons who knew my parents right from Italia. Some work for Pa, others are associates in some other way.

They bow their heads when I approach, and I do the same.

I walk in through the glass doors that swing inward when I push them open. I'm greeted with the aroma of food that reminds me that I haven't eaten since lunch. There's only a handful of people in here tonight.

Good.

I'm already too worked up to be around a crowd and probably should have gone through the back. I'm furious as fuck about Mark's daughter tied up in this. In all honesty, there's only one way I should handle the shit of the situation. Too many have already suffered because of his selfishness and recklessness.

I go through the *Staff Only* door and walk down the corridor past the kitchen, where the chefs are joking around about who's doing the late shift.

They don't see me.

That's good too. The rage inside me wants to unleash. It's times like these when I'm irrational and I can't get a handle on myself. Unfortunately, sometimes the people I care about the most get bruised from my wrath.

One chef, Chef Romi, has known me since I was a kid. I don't want to make a guy like him scared of me tonight.

The air changes when I near the end of the corridor. It's like the line of demarcation, warning that what's to come next is violence.

I take the stone steps down, listening to the slow drip of a broken tap outside. We need to get that fixed. I swear on nights like these, though, it's part and parcel of the danger that lurks in the dark. Mobsters at their finest.

Mobsters and monsters. Sometimes we're the same thing. I don't think I'm much different.

Salvatore meets me at the door as I go down the last set of stairs. I'm in the basement now. He doesn't look good. He looks as tense as I feel, and I know it's to do with the girl. I wish she weren't here too. This kind of thing hasn't happened in a while, but it's always messy when there're witnesses or people who get caught up. Wrong place or wrong time.

"Hey, they're down there," Salvatore says with a sigh.

"They give any more trouble?"

"No, they're just scared."

I'm glad he and Gabe have been on the case with me. The whole damn problem started at Renovata, my investment company, but Mark dragged everyone else in too when he thought it was a good idea to try and steal from the family business.

My damn fault again.

Mark has worked for me for the last eight years. I thought he was the best person to trust when it came to handling my business accounts. That just gave him access to fuck with our lives.

All the man did was make me look bad in the worst way. Now I have my brother looking at me with a question in his eyes. I know what it is even before he asks.

"Ava Knight, age twenty-six, magazine editor. *Journalist. Press. Media.* What are you going to do with the girl, Vin?" he asks cautiously.

That info was him laying the cards on the table. Laying down things I would have found out and known they put us at risk of exposure.

"She's seen too much," he adds.

Seen too much, but what does she know?

I wonder if Ava Knight knows what her father did.

Does she know how much he owes?

How long he's been stealing from me and taking me for a fucking fool? I think this grates me the wrong way because the records showed that he stole from me when I was at my lowest. Right after Sorcha was killed in cold blood. The man used that as a gateway to rob me to fund his little habits.

That's not what tonight's about though. That's small fry in comparison to the recent shit. Mark deserves death at least, for the dumb fucked-up shit he did that could have gotten people killed.

Salvatore looks at me waiting for an answer that I can't give just yet.

"Vin," he prods, then his eyes go wide. He must think I'm going to kill her. "*Vin,* think before you do anything. Hurting women isn't our way."

It was me who instilled that concept into him, and the rest of them. *Me...* not even Pa. I've been the eldest for close to ten years now, and it's me who made sure all the boys knew the code we live by.

I get it though. I've changed. That's what happened. I've changed, and everyone knows it. When Sorcha was killed, I became the beast.

A heartless, merciless, soulless creature.

That's why my brother is giving me the reminder.

I look at his face and think of how similar we look. He's not like me though. He hasn't been through the same things as me, so he won't understand that rage is what courses through my blood, as it does my mind.

I look away from him and move to the door of the room holding my captives, leaving him staring after me with worry in the dark hue of his eyes.

Pushing the door open makes it creak, and I'm greeted with the sound of a woman sobbing.

It's the girl.

My gaze lands on Mark holding her as they sit in the corner

of the dank room. The lighting is dim, but it's bright enough to see them. Mark with his salt and pepper hair pressed against his daughter's long brown hair that's a matted mess. Fear oozes from them. It's so thick it could be tangible.

The fear is visible when he looks up and sees me. At least I can give this motherfucker some credit for looking ashamed. *Ashamed*, and from what I can see, stoned.

Stoned from drugs he bought with my money.

I'm not a saint, and I won't claim to be anything other than the mobster I am, but fuck, the first rule we know to follow as Giordanos is to keep our heads out of shit. This man has not only turned cops toward me but the fucking feds, *again*.

Bastard.

I hate feds more than I ever did because they were involved in the whole plot to destroy me which resulted in Sorcha's death.

"Get up and fucking come here," I order him, and I'm glad he has the good sense to do as I say.

He shuffles out of the girl's arms and is visibly shaking. I look to her, and my frown deepens when I see her tear-stained face.

She's beautiful, has the kind of beauty that's striking and makes you want to stop and stare. It's pure beauty, and the innocent plea in her eyes makes me think she couldn't have known what her old man's been up to.

At least I don't think so. She looks at me, and more tears stream down her blotchy cheeks.

My eyes drift down what I can see of her body, curled in as she hugs her knees to her chest.

She shouldn't be here. Something about the way she looks at me gets me though. Her stare seeps into me and touches something deep down. Something locked away. I don't know what that something is... it's not my soul, and I can't take the time now to acknowledge it. Eight years I've known Mark, and I never thought to look a little deeper into his family.

I never had any cause to, and other than the standard checks to make sure my staff are suitable for my business, I don't dig deeper than that.

I snap my gaze back to Mark and reach for my gun in my back pocket. Ava cries harder when she sees it.

"Kneel!" I shout. My voice carries across the room.

Mark drops to his knees, and I look at him.

Mercy is the thing that cripples us.

I will not give it tonight. People don't take the act of mercy to mean what it should—they see it as weakness for a guy like me.

"So, how are you going to pay me back? Two million dollars, Mark, and my name gone out the door just like that. You gambled away two million dollars of my money and tied me up with drugs and prostitution," I begin.

I'm not looking directly at Ava, but out the corner of my eye I see her flinch at the snapshot of the revelation of the truth.

"I'm sorry, Vincent. I'm so sorry. Please... I'll pay you back," Mark says with a nod, like he really believes he can pay me back.

I actually laugh, although I feel like starting my damage with his knees. Blow off his kneecaps and work my way up. I laugh, and it's not laughter or humor. It's a crude sardonic sound that pours from me.

"How the fuck are you going to do that? I want it now!" I lash out and knock him over with the back of my gun. Ava screams, and it throws me off. It's another reason why she shouldn't fucking be here. "You motherfucker, evil bastard. You know you can't fucking pay it back. I'm your boss. I don't pay you that much, and obviously, you no longer have a fucking job with me. What do you really expect me to do here?"

Mark wiggles back on his arms crying like the motherfucker he is.

"Please, Vincent. I had some problems... I wasn't thinking straight," he sputters.

I cock the gun and fire one bullet that hits the wall. I can't take this shit. "You have problems? You fucking bastard. You started stealing from me when *I* had problems." I'm talking like I still don't have those same problems. "That's when this started. What do you want me to do? John was beaten to near death because the Montagues thought it was him who was stealing from them. But it was you. He's in the hospital now with two broken legs. Wife and children at his side. How is that fair? Dino nearly lost an eye and got a bullet in his arm because the Stevensons thought it was him who was stealing from them. But it was you. Should I continue?"

I prod because there's fucking more. The two million is just the start. That was what he took from me personally.

To date, the total amount of money Mark has had in his fucking hands is two and a half million. *Motherfucker.*

"I'm sorry," Mark wails, but I can't take it. Not another second more of his sorrys.

I fire a round of shots at the wall and grab his throat. I hold the gun to his head and growl, "I should kill you dead!" I get ready to cock the gun again.

"Noooo!!!" Ava wails. I don't know how she moves so fast. She rushes over and throws herself on me, at my feet.

I don't know anyone who would dare do that. She doesn't know me, or know of me, and she doesn't seem to care that the look of me is warning enough to stay away.

I glare at her as she starts begging, and *this*…. this is another reason why she shouldn't be here.

"Please, have mercy! Please, please, have mercy on him."

Fucking fuck… she's begging for the very thing I've learned to hate.

Mercy.

I have her father by the throat in one hand, looking like he's ready for the end. And she's at my feet begging me. She looks up at me, and I see her eyes properly for the first time, couldn't have seen them before from all the way over here. Not in this light.

They're bright green, but there's a slight hint of brown around the rim of the iris that blends into the green. Rare and striking.

Our eyes lock, frozen in time, and I look beyond the terror and see pain. I recognize it. It's pain as dark as mine.

Pain filled with suffering. Pain mixed with guilt. Pain mixed with terror. It's not the terror from the situation at hand.

It's older.

What I see in her eyes is older. Maybe that's the something I felt moments ago. It's back now, and it beckons me to stop. Stop what I'm doing.

I'm shocked to shit when I feel my grip loosen around Mark's neck. I continue to stare, and while I've loosened my hold on Mark, the gun's still cocked.

She sniffles and gulps air, breaking the trance. "Please, I beg of you. Don't kill him."

"He can't pay," I counter. I don't know why the hell I say that. We all know that fact.

She glances at her father and pants, then she returns her gaze to me.

"Take me..." she stutters, her voice a hush.

"No!" Mark cries before I have time to process her words. I look from one to the other and tighten my grip on Mark once more.

"Take me instead. I'll do anything," she says with more insistence.

My gaze intensifies on her. I can't believe what I'm hearing.

"Ava, no, don't!" Mark wails.

I glower at this bastard. It shouldn't have come to this. I squeeze his neck hard, and he gasps for air, trying to catch his breath.

"Take me!" Ava screams, taking my hand, surprising me again. The gun isn't far from her. "Take me instead. Please don't hurt him. Don't kill him. Please."

She's serious.

Fucking hell, what the hell am I supposed to do with that offer?

I look to her and know what she means.

Take her instead of killing her father....

I don't know what to be furious with more. I'm not a good person, but maybe I'm not evil enough yet to kill a man because he owes me millions and damaged my na... when his daughter is pleading with me for his life. Begging me to... ... M... m not evil enough to avoid showing *her* mercy.

It's not him. It's her. It would be her I would be giving this lenient act.

I can't leave here with nothing though.

I lower the gun and look her over. Now her eyes show a different panic as she realizes what I'm doing.

It's like she can't believe it. I can't either. I can't believe my rage isn't emptying a round of bullets in Mark's gut.

"Salvatore!" I call out, and Salvatore comes through the door.

He freezes when he sees them at my feet.

"Vin," he says my name tentatively.

"Take her to the house," I order him like he's my servant. He might be second in command to me, but he's not my slave.

He won't question me here though. He wouldn't in front of people like this. The look he gives me is enough, but he knows not to fuck with me.

Mark starts shouting the minute Salvatore takes Ava.

"What are you going to do to him!" Ava screams. It mingles with Mark's agony-filled shouts. "Wait, no," she cries, pulling against Salvatore's arm.

She may be ballsy, but her petite frame is no match for anybody.

"Get her out of here," I tell Salvatore.

"No!" she cries.

"Look, lady, you better shut the fuck up, or your old man gets it now."

That silences her, but she's still looking at me.

"Come on, doll," Salvatore says and has to practically lift her up to get her to go with him.

She's crying as she goes, but I can't worry about that.

I have to think about what I'm doing. This is the first thing to truly test me in years, and it's a big test.

I look back to Mark as he shakes and cries so hard my own hand shakes.

What the hell am I going to do with this fucking prick? And his daughter... what am I going to do with her too?

Am I seriously going to accept her offer?

CHAPTER THREE

Ava

I'm taken away from the place blindfolded. We drive in silence, or rather as silent as I can be while I sob.

What just happened?

What really happened tonight?

Is it real or a nightmare?

Dad... how could he have gotten himself into so much trouble? The drug use was just the tip of the iceberg. I just got the visual of so much more.

And... what did I agree to?

What did I offer?

A swap, a trade.

A swap for what? I said I'd do anything. I can make some very foolish decisions. But this... I didn't know what to really call it. I was trying to save Dad. So, what did I offer?

My body. The answer comes to the forefront of my mind and pangs of terror race down my spine. What else could my offer mean?

It's clear I'm offering my body.

After all I've been through, how could I do such a thing? But... what else could I do? I have nothing left to give.

My mind flutters and my stomach churns. *Jesus*... I start whimpering and trying to cry without making too much sound.

The blindfold is only removed once the car stops about forty minutes later.

I blink and register the fortress of a house before me, rising into the night like a castle.

It's large and impressive, comparable to a stately home. The architecture has a gothic European feel to it, but even in the dark I can see it's been modernized. I don't get the chance to look properly, of course; it's so I can't identify my surroundings. Salvatore opens the door and picks me out of the car the same way he put me in. Not rough and forceful, just dominant, and I know if I want to have some hope of saving Dad, I need to comply.

I'm numb, so I don't even register that I'm barefoot until my feet touch the cold ground.

Guards meet us at the entrance of the house. And as we walk into an expansive entryway with double doors and a high ceiling it feels like going into some official's home. I guess it must be. They all called that guy—Vincent—boss.

This house already looks like someone wealthy and important lives here. I guess too that if Dad stole two million dollars from him, then that's the kind of wealth I'm looking at, or more.

Salvatore leads me up a wide set of stairs with an ornate crystal chandelier hanging from the ceiling. We continue down a corridor with marble flooring and go into a bedroom. I walk in, but he hangs back at the door.

Once again, I'm in the biggest shit life can throw my way, but as the lights go on, I take note that the room is beautiful. Fit for a princess. There's a queen-sized bed in the center with a gold chandelier hanging above it. The lights look like pure starlight. The colors of the room are cream with soft ashes of rose pink.

Nice... but maybe for someone else.

Not me, who's being held here, captive. Or... whatever it is I am. I have no idea what's going on.

He didn't say.

Vincent.

He never said anything when I posed the offer. He lowered his gun, and while my heart lifted, my poor soul wept for myself. I still don't know, though, if it's a yes or no to my offer. What if it's not what I thought?

What if Dad's dead? What if Vincent killed him already?

"You will stay here," Salvatore says, cutting into my thoughts. "Someone will bring you up some food in a few minutes."

I open my mouth to say his name, but I stop myself.

I shouldn't do that. No names.

I don't think it would bode well for me if I showed that I know their names. Although they didn't exactly make any attempt to hide them. I picked out a few: Salvatore, Gabe, and Vincent.

"Please, can you tell me what's happening?" I ask, my voice quivering.

He looks me over, and there's a softness about his expression that's not as vicious as his brother. They're all brothers. I can tell. They all look too similar not to be. The boss looks the toughest.

Salvatore looks hesitant. "We'll just have to wait and see."

"What will happen next?"

"Doll, please... no more questions." He shakes his head, and I bite the inside of my lip. "We don't like questions and definitely not the kind we have no answer to. I don't have to tell you that your father is in a lot of trouble. We'll just have to wait and see what happens."

His phone rings, and he answers, glances at me, then starts speaking in Italian. That's because of me. He doesn't want me to hear what he's saying, or rather understand it. But I do.

Mom wanted me to learn it, so I did. It's one of the five languages I speak and understand so well I could be native.

Salvatore is saying he's going home to his wife and child.

I notice a wedding band on his finger. What kind of woman would marry into this? The mob.

These men are all mobsters. The kind that frighten me. I'm well versed in their type. No matter where they come from in this world, they're all the same. You can't trust them.

It seems like he's talking to Vincent. He asks about Dad but gives nothing away in terms of whether Dad's alive or not.

Salvatore ends his call and returns his attention to me. "Stay here and do not move. Enough shit has already happened tonight. You understand me?"

I nod my understanding quickly, and he leaves.

There's a chair nearby for me to sit on, a bed for me to lie in, a little sofa by the window bay, yet I move to the wall and sink down to the floor, resting my back against the wall with my knees hugged to my chest.

It's then I allow the tears to truly come. The numbness leaves me as I cry. Someone does bring me food. I don't know who it is, or touch it, because I'm too numb to eat. Eating is the last thing I could possibly think of doing in a situation like this.

I don't know if Dad is alive or dead. I have no idea.

All those things he did, all those people who were hurt by it. He's right. He did do terrible things. It's terrible. All so terrible.

I can't excuse his behavior. How could I? It all involved money. All of it, and there's only one thing Dad uses money for: drugs.

Nobody would have two million dollars in their possession and live in that gritty little apartment. It's drugs. He used all that money to buy drugs, and there was mention of prostitution.

It makes me sick to think of him with hookers, but shit, I'm not even thinking of the glaring thing I never knew. Dad worked for mobsters.

Vincent is his boss.

Why would he take a job like that after all we've been through?

He's been working with Vincent all this time at Renovata, and I didn't know he was working for a mobster. I thought he had a normal job. I'm so stupid. Dad's the kind of man who does what he has to, to survive.

Mobsters though? And, they seem to be the worst kind. They have serious money.

Now, what the hell's going to happen?

I'm still trying to figure out how I missed all the signs that Dad was in so much trouble. Have I been so wrapped up in myself that I didn't see all the signs? This occurrence tonight isn't just a sudden thing that's happened. It's been brewing a while. I've had my own stuff to deal with at work though.

The opportunity that would change everything for my career came about a few months ago, and I got sidetracked. I know I did. I won't deny it.

There was a competition to do the special edition issue on Coral Winters, and I got down to the final two. It was something I could only dream of. I was excited, and apart from getting to study at Browns, it seemed like the first time I was truly getting to do something I loved. Browns was the steppingstone. The place that furnished me with my journalism talents. But coming home and landing the junior editor's position at *Escada*, one of the most prestigious women's lifestyle magazines, was something else. It almost felt like I could have some part of my life back.

Now this...

What am I going to do?

Assuming they don't kill me, what will I do?

Hours pass while I sit and worry. The tears dry up, and my head dips as sleep claims me.

I must have been out for a few minutes when the door creaks open. It startles me, and I jump.

It's him.

Vincent.

My gaze goes straight to his face. He's looking at me, and I can't quite read what he's thinking.

All I want to know is if Dad's okay.

The shaking resumes, but cautiously, I rise to my feet and run a hand through my hair while I press into the wall.

"There's a bed you could have lain on if you were tired," he states, glancing over at the bed. "Why didn't you sleep in it?"

With his piercing dark brown eyes trained on me, he walks in, and just from his stride in those black slacks, it's evident he's the leader.

He's tall with solid muscle and has that edge to him that's rugged and raw. I place him at being in his early to mid-forties for the slight gray that graces his temples. He's one of these men, though, who could be a hundred and would obliterate a twenty-year-old guy in a fight.

He unzips his black leather biker jacket, revealing a gray T-shirt, then quirks a dark brow to study me. Probably as much as I study him.

He wants an answer to his question. It's clear he's not the kind of man you don't answer, even if you're scared shitless.

"I didn't want to sleep," I reply.

He walks up to me, filling up my personal space, and stops far too close. I try to hold his gaze but can't, so I bring my hands together and look down at them instead.

I can't look at him because I don't know what he's done to Dad, and if he's killed him, I don't want him to see me crumble if he confirms that as truth.

To my surprise, however, he reaches forward and catches my face, lifting my jaw up with his forefinger so my eyes can meet his.

He's tall, tall, at well over six feet, and I have to crane my neck to truly look him in the eyes the way he wants. I hate myself for thinking in that moment that he's handsome. Dangerous and beautiful all at the same time.

"Did you kill him?" I ask, my voice weak and broken with a rasp.

The corners of his mouth slide up into a little smile. It's like the laugh of sarcasm earlier. Not funny. Not even close. "No, I did not. I'm still trying to decide what to do with the two of you. Especially you, Ava Knight."

"You... know my name."

"Don't you know mine? Your father said it several times. I guess that skipped over introductions."

A chill races through me. He's obviously checked me out. What else does he know?

"What are you going to do with him? Is he safe?"

"For now. He's safe for now. What I'm not sure about," he pauses and drops his hand from my chin, "is if you truly know who your father is. I don't know if you'd still think he was worth a trade."

"He's not a bad person. He just lost his way," I say quickly, too quickly.

His brows knit together, and his eyes crinkle. He tilts his head to the side, allowing a lock of his hair to fall over his eye. It draws my attention to the silver taper of the edges.

"Bellezza," he begins.

Bellezza... I'm familiar with the Italian endearment used often to describe a beautiful woman. I just don't like it coming from him.

"Bellezza," he says again with slightly more emphasis. "I think you have a very clouded view of who your father is. No one in that room with you tonight can be considered not bad." He's talking about himself too. "You know what's worse? I keep finding out more things that your father did to rub me the wrong way. Right now, I'm not sure if I should be more upset that my money was used for him to sleep with barely legal girls or if I should be mad as fuck that he tried to drag me into the shit too with the cops or feds."

I blow out a ragged breath. It can't be the same person he's talking about. That's not my father. He wouldn't do that.

I look down again, then back to him. "He has a drug problem, and things haven't been the same for him since my brother died," I say, but I know it's useless.

Maybe I'm looking for some kind of explanation that won't make me feel so ashamed, clutching at whatever I can to explain this whole occurrence. I'm saying all the things that I know are true, but it doesn't excuse any of what he did.

"I sympathize, but I'm still screwed. If I were to act like your father and truly give into what I'm feeling now, you'd both be dead."

My breath catches because I know he means it. He's serious. He's being serious as fuck, but I don't know what that means in regard to what he's actually going to do.

"Are you scared, Ava?" he asks. I'm not sure why he would ask me that. Anyone who looks at me can tell I'm so frightened I might just die from the fright.

"Yes..." I rasp.

He leans closer, and the scent of his musky aftershave tickles my nose.

"I don't think you're nearly as scared or frightened as you should be. If you were, you wouldn't make such an offer, and not to a man like me. *A trade*. A trade where you'll do *anything*."

He's right. I hate to admit it. He is completely right. However, he's just right about one part of his analysis. I'm terrified, but I made the offer because that's all I have. I can't pay back two million, and from what he said, that's just the start of it. It sounded like there was more.

He doesn't know that I would offer myself because of how much I owe my father.

I owe him everything, including my life. It's nothing in comparison to what he lost just for loving me and my mother.

"Do you accept my offer?" I ask, surprising him.

Fury re-enters his eyes. "Ava Knight, do you know what it means to offer yourself to someone like me? In my world, a debt repaid in the way you offer means you trading your body for the repayment."

He means I become his whore.

I can't take my eyes off him now. I'm not stupid. Of course, I know what it means, but I'm not thinking straight. I haven't been in years. I think the part of me that used to be able to do that is gone. Damaged by the past. It exists now as a shimmer that may lend itself to me from time to time. This, however, doesn't feel like one of those times. What I'm acting on is that fight for survival. The instinct to protect... no matter the cost.

"Bellezza, it means you belong to me. You would be mine to do as I wish. Anything... you said anything, so that's permission you give me to do what I want to you." He speaks in a low voice that captures my attention. It works its way into me slowly and purposefully. It lingers with effect, along with his stare. A stare that draws me in and makes me take in the full beauty of his face.

Angles and planes all chiseled to perfection. He's the kind of man who looks better as he gets older, and everything about him has more effect.

What he's saying though... I don't know what I'm supposed to answer because what else am I supposed to do?

This is a nightmare. Is there a difference between being forced into it and offering it? Forced into using my body or me offering it to save Dad.

"Ava... listen to me carefully," he says, probably seeing my internal conflict. "I will only say this once. Think about what you're offering. Maybe this one time you should walk away and allow your father to suffer the consequences of his actions."

Consequences... I swallow hard. He's giving me a chance to walk away. How can I do that though? How am I supposed to allow Dad to be killed?

I won't excuse his mistakes and all the wrong Dad did, but I can't do nothing either and just accept that he deserves the consequences.

If I walk away, that's it. It would mean death.

Vincent must be considering my offer if we're here talking about it. He must be. It must be the only thing keeping Dad alive.

If I am, then that's something. It's hope.

"No, I can't let you hurt him, or kill him. He's my father."

He growls, and I shy away when he looms even closer. "I gave you a chance."

"And I'm still offering."

"You are foolish."

"He's my father."

"It doesn't matter who he is."

"Don't you want me?" I throw back. It sounds like the last part of my soul speaking, crying out.

He steps back, away from me. He looks me over, and desire fills his eyes, but his face is still hard.

"Yes," he answers, and it's a shock to my system.

A spark of arousal flickers deep inside me, and my nerves scatter. It's crazy. I'm crazy because I shouldn't feel that. His confirmation is enough to throw me, but maybe it's the way he looks at me. It's not really any different to how most men look at me. It just has more effect coming from him.

He sighs and stalks away, heading to the door, but stops just before he gets there.

"You have until lunchtime tomorrow to think about it. After that, everything is set in stone." The dangerous, dark look returns to his eyes, and he leaves.

The door closes, and I'm left wondering what tomorrow will bring.

I know I won't change my mind though.

I won't.

It's not even a question if it will help.

CHAPTER FOUR

Vincent

Don't you want me...
 I woke with those words in my mind. Ava's words.
 I fell asleep with them in my mind too.
 It was definitely the least of my worries, however, when the sun came up.
 The first shit of the day was my meeting with the cops who'd called last Friday alerting me to the situation at hand.
 Friday was when it all went down. The cops called first thing that morning. That was about the drugs and the prostitution ring Mark was helping fund as a valued patron. At that point, I still didn't know about the money. I found that part out at lunchtime when I started checking things out.
 Mark wasn't at work Friday. Most likely in the height of gambling away my cash.
 By nightfall, the feds called, and that was when I found out about everything else.

It unfolded like a fucking map pointing the way to the truth.

How Mark stole, how Mark was linked to a ring of drug dealers who were already on the feds' radar for lacing the real stuff with a synthetic compound.

How Mark gambled away my money at a high-stakes poker game run by Omar Al Sheikh, one of the wealthiest businessmen in Dubai. Then how Mark not only stole money from Giordanos Inc. using my passwords but also tried to set up a pump and dump scheme for securities fraud linking us in the shit.

I foolishly believed Mark wouldn't dare screw with me because of who I am. He knew it would mean death if I found out, yet me and death were the last things on his mind.

That fucking dog. He completely abused his position as one of my senior account managers and screwed me over all six ways from Sunday.

Bad enough that I didn't get to end him last night, but the meeting with the cops and feds made me want to breathe hellfire. From the minute they called, I knew they thought I was tied up in it. They thought they finally had a way to get me good and lock me up in the big house.

Not just me... Pa and the boys too. The whole famiglia if they could.

In my world, all you need to cause serious trouble is a couple of hot shot cops who want to be feds thinking they have a thing or two to pin on one of the biggest crime families in Chicago. What's fucking worse than that is the federal agents who try to twist the shit of everything to catch you out.

Cops and feds alike tried to catch me out, but I served them both the same answer that I hope like hell calls off the hounds.

With all the work my men and I did last night and over the last few days to clean up, I told them with *semi confidence* to make contact when they had real evidence to pin on me. Basically, find something to come for me, or fuck the hell off.

Usually, I play nice to keep things as cool as they can be. Today was different, but I think got the message across even though both meetings were a shit show where neither party got answers. While it made them piss off, it left it all vague. I hate vague.

As I make my way up the path to the family home, tension grips me.

We have a family meeting, and Pa will want answers. He'll want to know what happened with the cops and feds, and he'll want to know what I'm going to do about the situation with Mark.

He usually allows me to dole out certain decisions in situations where he doesn't need to get involved, but since this involved Giordanos Inc. and our investigation into what Mark got up to is still going on, I'm not sure Pa's gonna think it's acceptable for me to accept pussy as payment. A payment I haven't decided on... yet.

Fuck. I don't know how this is all going to play out. All because Mark was reckless. It's like leaving a box of important documents out in the street for all to see but you forgot where you left it. When the feds and cops start poking around other things we actually want to keep secret, shit will start to stir.

It's just pissed me off. It's barely eleven, and this morning has been a bitch, and I'm mad as all hell. I hardly got two minutes with my kid before I had to leave the house, and I knew even before I opened my eyes from the little sleep I got last night that this was going to be one drawn-out day with all kinds of shit happening.

Things I can't control, and things I can.

Like Mark.

He deserves to be taught a lesson, and I'm not teaching it to him because of his daughter and her offer looming over my head.

The same way it hasn't escaped me that she's more worried about her father than herself, it hasn't escaped me either that Ava is the only thing stopping me from killing Mark. It's a fact that's irritating the fuck out of me.

I won't be a prick and lie that I'm not attracted to her. The woman has a body that would make any man ache with need. My answer to her last night was truth, so I won't act like I'm some kind of saint and pretend I didn't think of all the wild, wicked, daring things I could do with my pretty little house guest when she threw her offer my way.

At the same fucking time, I have to remember who and what I am.

I push the door to the house open and am greeted by Philippe, our butler.

Pa hasn't said what this meeting will be about. It's strange for him to keep the subject of the meeting so hushed. If Pa hadn't scheduled it in before the shit with Mark, I'd be inclined to think it would be about that. I'm sure though that it will be mentioned, and sights will be turned to me.

I enter the meeting room, and it looks like I'm the last to arrive.

Everyone is already here.

My parents head the table, my father as boss of the family with my mother on his right hand as his consigliere.

There's a space on his left for me. My brothers Salvatore, Gabe, and Nick take up the seats to the left of Ma in order of their rank of authority. Whom I never expected to be here though are my uncles, and cousins; Christian and Georgiou. It's literally all the people who are important to the business.

I nod at Pa, acknowledging him in our habitual way, then take my seat next to him.

"Wonderful," Pa says. "Now that Vincent's here, we can begin. Vincent, what is the situation?" Pa asks, face stern.

Needless to say, he was furious as fuck about Mark and ordered his killing straightaway. That question right there is him asking me if he's still alive.

We have no secrets amongst us. That's the first code of honor. Salvatore would have filled him in on what happened last night. He knows too that Ava offered herself in exchange for Mark's repayment. We have no secrets, but I hope he didn't mention that part.

"I have it under control," I answer. My gaze flicks to Salvatore, who tenses his jaw, and Gabe, who looks off about the whole thing.

I know what's grating Gabe. He and Salvatore are like two peas in a fucking pod. Salvatore might not have told Pa about Ava's offer, but I'm sure as shit he told Gabe. Not Nick though. If Nick knew, he would have called me by now. The bottom line is, they'd all think it was wrong.

"Do you?" Pa asks, drawing my attention back to him.

"Yes, Boss," I reply. "The cops and the feds can't pin anything on us. Right now, it all looks like speculation aimed our way."

He gives me an uneasy look. He's my father, but I've worked with him long enough to know that wasn't the answer he was looking for, and not with the way I've been dealing out punishment lately to those who deserve it.

He tenses and bites down hard on his back teeth. "Vinny, we'll talk after in private."

Shit....

I groan inwardly. The last thing I need now is Pa on my ass. He's a lot harder on me than everybody else. He always has been, even when Frankie was alive. It was a clear demarcation of authority. Frankie and I were always going to be the muscle while the other guys would fall in line to run the business in the run-of-the-mill aspects of it.

Two years ago things changed, and everyone had to step up when our enemies tried to eradicate us.

Pa looks away from me and focuses ahead, looking at everyone. From one to the next. My uncles are silent. It's unusual. I get the feeling they know more about what this meeting is about than the rest of us.

Pa finishes looking around, and then he does something he rarely ever does in public. He reaches for my mother's hand, and she gives it to him. He then looks at her, and she gives him a coy smile.

My mother is anything but coy—she's like the Spartan queen who's as much an authority figure as the king.

It's curious.

"I have called this meeting today for very important reasons," Pa says. "Of course, the situation with Mark Knight has not been good for us, and I'm inclined to push plans aside until it is all resolved. However, I feel I must continue as planned. Everyone here is capable of their specific jobs. This meeting is about a restructure of our hierarchy."

He has my fucking attention now. He really does.

"What?" I know not to interrupt when he's talking. I was the hothead twenty-five-year-old when he first gave me the back of his hand in public and told me to shut the fuck up and never interrupt him ever again.

He doesn't do that now. When he looks at me again, it's with respect.

"The hierarchy of leadership in our family is being restructured because I wish to retire with my wife and go back to Italy."

There is a noticeable silence that spreads across the room.

My brothers and cousins look as shocked as I feel, but I was right that my five uncles look unfazed. They knew. They knew about this. Of course, they would. Our grandfather left specific instructions for things to be done a certain way. Everything in regard to the structure of leadership and ownership is to be handled by the six brothers. Pa is in charge and can overrule any of them, but he's not like that.

The question now though is, what next?

Pa straightens up and looks at me. "Your uncles and I have agreed that you will be boss of the family, Vincent. You take over the empire, with your brothers as your new leaders. That means that Georgiou and Christian will step up on the business side of things at the shipping company, where Georgiou as my eldest nephew will take care of your job as it is now, and you will have mine. Christian will share the duties Salvatore, Gabriel, and Nick have so everything across our business ventures can run smoothly."

Jesus.... All I can do is stare. This is something I definitely never saw coming at all.

Pa looks away from me. I noticed how there was no question

about it. Nothing for me to think about and get back to him because I trained my whole life for this moment.

"Angela and I will be leaving for Italy in three months. That is when I propose the official handover. I will remain in charge until then, and everything will be as it has been in regard to our leadership. Everything will, however, start to take effect immediately with an easing-in process so you aren't thrown into the deep end. I don't really think there will be a problem," Pa adds, and everyone shakes their heads.

He's right. We all do our parts, and we all tend to work together as a unit. However, if there's anybody who's going to be affected by his departure, it's me.

"Are there any questions?" Pa asks, and again, everyone shakes their heads. "Well, if there are no questions, then we'll adjourn this meeting and call back in a few weeks once I've ironed out my exit plan."

On his word, chairs shuffle as everyone gets up and starts making their way out. Salvatore glances back at me, as do Christian and Georgiou. It's funny, everyone does what they do, but I'm probably going to need those three the most. My brother more.

I stay behind.

Ma is the last to leave, which leaves just Pa and me in the room.

I look to him, and his face softens. "Which should we talk about first? The part where you well and truly want to chew my ass out for the fact that Mark's still alive? Or the bomb you just dropped on us?"

He chuckles. "Vinny," he begins. They all have their nicknames for me. Except Gabe and Nick. They're the only ones who full-name me. "I'm not gonna lie. I'm not happy about that fucker Mark. So, let's deal with that first. What the fuck happened? This wise guy shits on us, and he's still alive? Do I have to go take care of him myself?"

He's actually serious. One of the things I've always liked

about my father is that he's a hands-on leader. He gets his hands as dirty as the guy he's giving orders to. That's how he's always been.

"No."

"Listen, boy," he says, and I can't help but laugh.

"Pa, when the hell you gonna stop calling me a boy? I haven't been that in years." I lower my brows.

"Like fuck. You're my boy, no matter how old you get, so never Vincent. Salvatore filled me in, and I'm not happy about it. I'll tell you now that he never really wanted to tell me about the girl, but he had to. Vinny, I don't like it. It's not enough. I don't care that the fucker was high and lost his shit. Just imagine the worst things that could have happened. Those calls from the feds and cops could have been something else or started some shit we don't need."

"I know..." He doesn't have to tell me. I do know, and I can't argue because he's right.

"So, if you know, dole out the punishment... dole out the punishment and take care of the girl."

Oh fuck... *fucking hell*. My eyes snap open, but I don't know why I'm surprised. "Pa—"

"Vinny, you better make sure the next words that come out of your mouth are words I want to hear."

I ball my fists and growl. "Pa, you might not want to hear this, but how are you supposed to leave me in charge when you already try to test my judgment and decisions?"

That silences him. Honestly, I don't know how I feel about this news of his departure.

I'm not ready.

Deep down I know emotionally, I'm just managing. I'm not ready to take on the *empire*, as he put it, and maybe this is me acting out to try and deal with a situation I don't know how to deal with myself.

He wants me to kill Mark and Ava. I don't want blood on my hands like that. Not her. That's a different kind of killing.

My soul might have been taken from me, but that same conscience that makes me feel guilt is there telling me I couldn't do such a thing.

Pa studies my face, and it's clear he doesn't like my comment. "Can it be fixed? The shit. Can it be fixed?"

"For the most part. But I'm not sure what else we'll find."

"Right, well, hear this... as I'm easing out and you're taking over, I'm gonna leave this to you. But if I find out there's anything more to tie us in with feds, that's it, Vinny. I'll take them out myself, father and daughter."

I don't answer. Instead, I bite the inside of my lip trying not to seethe.

"Well, on to the next order of business, *the business*," he goes on. "Do you have questions? You must have questions."

I have a million. None of them will be anything he'll like.

"I wish I'd had a heads up... I know things have to be done a certain way, and I appreciate that. It's just... It would have been..." My voice trails off when I realize I'm showing more emotion than I should.

"Would have been nice?" he finishes with mock sarcasm. "Vinny, you aren't some fucker who pussyfoots around shit. You know what you're doing. That's why you'll be boss of the famiglia. Here in Chicago and the Giordanos in Italia. I didn't pick you just because it was a given. We all picked you because you're the best for the job." He gets a real uneasy look on his face, and I know what he's going to talk about next. I practically landed myself in it with my comments. "Vincent..." *There too*, he never full-names me unless he wants to make a point. "This is always hard for me to tell you, but as your father and the boss of the family, I have to. You need a wife."

The muscles twitch in my jaw, and I can already feel the vein starting to throb at my temple.

"I don't need a wife," I protest.

"Like fuck, you do. You need a wife to take care of the baby and take care of you. Take care of your house. You need a woman in your life who will do all the shit you're trying to do. You can't have that baggage on your plate when you're Boss."

"You think Timothy is baggage?"

"Vincent, don't do this. You know that's not what I mean. I'm speaking truth to you. You've been without a wife for two years now, and the effect on you is noticeable. I haven't allowed tradition to dictate to me and find you a wife because I know your loss of Sorcha runs deep."

Hearing her name and in this context stirs the rage. I have to brace myself to cool off.

"You got lucky with her," he adds. "You had the real deal, and no one can knock that, but business is business. We have to do what we have to do. Same as me."

I narrow my eyes, curiously. "What do you mean?"

"It's time for me to retire. I'm sixty-five, and I've enjoyed being boss. It's definitely time to pass the torch to you, but... I had to make the decision when I thought I was going to lose your mother."

I bite the inside of my lip. Ma may be his right-hand woman, but she's had to put up with a lot of shit from him. He cheats. He and all my uncles do. It's a known thing amongst them. They cheat and share women.

It's something that skipped the next gen because my brothers would never do that, and that was a word I would never even contemplate when Sorcha was alive.

Georgiou is married, but he shares his doll with his best friend, and it works. Christian is the last Giordano bachelor and is as wild as the rest of us, but I don't think even he would cheat.

So, what Pa is talking about is that.

"What happened?" I would never ask him that when I was younger. I probably shouldn't ask it now.

"She had enough of my unsavory habits. She's always wanted to go back to Sicily, so I decided I wanted that. I wanted her." He dips his head in a reverent way. It shows he loves Ma, but I'll never understand why she couldn't have been enough for him in every way. I guess maybe this is his way of showing her she is.

"I'll take care of everything, I promise. I will." I'm talking and telling him what I should say, but deep down I don't feel it.

I'm really not ready.

I'm still too broken from what happened to Sorcha. It's not something that you just heal from. Yes, it's been two years, and some people would have moved on and remarried as tradition dictates, but those people aren't me.

How the fuck am I supposed to be boss of the whole family when I couldn't even take care of the one person who mattered most to me?

"I know you will." Pa nods his confirmation. His belief in me makes me feel guilty. "There's also something more in the works that will change everything. It's the other reason I did this today."

"What is it?"

"The Bratva, the Ivanezh Brotherhood, want to form an alliance with us."

"Do they now?" I ask, on the edge of a breath.

"Yes, we own the seas, that means we own the world. It's something they don't have but want a piece of. That means money for us."

Fucking hell. Fuck, that's a whole other territory of alliance we've never crossed. There's a good reason for that. The last people in the circles we travelled who had any dealings with the Bratva ended up getting wiped out, as in their whole family killed. Nobody was ever given details of what actually happened, so all we were left to do was guess. It didn't take any real guessing to know that something happened to piss off the brotherhood. Then again, the way I hear it is that it doesn't take much to piss them off.

No one we know has revealed doing business, much less wanting to form any kind of alliance with them since.

So, why are we even considering it?

Pa temples his fingers. "Vincent you're like an open book. I can tell from the look in your eyes that you're thinking of past mishaps with the Romanos."

That was the family who got obliterated.

"Aren't you?"

He sighs. "Of course, but that happened well over fifteen years ago, Vinny. I don't see the need to hold on to something that never involved us and miss out on opportunity." He gives me a pointed stare like I'm being difficult.

I guess maybe I am, but I don't know about this. It could be good financially, but it could be bad too.

Back in the day, we might have needed them, we made our money mostly from smuggling cash and criminals from one country to the next. As we got wealthier, we didn't have to do that shit anymore. Now, we actually do legit business, and we're widely used by thousands of companies worldwide. So, we don't need to agree to this alliance with the Bratva.

"I want you to meet with them," Pa says. "Meet and think about the offer. We've had no end of trouble over the last few years with people wanting to usurp our control of the company. This is the first time anyone has wanted to have a sit-down-and-talk meeting to discuss an alliance."

I quirk a brow, but I'm listening. "You sound like you really want this."

"I'm interested in the opportunity for the family. So, set something up, meet and decide if you want to accept when you get all the facts."

"Alright, I can do that."

"Good. Deal quickly with Mark. I don't want to keep our Bratva friends waiting," he orders, and I nod.

Deal with Mark? I'll be paying that fucker a visit later.

To deal with him properly though, I have to deal with Ava.

I glance at the clock behind Pa. It's just gone eleven thirty. I gave Ava until lunchtime.

There are a lot of loose ends to tie up in regard to Mark. It is by no means anywhere near fixed. But I know what to do in the meantime if that offer of Ava's is still on the table.

She'll be an escape, stress relief, and some form of compensation for the shit her father served me.

I hear her words echo in my mind again.
Don't you want me?
My answer is till the same.
Yes.

CHAPTER FIVE

Ava

Darkness surrounds me, and the cold sting of terror runs down my spine, from the base of my neck straight down the length of my body. It always starts there once I hear the echo of footsteps against the stone floor. He's coming again.

Before I can think it, he comes, and his breath on my skin is the reminder that what is happening is real. It's hot, and it makes my nerves stand on end. Everything inside me struggles to flee, except I can't.

A firm hand grips me, holding me down, then laughter. That victorious laughter of triumph that kills my soul. The laughter gets louder, the grip tighter. It hurts, and I jump.

My eyes snap open, and I'm breathing hard. I look around trying to figure out where I am as the door opens and the face of an elderly woman comes into my view.

I was dreaming. It was ... a dream. But... looking around confirms I'm still stuck in a nightmare, just a different one.

The woman walks in. She's carrying a tray with cookies and a cup. I smell chocolate. She looks at me huddled on the floor in the same position I've been in since last night.

"Hello, signora," she says with a little smile. "I thought you might like this, since you have not eaten anything else." She speaks with a heavy accent and a warmth that's very motherly.

I'm surprised by the warmth as it's the first flicker of safety I've felt since I've been here.

"I mean you no harm. I just wanted to check on you. You were talking in your sleep. The kind of talk a person does when troubled," she adds.

"I..." I wonder if she knows why I'm here. She must know something.

She lowers to the floor and sets the tray down on the wooden surface. The sun catches the silver in her hair as she looks up.

"I'm half Italian. My mother was from Guatemala. Our people loved chocolate. The ancient Mayans and Aztecs believe it was a gift from the gods. We think we can tell what kind of person you are from the chocolate you like. I made yours with a kick of cinnamon and chili, sweet but fiery when you need to be."

I look at her and decide to smile. I like what she said. "Thank you. That's nice."

"It is, and it tastes good too. We also believe that chocolate calms the soul. Will you have some?"

I realize she's trying to calm me down.

I shuffle, and my legs ache from being in that position for too long. All night, I've been like this. I haven't even gone to the toilet.

I reach for a cookie and smile when I see they're the soft gooey type. I take a bite, and it ignites my taste buds, making me devour it in seconds, and reach for another and another.

She laughs. "I'm glad I was right. Try the hot chocolate. It's good to have something hot in your stomach."

"Thank you." I take a sip, and oh my God, this is something I would definitely savor.

It makes me think of Holly, my best friend, and I can't

believe this is the first I've thought of her. Holly works with me at *Escada* as a freelance photographer. She knew how worried I was about Dad. She would have called last night to check in. I can just imagine her calling me and panicking when the phone rang out. It was taken away along with my purse and keys.

As good as this delicious chocolate all is, thinking of her brings back everything to my mind, and I'm still left with the question of what I'm doing and what's happening.

I finish the hot chocolate though. I need it. I'm starving, and I don't think it's going to help me if I don't eat. I barely ate anything over the last few days as it is from my worry over Dad.

"Feel better?" she asks.

"Yes. Thank you for this. It's delicious."

"I'm Marguerite," she introduces herself with a wide grin that makes her eyes twinkle.

"My name's Ava."

"It's great to meet you, Ava. If you need anything, call me. I hope you do."

I wonder if she'd allow me to use the phone. "Is there maybe a phone I could use?"

Her expression gives me the answer to that. It's cautious, and her eyes are the same. She shakes her head. "It's probably better if you wait until later to speak with Mr. Giordano."

Giordano. That's his surname. I've heard that name before. There's a massive shipping company by the docks, and everybody knows it's owned by mobsters. *Giordanos Inc*. That's not where Dad worked though.

I nod, feeling weaker. I get that she can't help me more than she has with the food. That doesn't make it any less awful.

The door pushes open, and I straighten when Vincent comes in.

He's wearing a suit today that makes him look more alluring. His expression is still the same though. Hard and stern, his eyes cold and metallic.

I don't know what time it is, but I'm guessing it's lunchtime. He said he would give me until lunchtime today to finalize my answer. What I want, though, is to know if Dad is still safe, and where he is.

Vincent looks from Marguerite to me, then back to her as she stands up.

"Leave us, and do not disturb me for the next half hour," he says to her.

"Yes, sir," she answers and walks out, closing the door behind her.

His eyes zero in on me, and I see that same look he gave me last night. Not the look of interest. It's desire.

It was just after I asked him if he wanted me.

Now that several hours have passed and I've settled into the situation, I actually can't believe I asked him that. It was desperation talking.

I stand up, once again on shaky legs. He comes closer, and it's like déjà vu.

"Is my father safe?" I ask. I just need him to tell me yes.

The beginning of a smile tips the corners of his lips, bringing out the dimple in his left cheek. "The funny thing about it is, he is."

My whole body sighs with relief, but I try to control my reaction. He knows I'm scared, but anybody would be. What I'm trying to do is maintain some level of control, just something so I can protect Dad.

"Have you thought of an answer, Bellezza? It's not often someone rubs me the wrong way and gets the chance to walk away."

Walk away... freedom. Leaving this house. I could leave. I could have left. I'm sure there would be stipulations of never talking to anyone about what happened, but what would happen to Dad?

Death.

Not even a beating. Vincent had a gun and fired it several times. I won't be a hypocrite and pretend I'm not enraged by everything Dad has done.

He's gotten himself in some serious trouble with these

people. Enough for them to want to kill him. The fact that he's still safe means what I'm doing is working.

"My answer is still the same. I haven't changed my mind. I think you know that. You know I'm aware of what you want to do to my father."

He steps closer. "Yes, I am aware. I just want us to be clear on your offer... You'd be *mine to do with as I please, mine to do anything to.*"

He holds my gaze, and my breath hitches. I swallow hard. "Yes, have you accepted my offer?"

A devilish look comes into his eyes with a faint glint of lust. "I need to see what's on offer first."

I slow my breathing as something sinful enters his gaze. I exhale slow and slower so I can focus. *I can do this. I can do this. I can.*

"What do you want me to do?"

"Take your clothes off."

Here it is... what I knew was coming. I can't even act surprised. I'm infuriated, not with myself but this. The fact that this is happening to me.

I'm not some slut. I've never lived my life in that way, and here I am, about to take my clothes off for this man I don't know so I can show him what's on offer.

He smiles and seems taller, or maybe it's me shrinking away with fear.

"Something wrong, Bellezza?"

"I didn't think you'd want me to do this yet."

"What do you think this is? Some kind of courtship?"

"No, of course not."

"Well, you said you'd do anything. This is what I want." He stares back at me daringly, as if he's testing me to see if I'm really going to do it.

I'm not going to let him faze me. I got myself into this, and there will be a way out. Somehow. I take a breath and reach for the hem of my blouse. I then pretend he's not standing in front of me and take it off.

I tackle my jeans next and step out of those, leaving just my bra and panties on. His eyes rake boldly over my body, and I wish like hell I felt nothing, but his lust-filled gaze is so strong it's like it actually touches me.

"Bra and panties off too," he says.

Again, I swallow and breathe slower. I start with my bra by snapping open the little clasp holding it together across my back. As I move it away, my breasts pour out, free from the restraint holding them together.

His eyes go straight to my breasts, and I look away.

I slide my panties down my legs and step out of them.

I'm naked now. Naked before him, showing him what's on offer, and I can't look at him.

"Look at me," he says as if reading my thoughts.

I lift my head gingerly and meet his hungry gaze. His eyes eat me up and burn my skin everywhere it touches.

"Turn around, slowly," he commands, and I do as he says. I turn slowly, lingering with my back turned to him as I face the wall, and in those few seconds, I allow myself the respite from his predatory gaze.

It's just a few seconds, just seconds until I turn to face him again. This time though, as I stare at him, I notice he's looking at me the way he was last night, when our eyes first locked.

Something stirred inside me. I'm not sure what it was, but it was like he saw something inside me that must have come out in my desperation.

Just like last night though, the trance is broken within moments.

It's as though neither of us can stand it.

What is it?

I pray it's not that he's intuitive. I hope it's not that he's one of those people who can look at you and see right through you into the deep end and see you had to fight through shit to come out on top. I won't allow anyone to see that part of me. It's locked away so deep inside me that not even I can reach it, and I don't want to.

He steps forward, and instinct makes me move back. I'm already close to the wall so I couldn't have retreated any further than the one step.

"You.... you haven't asked me once if I intend to hurt you. You're so worried about your father, you haven't thought what I might do to you."

"I don't want you to kill him," I answer. I thought that was a given.

"But you're not worried I may hurt you? Do you think I won't?"

A chill runs through me, and I look at him, really look at him. The answer is, I don't know him so there's no way I can give him an actual answer to that question.

I'm so protective and worried about Dad that I've only thought of him. Things quickly escalated to this stage, and I've been so worried that my own safety was the last thing on my mind.

"I don't... I don't know," I answer, just to give an answer, and his smile turns sensual.

Closer he comes, and closer, until he rests his hands on the wall on either side of me. He leans right in, so close, too close. So close I see the lighter hue of his eyes while he stares into mine.

"Interesting...." he breathes, and his breath smooths over my skin like a gentle caress. It's striking for the tenderness in comparison to the formidable force he is.

It's tantalizing from the way it smooths over me and makes arousal crawl over my insides. It works its way through me and pulses through my skin, making my nipples tighten. "Very interesting," he adds, gaze dropping to my diamond-hard nipples.

"What is?" I falter.

"You... you fear me and want me at the same time," he observes, and instantly, I'm stunned.

I shake my head. "No... I don't."

A real smile dances on his lips. It's the first actual smile I've seen him give me. "Your body betrays you, Bellezza," he says, running a finger over the tip of my left nipple.

The slight touch sends a shiver of desire through me. I don't want this. How can I? It's crazy. If I do, then I'm more fucked up than I realize. So much more than I thought.

"No," I rasp.

This time, he brushes his finger backwards and forwards over my nipple and circles around it.

"No?"

"No," I repeat, but we both know it for a lie.

"We'll see about that, shall we?"

To confirm it, he shocks the hell out of me by reaching forward and smoothing his hand over the soft skin of my mound. I gasp when he slides two fingers slightly inside my pussy, and because I'm so wet, he slides in easily then strokes over the hard, sensitive bud of my clit.

I gasp, and my eyes turn to saucers when he takes his fingers out then holds them out in front of me to see the glistening juice.

I'm so shocked at myself I don't know where to put my face.

Heat creeps into my cheeks, and an unwelcome blush sweeps over my body.

"Liar, you're wet... and ready to be fucked." He grins wide, revealing perfectly aligned white teeth, then shocks me more by placing his fingers in his mouth so he can lick them off.

I can't say a word. Nothing comes to my mind, and nothing will come when he places a hand on the flat of my stomach and bends down to take my nipple into his mouth.

I draw in a sharp breath as he sucks me. I fight against emotion and everything inside me that wants to give in to pleasure. *Everything* that wants me to fall into the pleasure of the moment and enjoy what he's doing to me.

The second he starts alternating from one breast to the other in a wild suckle that makes my head spin, I know I can't hold it back any longer.

A moan falls from my lips, and he glances up at me and smiles.

His fingers return to my pussy, which is dripping with need, and he starts pumping in and out of me.

Slow then faster.

I press into the wall groaning and moaning as he finger-fucks me, the pleasure building and rising, beckoning me to enjoy it.

It's been so long since I was touched like this that I can't remember what pleasure is supposed to feel like, and he's about to give me more.

He crouches down, looks up at my shamed yet pleasure-filled face, and when he lifts my leg, I allow him to slip it over his shoulder so he can bury his face between my thighs.

His tongue presses up into my entrance, stroking over my clit. Stroking, teasing, tasting, taking.

He's taking me, making his mark on me in this way, and I can't stop the feelings that course through my body. I'm taken higher and higher as he sucks and licks, eating out my pussy like it's his last meal.

I'm not sure who could even pretend with this consuming pleasure designed to devour.

That's what he's doing, *devouring me*. And, I'm certain like any other woman, I come undone in his hands. The pull of orgasmic bliss takes me, swallowing me whole. It ignites from deep within. Deep, deep inside a place I never knew existed, then spreads over my body with fiery heat that sizzles and scorches, burning me from the inside out. The only thing I'm left to do is grab his wide, powerful shoulders and cry out from the intensity.

I'm left gasping for air, left trying to unscramble my mind from the buzz that fills it. I'm left undone indeed, but he seems the same as before as he lifts his head, licks his lips, and wipes his chin with the back of his hand.

I know my skin is crimson, and I'm so hot my throat feels like it's been stuffed with cotton, but he's unaffected except...

except for that look in his eyes. The predatory one that's looking at me with hunger, the type that wants to own and possess.

He rises to his feet with a wild smirk and comes close to my face, close enough to brush his cheek against mine.

"Ava Knight, I accept your offer. You're mine. Mine to do *anything* with." He speaks in a low husky voice. "I'll let you in on a little secret. I don't fear you, but I want you too."

I gaze deeply into his eyes. That makes his smile lift, deepen, and I wonder what the hell I've gotten myself into.

"I think we're in for a very interesting time. You'll get the terms and conditions of your stay at dinner tonight." He backs away from me, and something clicks. It's reality.

We just agreed to this arrangement, made this sinful contract, but how long for?

"How long?" I ask as the panic rises within me. "How long do I have to stay with you?" The words come on the edge of a stutter, and he chuckles.

He chuckles and doesn't answer me. He walks away, leaving me standing there wide eyed and naked against the wall.

The door closes, clicks shut, and fear claws away at my insides.

What the hell did I just do?
What have I done?
What did I agree to?

CHAPTER SIX

Vincent

I don't know how I didn't just take her against the wall.

What stroke of control could have come over me to resists such temptation.

Fuck, fucking fuck, maybe this is a bad idea, but now that I've tasted her, do I want to go back on my acceptance?

I own her.

Own her like she's mine to do with whatever I please. My damn dick is twitching at the thought of all the things I want to do to her, and we haven't even gotten started yet.

I walk down the corridor with the taste of her sweet nectar in my mouth and the hums of her pleasure ringing through my ears. In my mind is that look in her eyes of desire she's trying so hard to resist. I may be a monster, but at least I've never been a liar.

Never been one to resist, so I give myself credit for walking away, but it's only half credit because I know I want more. Greed fills my mind, and it makes me want more. Especially when just the taste of her has steadied my nerves in some sort of way.

I head to the playroom, where Marguerite is with Timothy. She's watching his train set go around the tracks I had built into the walls. The whole room is set up for it so the little red and black train set can drive around the room like it's real. There are mountains and a little island. Each stop has people he can put on the train.

It's one of his favorite things that makes him smile every day. Today is no different. He giggles in that seriously cute way kids laugh as the little train passes by some trees.

My boy's face lights up though when he sees me. As he sees me, all thoughts of his favorite toy are forgotten, and he rushes over, his little feet carrying him as quickly as they can.

"Papa, Papa..." he bubbles, and I pick him up. Marguerite smiles at us when Timothy's little arms circle my neck.

"Awww, this is always so beautiful to watch you two," she beams and brings her hands together, pride filling her face.

I chuckle at Timothy's wide grin. He looks exactly like me when I was a kid. He's going to be two in a few months. When he was born, he looked like Sorcha, then as the months went by, he became me.

I press my head to his. It's like we haven't seen each other in years. I don't spend enough time with him when he's awake, and I need to change that.

I look back to Marguerite. She has the look I expected her to have on her face. Cautious, but with an air of disapproval.

I wouldn't expect anything other from the woman who's like a second mother to me after seeing Ava. I know for a fact that if Ma were here, she wouldn't allow me to do whatever it is I'm doing.

She'd go mad even though she knows Giordano men have some very unusual ways. We're all sex crazed, even the ones who are happily in love with their dolls. It never started with a date and kiss.

From one to the next, it was something bizarre the rest of

the world would frown upon. So, I'm allowed this agreement with Ava if I choose it.

"Vinny, what's the girl really doing here?"

It's clear from her tone that she doesn't approve. Women know not to ask those kinds of questions, few like her are the exception.

"It's business," I answer, hoping she doesn't continue to press.

"*Business?* Vinny, she's frightened."

"She should be," I reply. Just now with Ava was just now. It was fun and sowed the seeds for more I'll be taking later. I want those breasts in my mouth again, and the taste of her pussy.

Marguerite sighs. She knows I won't be saying much more than that, so there's no point trying to push or press. "Whatever it is, please be gentle with her. I sense she's troubled. She was talking in her sleep."

I answer with a raised brow. Ava was probably talking in her sleep because she's worried for her father. I won't tell Marguerite that I left him chained to a wall, with the worry of his life and his daughter's hanging over him.

She sees me as the boy she took care of from birth. I'll keep that image in her head since she's the only person who isn't family I trust with my boy. No one else must touch him or be with him.

Her brows knit together when I don't comment. "How long is she going to be here?"

That's another question I'm not answering. The truth is, I don't know. I couldn't give Ava an answer, and I can't give it to Marguerite either. She bites the inside of her lip and inclines her head to the side.

"Ava will be here for a while. See to it she eats and is comfortable." That's enough.

She shakes her head at me and sighs. She'll never voice her opinions though. She never has.

She was my nanny and never voiced her opinions in our home when she saw things happening she knew were wrong, like

Pa screwing around with the maids and all the shit the other guys and I used to get up to. She won't now either.

She's here for support.

When Sorcha was alive, Marguerite came to help out from time to time. After Sorcha's death, our parents stepped up. Ma was here, and Evelyn, my mother-in-law. I couldn't bear to have Evelyn here because of the guilt, although no one has ever blamed me. And, Ma was just suffocating.

Marguerite is the only person I could tolerate around me. She's here as my live-in nanny five to six days a week. Unlike everyone else, she exists outside of the box. She just understands me in a different way. Maybe it's because, like me, she's a widow. She lost her husband to the violence of our world twenty years ago and never remarried. She treats me like a son, although she has two sons who both live in Italy with their wives and children.

"It's a good thing I'm used to you boys and your ways," she says and blinks several times.

"Yes," I agree with arrogance I know she hates.

"I'm sure you know best, *Boss*." She rolls her eyes at me and I smirk the way I used to when I was a boy. "Do you want lunch?"

"No. I'm just going to hang out with my boy for a little bit." At the mention of Timothy, I win back her approval. Her face softens, and she reaches up to tap my cheek.

"I love the way you are with him. So different to the way your father was with you boys. Not that I'm saying anything against your father. It's just that sometimes a child needs love. Especially during these years." She runs her hand over Timothy's downy head as he rests it on my chest.

"I'm trying," I reply.

As she looks back at me, I know she sees it. That thing in the depths of my eyes that's still broken.

"You more than try, Vinny. You never have to worry that you don't. Sorcha would be proud of you taking care of him the way you do. It's the way she was with him." She nods, and her eyes gloss over with tears.

She's the only person who mentions Sorcha like that.

Everyone else steers away from doing so. I understand why, but sometimes it's okay to talk about it. They think they're being helpful, but it's not always the case. Marguerite talks about her like she's just gone away.

"That means a lot to me."

"It's truth, and may God keep you safe for it, Vincent," she whispers.

I don't know why she bothers to bring God into it. I'm just another devil, one who can't seem to find redemption. Her words will fall on deaf ears.

"Thank you," I say just to be respectful. "I'm going out in a little while. I'll be back for dinner though."

"Okay." She nods and makes a move to leave us.

Just then, Salvatore comes through the door.

He greets Marguerite with the customary kiss to her cheeks, and she leaves us.

After that meeting with Dad, I expected him to come by. I expected all of them to come by. Nick and Gabe are at The Dark Odyssey early on Tuesdays though, doing the accounts with Christian and Georgiou. I'll bet they all left and went to talk because they'll be worried about the club with the new leadership structure.

They have nothing to worry about. I'm not changing much of anything.

The man whose life will change the most is here.

He's two years younger than me and I still see him as my kid brother, but he's anything but that. With Pa's departure, Salvatore will have to step up even more than he has as capo.

He'll become me. What I am now. He'll become underboss to the familia, and he'll have to decide when to involve the others and when not to.

He has a kid like me, and another on the way. My brothers each have two kids now. Becoming husbands and fathers made them grow up, and I can see the differences in each of them. I worry for Salvatore though because he'll be faced with many of the challenges I encountered.

"Hey Vin," he says with a nervous grin.

"Hey. Do you want to go sit outside for a little bit?" I offer.

He sighs and presses his lips together. "Yeah, air is always good."

We go into the garden, and I set Timothy down to play in the sandpit. Instantly, he gets to work on digging around with his plastic shovel.

Salvatore and I head to the patio across from him, and I reach for the humidor with my best Cubans.

"So, let's hear it, Boss." Salvatore smiles. "There's no way you can be this calm after the news Pa dished us."

I look him over, wondering if I should tell him the truth, that I'm not ready. He's the only brother who's truly seen me weak. At my lowest. When I found Sorcha dead on the floor, he was the first person I called.

He's the second oldest, and I relied on him a lot after Frankie died, but the guy is a good friend too. I think maybe a part of me wanted him to tell me I was imagining things.

This is different. It's a question of who I'm supposed to be.

"I don't know, Salvatore. I'm surprised, like everyone else. What about you?"

"I'm shit scared," he confesses and gives me a long, hard stare. "I can't fill your shoes, man."

"Of course, you can," I answer with a definitive nod.

"No. It's not even a question." He shakes his head. "I can't. I think we've all taken it for granted for years. I mean the handle you have on things. You've been underboss and head capo to the family for nearly ten years, Vin. It's a long time. Much has happened to you." Sadness enters his eyes as he says that, and I glance down at the cigar in my hands.

"Much has happened, and this is just change," I tell him with as much confidence as I can to make it believable, and he nods agreement. It's times like this when I miss Frankie because he'd know I'm lying through my teeth. He'd just know.

"It's just change."

"We'll do what we have to," I add, glancing up at the window on the second floor.

It's Ava's room. I wonder if she's looking outside, watching us. *Did she put her clothes back on?*

The displaced thought hardens my cock right up again. I'm gonna have to get her clothes, and there'll be a whole bunch of things I need to sort out when it comes to her.

Salvatore sees me looking and glances up at the window too.

"What are you doing with the doll, Vin? What's going on with Mark?"

"I'm seeing Mark in a little while."

"And what?" he prods.

"I'll keep an eye on the doll."

Salvatore tilts his head to the side as he lights up his cigar. I light mine too and take a draw.

"Keep an eye? And what of the offer, Capo Bastone?"

I hesitate to confirm that I've accepted, but he looks at me and knows. To my credit, I gave her several chances to leave. Sure, the price would have possibly been very hefty had she done so, but this is her choice.

She offered herself to me, and I accepted. It's not like the women who throw themselves at me daily. There's something forbidden and tempting about it that entices me. She'd be the youngest woman I've ever been with. I'm nearly twice her age. She's twenty-six, and I'm forty-four, eighteen years older than her. I know many who do worse. It's common in our world.

Salvatore chuckles deep and edgy. "Fucking hell, Vin. You exchange all that shit Mark did for a piece of ass. A fuck toy."

"Fuck, Salvatore, don't fucking say that to me." I straighten up. I'm not letting him take the moral high ground with me again. "I'll have a fuck toy if I want to."

"Vin, you know what I'm saying. I'll be the last guy to tell you what to do in that respect. It's just that Mark could have ruined us, and we don't know what more we could discover. He fucked around with drugs, so who knows what more we could find."

"I get it, and I agree. I just..." I'm thinking of the best answer. "The situation's in check for the moment. It's not resolved, and there's a lot to do, but we're doing it this way."

"Taking pussy as payment for two million dollars and counting?" He narrows his eyes.

I chuckle. "Hey, since that two million was mine and came out of my pocket, I think I'm allowed to take whatever form of repayment I choose. Everything else is shit that we have to deal with as it comes, and currently, I got the cops and feds in a corner." *Those fuckers.* I'm still pissed from the meeting this morning.

He laughs at that. "Alright, Vin... I hope the repayment will be to your liking. Does that mean my club won't be seeing you there for a while? You're going to break a few hearts with the news of your departure."

The Dark Odyssey... I'll take her there. I can just imagine how horrified she'll be heading into a sex club. I'll make sure she enjoys herself though.

"We'll see. There's something else we got to deal with," I state. Pa told me about the Bratva guys. Now it's for me to decide who to involve in my plans.

"What's that?"

Quickly, I fill him in, and when I'm done, he leans back in the chair and stares at me with suspicion in his eyes.

"That's real interesting, Vin. What's your take on it?"

"Far be it from me to raise the alarm of suspicion when this could make us even richer bastards than we are. We'll set up a meeting with them. You and Christian will come with me." I know what I'm doing, but Salvatore looks confused at the mention of Christian.

"Why not Gabe or Nick?"

"It's too much. Four brothers of power going into a meeting with powerful men is too much. Christian will provide a balance. He's like Gabe though, good at reading people. And you..." I pause. There's a lot about Salvatore. This new structure will leave a job opening for the most trusted advisor. My father chose my mother, and now I will choose my brother. "I'm going to need my consigliere with me."

His eyes widen, and I'm not real sure why this would surprise him.

"Me? You're going to choose me?"

I nod. "Yeah. I'm choosing you. You'll see through bullshit." He'll be my eyes and ears. I need the two of them because I can't think straight, so I'm doing the next best thing.

My eyes return to the window, and I can just about see Ava looking down through the frosted glass.

Beautiful and scared.

I take a draw on my cigar and blow it out slow and purposefully as I continue to stare back, allowing her to see that I see her.

We're far away, but I can sense that fear and want.

It's still interesting.

CHAPTER SEVEN

Vincent

Mark lifts his head as I enter the room.

He looks like shit, like hell came to claim him and he was dragged through the fire several times. He looks like that, and he hasn't really taken a beating from me.

I went easy on him last night but kicked his ass mainly for getting his daughter dragged in and allowing her to make such a swap.

He's chained to the wall, unable to move around. The guys outside on watch told me he started having the shakes late in the night, then begged for a drink. Not water. The fucker wanted a beer and pleaded with them to grab one from upstairs. He pissed himself when he didn't get it.

I pull up a chair and sit on it backwards. I'm still deciding what to do with him. Ava made the trade. The thing to do would be to let him go, but that's not how this will work. There are several reasons why I can't just do that, and it wouldn't be me breaking my end of the unwritten contract.

"Please, tell me she's okay. My Ava..." Mark pleas, and a tear streams from his eyes, dark and puffy with circles that look like smoke spreading around his skin.

"She's okay," I answer, sounding calmer than I feel.

"Please don't hurt her, Vincent, I beg you, please don't hurt her. She's had... a rough life."

I narrow my eyes. I know his son died a few years back, and that was a terrible time because it was gang related and the killer was never found. What I didn't know was that Mark had turned to the dark side and was in so deep into trouble. That rough life he's talking about could only have come as a result of something he did. Just like now.

"What are you going to do with her?" he asks.

"I'm not going to discuss that with you," I answer. He knows why. The fact that more tears stream down his cheeks confirms he knows exactly what I'll be doing with his daughter. His worry should be more focused on what I'm going to do to him.

"You accepted her offer?" Unspoken pain comes alive in his eyes.

"I did."

"Vincent... she's a bright young woman with a future ahead of her. She's in love with her writing. Please, don't bring her into the darkness of our world. I've tried my best to keep her out of the underground. I never meant for this to happen."

"We never mean for most things to happen, but they do."

"Please, don't stop her from living her dreams," he begs.

It's strikes me as strange that he would say this to me when he nearly ruined everything all by himself. "Mark, you owe me over two million dollars you used to gamble and pay for prostitutes younger than your girl to fuck you. Don't dictate shit to me. Be grateful I haven't rammed your head into the wall and fucked you up so bad you have to piss backwards." I bare my teeth, and he shudders, his red eyes bulging.

He's never heard me talk like that. Chances are he would have had better sense if he had.

"Vincent, I'm really sorry. I really am."

I hold up my hand and shake my head. I don't want to hear him apologize again. I heard it practically all of last night. Now, it's time for action.

What I'm about to tell him won't be enough. Not by a long shot, and I already know I'm going to have to take a hit with the stress of it. I figured it this way, I'm still fucked and everything's a mess whether he's alive or dead. The death would be punishment. That's all it would be and wouldn't help me fix the shit one way or the other.

That's what I'm telling myself to make it... tolerable.

"Ava will stay with me, and you... you will sort yourself out in whatever way you need to, so you can tell me all that you did." It really doesn't feel like it's enough, absolutely unfair in comparison to the repercussions of his actions. I should beat the fuck out of him and mess him up more than I did. The truth is, I can't.

It's her again. I look at him and see her face. She's payment, and I accepted, but even before I accepted, the beauty calmed the beast inside me.

"You will give me that chance?" His voice quivers.

I sneer at him. "Motherfucker.... Don't make the mistake of thinking I'm freeing you. I'm not fucking doing that, and definitely not until I know all the damage and shit you've done."

"I ...I don't remember anything much, and what I can remember is stuff you already know."

"I'm sure you can shed more light than that," I demand. "You will tell me everything. I want to know what happened and what you got me mixed up in. I can't afford to waste any time. Who else did you hang out with?"

"Omar and a few of his associates. I made deals to follow through on the securities."

"On Giordanos Inc.?" I seethe as he nods.

"And... the Odyssey hotels." I tense when he says that. *Fuck.*

Why do I get the impression that this fucker is going to tell me more that's going to make me want to kill him right the hell now? The Odyssey hotels are a venture I entered with Salvatore and Gabe. We own a chain of hotels on five islands in the Caribbean that cater to adult fantasies. They're like the sex club set in paradise.

"What about the hotels?"

The fear that fills his eyes makes my blood boil. What more is he going to tell me?

"I was siphoning money to an offshore account. There's a guy who wanted to set up some business in Antigua."

I bite down hard on my back teeth. "You fucker." I glare at him, and then it occurs to me he did all this without me knowing. He has access to the systems, but no one knew what was going on until he slipped up.

Then we couldn't find him for three days. That's virtually impossible, and not with a man like this.

Or maybe it's me who's wrong again. There I was thinking of him as the simpleton. Maybe it's me who's underestimating him. What simpleton can do all that he's done to a guy like me?

He looks a pathetic mess now, but I can't help but wonder if there's either more to Mark than I know or if someone was helping him to steal and fuck me over.

I have to factor in every possibility and leave no stone unturned.

"I wasn't thinking straight. He offered me a discount on some drugs if I could set something up for him in Antigua. Vincent, I... don't remember anything else. I can't." He lowers his head and shakes it. "I need to go to the clinic, Vincent," he states, and his cheeks flush with shame. "I'm not refusing cooperation, but I can't see for shit. I'm addicted to all manner of fucking shit, and no matter what I take, I can't forget." He lifts his hands against the clink of the chains, and they tremble.

The fucker strikes a nerve inside me. "Forget?"

"The loss... the loss. Lost her, and them to death." He's not looking at me. He said *her*.

I know he's not married. I'm assuming though there must have been a woman in the picture.

He laughs and lifts his head. "I'm just a dead man walking

without a soul, waiting for the fucking devil to take me. Drag me down to hell and put me out of my misery." He's tripping. I can see it. The shaking in his body and the tremor is voice is more than fear. It's the shit he's high on.

"What did you take before we got to you?" I ask, trying to calm down.

"A mixture of coke and ecstasy. I had some beer. It balances the effect. Not by much though. I need to go back to the clinic, and then I can help. Ava wanted me to go to the clinic. Please let me go, Vincent. It's the least I can do."

"I'll make the arrangements."

"Thank you."

"I'm not doing it for you." I give him a hard stare and he flinches.

Shaking my head I leave. There's nothing more I can do here.

Today is just as long as I knew it would be.

I get back home at eight after taking care of a few things back at Giordanos Inc.

It's dinner time. Ava is supposed to be joining me. I make my way into the dining room, where I find Marguerite at the table with Timothy.

When Marguerite sees me, she sighs. I'm interested to hear how the rest of the day went after I left.

My arrival has signaled the chefs to bring the food out from the kitchen. They've made roast beef and honey roasted vegetables at my request. As always, it looks amazing and smells even better. They set a plate for me and another for Ava.

"How is she?" I ask Marguerite when the chefs leave.

"She's not eating, Vinny. Other than the cookies and hot chocolate I gave her this morning, she hasn't eaten anything. I gave her a robe and a T-shirt to change into so she could shower. Lydia will be here later with some more clothes. It's... been weird, Vinny." She presses her lips together in disdain Timothy reaches for me, and I take him. It's his bedtime, so I don't want to take up too much time with him.

"I told her you wanted to see her here at eight," Marguerite adds.

"I'll deal with her when she comes down."

As if on cue, Ava walks into the room. She's wearing a fluffy white robe, and her face is bare of makeup. Without the streaks of mascara on her face and her hair ruffled, her true beauty is on display.

Her eyes go straight to Timothy. Surprise settles on her pretty face as she watches me holding him. Maybe it's how I look when I'm with my son.

Timothy gives her a wide toothy grin and reaches out to her gurgling and giggling. His angelic innocence breaks down the barrier of hardness on her face, which breaks out into an open smile that makes her eyes twinkle.

I haven't seen a smile on her face before, so it's something I note. I'm vigilant though, as always with my kid, so when she goes to reach for him, I move him to Marguerite so she can take him.

"Can you take him to bed?" I tell her, and she nods.

It may be weird, but I don't allow random women to touch him or bond with him. Nobody who isn't family or friends. I don't usually have women here in the house he can see, so I don't want him with her.

Marguerite takes him away and closes the door behind her.

I return my gaze back to Ava, who's looking at me with caution.

"I didn't know you had a son," she states.

"Because I never told you."

She hardens her gaze on me. "I wasn't going to hurt him."

"You don't have to worry about him while you're here." I'm trying to be firm and assert control. I have a few things to tell her she won't like. "Sit."

She sits at the place that was set for her, which is just over from me, and looks like she's readying herself not to eat.

"I heard you didn't eat anything today. Why?" Since I'm starving, I start on my food.

"Not hungry," she answers stiffly, and I ball my fist that's holding the knife. She cuts me a sharp glance, eyeing up the knife.

"Marguerite says you had cookies."

"I did."

"That all you eat in the days?"

"I'm here for sex. What does it matter if I eat or not?"

Oh... I see. Looks like it's just hit her now—the situation. I straighten up and smile at her much to her displeasure.

"You will not stay here and starve. When I fuck you, I need you to be alert and not perishing on me for lack of food." She doesn't like that answer one damn bit. I don't care. These people, *her*, she needs to know I'm doing them a favor.

"Where is my father? Did you let him go?"

Maybe it's a mixture of fear and anger talking, but she's gotten ballsy.

"No, I didn't let him go."

She visibly shudders and winces. "I thought you were going to let him go."

"Ava, your offer stopped me from killing his ass. I'm not letting him out on the street to do more damage."

"What are you going to do with him?"

"I haven't decided yet. All you need to know right now is he's alive." I intensify my gaze on her, letting her know to cut the questions about her father.

She draws in a slow breath. "You never answered my question earlier. How long will I be here? I have a life. I work. I have friends. People who will be asking for me. I have an apartment I pay rent on. *Fuck*... I don't even own my own car. It's on finance, and it's still at the docks." Her voice is shaky.

"All those things will be taken care of while you are here."

"What do you mean, taken care of?"

"It fucking means exactly as it sounds. I'll take care of it."

I'm tired and fed up. She's in her right to be pissed, but I can't deal with it tonight.

"So, you're just going to keep me here and pay everything. There are some things that money can't take care of. I'm working, and I was working toward a promotion that would change my life. I can go to work and come back here."

My hands still, and I intensify my glare on her.

This broad actually thinks she can tell me what to do? And not just that, seems like she thinks she can dictate the terms of this arrangement too, like I'm some kind of schmuck. Fucking fuck that. I have news for her fine ass.

"No. You will not do that," I inform her. "You are allowed in this room, the kitchen, the library, and your room. Your room has an en-suite shower. The library has books, the kitchen food. It's enough. You'll have dinner with me most evenings and I'll send for you when I'm ready to fuck you. There, that sounds good to me."

Her face is classically horrified. No—scratch that. It's the perfect illustration of mortified. She won't say anything though because a deal's a deal. *Good girl.* At least she knows that part.

I decide to continue reeling off the terms. "I will have one of my guys accompany you outside on the grounds, where you can take a walk and get some fresh air. That is what you will do while you're here."

"Like an animal," she fumes. "Walk me like a dog?"

"Ava, if you fuck with me, I'll put you in a cage like a fucking animal."

She stands up straightaway, almost knocking over the chair. She shakes her head at me.

"You'd really do that to a person! A cage?"

I choose to ignore her question. "You're going to the doctors in the morning," I state. She's pushing me, but fuck, if she wasn't enraged before, she's that now.

"The doctors?"

"For birth control."

"I'm already on birth control."

"He'll also be making sure you're clean."

She gives me an incredulous glare. "I'm clean. I'm not some slut."

"I don't know that."

Her eyes blaze. "You asshole. How dare you?"

That's it. I can't deal with her tonight.

I get up in one motion and march over to her. Panic washes over her pretty face, and she backs away.

I go for her, walking her right into the wall like earlier. The difference between now and then is, earlier, I was aroused and interested. Now, I'm aroused and pissed.

I ball a fist and land a punch right into the space by her elbow. She flinches but stares at me head on.

"How dare I? Really?" I fume.

"You don't know me. You can't just do this. You can't just keep me locked away. How long are you going to keep me here?" she challenges, and I get up in her face.

"Two million dollars!" I shout. It's a release of frustration. "Two fucking million dollars. How long do you think you should stay?" Better to pose the question like that to her so she can get the picture of what we're dealing with.

I lower my head, closer, and bare my teeth. "How long, Ava? What do you think is reasonable?" There's no good answer. That's why she can't give me one. There's no answer that works for either of us.

Her lips part. Her plump, full lips part, and my gaze drops to them along with the slight rise and fall of her chest. There's a hint of her cleavage peeking through the robe, and damn it, when my gaze flicks back up to hers, I see that distinct look of fear and want. It's there again, and I'm not mistaken. The fear just enhances the want. It enhances my want for her too.

I don't know what it is about this woman that gets to me. I've known her for less than twenty-four hours, and this... *thing*, whatever it is, chemistry, attraction, or madness has me wanting her.

I feel it deeper the longer I stay close to her. It's so strong she looks away from me, but I catch her face and focus her stare back on me.

Fuck this frustration. What am I waiting for?

I hold her face with one hand and with the other, I undo the belt to the robe. I look down at her as the cloth falls open, revealing her breasts. She's wearing panties. That's all.

Her breath hitches when I rub my fingers over her mound. I move the lace back from her panties then slip my fingers into her pussy.

My cock hardens straightaway when I feel how wet she is for me.

"You're wet," I point out with a devilish grin, and she tries to look away, ashamed. "Your body betrays you again, Bellezza. You're trying to leave, when it really looks like you want to stay."

"You can't keep me here forever."

I can't. I know I can't, but I can't give her an answer either. I haven't cooled off enough from the shit her father put me through to give her a sufficient answer. The truth is, she fascinates me.

She seems to be the first woman in a long time whom I've felt that spark of need for, and I crave it.

I add another finger to her pussy and start pumping harder, faster, and she does her best to look like she's not enjoying it. She fails after a few seconds and bites down hard on her lip to hold in a moan. I release her face, and she continues to hold the pleasure in, so I pump harder, faster, and thanks to the few minutes I got up close and personal with her earlier, I learned a thing or two about what makes her give in to her inner desires.

So, when I lower my mouth to suck her tits, I know she'll cave, and she does.

Her tits already look ripe and puckered, begging to be sucked. By the time I taste her nipples, they pebble hard like diamonds.

I move from one to the other, sucking hard, encouraged by her moans of pleasure, as I continue to finger-fuck her until I feel her clit harden up too. But fuck... it's the simplest of things that drives me over the edge.

It's her hand.

Her delicate hand smooths up my shoulder, soft and searching, caressing. Her long, elegant fingers run over my shoulders and flutter over to my neck, where she continues to stroke the skin there. I pause my suckle to look at her.

She's panting and aroused. Lost in need and want for me, completely at my mercy. It's that what makes me greedy.

It's that what makes me crave more, and I haven't truly had her yet.

I catch her face once more, and she comes to my lips like an obedient servant.

I kiss her, and she kisses me back with reckless abandon, giving herself to me. Our tongues tangle and twist, and I taste her.

The taste seals everything else. I pull away from her lips and gaze down at her lust-filled eyes.

"I'm clean... we're doing this now," I practically growl, ripping the robe from her. I want her body on show while I fuck her. "You hear me?" I ask because she looks numb.

"Yes," she answers, and I start undoing my pants.

CHAPTER EIGHT

Ava

I've gone past the stage of asking myself what I'm doing. I'm pretty certain now that I've bordered on the edge of madness.

It's the only thing that can explain what I'm doing.

I rest against the wall, naked again, with the same man before me. My damn mouth waters as I watch him undo his pants, the belt first, then his zipper. He pushes his pants and boxers down just enough to allow his massive cock to spring free.

It's big, and the fat mushroom head is glistening with pre-cum.

I'm crazy, completely crazy, and I won't admit anything, not even to myself, because I don't want this. I don't, but... I do.

I can't. *But*... I am.

All thoughts of what I want and don't want and can't want are wiped out of my mind when the godlike man takes hold of me. He lifts me up, and because I'm so wet, he plunges right into my pussy, my body welcoming him as his ruthless cock sears into me.

I arch my back to take the intensity, but he rights me and holds me to him as he starts pumping into my body. He presses me into the wall and angles me so he can fuck me harder.

My lips fall open, and I gasp at the thrilling sensation that races over me. Like wildfire, it spreads recklessly over my body starting with the endings of my nerves, then it sinks deeper and burns up my insides.

An orgasm takes me right away, and I throw my head back, crying out into the release. I come and I come, and the arousal of passion coils again. He drives into me harder and faster, rutting into me like an animal, fucking me like I've never been fucked before, claiming me and making sure I know I'm being claimed. He pushes me rough into the wall and holds my face so I can look him in the eyes and see the primal, animalistic need.

That's when things change, and I hold on to him. At the same time, he kisses me just like before but harder.

We move to the table, and he knocks everything that was at my spot to the floor. The chair, the plates which smash, the glass that shatters.

He sets me on the table, and I lower down to rest on my elbows. He lifts my leg up over his shoulder and starts jackhammering into me.

This position feels different. I close my eyes as sparks speckle my vision, but he holds my face again.

"Open your eyes. Look at me," he commands. He seems to have something about wanting me to see. I listen and do as he says. It seems to be the only thing I'm set to do.

He returns his hold to my hips, gripping tighter as he pounds harder. The shaking of the table causes something else to fall to the floor and smash. I don't know what it is.

When his cock pulses inside me, I know he must be coming. I'm there at the precipice of the edge again. It's seconds before I fall. It feels like falling, so I lunge forward and reach for him. He catches me, pulling me to his chest to rest against his ruffled shirt.

He holds me, and we come together. I cry out into the release that takes us and he growls.

His pumps slow as his cum floods my passage, hot and virile, all male and primal just like him, and even that has dominion over me.

His hair is ruffled. A lock of it hangs over his eye, showing off how truly sexy he is. His hot breath against my skin makes me want him all over again, and I realize then that I'm in trouble.

I can't believe I just had sex with him. A mob boss.

He releases me and pulls out, allowing his cum to leak down my legs.

I'm still trying to catch my breath. He's breathing hard too as he does up his pants.

He looks me over and holds my gaze, showing more fascination than before. It's more want, but a dark thought strikes me as his volcanic eyes stare back at me.

Would he still want me if he knew? Knew my past?

It's been years since I thought that, but then I've never been with anyone who looked at me like that before.

"You will stay here until I say when you can go."

"What if I change my mind?" I hear myself say. I know the price, and I'm ashamed to ask because I know what it means. I just don't know if I can do this. Be here, be here with this man who's looking at me with so much desire it breaks down the walls I've built up over the last ten years.

One corner of his sensual mouth slides up into an easy grin.

"You won't..." That answer isn't just because he knows I know what will happen to Dad if I leave. He knows I won't change my mind because of him.

Just like earlier, I watch him go.

This time, he looks back at me. He glances over his shoulder before he walks through the door.

It closes, and I'm no better off than I was before.

I look around the floor at the mess we made, at broken

pieces of glass everywhere. I fixate on the broken tumbler before me. I still have questions, I'm still worried, and I know people will be worried about me.

Morning comes...
I slept through the night. I can't believe I actually slept. In the bed too.
I guess I should be grateful I have my own room and didn't have to sleep in his bed. I'm sure though that I'll be there soon.
I woke late and only when Marguerite came into the room.
She brought breakfast. I'm so hungry I couldn't be difficult if I tried.
Clothes are brought in for me, the expensive stuff. Everything is designer made and cost more money than I make in a year.
Any other woman might be thrilled to have such lavish clothing, but I'm not. I have my own clothes, and I need to work.
I can't quite explain to anyone how hard I worked to get to where I am today. Mind, body, and soul. This is the second day I've missed at work, and I really doubt Freddie is going to understand any lame excuse I may give him.
Vincent said he would take care of it... What the hell would he have said to Freddie?
And Dad.... Where is he? I still don't know.
The rest of the day passes and infuriates me. Despite the way Vincent fucked me last night, I still had to go to the doctor, where I was given the contraceptive injection with instructions to come off the pill in seven days when the injection kicked in. I already felt it was a complete invasion of my privacy, but then the fucking STD test took invasion of privacy to another level.
I couldn't have been more humiliated. It brought up memories I don't want to ever remember. Other than my standard checkups at the gynecologists and pill checks, I tend to steer clear of the doctors.

Of course, I was clean, and I never had to go through any of that shit, but I guess I'm getting the picture of the type of control freak Vincent is.

To add insult to injury, I was informed on my arrival back to the house that Vincent wanted to see me.

I'm making my way to his office now. It's on the ground floor and at the back of the house by the turn of the corridor that leads into the kitchen.

I'm walking, but my legs feel like jelly.

I'm like a mindless automaton set to do what I'm told, no matter if I like it or not.

I hate it that I still don't know anything about Dad other than that he's safe, and I really hated today.

I know this is on me. I'm choosing to be here. I insisted and all but begged. So, that means I have to play by the rules. His rules.

I didn't know what to expect, and I'm not sure if anyone would be able to understand that my choice to be here barely felt like a choice.

This all feels like I'm in some kind of nightmare.

And... there's what happened between us last night.

Last night is still in my mind. Me and him together, having wild, out-of-control sex like we wanted each other.

My damn head is still spinning. I can't believe I behaved that way with a man I don't know.

All day yesterday, I wondered what the first time would be like. I wondered what he'd be like. I didn't expect him to take me in such a way that it left me breathless and so lightheaded. There were points where I felt like I was going to float away.

I shudder to think what that must mean, because it felt real to me.

I should know the difference between what's real and what's not. I think I can take claim to knowing if nothing else, and last night, there was genuine want and desire from both of us.

What will tonight be like?

I get to the door to his office and stop to catch my breath

and right my mind. I look over the door and try to imagine what he's doing inside.

The door is made of oak and old-fashioned with a golden lion's head set in the top center of it. It kind of gives me the creeps. Not that I've had the grand tour of the place, but this part of the house feels older, a little like the library. Marguerite took me there this morning and tried to do that comfort thing again with her cookies. She said I could read any book I wanted, and I could hang out in there or take a few books back to the room.

Pulling in a deep breath, I knock on the door and gear myself up.

"Come in," he answers, his voice a low timbre that's already doing things to me.

I turn the handle and push the door open, seeing him standing behind his desk. He looks like he was just sorting out some paperwork. He stops when he sees me and gives my body a full sweep.

I take the moment to look at him too. He's dressed more casual in a black long-sleeved T-shirt and black slacks that look similar to the pair he wore when we first met; these have a little dragon insignia on the pocket though. I've seen him in a suit and slacks. I wonder if he ever wears jeans.

"Come in and close the door," he commands, and I walk in allowing the door to close behind me.

"Good day?" he asks. The humor on his face is a tell that he was most likely informed about the day I had. I gave the driver who took me to the clinic a mouthful because he stayed with me through the whole examination. He was told he had to.

"What sort of answer do you want me to give you?" I throw back. I know my tone is way off and I should watch myself, but I can't help it. I'm pissed.

"The truth," he answers.

"You don't want the truth."

"Try me."

It's an invite I think I might accept. "Well, for a start, when I tell you something as personal as I'm clean and I don't have any STDs, it would be decent at least if you believed me. I don't wish to spread my legs for the fucking doctor and driver all in the same afternoon. You didn't have to have the driver in there with me. It was humiliating." I didn't think I was going to launch into such an attack. Now that I've got it off my chest, I feel better for it, but I don't know what it will cost me.

His face is completely unreadable. I don't know what the hell he's thinking. He's just looking at me without answering.

"If you wanted me to go to the doctors with you, you should have said so," he states, and I glower at him.

"What? That's what you got from my answer?"

"Well, I think you're right. Your pussy belongs to me, so it should just be me who sees it. I'll bear that in mind next time."

Next time?

What the hell would I be going anywhere for next time? Shit… if he's thinking in terms of next time, there's still that issue of when I'll be allowed to leave here.

"There will be no next time." The words fall from my mouth mindlessly, and the instant they do, I realize my mistake. I forgot who I'm talking to and why I'm here.

Much as I hate to admit this, he actually did me a favor. He spared Dad's life and showed mercy. I'm thinking all these things, reminding myself that I need to keep them at the forefront of my mind, but this just feels like I'm in prison.

When he steps from behind his desk, I tense but try to act like he has no effect on me.

He sees through the shit though. As he comes closer, the cunning look in his eyes intensifies.

He gets right up in my face, and I don't back away. Instead, I stare up at him with expectancy, waiting. Waiting for an answer or an action.

"Ava Knight, what do you think ownership means? It appears you and I have some very different understandings of the term. Mine is the Oxford definition, which is generally acceptable by most. *'The act, state, or right of possessing something.'* Right of possessing. That means I get to make the decisions I want over my property. That sort of thing. What do you think it means?"

I close my eyes and seethe. What do I do here? This is more than humiliation. So much more.

Don't make the situation worse, Ava. You'll suffer. I can't make it worse.

I will myself to think straight and block out the rage.

"I agree with you," I say, except the quiver in my voice makes it sound so shaky it doesn't sound like the voice comes from me. His eyes darken with a sexual heat that reaches me. He touches the edge of my cheek and traces the outline of my jaw. It makes my nerves scatter. "Ownership means that."

"Good. Now that we're on the same page, go and sit over there and spread your legs for me. Let me see your pussy."

CHAPTER NINE

VINCENT

Her cheeks flush red at my words.

The coloring starts there and works its way down her elegant neck. That damn look of want and desire in her eyes comes right back and gives me permission to do whatever I want to her.

She wouldn't know it's the only thing keeping me from breathing fire at the moment. The look and the scent of her.

Her scent reminds me of jasmine and gardenias like the flower gardens at our family home in Sicily. That's what she smells like. It's a very distinct smell, so when she's aroused like she is now, it's stronger.

So much stronger, and it hardens my dick when I think of tasting her and feasting on her hot, wet pussy.

After the day I've had, I need a good fuck, and she looks like she needs it too with the way she's so wound up.

That wild fascination takes over as I watch her cross the distance and sit on the leather armchair I directed her to.

"Panties off," I say. She doesn't look at me though.

She just does as she's told. Her long brown hair drifts over her shoulders and flows past her breasts when she bends to shimmy out of her panties. She's wearing a little dress, which is perfect for fucking.

I want her to keep it on.

She's a sight for sore eyes and blue balls.

Both of which she gave me today from thinking of her. Sore eyes from lack of sleep and blue balls from wanting to be inside her again.

It wasn't what I needed to be going into work with.

Today saw me dealing with more shit from her father.

It was so bad I had to call Christian to help me. He and Salvatore are the best guys at dealing with anything technical. I have Salvatore working with the investigation team, so I grabbed Christian instead and learned that my systems were fucked.

Mark screwed with all the records. Everything was a fucking mess with discrepancies going back for months. At least six months, but it looked like it could have been more. So much fucking more. At first, it looked like he was trying to cover up stealing money, but then he got sloppy and mixed up all the figures.

I need my figures right, always, so I can do what I do to shift the dollars around and make it clean. When fuckers like Mark fuck with me and fuckers like the feds try to investigate, I'm leaving myself out in the open for attack.

So, I will have this moment, and I don't care that she's pissed about today. I will definitely be doing what I want to her.

I move over to her as she pulls her dress up, revealing her perfect pussy.

She spreads her legs and straightens up so I can see. What I see is that she's practically dripping wet and her face is almost the same pink color as her pussy.

Those eyes of hers are doing their best to avert my stare.

I chuckle. "You know you don't have to try so hard not to like it. It's okay to want to be fucked."

"I don't like it," she lies.

It's fine. I don't need to convince her. She can do that all by herself.

"Touch your pussy, Ava," I tell her.

Her eyes are weighted with a mixture of shame and disgust. She presses down hard on her back teeth, a last resort to hold back the mountain of words she wants to say to me. I watch her give up the fight, and I almost laugh.

The joke's on me though because when her fingers slide down to her mound and move past her pussy lips, the beauty has my mouth watering so bad I have to swallow. The sight of her touching herself is so fucking hot I nearly blow my load.

Her face turns crimson when her fingers come away with the slick juice.

"Do it again and push right in," I order, and she obeys, sliding her finger right inside. She's so wet there's a slicking sound that embarrasses her further.

She looks away shamed but turns her head back to me when I take her hand touching her pussy and guide it to her lips.

"Taste." I want her to taste so she can see for herself what I'm doing to her.

She looks appalled that I'd ask her to do that, but thank fuck she doesn't protest. She does it, she tastes, and it's arousing as fuck watching her do that too.

"Looks like there's much I have to teach you," I begin. "When your body speaks, Ava, it's telling you the truth. That is what I do to you, and now that you know, you will never say no again."

"That's not fair."

"Why? What else do you think it means?"

She can't answer. Good, she knows I'm right.

It's time to stop talking now. No more of it. Time to take care of our needs.

I smile and love it when her soft, full lips fall open as I dive in to feast on her pussy.

I bury my face right in between her soft thighs and start licking her clit.

That first to mellow her out. I go slow with intention to my strokes. Slow will drive her as crazy as I was today. Slow will tease her to give in to me. Slow will take her inch by inch to the point where I need her to be. Right where we left off last night.

I lick, and she gets wetter. I hold her pussy lips open so I can get deeper, and that's when she starts moaning. It's a glorious sound, and my damn cock gets so hard when I hear it, I almost explode.

What I better do is stop and look at her.

"You like that, Bellezza?" I ask, and the whimper she was holding back is answer enough. "Don't worry. There's so much more where that came from."

I give her a wicked grin before I go back in. Feasting is definitely what I'm doing to my pretty little guest.

"Ahhhh.... Hmmm..." she moans, and I lick her clit, coaxing her release. I won't get her to hold it yet. I can tell she's not used to this. I'll bet anybody she's been with in the past never went down on her and ate her out the way I do.

She wants to know when she's leaving here. Fucking fuck that. By the time I finish with her, she'll be begging me to stay. Begging for more.

It's the look of her now as I glance up. And fuck, she reaches forward and takes hold of my shoulders just like the other night. It's then I know I have her right where I want her. Exactly at the point where she can no longer resist and has to yield to me.

Her sweet, juicy nectar flows right into my mouth.

It's a gush of syrup that flows right into my open mouth, and I drink from her, lapping it all up. Her hands on me aren't gripping anymore. She's stroking. I don't know if she realizes what she's doing as she glides her hands over my shoulders like we're lovers.

I look up at her and have to stop. She's never looked more beautiful, captured in the height of pleasure, claimed in its claws as it beckons her to feel passion.

Feeling my gaze on her, she opens her eyes and stares down

at me. Her cheeks grow rosier with surprise at her reaction, and her hands still.

Here's the part where I need to stay in control. Last night, I realized all too quickly that I have a fascination with her. An unhealthy one. It started the night we met and I saw that old pain in her eyes. Since then, I've been able to see everything she's feeling, and I'm not sure if she knows that.

I stand up and look down at her, regaining my dominance as she tries to catch her breath.

"Get up and bend over the desk," I command her.

My harsh words break the spell of the moment. In fact, they shatter it, but my mind is taken up with the way she follows instruction. My command over her is turning me on, making me love that she does what I tell her. What I love more is that she wants it too.

There's no part of her that doesn't want me.

She goes to the desk and bends over. Her dress is too long for my liking though, although it only stops by her thighs. She's trying to bunch it up, but it keeps covering her ass. I want that ass uncovered.

I take the edge of the dress and pull it off over her head in one swift action, making her turn and gasp.

"I could have taken it off," she protests.

"Don't worry about it," I answer with the smile and unhook her bra so her breasts can fall out.

They do, and I back off the straps down her arms.

Her puckered nipples call to me to suck them, so I hold her in place on the desk so I can give them a good sucking before turning her to face the desk. As I bend her over, her fully rounded behind is on perfect show. Exactly the way I want it.

I take out my cock and plunge right into her pussy. She winces, and her knees buckle, but I slip my arm around her waist to catch her. I'm not an inch-in sort of guy, and not when I give her good foreplay. She takes me whole, and I start to fuck her hard, giving her the fuck I wanted to give her since I woke up this morning.

Fucking hell, if I could have been late, I would have gone to her and this would be the second time today.

I plunge into her relentlessly, allowing my body to guide me and drive my movements, her moans and cries of ecstasy fueling me to continue.

Then something slips away from me. I don't know what it is —control or reality. I felt it last night too when I had to put her on the table. It's happening again and drawing me in to consume her. I start pounding into her. I know she must feel it too when she starts moving on my cock, fucking me too.

We both go crazy on each other. I never expected that. It's worse than last night.

I know I've lost my mind when I hold her right down on the table and fuck her so hard she screams out loud with pleasure. It's a sound that makes me wish I could go on, but I can't. I was already a goner, then I heard it, and blew into her like a storm, filling her hot passage with my cum.

It was wild again. Another wild session with this woman that's left me drained. It's the second time, and I feel like I want to devour her. The need is more.

She's panting, trying to catch her breath, but I notice something else that has me hardening up again inside her. She's stroking her left breast. Fucking hell, she's still so aroused.

The fascination comes back to my mind, and I lean over, placing my mouth to her ear while I still her fingers and take over. I stroke over the swell, and she presses into me, enjoying the thrill of the afterglow. It's practically burning my skin.

While I stroke her tit and stroke the nipple, she starts wiggling her ass against me, and I allow her to for a few seconds until I feel the need to put up the wall again.

I've been a quick study with this woman.

Touch her the way she wants and give her what she needs, and she's all mine. Piss her off, and it brings back reality and returns the control to me. Control of what we are.

We aren't lovers, although as I look at the vague reflection of us in my window against the dark night, even I have a hard time believing that's not true.

It can't be though, and no matter what magic she's worked on me to give me this fascination, I can't let it take me.

I rest my hand on her ass and give it a good squeeze.

"Naughty Bellezza, you want me to fuck you again. Dirty girl. I have work to do." The minute I say that, she stills and tenses in my arms. My words severed the erotic trance, and I almost feel like a prick. But this good girl who looks like she'll give her heart and soul to save a man from the devil mustn't confuse what we are. I whisper now against her ear while I put my dick back in my pants. "I'll tell you what, since you want my cock so badly, I'll allow you to ride it in the morning."

I chuckle as she tries to pull away from me in clear disgust. I don't know why she keeps forgetting who I am.

She actually thinks she can run away from me when I haven't dismissed her.

I grab her arm, and she tries to cover herself.

"I hate you," she wails.

Good... she should hate me. She should at least think she should. There was no part in this contract that included love, or even lust.

We're not supposed to feel anything. I can't resist though, can't resist one last taunt for the evening she won't forget.

"We both know that for a lie," I say, releasing her. A tear runs down her cheek.

"Must you be so awful?" she counters.

"Yes. Now, go to your room. I'll see you in the morning at eight. Make sure you're up."

She grabs her clothes, shoving her dress on inside out and her panties backwards. She flees without her shoes, and I watch her go.

I watch her go, watch her rush down the corridor and turn the corner, and even after, when I can't see her anymore, I still stare.

Awful... yes, I am.

She makes me not want to be though.

I fight against the warm glow surrounding my cold, dead heart. I fight it because I don't want to feel good nor bad.

I don't want to feel anything.

Misery doesn't always love company.

Wanting and needing are two very different things.

I want her. I must never need her though.

So, I can't confuse what we are either.

CHAPTER TEN

Vincent

Ava was colder toward me this morning.
Ice cold.
We still ended up the same way as yesterday, slaves to passion when it came to claim us. It left me wanting more and on edge. Two things I can't be right now. This instability of emotions is not good for me. Today is the meeting with the Bratva guys.
It's happening in a few minutes.
I got to Giordanos Inc. early. It was so early I had to open up the building myself. We have a custodian who usually takes care of that.
I've been standing by the window of my office looking out at the shimmer of the lake as the sun graces the water.
My office here is bigger than the one I have at Renovata. I like it more here because of the view. It makes good for times like these when I need to reflect and get lost in my thoughts for a while. Or rather just think of anything. The problem with thinking is *over*thinking.

Right now, I have Ava and her gorgeous body stuck in my head, and I have this meeting I'm really not looking forward to. The two things are competing so badly for my attention that I'm not even thinking about Mark. Ava has replaced him in my mind.

My phone buzzes in my back pocket, and I reach for it.

It's Claudius Morientz, another mafia boss and a friend of mine. He has a PI he works with who's helped us out a few times. He's a powerful man in Chicago and has seen his fair share of trouble, which means he knows the right people to get certain things done that the usual Joe can't do.

His text says: *Gibbs is on the case.*

I message back my thanks.

I contacted him yesterday when I realized it was best for me to delegate some of the investigative tasks I needed to do on Mark. The shit of a mess he left in the office was too much to handle with the investigation as well.

Now I'm glad I did it because last night, I got a message from the rehab clinic Mark booked himself in letting me know he was being placed under a medicated detox.

The doctors said he wouldn't be able to talk business for the next three days while they weaned him off the drugs. He'll be in there for a minimum of three weeks.

Three fucking weeks. It pissed me off, but at the same time, it made me aware of how serious his situation must be.

Gibbs on the case will give me a break. I need it all resolved so I can be sure there's nothing left to worry about. Then all it will be about is my lost two million. I can deal with that and anything that directly affects me. What stresses me out is shit that affects everyone else.

So far, I have those things under control. Various clients Mark was stealing from have been paid back, out of my damn pocket to smooth things over, and we've managed to put a block on all the shit he set up to siphon money from the other business.

I am absolutely still left in wonder as to how the fucker did it while I never knew what he was up to, but I've decided I'm not thinking about it today. I don't care if someone holds a fucking gun to my head, my focus is going to be on this meeting. And being objective.

A knock sounds on the door, and I glance at the clock on the wall. It's time.

"Come in," I call out, and Salvatore comes in with Christian and two bulky-looking Russian men who look like cage fighters.

That's my first clue of personality. One has dark hair, the other is blond.

The dark-haired guy is Dmitri and looks like my age. He's the Sovientrik, advisor to the Pakhan, the boss. He's the same rank as my mother to my father.

Yuri, the other guy, is a Brigadier, like Salvatore is capo to me. The structure is different though to the way we are in the Italian mafia. My family is Sicilian, and we tend to be old school La Cosa Nostra. Born and bred. The first thing we know to do is to go with gut instinct. Mine is on high alert right now.

"Good morning, gentlemen." I beam, becoming the leader I'm supposed to portray.

"Good morning," Dmitri says to me. His accent is thick. He makes his way right over to me with Yuri. Both shake my hand. "Great to meet you. I hear congratulations will soon be in order."

Although I smile at him, I get that uneasy feeling again. He's talking about Pa's retirement and my ascension to be the new boss. News travels fast in the underworld.

"Thank you. I appreciate it. Please sit."

They sit on the opposite side of the table, and Salvatore and Christian sit to my left, leaving me at the head. I quickly glance at them, grateful they're here. Yesterday, I had Gabe on the phone asking me if I needed help. I couldn't tell him that I felt like I needed all the help I could get.

I certainly can't look like that now in front of these men. They're like sharks. I don't need to know them to know that if they get a whiff of blood, they'll eat me alive in one gulp.

I straighten up but rest back against my chair, casual and cool, crossing one leg over the other. "So... my father has told me the basics. I'd like you to tell me more about what you're hoping to get from an alliance with us."

Dmitri nods his head and runs a hand over his beard. "Of course. The idea came about because we have a new business venture and we're looking to be aligned with the best people to make the most money."

To my knowledge, most Bratva guys are into drug trafficking — *heroin*. We don't get our hands dirty like that. If it's that, we're out because if we get caught, we'll be well and truly fucked.

"And what is this new business venture of yours?" He doesn't like the way I say that. I wonder if he expected me not to ask.

Dmitri shuffles in his seat, sitting forward so he can rest his elbow on the table. "I hope you understand me asking you to keep this under wraps."

"That goes without saying. Don't worry, I didn't think you needed us to ship daisies." I smirk.

He smiles at me. "I like that. I must use that one. We're into diamonds. Mining in Africa. We need them shipped to various parts of the world."

Diamonds. That is definitely a new one for us, and from Africa?

Jesus Christ, it has illegal written all over it. Africa has extremely strict laws with regard to their diamonds. Of course, they would. It's their countries wealth.

This agreement here means we'd be smuggling those diamonds, and I'm sure as fuck they're not going to be any old diamonds.

"What kind?" I ask. "What kind of diamonds are they?"

Dmitri smiles wider. "I see you are a man of taste. They are the kind that would draw a lot of attention if discovered we had them. We have a very sophisticated setup we're proud of."

I look at him and think about it all. Pa told me they're offering a contract for one billion dollars. That's to secure our services for five years, after which there will be an increase. It all sounds good, and we could do it.

The thing about our company that everybody wants is, they know we can bypass certain people and laws. We're like pirates, and to say we own the seas is no underestimation. We actually do.

What gets me though is, sure we're powerful in the sense of what we can do, but we're the little guys in comparison to these people.

"Why us?" I ask. "You could pick anyone. We're just humble criminals who're good at making a buck." Like fuck, I make us sound like we're more honorable than we are. In actual fact though, we're probably a lot more honorable than these guys.

In the Bratva, it's always about who has the most money. It's a different kind of greed. It's heightened right here and now with me questioning a billion-dollar contract.

"You guys have the ability to smuggle any shit without being seen. We need efficiency, and sometimes small is good. Looks more legit. Especially when the feds have their eyes turned to prior alliances."

Ah. There we go. That's it. Makes sense now. "Didn't work out with your other associates?"

"No. You and I both know that feds are not the best people to have on your ass."

"Hear, hear," I agree.

"So, what do you think?"

I draw in a breath. "Sounds like something we can help you with."

Dmitri nods his head, satisfied with my answer. I'm not done yet though.

"That's fantastic. So... when can we sign contracts?"

"Wow, you move fast. I'd like some time to think about it, if that's alright. I'll get back to you as soon as I can, and we can talk contracts then. If you get your people to send over all the paperwork so my people can go over it, that would be great."

His smile stiffens. "Oh, I see. Well, we're hoping to get this project and agreement underway in the next eight weeks. We'd love to have everything in place before then."

This is where people who assume they have some control over us falter. I know we're small fry to him, and he probably expected me to jump like a dog and catch his bone.

I won't though. I gave my answer.

"I'd like some time to *think* about it. I'll get back to *you* as soon as I can," I merely repeat. I almost laugh at the flicker of anger that sparks in his eyes. I know what death looks like, and I'm sure this guy is the kind who would kill me dead just for my insolence if he could.

He needs me, and that's my leverage.

"Okay. Well... I guess we'll be waiting eagerly to hear from you."

"Four weeks tops," I answer. That will give me time. It's standard waiting time across the board that is usually acceptable. I think for an alliance, and with so much money involved, I'm within my right to take the time I need to make sure I'm doing the right thing on all fronts.

Dmitri bows his head, and although he looks calm and cool, his eyes still give him away. There's a lethal iciness in them that I pay attention to.

Fucker... he can wait.

"Thank you." He stands, as does Yuri, and they both leave.

The tension leaves the room too, and the air is less tight as the door clicks shut.

I look to Salvatore, who leans forward onto the table. Christian shakes his head.

"I do not like them," Christian says.

"You and me both," Salvatore agrees.

I'd jump in there and say the same, but I decide to take the high road and talk out the shit.

"What don't you like?" I ask.

"Shady as shit," Salvatore says.

I raise my brows. "We're shady as shit."

"Come on, Vin, you know what I mean. Diamonds as well? We've never done diamonds."

"And there's a reason for that," I add.

"Yes, we're done if we get caught," Christian puts in.

"But we've never got caught, not once. I want us to think about this objectively. I'll admit there's something I don't like. They won't be telling us everything the same way we'd never tell. Business is business. So, the focus needs to be this: we stand to lose a shitload of money if we get this wrong."

Salvatore narrows his eyes at me. "I don't know, Vin. I feel like there's more that could potentially be damaging to us."

He's right, at least I sensed that too. This alliance could be no different to any other we've agreed to, but then it might not be. And it's an alliance. Different to just a simple contract. It means working together above the rim.

"The problem I see is, there'd be a clash of titans," I point out. "We know how we run things but don't know how they do. We don't know what else we could be getting into with guys like that."

"So, what do we do?"

"We'll do our standard checks and make sure it's all for our benefit. If it is, then we'll do it." There, that's me being completely objective, although my gut instinct is already telling me not to trust them.

The pressure is on more than ever to make the right decision. I already feel inadequate to take the lead. I don't want to be the guy who starts his leadership and brings about ruin to the family and business.

CHAPTER ELEVEN

Ava

It was Holly who first told me about The Dark Odyssey.

She went for her twenty-first birthday with her then boyfriend, who was into BDSM.

I think every girl needs to have one of those friends who have a taste for the wild, but Holly was a little more than that. Wild for me is skydiving, bungee jumping, eating bugs, or some shit like that. I've never done any of those before, but that would be my definition of wild.

Unreal and far outside my comfort zone would be going to a sex club. So, when she first told me about her experience there and all she saw, yes, it fascinated me, and I might have hung on to every word she said, but that was all. I never planned to go.

Like most things that have happened in this one week, tonight doesn't feel real as the car I'm in pulls up at the entrance to The Dark Odyssey.

I'm actually here. Apart from the doctors, this is the first I've gone outside in days, and this is where I've been taken to.

I'm in the back of a Bentley, and a driver Marguerite called Pierbo has brought me here to meet Vincent. Under the coat, I'm wearing some type of lingerie I've only ever seen in a Victoria's Secret catalogue.

Lydia, a younger woman a little older than me who works at the house, gave it to me earlier, informing me that Vincent wanted me to wear it.

It's a silk rose pink baby doll negligee with cream lace on the edge. There's a matching thong, and my mask is cream with pink feathers and diamantes going around the rim.

I look like... I don't know. I look good. Marguerite did my hair for me, and yes, I do look good, but I don't feel it.

I'm still furious from the other night, and this is just... I have no words to truly express what I'm feeling.

As I'm ushered out of the car, I try to calm myself and remember why I did this. Maybe after it's all said and done, I'll feel better about the past.

Maybe I'll be rid of the guilt I still feel when I think about it.

Maybe I can then feel free and like I don't owe Dad so much. Like I don't owe him everything. I feel bad for my thoughts because I know wherever he is, he doesn't want this.

He never wanted this for me and never saved me from the horrors I faced so long ago to have me end up here. Captive again, although this was my choosing.

Another man takes over from Pierbo at reception, and I feel like property again. Like a package hand delivered and passed from one hand to the next.

We walk past with the line of people checking in and stop at coat check.

Awkwardness takes me when I take off my coat, exposing my body in this barely-there negligee. I've never worn anything so sexy outside the bedroom, and definitely not in public like this, with so many eyes on me.

I don't miss the way the guy taking my coat gives me a once-over but rights himself quickly when the man I was delivered to clears his throat. It's like a warning, which he seems to understand very quickly. I do too. It's obvious that he wasn't to look at me because I belong to Vincent.

I draw in a breath to clear my mind and follow the man who now feels more like a bodyguard.

I'm all worked up, but at the same time, I take in how beautifully decorated the place is. My heels click against the marble flooring that leads to a set of the large doors which open for us. At that moment, my breath is stolen away completely.

It's like I could be in Venice again with my parents. The architecture of some of the buildings in Venice is similar to Russia.

The club has that feel to it with the gold ceiling that mingles with the club lights and the European décor.

The music is blaring with vibrancy, and the people around are taking fun to the next level. They're all dressed in super sexy lingerie and masks, dancing the night away without a care in the world.

I was about to think the place looked like a normal, very classy club when my gaze lands on a couple having sex to my left.

My mouth falls open. I'm not the kind of woman who would want to watch people having sex, but looking at these people fucking out in the open is the thing that shocks me to the core. I don't get the chance to continue my stare though because I'm escorted away. What I did see, however, was that the whole sideline area had cubicles with couples. All having sex.

We go into an elevator that's to our left. It has one of those glass doors, and as we go up, a couple of acrobats float by on an aerial hoop. They're naked except for the gold and green paint on their bodies and the traditional carnival masks. I'm so fascinated I move closer to get a better look and get a shocker when I see they're having sex on the hoop.

I don't even know how they manage it. The woman has her legs wrapped around the guy's waist while he's keeping them on it with his legs spread into a full split and his feet wrapped around the hoop. He's moving into her slowly while she gives him complete control of her safety. They remind me of animals who bond together and are mated for life.

The elevator goes further up, and they're lost from my view. We stop on the fourth floor and step out to an elegantly decorated lounge area.

"This way, please," the guy says, guiding me by my elbow when I accidentally walk the wrong way.

I'm not thinking straight. I'm just walking like that mindless automaton again. Not knowing what to expect. Then I see him.

Vincent.

He's standing by the private bar waiting with another guy who looks like him. Another brother. One I haven't seen. There're definite similarities between them, except this one has striking blue eyes.

Vincent says something to him, and he glances over at me and gives me a curious look. When he looks back to Vincent, he raises a brow. I don't know what that means, and I'm not introduced either because he walks away before we reach Vincent.

"Boss," the guy says.

"Thank you, Tony. Arrange for Pierbo to get back here to take my guest home in an hour," Vincent orders.

"Yes sir," Tony answers.

They all have such respect for him, all doing as they're told. They don't owe him anything, but they do it because he has power over them.

Tony leaves us, and I straighten up trying to look unfazed by how uncomfortable I am. It's hard to do it though, with my breasts practically on show, and my ass too for the matter. The slight breeze from a passerby would lift the silky hem of the negligee, and everyone would be able to see I'm wearing a thong.

"Hello," he says, looking me over. A light of interest flashes in his eyes my damn body doesn't ignore.

"Hi," I answer. I'm so worked up though that I can't keep the tremor out of my voice. "Is my father safe?" I ask, not caring that I sound a little harsh. I need something to work with.

Something to take the edge off.

"He's in rehab," he replies, and my whole body sighs with noticeable relief.

God... he's there. Dad went to the clinic. He's there. I wonder how long he'll have to stay and what's happening.

"Did he go in on Monday?"

"He went Wednesday night."

I try not to fume. It's Friday, Vincent could have told me that from yesterday when I asked. The fact that he didn't just highlights how controlling he is.

"How long is he going to be there?" I ask keeping my tone even.

"Three weeks."

Jesus... that's much longer than last time. The last time was just ten days followed up with outpatient care.

"When can I talk to him?" Tears threaten to fall when I think of Dad alone at the clinic. He's had to go in for inpatient care three times. This is the fourth. It seems like the most serious as well. I've been with him every time—this will be the first that I won't be.

I'm grateful when Vincent's face softens and I see some element of compassion enter his eyes.

"Your father is in rehab and needs to focus on getting better. That's all you need to know right now. I will let you know when you can speak to him."

"Will you?" I challenge.

"We are not talking about this anymore." He smiles.

I hate that he has so much control over me. At least I can take some comfort in knowing that Dad's safe and is where he needs to be.

So, now I can think of me for a little bit until I have to think of him again.

"Why did you bring me here?" I ask.

"It's our playground. The house can become too boring. I don't want that."

"Playground?" God, what is this man going to have me doing?

I have no idea what to expect here, and what I've seen so far has thrown me for a loop.

"We'll be coming here sometimes to do things," Vincent says, running a finger over the flat of my stomach. His fingers brush over the material, but I feel the heat seeping into my skin.

Dare I ask what kind of things he means?

"Have you ever been to a sex club before, Bellezza?"

"No."

"Don't worry. I'm sure you'll have a good time. I'll make it enjoyable for you, especially as it's your first visit."

I don't answer. What am I supposed to say? What he means is sex, sex, and more sex, except I get the feeling that we're about to go over to the dark side. I see it in his eyes.

He walks around me, circling me in that predatory manner. "This is your color," he states. "It makes you look sexier. Now if only you didn't have that *miserabile* expression on your pretty face."

He takes his time to enunciate *miserabile,* and he actually says it with an accent. It sounds sexy when he says it.

"Maybe I look miserabile because you are a *maniaco del controllo*," I answer, giving away that I not only understand Italian but speak it too. I knew what I was doing though when I said it. There's little point holding on to something I don't have to.

It's much to his fascination.

He chuckles. "You think I'm a control freak?" He raises his brows.

"Yes."

"And you speak Italian?"

"Yes."

"Never told me that." He looms closer and makes an obvious show of searching my eyes through the mask.

"You did not ask."

"*Fiery*... I like it." He dips his head, and a lock of his hair falls over his eye. "Take off your mask. It's customary here to do so when you're with the person you're spending the night with."

"I thought I was going to be here for an hour."

"I want you later when I get home." He holds my gaze, and the crackle of energy that passes between us stirs hunger inside me.

That's how it starts. Always with a spark of something I can't control. He says something or does something that throws me, so I never quite see it coming until it hits.

He gives me an expectant look that nudges me to take off the mask. I slip it over my head and notice the way he studies my face.

I'm wearing makeup. The last time I had on makeup was Monday night when it was smudged all over my face from crying. It wasn't a good look. Tonight is different. It was odd getting ready with Marguerite doing my hair and Lydia my makeup, like I was getting ready for a date. Because I've taken to them, I humored them with excitement despite my anxiety.

"You look beautiful," he states, and that sensuous baritone of his voice slips over my skin.

"Thank you..."

"Come, let's get lost in a wild fantasy." He stretches out his hand for me to take, and I do.

His large hand swallows mine as he holds my hand and leads me to a room just behind the bar area.

He opens glass doors which slide open for us. As we step inside, my breath is swept away again by the beauty of the décor. Again, it hands down has that European feel to it but with a modern edge. Everything about it looks like a bedroom, except for the floor. It's mostly made of glass then tapers off to marble like the flooring downstairs. There's a king bed there set against the marble with silk burgundy sheets.

We walk further into the room, then I see why the floor is made of glass.

It's so we can see what's happening beneath us.

Numbness fills me as the blood drains from my body, then I'm parched when it rushes back in a wild streak of fire as I watch the bodies moving around below me in sinful ecstasy.

There must be about fifty people down there. Men and

women, all naked, having an orgy. Where they are looks like it was designed for it too. It's a room with a padded floor that looks like one big bed designed for fucking.

I try not to look, but I can't tear my eyes away. When I do, my attention is drawn to the corners of the room where there are people lying on tables with fruit and cream covering their bodies from head to toe.

They're laying there like human desserts while others gather around to lick, eat, or suck the fruit off their bodies. The fruit and body parts. Breasts, cocks, pussies. There are men and women all partaking, no one caring about differentiation.

My mouth drops open, and I'm not sure how it doesn't hit the floor. It's sexual overload, and I don't know what sort of dimension I've entered.

Nothing has quite felt real since Monday.

It's just Friday, and I've had all sorts of things happen to me.

I don't even realize I'm squeezing down hard on Vincent's hand until he lifts it and gives it a wave.

It's then I'm able to look up at him and see the wild curiosity he's staring back at me with.

If this was designed to shock me, it worked, and like most encounters with this man, I'm left wondering, *What next?*

"You look scared. My darker tastes aren't too much for you, are they?" His burning eyes hold me still.

I glance back down at the bodies again moving beneath us then look back to him wondering if he's ever done that.

"Is this what you do?"

"Not this. I just like watching. The glass is like one big mask that I hide behind as I watch. The way they fuck is so outrageously wild that you lose touch with reality. It's an escape. You look at them, and they don't care about anything besides the pleasure. It's like they've gone insane on it."

As he speaks, my jaw loosens. I look down again. Just below me is a woman on her hands and knees with one guy pounding into her mouth as she sucks his cock and another guy pounding into her from behind. There's another guy sucking her breasts.

Vincent's right... they look completely lost in what they're doing to each other. It's only when they switch around that my stare brakes and I return my focus to him. I'm already hot from all I've seen, but he makes it worse with the molten heat in his eyes.

"What do you think?"

I pull in a breath. "I don't know."

"Don't you?"

I'm lying, and he can tell. I'm so aroused I don't think I can move, and I'm thinking about sex... with him.

He releases my hand and touches my face. I look away and wince at his touch because his fingers on my skin feel like fire.

"Watching others lose themselves in pleasure like that is like an aphrodisiac. It makes you naturally give in to what you want most," he taunts, guiding my face back to meet his gaze.

"Is that why you brought me in here?"

He smiles and slides his grip down my throat. It's almost tight but just loose enough that it doesn't appear threatening.

"Yes... I thought it would be easier for you to give in to your desire for me." Without any warning, he lifts up my negligee and slides two fingers past the lace of my thong and right into my pussy. Instead of the usual tease, he strokes my core, but it's just as tortuous. "I see it's worked. You're soaked."

I hate feeling so exposed. I hate having my feelings and emotions so transparent to him. I can't keep anything inside or away to myself. He knew I was wet before he touched me.

"Still saying you don't want this?" he taunts.

"I don't..." I'll keep saying it, even as I moan from how damn good his fingers feel inside me.

He narrows his eyes at me, pumps harder, and leans in closer.

"Tell me to stop then, Ava...." he says, finger-fucking me now. His thrusts drive in and out of me hard and fast while his hands at my throat burn me.

I open my mouth to say the words, but I can't.

The devil has me exactly where he wants me at the point where he's giving me so much pleasure he knows I can't resist it.

I try to look anywhere but his eyes. It's his eyes that do the damage.

What I see though is a couple off to the corner of the room below. Like everyone else, they're naked, but they're making out. The way they kiss is almost comparable to the relentless movements of everyone else.

I watch them and almost forget what I'm supposed to say.

I look back to the man who's giving me this insane pleasure and see he's smiling at me with pure satisfaction.

"Tell me to stop, Ava... I'm waiting. Giving you the rare opportunity to take back control. Use it, or... lose it."

"I... can't..."

He gives me a wicked chuckle, looks to the couple I was watching, then shocks me by cupping my face and guiding my lips to his for a kiss.

He pulls his fingers from my pussy and holds my face so he can deepen the kiss, and shit... I lose it.

I kiss him back too high on lust and arousal. Our tongues tangle in crazy need, and even though he's kissing my lips, I feel him everywhere, all over me. Inside and out.

I find myself tugging at his shirt while he cups my breasts. I pull harder, and the sound of a button popping off and landing on the glass floor registers in my mind. Just that and his hands are all I'm aware of.

He claims my mouth, crushing his to mine, deepening the pressure as he exploits my lips. Then he stops and pulls away.

I look at him not knowing what he wants now. I don't want to accept what I want, because this can't be me.

My hands are still on his shirt. The bottom two buttons are gone.

"Finish taking it off, Bellezza," he says. His eyes entreat me to give in to what I want most, but my hands shake with nerves and the conflict of emotions roiling inside me. "Take it off, Ava. Do what you want to me."

As he says that, it sparks something deep inside me. *Do what I want?* It's been so long that I've done that. It feels like it's been so long since I gave in to the call to do something I truly want to do.

He feels like that, and the temptation to take what I want from him is something I don't want to say no to. Boldness takes over.

His smile widens when I start undoing his buttons. It's the kind of smile that belongs to a man who's confident about his appearance.

I conjured in my mind a masterpiece of a physique based on the sharp outline of muscles I've seen straining against his shirt. When the soft cotton lies open and he takes off his shirt, I see I was right... *partially*. He does have a body to be proud of, but what I'm looking at could rival the Greek gods.

Muscle on muscle is all I see running from the top of his shoulders right down to the V cut of his torso. He has a tattoo of a dragon on one arm and a snake on the other. His chest is covered with more tattoos.

There's a black inky dragon. Something that looks like it flew straight out of a fantasy. It looks like it would breathe fire. The tail runs down the length of his abs and curls around the edge of his hip, calling to me to explore, so I do. I follow it all the way around and see the end right around his back, which shows five sparrows in flight.

I touch his tight taut skin, tracing my finger over the dark inky birds.

"Five," I whisper.

"The five Giordano brothers," he replies.

"There are five of you?"

"Four now," he answers with hesitation and my heart stills.

"Four." One died... death is always sad.

"Story for another time."

I walk back around to face him, and he gives me a scandalous look so hot my blood heats up in my veins.

"Come here." He reaches for me, taking my waist and lifting me up like I'm weightless. I rest my hands on his shoulders and look down at him. His muscles tense as he holds me out just looking at me. "Doll," he says with admiration.

He walks with me over to the bed and sets me in the center, lowering to kiss me again. This time when we kiss, it feels more sensual and personal, like we're tasting each other. It's an exploration driven by hunger and passion that leaves my mouth burning with fire.

He licks my tongue and allows me to do the same to him. I get the feeling we could do that all day. Just kiss. It's a chaste thought to have in a sex club.

It's not like we're here though, and it feels like this room was just made for us.

I'm not ready for him to pull away when he does. The wildness, however, is back, and he pushes me down to take off my panties. They go sailing across the room when he tosses them.

"This stays on," he rasps, tugging on my negligee. "And these fuck-me heels." He gives my feet a little tap.

The need for him to be inside me makes me crave him like I'm starving.

He backs off the bed and undoes his pants, shrugging them off along with his boxers. His perfectly erect cock breaks free and juts toward me.

With his pants gone, I see he's got more tattoos down his legs. *My God...* I've never been with a more sexier man.

He gets back on the bed and moves back to me. Parting my legs, he runs the fat head of his cock over my entrance then plunges right in. There was no need for our usual foreplay. My body welcomed him like he belonged there. Like I belong to him.

It's funny though. I don't feel like property as he pumps into me. As I lie beneath him and he claims me, I don't feel like a thing or a whore. I feel like a woman he wants to be with, and he feels like a man I want.

I don't know what's happening to me, but I know when I'm with him, I give in to my inner desires because he pulls them out of me.

Vincent holds on to my hips and starts fucking me hard. I writhe beneath him taking his rough, hard strokes that quickly send me over the edge.

I arch shamelessly into him and wrap my legs around his waist, digging my heels into his back.

"You're fucking perfect," he growls. "Fucking perfect."

Heated licks of fire torment me as he speeds up and the tug of an orgasm brews deep inside my core. It's divine ecstasy that sends a shock wave through my entire body.

"Vincent!" I cry as the tension builds.

He glares at me and stops. He stops right in the middle of sex, and I'm so hungry for his wild pumps that I thrash against him.

"Say that again..." he says, capturing my gaze with an intense stare. "Say my name again, Bellezza."

"Vincent." As I say his name, I realize that's the first time I've ever said it. "Vincent..."

"I want you to scream my name." A sinful grin dances across his perfect lips, and he flips me over onto my hands and knees.

I gasp as he plunges back into me and a new wave of pleasure takes me over the edge. In that moment the insane wildness I've grown accustomed to with this man comes back with a vengeance and he starts to fuck me with a manic speed that rocks my body. It has me screaming his name, just the way he wanted.

Fuck... it's too much. It's all too much. *He is.* I'm dizzy with pleasure, my body humming from the satisfaction of it. I come again and I feel like I'm going to collapse, but I want more. He's made me greedy for him, greedy for what he's giving me and I want more.

"You're perfect baby," he groans still pumping into me. He runs his hands up my waist then his fingers flutter over the small rosette of my asshole. Panic fills me when he stills and circles his finger around it.

"I want your perfect ass, Ava," he says, giving my ass a hard smack that jolts my body forward. Despite the pain I feel from the sting on my cheeks, I moan, and he slaps me again then places soft kisses all along where it stings. "I want you here."

The same wicked, sinful streak that took him must have me too because I can't shake the ravenous thought of him filling me there and owning another part of me.

It's that need for him to touch me everywhere coming out. The fact that he's still got his fingers on my asshole makes it worse. I've never done anything like that before, and I've never been with anyone who I wanted to do it with.

"You can say no, baby. Tell me no if you don't want me to, Ava. I mean it." His voice is gentle, making me trust him.

"I... want you to," I answer, and the desire intensifies on his handsome face.

"I won't hurt you."

Those simple words mean so much.

He pulls out of me, moves over to the nightstand and returns with a small container of lube.

I watch him over my shoulder as he gets back on the bed, opens the container and takes out some of the clear solution. When his fingers return to my ass a shudder races through me. It's from his touch and the anxiety over how this will feel. He smears the lube over my asshole and I squirm when he pushes his fingers inside.

"Be still," he commands and I obey.

He adds more lube, coating his cock with some of it too. He then adjusts himself behind me and takes my hips again. I brace myself as he rubs the fat head of his cock over my asshole, and I suck in a sharp breath as he starts to slide in.

"Ohh..." I moan. It feels weird, like I'm being forced open.

"Good girl. It will feel better in a second baby," he promises and he was right. It does. His cock in my ass starts to feel good when he gets in a little more.

"You okay, Bellezza?"

"I'm okay." I pant.

He goes in a little deeper and ... Oh. My. God. Fuck, it feels too good.

He starts with a slow pump and grind and speeds up a little more. His cock pumping into my ass sets my whole body on fire. Convulsive reams of it lap over my skin and then explode in raw, carnal pleasure that has me screaming his name again.

"That's right, baby, scream my name," he growls.

I'm lost in the combo of the pleasure filled sensation that ripples over me and his cock pounding into my ass. As his cock pulses, however, I know his release is coming. The thought takes me to mine and I come. Moments later he pounds to his and the warmth of his cum fills me right up.

The electric buzz stays with me although we've climaxed. It awakens passion, awakening a flame inside me that shouldn't be alight. It radiates from my core and spreads over my body. It's amplified when he smoothes his hand over my waist.

Vincent pulls me into his arms as we collapse on the bed, and cradles me. The mere touch sends a warming shiver through my soul. I turn to face him and we stare at each other. My heart races as he strokes my skin and it feels like his embrace encompasses more than my body.

I drop my guard the longer I stare back at him, finding I can't place the walls back up to shield my emotions. We're not saying anything but the silence speaks of the desire that ripples between us.

It's so intense I look away, but Vincent catches my face and reclaims my mouth, soul kissing me. The sensual kiss he gives me is so different to the animalistic madness that took us moments ago. It quickly becomes exactly that, however, taking me deeper down the rabbit hole.

And I allow him to.

CHAPTER TWELVE

Vincent

I've never been a coward.

I can't remember a time in my life when I've run away from anything. Not even when I should have did I run away.

The last two days have been a first for me.

The whole weekend has seen me doing my best to avoid Ava because Friday night was too intense.

Too much.

Too damn much.

I indulged in the woman the whole damn night and had to tear myself away from her so she could sleep. That's when I left and arranged for a car to pick her up early in the morning.

I haven't seen her since.

I'm at Giordanos Inc. again. I got here early to get a head start on my work for the week so I can spend more time at Renovata.

I've decided I'll go over everything myself with a fine-toothed comb and organize the accounts to my liking. If all goes well here, I should be able to go to Renovata on Wednesday and spend the rest of the week there.

I'll be busy. That's what I want. I'm assuming too that we'll get the checks back on our Bratva friends any day, so I want my schedule flexible for that.

I'll be sure to see my boy first thing in the morning and last thing at night. That's all I need. I gotta stay away from Ava for a few more days. Just so I can cool off.

It's the middle of the day, and I've been working harder than usual to keep my mind busy.

Keep busy and not face the fact that I don't know what to make of this fascination I have with a woman I've known for exactly one week.

The worst thing about it is, I don't know how to deal with what she does to me. I've never been a liar, so I won't start now and do worse by lying to myself. The truth is... I've never met anyone who's had the effect she's had on me, and I'm ashamed to admit it because Sorcha was the love of my life.

I've never been with a woman who wanted me the way Ava does. When she touches me, it's enough to transform that raw, carnal force of rage inside into undiluted passion that takes over my whole being.

Fuck... I don't know what the hell I'm thinking. She's driving me crazy, and I'm driving myself crazy.

Crazy is not what I need now. With my impending takeover of the business, I can't afford crazy, or sloppy.

I shouldn't feel like this about a woman who is a debt repayment.

That's what she's supposed to be. I'm supposed to see her that way, but that image is fading. I'm losing control, and I can't allow that to happen.

Christian knocks on my open door and comes in.

"Man, this chick must definitely have done some kind of number on you," Christian states, shaking his head at me.

He's dying to know what's going on with Ava and knows a

little more than I want because he's been helping me sort out the shit Mark left at Renovata. He guessed right away what the situation was if I had Ava at my house and hadn't killed her father.

Most of that side of my family are used to arrangements like that. Taking women as payment or in exchange for something is nothing new to them. Although I think it's safe to say that the debt owed in my case is a little higher than I've heard.

"I really hope the pussy payment is worth this shit. Maybe it is. Haven't seen you at The Dark Odyssey the last few nights, and the last time I saw you there, you were with her. Makes me wonder if you're satisfied with what you have at home."

"What the fucking hell is it now?" Clearly, he's found something.

"I'm just saying this woman must have worked some kind of hiyaka on you, or her pussy must be really good for you to forgive her old man for so much. I just found another two G's missing from the business account. Looked like some prearranged order. It went to a hooker called Mindy." He starts laughing like it's fucking funny.

"Fuck... fucking Mark." I ball my fists. "And fuck you too Christian. It's not damn funny, you prick," I snap at him when he continues to laugh.

"Come on, Vincent."

It's days like these when I see the split in differences across the family. His side is far too jovial in times when I need them to be serious. Both Christian and Georgiou talk to me like we're always hanging out, never serious. Georgiou is a few months older than me, yet he acts like he's living in a perpetual fantasy. Christian is thirty-seven and is still the billionaire playboy.

"Christian, you gonna push me right now?"

"Basino, if it's funny, it's funny. If it was me, I'd go check out Mindy and get my money's worth. Why should she get paid for nothing?"

I sneer and look away from him.

He chuckles. "Okay, on a serious note... you do have two G's gone from your business account, and I'm guessing if Mark set something like that up once, there'll be more things like that to look out for. So, I've set a note on the account to query any transactions like that. I also spent some time at Renovata this morning shaping up things up. I think between the two of us, we'll be able to get everything back on track by the end of the week. Maybe before."

Okay, he's definitely back in my good books now.

"Jesus... Christian, thanks, man."

That's the first piece of good news I've had since this nightmare with Mark started.

"No worries. You'll also be glad to hear that everything looks fed-proofed. If anybody wants to check things out, they're welcome to it. The accounts look the way you need them to."

I laugh now. "That will help big time."

"Yeah, well, I'm hoping you give me more contracts and a raise when you become boss." He grins.

"You need more money, Christian?" He co-owns The Dark Odyssey with Georgiou, Salvatore, Gabe, and Nick. The five of them make millions from people's sexual fantasies. He's not broke.

"Hey, if you can make it, do it. I just know what I can do, and I know my worth, so you remember me when you collect your old man's crown."

"You fucker." I smirk, and he gives me a nonchalant smile. "Thanks for all your help though. I don't want to think about this Mark situation anymore."

It must be some kind of sign for me not to because the instant I say that, a beep comes through on my computer. It's an alert from the secret squad, the guys who do our checks.

Christian knows what the beep means too, so he tenses up and looks at me with expectancy.

I open the email quickly. Part of me hopes they'll find something, and I won't have to worry about the discomfort I feel about this alliance.

My damn heart sinks when I scan through the email and see every fucking thing came back clean.

They're clean, good to go, good to do business with.

Shit.

"What, Vincent?"

"The checks on the Bratva guys are clean," I answer.

"Oh... okay. I guess that's good, right?" He raises a brow.

"It's good."

Our checks are good. They're high level and the type the feds use, so that means we can dig deep. If we run a check on a person or group of people and they come back clean, it means you can trust them with your babies.

So, why do I still feel the same?

Like shit. Like there's still something to find to explain this brewing feeling of distrust I have for them.

I look at the paperwork on the screen and see we didn't just run the checks on Dmitri and Yuri but their Pakhan too: Ilya Lobonov. He's the actual guy we'll be doing business with.

Everything's clean by our standards, and it looks like they don't get their hands dirty either, just like us. We don't get our hands dirty unless we have to.

"What now?"

"I don't know."

He narrows his eyes at me in confusion. "Is there anything else you want me to do?"

"No, I don't think there's anything else."

"Vincent... you don't look that... confident. This isn't like you. It's normally *pass check, next please, we have other things to worry about*. What's with you and these guys?"

"I don't know. I'm being crazy stupid. It's just that..." I sigh. Maybe I'm seeing things that aren't there and am being overprotective.

"What?"

"Christian, if these people were guys who'd worked with

someone we knew, I wouldn't have a damn thing to say about it. It would be cool. But what I can't stand is instances where there's little to no info. I know they're different units and syndicates like us and we aren't the same across the board, but there's something about them in general I don't like."

He nods, agreeing. "What can we do about it? Your pops looks like he's already got this in the bag."

"I know."

"Vincent, they came back clean, so maybe these guys are straight up legit. It's hard to be suspicious when everything is good by our standards." An uneasy expression fills his face . "But if you don't trust them, maybe you need to think about why."

He's right. That question of why I don't trust these guys is a good one. Now I have no reason not to.

"I'm gonna... take the rest of the time to think. I told them four weeks. They'll be expecting to hear back from us in that time frame."

"I think you should do that. Maybe talk things through with your pops too."

I nod, appreciating his advice. I can't talk with Pa though. No way. He would have gotten a copy of that email and will be on my ass by nightfall about it.

I think I do need to talk it over with someone though. Not any of my brothers. This feels like I need someone who's used to making these types of decisions.

I have just the guy in mind.

I get off the phone with Claudius, making arrangements to meet in two days, when a knock sounds at the door.

I frown. I was about to go home. It's already late, bordering eight. I've been here for over twelve hours.

Janice, my secretary, would have called me to check if I was seeing anybody, but she's already left for the day.

Whoever that is better have a good excuse for knocking on my door at this hour.

"Come in," I call out.

The door opens, and I'm surprised when I see Dmitri.

Fucking hell. This is completely unexpected.

"Hello, Boss," he begins, raising his hands. He doesn't look as uptight as he did the other day. His face is also less tense.

"Good evening," I say, making a point of noting the time of day.

"I apologize for my impromptu visit. I know it's late. I called your father earlier, and he said you'd be working until late and it would be better to speak to you then."

Shit. Bad enough I feel like my damn hands are tied behind my back when it comes to these guys, but must Pa rule my time too?

"That is okay. What can I do for you?" I ask.

"I'll only be a minute. I just wanted to check that we didn't get off on the wrong foot last week," he says. "I hoped my eagerness to get things going didn't overstep boundaries. I apologize if it did."

I'm not exactly sure what it is I'm supposed to say to that.

"No worries. It's understandable that you'd want to get a thing like this sorted out as quickly as possible," I answer.

"I appreciate your understanding. I thought I would ask the question of trust too, just to make sure I cover all bases."

"Trust?" Interesting he would say that.

"I wanted to know what it might be about us that you don't trust? I assure you we don't hope to repeat mistakes of the past."

He nods.

It's curious he would mention the past. When bad things like that happen, people tend to steer clear of any talk of it, especially when it had nothing to do with them. The past involved a different brotherhood, although they're Bratva all the same.

"I want to make sure I do what's right for my people," I answer. I won't make any reference to the past or engage in any discussion about it. Nothing for him to take away and use against me.

Dmitri nods. "Well, that's a sign of a good leader. You would like our Pakhan. Please, take the time you require. I thought it was important to have this meeting with you just to make sure you see we're very interested in making this work."

He's saying that, but my trepidation is still there. I smile though.

"I appreciate the visit."

Dmitri smiles. "I hear you guys have a club to our tastes. We could come by and hang out in a more casual setting, not business. Just a drink."

I nod. "Yeah, sure."

"Thanks for your time, Vincent."

"You're welcome."

He dips his head for a curt nod and leaves. As he does, I take a moment to think.

He seems like a decent guy. That's the appearance he portrayed. It was just that it didn't feel real to me.

Most often when something feels too good to be true, it's usually not.

I get home late and head to my office.

There's a private room in the back where I have some CCTV set up.

The house is like a fortress with security comparable to a prison. There's no way I'd make the same mistake as I did at the old house.

That was different though. With my best men protecting the place and guards at the door, nothing would have stopped the infiltration because we had a rat.

I don't want to think about it now, and I wish I could stop seeing the image of my dead wife's body in my mind.

Some nights when I can't sleep, I end up here and just watch the place like I'm triple-checking the house is safe. Checking my baby is safe in his room and Marguerite in hers when she's here.

I do that looking in on both, and then I look in on Ava. This would be the third day that I haven't seen her. I told Marguerite to tell her I'd be working late. Ava's not stupid though.

I'm a fucking prick, but I wasn't that to her last Friday. All I did in that room with her was real.

She'll know that's why I haven't been around her. She'll know straight up that I've been avoiding her. No matter what excuse I tell Marguerite to give her, she'll know the truth.

We crossed the line. We crossed the line big time, and I'm trying to make my way back.

She's awake but lying down on the bed in the dimly lit room.

She's gazing out the window with an expression that shows a million questions on her mind. I can practically see them swirling around her pretty little head.

She wants to see her father, she wants to speak to him, she wants her life back, she wants to leave here. She wants to leave me.

I watch her sit up and pull her top over her head, showing me her naked

breasts.

Those fucking guards better not be watching. She doesn't know there are cameras in the room. There's a camera in every room of the house that connects to my phone. If anyone would be idiot enough to break in, they're dead. Pure and simple. *Dead.*

I tap on the keyboard and disable the view of her room from everyone else.

It's only me who can see her now.

She gets up out of the bed. It's torture watching her parade her body like that in front of me when I can't touch her. She walks over to the window and cracks it open.

It is hot, so I don't blame her. She gets back in the bed and covers herself slightly then rolls onto her side, where she resumes her thoughts.

I wonder what crosses her mind when a tear rolls down her cheek.

What is she thinking about?

I look into her eyes and try to see.

I find myself looking at that old pain again.

Old pain never goes away.

Pain and guilt. It's the same.

I wonder what her story is.

CHAPTER THIRTEEN

Ava

I'm not stupid...

I may make stupid decisions sometimes, like deciding to drop my guard and allowing him in, but I'm far from stupid.

I know it's because of the way we were on Friday why Vincent's staying away. It got too real.

It got too real for me too.

I never really felt like I was a slut when I was with him until I woke up that morning and saw that he was gone.

It was just a feeling that came over me, and as the days went by, the feeling stuck, reminding me that I'm his whore so he can pick me up when he wants to fuck me and toss me to the side when he's done with me.

I wonder if it was because he could sense that I'm damaged and broken. Like he knew there was something that wasn't quite right about me.

He's avoided me for the last few days, and today looks like it's going to be the same.

I've pretty much stayed in my room watching day turn to night like a prisoner would.

I've barely been eating, and last night, I cried myself to sleep when images of the past came back to haunt me. It was that thought of being damaged that made the memories flow back, and I couldn't stop crying. Then I was crying for everything and wishing life could have been better.

It nearly was with work at least.

I barely ate anything again today.

I felt bad for poor Marguerite doing her best to try and make me feel welcome, but to no avail. There's only so much she can do with the little information she probably gets from Vincent.

There's only so much I can do, and I wish to God none of this happened.

Maybe I should be more grateful for the days when I'm not a whore. Then I'm just a prisoner.

It's watching and waiting that makes me more in tune with my surroundings. So, I'm more inclined to hear what's happening around me.

It's extremely late when the front door creaks open. I just know it's him. He's been coming in around this time the last few days.

I get out of the bed, careful as I pad across the floor, and open the door. The lights are off. I know I shouldn't be roaming around the house at this hour, but I've decided I no longer care.

I no longer care about Friday or his stupid rules. It's almost Friday again, and last week will be just a memory to file to the back of the shelf.

I want answers. That's what I want.

All Vincent has told me is that Dad is at the clinic. I need more information than that. And I need to know when I'm leaving here. It's not good for me emotionally and mentally to be in this house. It never was.

I step out into the passageway at the end of my corridor and see him across on the other set of stairs.

He's about thirty feet away from me, so he can't see me.

I was about to call to him, but I stop myself when the dim stair lights come on and I catch a glimpse of his face before he proceeds up to the third floor.

He doesn't look like himself. He looks drained.

It's curiosity that makes me follow.

Carefully and cautiously, I follow him up the stairs, keeping to the shadows and making my steps light.

When I get to the top of the stairs, I stop and hide in between the crevice as he enters a room. He leans against the mantel piece of a wall-mounted fireplace and rests his head against it.

I watch him and wonder what could have happened today, then I look up as he does at a painting of a very beautiful woman.

She has long brown hair and is wearing a wedding dress. There's a hint of a smile on her face that reflects in her bright brown eyes.

Vincent gazes at the painting. His stare lingering on it, *on her*. It's then I realize the woman meant something to him.

I've been so caught up in being here and Dad that I haven't thought of the glaring questions.

Vincent has a son, and the only women I've seen around the house are Marguerite and Lydia. No one else.

Was the woman in the painting his wife? An old girlfriend? Is she his son's mother? I feel she is, so what happened to her?

Vincent continues to stare up at her, then he shakes his head.

"It's not right, baby," he says. His voice is just above a whisper, fueling my curiosity. "It's not right that you aren't here. I can't forget you."

I can literally feel the love rippling from him. Something happened to her. I can sense it. Something bad.

I shrink away when he looks over his shoulder, probably sensing my presence.

He closes the door, and I take the moment to leave and go back to my room.

I think of the woman in the painting.

It was strange to see Vincent so ...different when he looked at her. That was definitely love I sensed in him.

What would it feel like to be loved by a man like that? A man so full of mystery and danger.

The mystery and danger is all there with enough warning to stay away. At the same time, there's a side to him I'm drawn to. Maybe it was the same part of him that drew her in too. That woman.

In my case, that's the part I need to be careful of. It wears me down and I can't allow that to happen. That opens the door for confusion.

I need a reality check. I'm a debt repayment. Here for sex.

I need to remember that. I'll do what I'm told and pray for freedom. I'll do it, and I'll try to feel nothing, no matter how real I think it is.

I've come too far in my life to mess everything up. When bad things happen to you that you can't even speak of or think about, and you can rise above them, there's definitely a sense of accomplishment in it.

I worked hard to rebuild myself and have some sort of a normal life after the nightmares of the past. It was years ago, but to me, it will always feel like yesterday.

I sound like I faced my fears, but it wasn't that. What I did was move them out of my mind. Maybe that was wrong. The shrinks tell the broken and damaged to face their fears and problems. I didn't think that advice applied to people like me. So, I took my fears and problems out of my consciousness and locked them away somewhere.

My mind is filled instead with my dreams to write.

That's why I can't throw away my future.

I won't allow the mafia to take everything away from me. *Again.*

The strong scent of smoke burns my nose.

Cigar smoke, like the ones grandfather used to use. And him, that man. No, that *monster*... Even as I stir from my sleep, I know not to think of his name. I think of him only as one of the shadows in the dark I don't want to remember.

It's the smoke that conjures up the memory in my mind of the large Cuban cigar dangling between thick fingers.

I roll onto my back and turn my gaze to the man standing by my window, basking in the morning sunlight.

Vincent.

He's standing there smoking a cigar. He's wearing a tank top that shows off his massive biceps and thick tattooed forearms. His hair is ruffled like he just got of bed, but the alert look in his eyes suggests he's been up for a while.

The sight of him startles me and makes my heart flutter at the same time. This is the first I've seen of him since Friday. I sit up straight away.

We're staring at each other. Seconds pass, and I think back to last night. Normally, he would have said something to me by now, so I wonder if he knows I was watching him in that room before he closed the door.

He puts out the cigar and leaves it on the side plate Marguerite left me yesterday with cookies.

"We're making an early start," he announces. There's an edge of annoyance in his voice that suggests I'm right. He might not have seen me, but he sensed my presence last night, and he's not happy about it.

"Does that mean I get to ask you if I can call my father?" I'm pushing my luck, but I want to get in my request before something happens to piss him off more than he looks.

"No. It doesn't mean that. You won't be speaking to him today."

"Why not? Why can't I speak to him for a minute just to see if he's okay?" I bite the inside of my lip, but then a dark thought hits me. What if he's so adamant that I don't speak to Dad because something bad happened? It's not impossible.

Vincent is a mobster. He's a mafia boss, and I've been here

spreading my legs for him, trusting that he was going to keep his end of the deal.

"You hurt him, didn't you?" I ask, unable to keep the shaking out of my voice.

"No." He eyes me dangerously.

"How do I know you're telling the truth if I have no proof?"

"Bellezza, it's wise not to push me this morning. Not when I'm already pissed."

I hold my tongue on my next words.

"Take your clothes off," he husks, and I narrow my eyes.

"I didn't know we'd be starting the morning like this."

He comes over to me and lowers to sit on the bed next to me. He reaches forward and fills his palm with my right breast, feeling me up through the silky camisole top Lydia bought for me.

He keeps eye contact when he moves away the cloth and lowers his mouth to suck on my nipple. It's brief but effective. The pull between my thighs makes my pussy clench with the anticipation of having him inside me.

Heat climbs down my neck and spreads over my body as he continues to suck.

When he pulls away, it's like that heat leaves my body.

There's a devilish grin on his face. Today, it has an air of menace in it that shows he knows how helpless I am.

"As long as you're here, you belong to me. Mine. If I want to start my day with your tits in my mouth and my cock in your pussy, I will."

The crassness in his words makes my cheeks sting, and I have to remind myself of the strategy I came up with last night.

Do as I'm told. Do it to keep the peace with the hope that I get what I want, which is to get out of here.

He gives my breasts a gentle squeeze, and his smile widens. "Take your clothes off.

I lift the hem of the top and pull it over my head, showing him what he wants: my naked breasts. I then slide my panties down my legs.

The second I do, the door pushes open and Marguerite comes in, stopping at the entrance when she sees she's intruded on us. I grab the sheet and shield myself.

"Come back in twenty minutes," Vincent says to her. His expression is the same. Stern.

"Of course, I'm so sorry," she apologizes. I don't look at her as she leaves.

Vincent turns his attention back to me and moves the sheet away from my breasts. "Get on your hands and knees."

I do as he says, watch him as he gets on the bed behind me and takes out his cock.

He runs his fingers over my ass and gives the cheeks a firm squeeze before tracing a line down to my pussy. Of course, just like all the other times I've been in the presence of this man, my body reacts to him, betraying me.

Wanting him.

"Naughty Bellezza, always wet for me..." he taunts, sliding two fingers into my passage.

My traitorous body loves it, awakening at the memory of us at The Dark Odyssey.

I turn my gaze forward when his tongue licks over my pussy lips and then over my clit. He holds my ass firm so he can press his tongue right into me. I moan from the pleasure. The sound of me moaning seems to encourage him to give me more.

He does, licking and sucking over the hard nub of my clit. I already feel close to orgasm. When the fat head of his cock presses against my entrance, I'm there.

He plunges in, and I come straightaway, feeling the gush of wetness flow from me and coat the thick length of his cock as he claims me. I'm not given any time to catch my breath or recover. He just keeps going.

The grip he has on my hips tightens painfully when my passage adjusts to take the magnitude of his cock and he speeds up, fucking me hard. Fucking me so hard our skin slaps together and the sound of flesh hitting flesh fills the room. That and us. The sounds of us. I felt the moment when his control slipped and his body took over. It was the same time mine gave in to him. The moment primal instinct took over and surpassed whatever it is I want to tell myself about this crazy relationship we have. It took precedent and took over, making me move against him too.

Damn it, I can't control myself. It's just like the other night. There was a moment when it all became so raw and greedy, like we'd both been starving for each other. I'm sure that's not true for him though. It can't be. I'm sure he has his harem of women at his beck and call. The power of who he is, is one thing, but the man is gorgeous.

"Fuck," he groans as his cock tenses inside me. It came as a response to me grinding back against him.

He catches my waist and holds me, so I stop, and he pounds harder, taking back control. It's too much. Much too much. Worse than Friday. It's like our bodies missed each other and this reunion is an explosive blast of ecstasy and passion.

I'm not surprised by the force of pure scandalous pleasure that takes me moments later that has me screaming. Not even just simply crying out. I scream, and I hope like hell Marguerite isn't anywhere near the door or on the floor near the door outside.

Anyone out there would definitely hear us. My screams are filled with the kind of pleasure a woman would feel from a man who wants to possess her and make her his for real and not this... not this façade of what we're doing.

He grunts his release, filling me with hot cum that feels so damn good as it sprays up into me. It feels good, and I'm so upset with myself for the thought and the moment I actually allowed myself to savor it.

I can't want this... I can't want him. I can't allow myself to think this is anything other than fucking, no matter how my body responds to this man who is my enemy.

The reaction I'm having to him is not normal, not for someone like me, and as my hand smooths over my stomach while we calm, I know as bad as he is. He wouldn't want me if he truly knew what happened to me.

I can't give him control over me like that. I've never given it to anyone. As he pulls out of me, I harden my heart, the same way he does.

He slides off the bed, and I roll over and watch him move to the bathroom. He comes back with a wad of tissues seconds later, his pants pulled up, his face unchanged and emotionless. My gaze follows him as he sets the tissue down on the bed next to me to wipe off his cum.

I do, pull my clothes back on, and chance looking at him.

He looks like it was nothing. He looks like it was all nothing while I'm left with this clash of emotions that's threatening to push me over the fucking edge.

Since I'm not the kind of person who has sex on the regular, I'm not sure if this is a situation I'll get used to until it will eventually be as meaningless as he treats it, or if it will be more for me.

That can't happen.

He straightens and tenses his jaw.

"I'm going to be away all day. You are to keep to your quarters," he says. It's confirmation enough that he knows it was me who was watching last night.

"I–"

He holds up a hand to wave me off, so I stop talking.

"You're not a guest here, Ava, and you won't do yourself any favors with me if you go snooping around the house at night, or any other time."

I barely did anything for him to be so worked up. My first thoughts are that there's something in the room he doesn't want me to see. But the look in his eyes suggests it might not exactly be a thing. It's more to do with how he was last night. I remember the way he looked as he gazed up at the painting of the woman. This is about the significance. It's personal. That's why he seems meaner.

"I was just looking around. I couldn't sleep," I explain.

"You are not here to look around. You're paying a debt. That's why you're here in my house."

To be his whore.

I ball my fists, and my chest constricts. The reminder of what I am makes me sick, especially with the way I just gave myself to him.

I can't do it. I can't just do as I'm told to keep the peace. When you allow people to treat you a certain way and you say nothing, they keep doing it.

He turns to leave, but I stand up and steel my spine. "I'm not a whore," I call out, and he stops midstride.

Turning back to me, he cocks a brow. "You'll be whatever I want you to be."

I must have some type of death wish because I shake my head and say, "no, I won't."

That did it. It snaps the tension that already existed in the room from the moment I woke up and saw him.

He rushes over to me, but unlike the other times, I don't back away.

I stand up to him and shock him.

"What did you say to me?" he barks.

This is about money and whatever trouble Dad caused. It's not about me, and I've done what I can to fix it. I can't allow him to take the last part of me.

Standing a little taller, I lift my head and gaze straight at him, a challenge I know I won't win.

"I'm not a whore," I repeat.

"I'll be the judge of that. I—"

I don't give him a chance to finish. Red flashes in front of me, and it's like I'm transported right back to the last time I was made to feel like a whore. As rage fills me, my hand lifts, takes on a life of its own, and slaps him straight across his face.

The feral look in his eyes is all I get to register before he lunges for me. This time, I decide not to be stupid and stand up to him. Him with his six-foot-six stature, and me the little woman at five four.

I try to run, and I scream, but he reaches for me, and we fall back onto the bed.

"Let me go!" I wail, thrashing beneath his heavy frame.

He has me pinned, and the growl that tears from him is so animalistic it makes my soul shudder with pure fear. We couldn't be the same people who were having sex on this very bed not five minutes ago.

Tears run down my cheeks. I cry not knowing what he's going to do to me.

Is he going to kill me?

Did I just fuck things up completely for myself and Dad?

"Let me go," I squeak.

He raises my hands over my head and holds me down scowling.

"Don't you ever hit me again," he says, getting right up in my face.

Through the blindness of tears, I try to see him.

"Vincent. You're a monster!" I sob, and he seems to still. "You're a monster if you think I'm a whore because my father owes you money. It doesn't matter how much it is. I gave you my body, and now you want to steal my soul. *Monster*... I hate you."

God and all his angels must be watching over me because in that moment, my words, spoken straight from the agony of my heart, seem to reach him, and he stops.

His grip loosens, and he releases me.

I shuffle up to my elbow and watch him walk out, slamming the door.

CHAPTER FOURTEEN

Vincent

I hate you...

She said it again. Not the first I've heard those words from her, but it was the first time she meant it.

That first time was an attempt to hate me. I probably should have allowed her to because hearing those words again this morning wouldn't have stung the way they did. I deserved it.

It's the first time in my life I've ever felt so ashamed of myself.

She didn't deserve to be treated that way.

I've never thought of her as a whore.

She called me a monster, and she was right.

I truly, truly behaved like a monster. I'm a monster, and that's why she shouldn't have offered herself to me.

I don't know how to take care of things, not even what's mine.

My behavior wasn't about money. Sure, I was pissed that she was snooping around the house, but what I was more pissed about is her intrusion on a private moment I was having with my wife. I was pissed at Ava because of how she makes me feel, while the person who used to make me feel close to that is no longer here.

I didn't actually sleep last night. I stayed up in that room that's become a shrine to my late wife.

I'm like a ghost that needs to move on and can't because I'm fucking stuck in limbo.

Now I'm losing myself too. There's a line between being a badass and being a monster. Asshole and prick. I was all earlier.

That first night I was with her was the start of my emotions going eschew. Screwed and fucked. It made me sloppy. Then this morning, it was like emotion overload. I think the fun is over. It's time for me to calm the fuck down and think of a

reasonable date for Ava's departure.

Business first, however...or rather, guidance.

I'm on my way to see Claudius. I haven't seen him in a while, and today's visit is more of a guidance session. I've never needed anything of the sort before, and I don't need it because of the hot mess I am with Ava.

I need it to help me figure out what I'm doing with the Bratva guys. That's what.

Pa messaged me yesterday wanting to know what I was doing. Knowing him, he probably expected me to contact Dmitri straightaway and talk contracts.

Although I didn't speak to Pa, the tone of his next messages did not sound like he was in agreement with my answer—to wait and take the time to figure things out.

So... my answer to that and my flux is to go to a boss who's the same level as him—higher, if I'm honest. I won't pussyfoot and talk big because I'm a Giordano. It doesn't mean squat when you're put next to the Morientzs, who practically inherited Chicago from the Rossis.

Before Raphael Rossi died, he was the *capo dei capi* of Chicago. Boss of all bosses. My old friend Claudius was the perfect man to slip into his shoes.

When I walk into Claudius' building where he holds his business meetings, the receptionist takes one look at me and calls up to him straightaway.

She knows my face, as do the security guards who instantly straighten up and stop their casual conversation as I walk by them to take the elevator.

There's an obvious hush of silence as the women by the coffee machine see me step out of the elevator when the door dings open. I get to Claudius' door down the corridor and knock.

This here is where that respect and fear I was just shown recedes. Whoever's in that office with him will be guys on par with me, even if they are capos. He has a different setup to us in who he's chosen to fill his hierarchy. They're his closest friends. The Giordanos, on the other hand, are more family orientated.

I push the door open when he gives me the go-ahead, and I see exactly who I expected to see inside.

Claudius is sitting around his desk with the bright morning sunlight beaming on the tattoo of a cross on his cheek. His father, who is his consigliere, is to his right.

In front of him are his three capo sitting in order of rank. Dante, Gio, and Alex, who have tattoos of crosses on their necks.

I know them all. We grew up together. We were boys together and went through life together. In this business setting, though, it's professional, so when each looks to me, it's with acknowledgment of my presence.

"Vincent Giordano. Hello, old friend," Claudius beams.

"Boss," I say with a curt nod of my head. These men have been in the height of battle with me more times than I'd like to count.

They are what you call friends. Our alliance with them is strong.

Claudius looks to everyone and nods. "Leave us. Report back on the situation later," he directs them, and they rise, his father included, and walk past me.

With them gone, I make my way inside and take a seat in front of the guy whom I trust like one of my brothers. He is my oldest friend. He's the youngest boss in Chicago, and when I become boss, I will join him. We're the same age.

"It's weird hearing you call me boss, *Boss*," he says to me, and his lips tip up into a small smile.

I chuckle. "*Boss*, there's no way I'll be calling you anything other, especially in front of your men. Pretty sure your father would hand me my ass if I showed you any form of disrespect."

Claudius laughs. "The way he did when you smashed up his car several moons ago?"

I grin. No one will allow me to forget that story. "Yes, a little like that."

It started with a stupid fight in our senior year of high school over a girl. I can't even remember her name. I lost my mind when Claudius set my motorcycle on fire, so I smashed up his car. But it wasn't his car. It was his father's, and that day, Marcus Morientz taught me a lesson I'll never forget.

"What's going on, Vincent? You don't usually request to see me in the middle of the day, definitely not so early in the morning. Not that I mind."

I pull in a deep breath. He's right. This is unusual. It's unusual for me too to feel this way without reason. I'm just unsettled, and truth be told, it's the wrong time to have a woman in my life screwing with my mind.

"There's something going on that I need some help with."

"I gathered," he answers, looking me over. He has one blue eye and one brown. The blue eye is the one I refer to whenever I want to try and figure out what he's thinking. Right now, I see he's curious. "What's the something?"

"It's the kind of something I shouldn't be talking to you about until all arrangements are made and deals closed." He knows from that it's family business related. I would never insult him by asking him to keep something secret. He knows though too, that's what my comment implies.

"You have my word, old friend. This conversation never happened."

"Thank you. I appreciate it." I draw in a breath and clear my head so I can say all that I need to in the right words. As I clear my mind, I clear my shame over Ava. I try to forget her tear stained face and push aside the echo of her calling me a monster. "The Ivanezh Bratva want to form an alliance with us."

The second I say that, his face tenses up. A seriousness I never expected washes over it, and he stares at me long and hard.

"The Bratva?" he confirms, and I nod. "And your father would allow this?"

The question is phrased in such a way that it actually gives me the answer of what he might think of the whole idea.

"He wants it, Claudius. You know us mobsters, greedy." I won't excuse myself in any way. Greed runs through my blood. It doesn't with this guy though. He knows when enough is enough.

"Vincent... I don't like getting involved in things like this. It's like me pissing on your ability to run business the way you want. Please don't expect me to tell you what I would do."

I laugh again. "That's exactly why I'm here. Our checks came back clear. All legit by our standards. So, who am I really to question it? My father has been boss for close to thirty years, and he's had a handle on things. He knows what he's doing."

"And you don't?"

I bite the inside of my lip. This is a guy I can be real with. I don't have to pretend with him because we owe each other nothing. We're on neutral ground.

"I'm not sure I do," I confess. "I always go with my gut instinct, and right now, it's telling me no. It's telling me to say no, but maybe it's telling me that because I'm afraid." There, that's the crux of the problem. *Fear.* It's the thing I could never tell Pa, or anybody else for the matter. I'm ashamed to even say the word to a man like Claudius, but he's that kind of friend to me. The kind who will keep my secrets.

I'm afraid and that eerie vibe of distrust I keep getting when I contemplate the alliance isn't helping.

"What are you afraid of, Vincent?" He tilts his head to the side.

"The past saw these people wiping out a whole family, close to a hundred people. Men, women, and children. I already got caught up in a blood war and lost my wife. Could have lost my child too. I don't want that to happen again for the sake of money." It's probably the most heartfelt words I've said in a while.

He nods understanding, and his face softens. "I get it."

"So, I think what I'm trying to say is, I'm conflicted, and that gut instinct of mine might be biased because of my own past."

My past wasn't even that long ago to be referred to as *the past*. But... the shit started with Frankie's death nearly ten years ago.

The same man who killed my girl killed Frankie. Stephanou Portaleu. That was his name. The killer of two people who meant so much to me.

Stephanou killed Frankie because he accidentally killed Stephanou's wife. That was how it all began. Then the shit two years ago was him and the Fontaines trying to eradicate us. They wanted the whole Giordano line of power gone. That's how Sorcha was killed. Except... Stephanou not only killed her to send me a personal message, he raped her too.

The thought makes me sick and I still feel like I didn't make him suffer enough before I hacked off his head.

I think that I'm wary because these Bratva guys have the same vibe as him. The same malevolent vibe as Stephanou.

"What's the status of the situation?" Claudius asks.

"They know they have to wait four weeks to hear back from me."

"Let them wait," he says, and I feel some semblance of relief.

"You think so?"

"Yes. First, no harm in waiting. Next, if you distrust them for any reason at all, you need to work through those issues, no matter what the checks say. Want me to get Gibbs to look into it a little more for you?"

I nod. "Thank you. I think I'd feel more confident if he did."

Gibbs is already working on Mark. I have every confidence that he'll leave no stone unturned in regard to any work he does on him. It would be the same here. Not that I don't trust my people. It's just that this is a little outside the box.

"I'll get him on it straightaway."

"Thanks. Claudius... would you form an alliance with them?" I have to know.

His jaw clenches and eyes narrow. "No. No fucking way. They would not be bold enough to even mention such a thing to me."

I'll consider that too in my thoughts.

"Do you have any idea what it was that happened in the past?" We've never had to talk about things like this before.

Claudius is a man of many secrets. He has them and knows them.

"I don't, Vincent, and there's not a damn thing I can't find out." He eyes me cautiously. Both eyes have the same warning in them that I take heed to. "Have I tried to find out? Yes, and there was nothing to find... a little like how clean your checks are. That's how they work. They're bigger than us, more powerful on a worldwide level. When they want to erase a path, they can. They can make something look like it never happened, make people disappear without a damn trace. Those are not the kind of people you want to do business with if you want to control any ounce of power."

CHAPTER FIFTEEN

Ava

I haven't seen Vincent since yesterday.

I don't even know if he came back because I was up until quite late and never heard him come in.

I fell asleep in the early hours of the morning, so he could have come back home then.

This is a nightmare. All of it. As is he.

Yesterday, I was so upset I stayed in my room all day and barely ate anything. *Again*. I can count the things I've eaten this week on one hand. The week hasn't ended yet, and I'm already a mess. A mess in my mind and body.

It's one thing to agree to this shit charade, but not knowing how long I have to do this for is killing me. It's eating away at my insides and making me crazy at the same time. Even convicts know when they can leave prison.

Even when they get the life sentence, they know the only way out is death.

Will it be the same for me?

Am I to stay with this man for life for the two million? Is that what he intends?

It's that worry that played in my mind over and over again all through yesterday and then today.

I don't know how long I'm going to be here. I don't know if Dad is okay, and I have to be real—I probably lost my job.

I wanted that chance to do the interview on Coral Winters for more reasons than the prestige it would carry. She's famous for her notable charity work across the world. She's one of those strong women who help people.

Doing an article on someone like that would be amazing. For me, it's a little more personal than that. She wrote a few books of inspiration to heal the soul.

Her words helped heal me.

Simple words that spoke to me.

Remember who you are and never give anyone permission to treat you less than that.

It was those words that snapped me out of my funk. A slump I'd been in for years, something I never thought I would break free from. With my mind damaged and my heart in pieces from all the things I saw and all that I lost and was done to me, I don't know how I made it back.

This whole thing... being here with Vincent feels like I let myself down.

Today, I could only calm my troubled mind by going to the library. The goal was to read to escape the shit my hard-fought-for life has turned into.

Everything is shit, and I'm so worried I think that by itself will kill me. That along with its friend—helplessness.

I stayed in here the whole day reading Shakespeare. I'm shocked Vincent has such books, but he does.

The library is quite big for a house, and I wonder if the woman who lived here before created it. I look around the rows of shelves and see good books, old books. All the classics and more.

Today, I read Julius Caesar and King Lear. They're my

favorites. I've read every single play and sonnet written by Shakespeare because in my household it was a must. My parents wanted me to read the greats and be strong minded.

I moved on to Macbeth an hour ago, but now I am really tired. It's super late.

At eight, Marguerite came in to ask me if I wanted dinner, the same as she did a few times today to ask me if I wanted something to eat. Each time, I told her no.

That last time she was prepped for the answer and came with those cookies I liked when we first met.

I ate those, but since my appetite is screwed, I couldn't taste the flavors.

It must be after midnight now.

I close the book, get up, and place it back on the shelf. I'll just go to bed and hope that tomorrow will be different. Just like last night.

I'm about to leave when my gaze lands on the other door across the room. It's between the shelves with the encyclopedias.

Curiosity takes me over to it.

I try the handle assuming it will be locked if I'm not to venture and go *snooping* around the house. It's not locked though. The handle turns, and the door opens.

I'm staring at a winding set of stairs that goes up. That's all it is. The library is on the ground floor, and the stairs must just go up to the floors above.

Snooping around enters my mind as I go through the door. If the door was unlocked, then this must be somewhere I'm allowed.

Shit.... *Allowed*. Like a child or a pet, and my master has forbidden me to do certain things. I shake my head at myself and walk up the steps. They're wooden, unlike the other stairs in the house that are made of stone and marble. I haven't actually been outside to look around properly, but I get the feeling that the place is quite old. This part feels old, like it was part of the earlier features and the rest was just a refurbish.

I continue up until I see to my actual horror that I'm on the floor I was on the other night.

Across from me is the staircase I came up. The room I saw Vincent in is closer, and there's another room next to it with a smaller door.

God... this is the part where I should turn and walk back the way I came, or go down the other stairs that will lead me back to my room.

I don't know if he's home. Apart from that night when I saw him in here, last night has been the only night he's ignored me.

The warning of our altercation yesterday morning is screaming at me to leave.

Why put my fate to the test and make things worse for myself?

Why piss off the man who's keeping me captive here any more than I already have? A captive is what I am, and those who can't do any better should preserve what they have control over.

In other words, stay the fuck away.

Except... curiosity whispers to me. Maybe it did at the door in the library, enticing me to go through it. Now I'm here, and the whispers have a hold on me.

There's an answer inside that room, but why do I care? Do I care to find out what the answer is?

And what's the question? What's the question I want an answer to? There's nothing for me here but misery and distress. I already know the reasons for it. It's Dad.

Looking at the room, though, I remember how Vincent had seemed from the glimpse I saw of him and what he'd said.

Maybe there's a part of me that wants to know him that way. Know what he's like that way. Just a man who looked up at the painting of the woman who he seemed to love.

Maybe I want to see that softer side to him... the passionate side, because I felt it every time we had sex. Every time, it grew stronger and stronger.

Maybe I want to feel like more than just his whore, and I'm looking for something to hold on to, to make myself feel better.

The thought moves me.

I look around and see the passage is clear. There's no one up here but me. From what I noticed so far, the guards don't tend to come upstairs. Not to the private quarters.

There are enough guards around though. Enough to make sure I don't entertain any bright ideas of escaping. As if I would.

I almost laugh at myself. No one in my position would think of escaping, certainly not when I don't know where Dad is.

The guards are always downstairs guarding the entrances to the house inside and out.

I see them when I go down the stairs and when I've gone to the kitchen. There's a door in the kitchen leading to the garden.

It would be one of them who would walk me like the dog I've become.

I pad across to the room. Again, I assume the door would be locked, but I see it's not. Opening it confirms it's not a door with a lock on it.

I close it, and fear fills me just for being here. I look at the painting of the woman, and I don't know why, but I feel at ease for the subtle warmth that emanates from it.

It's her eyes. I get closer and notice the way the artist did a great job of drawing the focus to them. It captures the emotion of contentment. That's how she looks. Content and happy.

I stare at her for a few moments, my mind racing with questions. Who was she? What was she to Vincent? Was she really his wife?

The dress she's wearing is a wedding dress. I'm sure of it.

I try to imagine him asking her to marry him. She seems so angelic and perfect. *Gentle.*

I look away and turn my attention to the rest of the room. It's quite large. In the center is a black leather padded sofa. Over by the wall is a wide flat screen TV that takes up most of the wall. Then, next to the TV, there's a row of shelves, glass cases, and cabinets. The glass cases have a museum feel to it. Like they're preserving the contents inside. Or... memories.

When I walk over to the closest one, I see pictures in elegant silver frames sitting on the rows of glass shelves.

They're all pictures of her.

What happened to her?

They're all her at various stages of her life leading up to one last one that looks like her in the portrait. She's wearing a wedding ring in that last picture and is smiling wide.

The next two cases have some collectable ornaments made of porcelain. They're little jewelry boxes and trinkets. The next has figurines made of glass. It's the last case that captures my attention completely, however.

The whole unit holds a display of ballerinas. Beautifully crafted porcelain ballerinas. Looking at them takes me to a time of happiness when I used to dance.

I was the dancer before I became the writer. Long before. Sometimes I wonder if it was real. I tend not to think back to my life before I was sixteen. That was when everything changed and I seemed to slip into some nightmare world where nothing quite seemed to fit, or feel real.

I was a dancer. Or at least that's what I was going to be. Then the dream was stolen away from me along with everything else. I dare not think of dancing again. It reminds me too much of the past and my parents.

Looking at the display of ballerinas, though, is nice. The nostalgia takes me back, and I can't resist opening the door to the case and picking up one with a little pink dress.

It reminds me of the dress I wore at my last performance. I'd just turned sixteen the day before. I didn't know that everything I knew was about to change. I never knew that was the last time I'd experience true happiness.

Dancing in front of my parents at the Royal Opera House was possibly the best thing I've ever done in my life.

I'm so lost in the memory that I don't hear the click of the door behind me. It's already too late when heavy footsteps echo against the floorboards. In that moment, I know I've truly fucked up. *Again.*

I turn to face Vincent...

His eyes blaze and nostrils flare. He looks like he could breathe fire and incinerate me right here.

What do I do? What can I say?

I know I'm not supposed to be in here, and I directly disobeyed.

"What the fuck are you doing in here?" he roars as he marches over to me. My soul shivers.

"I..." I try to rasp out a breath and some words, but I don't know what to say, and I definitely don't know what to say when he looks at the little ballerina in my hands.

He swipes it out of my hand, and I actually believe he's going to hit me next, so I back away from him, bumping into the table. Something falls to the ground. It's the TV remote.

I bend down to pick it up but freeze as the TV comes on, and so does she. The woman in the painting and the pictures.

She's on the screen.

"Vinny, this is ridiculous," she says with a hearty laugh, and we both fixate on the screen.

She's walking up the path and carrying a baby.

"Sorcha, this will be one of those funny videos we show him when he's older," a male voice replies.

I recognize it. It's his.

Vinny... that's what she called him, like Marguerite does even though she tries to keep up the façade that she always calls him sir, or boss.

Sorcha... that's the woman's name.

"Couldn't we do this on a different day when I look better? Vinny, I just gave birth. I look terrible." She shakes her head and holds the baby to her chest. That's Vincent's son.

She's standing by the door. It's the front door of the house, but I don't think it's this house.

"So, the first thing I want my son to know is his mother is a goddess and will always look beautiful to me, even when she thinks she doesn't." That's him again, his voice, but I don't recognize the lightheartedness and love in the tone. "Sorcha, just give your message. He's two days old. What do you want him to remember most about today?"

Sorcha smiles and looks back at him. Her eyes come alive when she holds her baby closer.

"I want him to know how much I love him and that his father is the love of my life," she answers, and then I hear something snap. The sound drowns out everything else as I turn to Vincent and see he's snapped the ballerina in half.

He does it again. This time, blood trickles from his hand. He growls and grabs the remote, switching the TV off.

As he whirls around to face me, face hardened and teeth bared, I rise to my feet and swallow hard, feeling terrible for my intrusion on his privacy. I feel worse and shock fills me when a tear tracks down his cheek.

It's then that I know. I know deep down what happened to her.

She died.

"Get out!" Vincent snarls, furious. "Fucking get out!"

Shame fills me as I rush out.

It takes me to my room, and I wish I could run away, run outside and never come back.

I can't do that though. I'm bound here as long as I owe him.

And I just made things worse.

CHAPTER SIXTEEN

Vincent

"Fuck!" I bellow and throw the remains of the fucking figurine into the wall. The shards of glass bounce off it because there's nothing left to break. Nothing left to crack.

A little like me.

I've played that video one time only. It was when I set up this room. It was just after I moved here.

I wanted Sorcha to have something, something that said I didn't forget her. I couldn't stay at the old house after what happened.

I barely went back to move out. Within weeks after her death, I got this place and moved away from the nightmare of what happened to my girl.

The last time I played that video, it left me in a mess. The same mess threatens to take me now.

It was hearing her voice. Hearing it on the TV, like she's here. Like nothing ever happened. That day I made that video felt like we had forever to look forward to.

It took us five years to get pregnant with Timothy, and we went through so much we called him our miracle baby. We were planning to have more children, and that day felt like the start of something amazing I would share with her forever.

I never knew it wouldn't be.

I wipe away another tear and feel disgusted with myself. Look at me crying like a pussy. Look at me pathetic.

When am I going to stop feeling like this?

Sorcha's gone. *Forever.* I can't bring her back, and I can't do anything to change the past.

I'm just left here blaming myself.

And damn Ava. Why the fuck did she come in here?

Anyone else would have some death wish defying me like that. Not her though. Just like everything else since I met her.

It's like she doesn't have that survival instinct for herself. What was it this time? Was she so fascinated to find out what I might have in here that she came in here snooping around my wife's things... fuck!

Wife. I keep saying that, but I don't have a wife. I'm a widower and a single father. That is what I am, and I'm deluded if I keep referring to Sorcha as my wife.

I leave the room, locking the door, and head down to my office. I go straight for the cabinet where I keep my good drinks and grab some whiskey and rum. Those are the only things that are going to help me when I get like this.

That, fucking, or killing. Since I definitely don't feel like fucking, and I can't kill the guy I'm supposed to kill, I'm doing the lesser of the three evils.

I don't bother with a glass. I start on the rum first and practically down it even though it burns my throat. In fact, it fucking scorches it.

Whiskey next, and the same thing happens, but it does the job to calm me. I grab more rum, and one sip takes me to the place I want to be.

It's a place where my mind is so numb I can't think.

I don't think.

I remember sitting down behind my desk and closing my eyes. I remember registering that part, then feeling like I'm having an out-of-body experience and watching myself.

Then I'm somewhere else, taken somewhere else in my mind. I'm still watching, and I turn around. I'm back at the old house. I see it just as it was. That day I came home. It was the middle of the day, although maybe the devil had gotten there the minute I left the house. I don't know.

I was gone since the night before, covering the streets with the guys, scouring them for Stephanou. How twistedly ironic that he was at my home when I was searching the streets for him.

It was the bullet holes in the door that made me burst in, then I saw more in the passageway with my dead guards lining the path up to the stairs.

I head straight to the kitchen because that was where I built the safe room. It led down to the basement, where Sorcha and the baby would be safe. Only I knew the code to open the door, and the metal door was bullet proof.

In my mind, I walk the path I took two years ago. I see myself go into the kitchen. And there she is. My girl lying on the floor covered in blood, her lips blue, the baby crying behind the metal door.

I know she's dead, but I don't want to believe it.

My phone rings, and I hear his voice as I answer it.

It's Stephanou... "I raped her as she begged for her life," he says with a devilish laugh, and then I hear screaming.

I jump out of the nightmare as someone shakes me. Instinct makes me want to reach for my gun, but I stop when I see Marguerite.

She's staring down at me, worry in her eyes. It's morning, and the sun piercing through the window picks out the silver in her hair.

"Vincent..." she says. She keeps her hand on me and runs it over my shoulder the way she did when I was a child. "Are you okay?"

I shake my head. "No." My answer is short and succinct but tells all.

"What happened?"

"Everything. It's everything, Marguerite."

"There's broken glass in the room upstairs. Did something happen in there?"

I run a hand over my face and settle on my beard.

"Vinny," she prods, and I return my attention to her. "I have been in this family since I was a girl. My mother worked for your grandparents and parents, and I have worked for them all my life. The one thing I know is my place. I know not to step over the line, but today, I will because I love you like my own child. I will step over the line and say, you... need to move on."

My lips part, but I press them together. "How?"

"You have to find a way. Sorcha wouldn't want you to be like this. Miserable and a shadow of the person you used to be. She would not want that for you. Things happen, the life we live makes it so. Even when you try to leave it behind, it follows because you can't run away from who you are. The problem is, you keep blaming yourself, and you shouldn't."

I'm as numb as the drink made me earlier. I hang my head down, but she lifts it back up.

"You cannot blame yourself for her death. Now, get up and clean up. Your father wants to see you. He wants a report. I assume you know what that means."

I nod. Sure, I know what that means. He wants to talk about our Bratva friends.

I walk into Pa's office at Giordanos Inc.

He's sitting behind his desk doing paperwork.

I already know he's not going to be happy when I tell him I'm still in two minds about the alliance.

He frowns when he sees me. "Vinny, you look like shit. You

come see your old man looking like that? Unshaved with red eyes?" He's being serious.

I could have shaved, but there's nothing much I can do about the red eyes.

"I'm sorry, it's been a long night."

"I don't know if I want to know what that means," he answers, giving me that look I used to get when he knew I was getting up to no good with a woman, or at The Dark Odyssey.

He'd probably be surprised to know I did neither last night.

I take a seat in front of him.

"So, what's the status with your decision for the Russians? Everything looks all good to me. I'd say yes to them... what say ye?"

I tense and stare at him. My stare makes him temple his fingers at first then ball his fist and bar his teeth the way I do when I'm mad.

"Vincent," he prods.

"Pa... I'm not too keen on them," I answer simply, deciding to opt for the truth.

"Why? Why the fuck not?"

"I don't know. Something... feels off."

"What feels off, boy?"

"Them," I say, leaning forward. His frown deepens.

"Working with the Bratva is going to be good for us. Alliances between groups like us are a powerful form of collaboration. These are *powerful* men, Vincent. I dare say that some of the problems we've had in the past would never have happened with such an alliance."

He's not wrong about that. In Chicago, we have an alliance with a lot of the other crime families, but this would be on another level. The Ivanezh Brotherhood are worldwide, strong in Moscow, and I know we should be grateful that they want to do business with us.

I just can't do business with men I don't trust.

"Pa, I agree. I absolutely agree. No one would fuck with us if we had men like that on our side."

"So, what is the fucking problem, boy?"

"I told you, something feels off. I don't know what it is. Pa, there's no harm in them waiting until I take the time to feel comfortable with my decision." There's no way I'm even going to think about what that decision will be until I hear back from Gibbs.

"Vinny, taking so much time to think suggests distrust. It shows we have something to distrust them over, and there's nothing," he stresses.

"Pa, the fact that none of the families in our existing alliance have ever worked with the Bratva is enough to make me want to take the time to think about it."

That silences him. He can't refute it. It's a fact, one I think we should consider.

"Vincent." He sighs with frustration. "Don't think I haven't noticed the change in you since Sorcha's death." Pa straightens up and glowers at me.

I narrow my eyes at him. What the hell is he going to say to me now?

"Do you expect me to be the same?"

"No, I don't, but fuck, you're neither here nor there. One end of the spectrum to the next. Never in the middle. You can kill a man for selling drugs to kids right off the bat, but you can't kill Mark when he steals two million from you and fucks with us. You can kill a man who stabbed his wife, but you can't see for shit when you have something good in front of you."

He could continue. The list of things I've done since Sorcha's death is long. I became a no-chances guy after. It was enough for me to know that a guy was evil, doing evil things, and I didn't think it was right for me to know that and let him walk away.

It's rage. I won't claim that I was being heroic. It's more the case of me dealing out death to those I thought deserved it. But what happened with Mark was Ava. She was his get out of jail card. He did bad things too, and I practically let him go.

"Pa—"

"No, Vincent, don't make me regret my decision to make you

boss of this family. It would break my heart. My other boys are each as deserving of the position, but you are the only one who earned it. In the end, though, I will do what's right for the family the way I always have. Take your remaining three weeks, but no more. If at the end of that time you still feel the same and can't come to me with a solid reason for why we shouldn't follow through with this alliance, I will take matters into my own hands. I will do it, and you will not like it. This opportunity is too big to fuck it up."

I'm listening. Listening loud and clear, and hearing him, knowing that I better take that month to shape up in more ways than one.

Even if I don't want to.

CHAPTER SEVENTEEN

Vincent

Her favorite flowers were lilies.

Calla lilies.

She had them in her wedding bouquet and had the flowers pressed so she could save it forever.

Sorcha was always doing things like that. Always creative in some way. She loved collecting things, and she loved the ballet. It was me who got her started on that figurine collection. I bought her one, and she got the rest.

I don't know why I'm here again today.

At the cemetery again, standing by her grave, the confirmation that she's gone and never coming back.

I don't know why I think coming here would help me in any way.

I was here twice last month.

Once for my usual visit and then weeks ago for the memorial. Both times, I brought her flowers.

Today is no different.

I just arrived, and I see that someone's been by since I was last here. I have a custodian who tends to the grave on a daily basis, but I can always tell when someone else has been by. Today, it looks like it was her mother. She always brings dahlias with a little blue ribbon tied around the bunch.

Like always, I'm stumped for words, and I feel selfish because I came here straight after speaking to Pa.

Emotions drove me back, and I feel like I need her.

"Hi, doll, me again," I say and scan over the grave. "I really miss you. I miss everything about you, and I'm trying to be okay but making all kinds of shit decisions."

The Bratva and Ava.

Those are the current thorns in my side.

I've possibly sent Gibbs on a wild goose chase, pissed off Pa because he thinks I'm going to mess up a good opportunity, and I have Ava at my house, still there for sex.

This week has been so up and down that I haven't really thought of what to tell her in terms of her leaving.

There has to be an end date. There has to be now more than ever because she's moving too far over the damn line.

Last night was absolute shit, and I was so mad at her again for the intrusion on my privacy. I allowed her to see my weakness and the thing that gets me good.

Love.

When I love, I love hard.

Despite knowing the fucked-up shit that can happen in my world, I foolishly thought I was above it. Even after Frankie was killed, I never really believed that my wife could be killed just like that. There one day and gone the next.

I never believed it could happen, not when I had the best security and the best of everything. I thought I'd be settled for life and couldn't have been more wrong.

If there was any part of that, that was right, I wouldn't be standing here today, and she wouldn't be six feet under.

Marguerite is right. I need to move on. Sorcha wouldn't want me like this. How do I move on though?

I look past the grave and scan over the rolling hills and on to the river before I make my way over to the gravestone and sit next to it.

I stay there until night falls, and I don't move. The most I do is send a text to Marguerite to let her know I won't be back tonight. I don't lie, and I don't tell the truth either.

I don't want the fuss over me and anyone telling me I'm crazy. So, I don't say more than I need to.

At some point, I fall asleep. I fall asleep next to my wife's grave until bright sunlight stirs me along with the shimmer of a man standing before me.

The sunlight covers him, and I can't quite see his face, but when he steps into the shadows, I see it's Salvatore.

He's the only person who would have known where to find me. Not that I've done this before. I used to come here every day when she was first buried, and it was him who always knew where I was. I never had to say.

Once again, though, he's seeing me at my lowest, and I feel like shit.

He comes and sits next to me on the cleared path.

"Vin," he says, looking at me with concern.

"Hi."

"I thought you might be here. I was looking for you yesterday, and when Marguerite said you weren't coming back, I figured this is where I'd find you."

"Yeah..."

"You stay here all night?" he asks, and I nod.

I turn my gaze away from him and glance over to the nearest grave, which is just over the hill. I know what he's thinking, and I don't want to talk about it.

"She told me to make sure you didn't work too hard," he says with reflection.

"Marguerite knows I'm always working hard." I shake my head.

"Not her. Sorcha," he clarifies, and I turn to look back at him.

"She did?"

"Yeah. The thing about me is, I'm the guy who makes the promises. I promise to do various things. Most often, it's to take care of others. Because our lives are so dangerous and you're not exactly a calm person, Sorcha was always making me promise one thing or another." He chuckles. "Make sure you eat, make sure you rest, make sure you don't work too hard, make sure you allow me to take care of you. Now, that last one threw me, took me a minute, but I got her meaning. You've been in charge for a long time. Pa's right-hand man. You're busy taking care of everyone else and never actually allowing anyone really to do the same for you. She knew I was probably the only guy you'd allow to do that. So, here I am, Vin. Keeping my promise to my sister-in-law. Please allow me to."

I bite into my bottom lip so hard I taste blood and hang my head.

"I don't know what I can do, Salvatore. Everything's a mess."

"It's kind of like that all the time. The mess things are, are just a different kind of shit. This situation with you is not about everything else. I'm just going to tell you straight that you can't blame yourself for Sorcha's death."

I close my eyes for a few seconds. "I can't help it."

"Vin... the way that fucker came for us, everything was all set in motion to play out exactly the way he wanted it to. *Everything.* Stephanou wanted to send a message, and he did. He was hoping he'd get to kill you in the end, but that didn't happen. There was nothing you would have been able to do to save her, because you were already doing everything."

I'm listening, and I want to believe it. What he's saying sounds like truth, but I don't want to excuse my guilt if there was more I could have done to protect her.

"You can always do better," I impart.

Salvatore shakes his head. "No, not when you do your best. You can't do better when you've done your very best, and I watched you with her. You loved her with your soul, the same way you love your child with your soul. They are the same, and you did everything to protect them that day. If you'd been there, Stephanou would have killed you too. You'd be an additional dead body in that house because you would have been vastly outnumbered."

He holds my gaze and strikes a nerve. I can believe whatever I want, but truth is truth, and he's right.

Everything he's saying is right.

"I just... wish it didn't happen. I wish it never happened."

"Me too. Me too, Vin. I can't tell you how much I wish it never happened because we all loved her. We all did, and it was hard to have something as horrifying like her death happen and feel like you can never get justice."

That's it. He hit the fucking nail with the hammer. The reason why we can never get justice is that we can't have what we want.

Her.

Nothing can bring her back.

Salvatore pulls in a breath and continues. "If I feel that way, I can imagine how you feel. What I know, though, is she was always happy, and I don't think moving on means we should forget that. I think you need to remember how she loved you and how happy you made her. She'd want you to remember those things and live. Not like this, but as the guy she fell for."

It's like he's echoing the words from the video.

I nod, and he stands, putting out his hand to help me up.

I take it, and he pulls me to stand.

He smiles at me. "Come, let's go."

I follow him when he takes a step away. I look back once to the grave and promise myself and her that the next time I visit, I'll be better.

That means I need to try and find myself.

Try to move forward.

Just try...

CHAPTER EIGHTEEN

Ava

I've been listening out for him to come back. I heard when he did. It was an hour ago. It's nighttime again. It's not as late as he's been out, just gone ten.

It's the first day, though, that I didn't spend feeling sorry for myself.

I spent it feeling sorry for what I did.

I've spent the last hour trying to figure out the best way to apologize. He hasn't come to see me, and I doubt he will tonight. That doesn't mean, though, that I shouldn't see him. Even if I'm walking dangerously close to disobeying him again.

Gathering my courage, I leave the room and venture out into the passage.

I head downstairs to the office. The second I get down the stairs, the two guards nearby look at me. I don't pay them any attention though. I keep walking and stop at the end of the corridor when I see Vincent inside his office talking with his brother Salvatore.

My presence makes them stop talking and Salvatore looks at me with an uneasy expression.

"I was about to head out. See you in the morning, Vin," he says and glances at me as he walks past.

I look back to Vincent feeling his glare on me.

"What?" he demands.

"I'm sorry," I say, but it doesn't feel like it's enough.

"I'm tired of you people and your sorrys." His face is set and his mouth twisted wryly.

"I know, and I have no excuse for being in your room, touching your things. I am sorry. Um... my first love in life was dancing. My... mother, she used to do ballet." God, that's the first time since the incident that I've actually told anyone that. Not even Holly knows. Saying it, though, has broken down something that I held in place to keep those precious memories. "I was a dancer, and I had... an accident that meant I couldn't dance anymore. That was when I started writing."

It's best to put it that way and call it an accident. It wasn't, not the way I made it sound. The whole incident was life changing enough and comparable to an accident that takes everything away.

I pull in a breath and keep talking. "The ballerinas just reminded me of when I used to dance. They reminded me of happier times. Maybe they can remind you of happy times too."

He doesn't say anything, but then I didn't expect him to. Something changes in his eyes though, in the way he looks back at me.

That's all I have to say, and I hope it's enough.

It's all I can offer. I turn and walk back to my room.

I didn't apologize so that he would forgive me and treat me... well, treat me a little better than a whore. The apology actually came from my heart.

I resume my usual stare out the window the next day and the days that follow see me doing the same. The nothingness of the days and the worry over Dad makes me digress into a deep depression comparable to what I faced years ago.

The only people I see each day are Marguerite and Lydia. Vincent avoids me completely.

Friday comes and I wake with the sun. Marguerite comes in a few hours later with her usual tray of pastries and hot chocolate. And as usual she does her best to make small talk and make me feel better. She can see my debacle though. I know she does. There's no way she can't see that being here is slowly destroying me.

Today I eat the cookies not because I'm hungry. I eat them because it's something to do.

The tastes takes my mind off the shit. For those few moments as I eat I stop thinking.

It's Friday again which means I've been captive here for almost three weeks. Friday again and I think back to weeks ago at The Dark Odyssey and the way I was with Vincent.

I remember the first time I had actual sex. Not the times before. It took me a long time to push anything previous out of my head and class the first time as the first time. I was twenty-one.

There was something about being with Vincent that night that reminded me of it because of the way I dropped my guard. I did it then too and gave myself completely.

He would never know what it meant for me to do that. Of course he wouldn't. I'm a whore to him. *A nobody. A thing.*

I was just finishing the last of the hot chocolate when the door opens and Vincent comes in.

He looks better than when I last saw him, although I did not mind the rugged look he sported with a fuller beard. It's completely gone today. His clean shaven face makes him look younger.

He's wearing a suit again, so I assume he's going to work. I don't know what version I'm going to get of him today, but at least he doesn't look like he's still pissed at me.

I stand when he approaches.

"Here, you have five minutes with him," he says, and my heart stills in anticipation. I could cry when he takes out his phone and clicks a button.

A tear runs down my cheek when he hands it to me. I recognize the number he's calling straightaway. *Dad...*

"Dad," I gasp when he answers.

"Hi, sweet girl," Dad says, and that's when the tears come.

I'm glad when Vincent leaves, giving me the privacy I need, but I doubt he's gone far.

"Please don't cry, my darling," Dad says. "Please don't."

"I'm sorry. It's just so good to hear your voice. I thought you were dead." I really did think that. What else was I supposed to think?

"I know. I'm so sorry, Ava. Please tell me you're safe. He hasn't hurt you, has he?"

I shake my head even though Dad can't see me. "I'm safe." It sounds like a lie. Honestly, though, it's true.

"Thank God in heaven. Oh God, you shouldn't be there. I wish you didn't make such an offer, Ava."

"Dad, don't. Please don't say that. Please, let's just talk. We have five minutes. Tell me what's happening." I try to hold the tears in.

"I'm at the clinic. I've just been under a lot of medication for the last few days while I detoxed and did a few other things," he explains.

"How are you feeling now?"

"Like hell. It's worse than last time, I guess because I've been taking stronger... drugs. I've arranged to stay another week to be on the safe side. I'm trying...harder this time. I want it to be different, Ava..." His voice trails off, and I hear him sniffle like he's crying. "Ava, I fell off the rails when I lost Sasha. I blame myself that I didn't see he needed my help, my attention. We came to this country, and

I thought we'd be free of the monsters. The darkness. But we weren't."

I cover my mouth to keep from crying out as guilt sweeps through me. We came to this country because of me. Only because of me. No other reason.

He only got in trouble because of me, lost everything and had to start anew.

"It's my fault," I breathe.

"Don't you dare... don't. I didn't go through all that hell for you to blame yourself. I failed you and her, your mother. And I have to be realistic. Your father would kill me just for the danger I've put you in now."

My breath hitches, and I shake another memory away that I don't want to remember.

"You are my father, and you've done everything for me," I remind him. The same blood might not flow through our veins, but that doesn't matter.

"No, Ava, what happened should never have. I lost my way, and I can't even remember half of the stuff I did. You shouldn't be paying the price for my sins. Sins I can't fix. Not you."

"Don't worry about me."

"I do, dorgoy" he replies, and I get that ominous feeling I've had looming over me again.

We don't talk about the past, and we never speak in Russian.

"Ava, I'm going to do better. For you and her. She would want me to, so I will. I pray your father isn't turning in his grave at what I've done. I love you."

"I love you too."

Tears stream down my cheeks as memories fill my mind of the past and those who died. I see their faces, and I can't shake them out of my mind.

My mother and my father—*my real father*. Dead. I know it wasn't my fault they were killed, but I still blame myself.

I always wonder what would have happened if things turned out differently. That last ballet was the last time we were together and happy. They wouldn't have been where they were if not for me, and what happened to me next wouldn't have happened.

I'm crying so much that when the door opens and Vincent comes in, I barely register it.

My hands are shaking, and I hate that I'm still crying.

He takes the phone from me and ends the call.

I turn away and face the window so I can have the privacy to cry. He stays. I wish he would go. Just leave me. It's been years since I broke down like this, and I can't have anyone around me right now when tears of pain flow down my cheeks.

Pain from death, horrible deaths, all of them, especially my mother. Both my parents were killed right in front of me.

I'm stunned, shocked even, when I feel warm hands on my shoulders. I'm crying so much, though, I can't move.

Vincent smooths his hand down my back and slips it around the midsection of my waist, pulling me to him. I rest against his chest and look up just to check if this is real. It's that moment when I feel the answer I searched for that night.

It comes as a feeling as he holds me and I allow him to.

Something bad happened to him. Something bad happened to me too.

The memory of my parents has filled me with darkness. Darkness I left in Russia ten years ago.

Darkness I left with the Bratva.

CHAPTER NINETEEN

Vincent

I walk up to Ava's door and stand by it, looking over the grooves in the wood.

I couldn't leave her to cry earlier.

I just couldn't do it.

I couldn't be the heartless monster, or keep up this... distancing from her.

I'm still in this state of flux when it comes to her, but I know that keeping her in this room, locked away in this house, is wrong.

I stayed with her for a while and only left when I felt she wanted to be alone.

As I watched her, I got the impression that she was crying for more than Mark. It was the way she was crying that gave it away. It was like that night when I watched her through the cameras and I just knew. It felt like that old pain again.

I just got back from work, and Marguerite told me Ava

stayed in her room all day and hasn't eaten anything. Not a damn thing. Not even the cookies she likes.

It's the earliest I've been home in days. It's just gone eight. When I started off this charade, I set dinner time for eight so I would eat with her. That hasn't happened in weeks, and it's not going to happen today.

I never usually knock on the door, but I do tonight, at least before going in.

She's sitting by the window again. She looks surprised to see me.

Her eyes fill with it, and her cheeks turn pink.

"You knocked," she states, standing.

Her eyes are red and her skin blotchy. It's clear she's been crying all day.

"Yeah."

She steels her spine, and there's a visible determination in her face to shield whatever she feels. It's a good attempt, but I don't know if she realizes that her eyes still give her away.

Want and desire are still very much there. It throws me off guard.

I don't know what she sees when she looks at me. I just pray I'm not as transparent as she is. That Friday when we were together at the club, it was real. It's fucking real every damn time, and I blame myself for allowing her to feel for me, teasing it out of her then being a prick. There was so much I did wrong.

"Was there something you wanted from me?" she asks.

"You haven't eaten all day."

"So?"

I know from the tick in her jaw that she's in that mood again where she's being difficult. What she wants is an end date. I'm not there yet though. I'm not at the stage where I can give her one.

When she first got here, I was mad as fuck because it felt like Mark got off too lightly. Now that I've been with her, there's a part of me that's eager to explore this insane chemistry between us. Both those things are holding me back on telling her when she can go.

"I told you I need you to eat."

"I'm not hungry."

I didn't come in here to argue about food, and I didn't come in here to get pissed at her. I have something else to talk to her about. I guess maybe it's my way of lightening the tension and meeting her somewhere in the middle.

"Suit yourself," I say, pushing my annoyance away. "You can go to your apartment tomorrow to get some things. Clothes and your computer for work. I'll have a car ready to take you at nine in the morning."

First, she looks surprised, then the guarded look returns to her eyes.

"Thank you."

I turn to leave thinking it best. The last time I had sex with her I was a bastard. I can't be in the same room with her for too long without wanting to strip her naked and fuck her. I don't know if going to that place tonight will be good for either of us.

"Is that all? Doesn't my master require the services of his whore today?" she calls out, and I freeze mid-step.

I turn back to face her. Although she's standing tall and defiant, her hands are by her sides, shaking.

"Ava..."

"I was just checking to be sure."

I totally deserve that.

I walk closer to her, and fear comes back into her eyes. She's afraid of me, definitely afraid of me, and she probably thinks I'm going to do shit to her for smart-mouthing me.

I take another step. I'm too close, so she steps back. Another step forward, and she takes one backward. She's right back against the wall now, and the quick rise and fall of her chest shows how panicked she is.

I allow instinct to guide me, mentally screwing the fucking worries and flux I'm in with her.

I am too close, and now I'm trapped in this space with her.

So trapped arousal knifes through me, splintering the guard I placed over my heart. Need and greed want me to take her. Take her the way I did last Friday. Take her like she's mine.

She *is* mine, so I reach for her. Slipping my hand behind her head, I bring her to my lips. Straight to my lips, where I claim her mouth.

At first, she's still tense and uncertain. She holds back, so I pull away and look into her eyes. They're glassy and brimming with tears. What I want is for her to look at me and see that I want her. I want that wild connection we had before.

A flicker of light sparks in her eyes the longer I stare.

Good. It's back... she's back.

I press my lips to hers again, and this time when she kisses me, it's with that unyielding desire.

My body remembers hers and wants to touch her everywhere.

The wild kiss turns hungry as I press into her head and harden the kiss, delving deeper.

She starts pulling at my shirt with both hands. It's like greed has possessed her. It comes for me too.

I allow her the second it takes to pull my shirt over my head. Our lips barely leaving each other.

Since she's wearing a little dress, I pull that down her shoulders and practically rip off her bra.

Her long legs wrap around me when I pick her up and carry her to the bed. I settle her down in the center, take off the rest of my clothes then her panties.

Her long arms slip around my neck when I climb onto the bed to take her.

While she kisses me, I part her legs and guide my cock into her slick, wet opening. She's ready for me, always ready for me.

Her lips part slightly over mine when I start to move inside her. I adjust myself so that I'm on top of her, so I can fuck her properly and kiss her at the same time. It's hot like hell. Our movements are filled with passion and need. It's no longer a simple matter of *want*.

I'm touching her like I need her, and she's holding on to me and kissing me like she needs me too.

I pump deep and hard, and her moans of ecstasy drive me wild. I know I won't last. Not like this. It's too much. Again. It's all too much and too intense.

We are.

We're at that point where we're so far over the line I don't know where it is anymore, or where it was.

We come at the same time, surrendering to pleasure, relinquishing everything. That's what it feels like for both of us.

I try to catch my breath after, and she holds on to my shoulders. Her delicate fingers brush over my skin, heating me up when I'm already alight.

As our breathing stills, worry floods her beautiful eyes. That look of *what next* is written all over her face. She looks away from me turning her head to avoid my stare.

"You aren't anybody's whore," I whisper, and she looks back to me. "You aren't anybody's whore. You hear me?"

A tear slides down her soft cheek. Briefly, I press my face to hers, taking the wetness of her tears.

As I hold her, I feel it. There's something about her that I feel I can't put my finger on. When her fingers flutter over my chest, I focus on her again although she doesn't say anything.

I see that pain in her eyes though.

"What is it, baby? What... hurt you before me?" I ask.

When she shakes her head and another tear makes its way down her silky skin, I know I'm right.

Something happened to her. Something bad.

I just know, so I hold her.

CHAPTER TWENTY

Ava

The shadows move like figures in the night. I know it's daytime though.

I can sense it, although I haven't seen daylight in forever.

The darkness is scary, but what's scarier is the shadows. I know they're there, and they know I know. It's a game to them. All of them.

A laugh sounds, and it triggers the fear of God deep inside me.

Rough hands grab me, and flashes of light go on and off. I don't know why they bother. I wonder if it's so I can't identify them, or maybe it's part of the game. I know their faces. I know who they are and what they are. Men who are monsters. Men who are nightmares.

Laughter and more hands. It all comes at once. Terror comes next. It feels like falling to death. I'm falling, and there's no one to save me. Those who could are dead.

I'm next... but these devils will only let me have death when they're finished with me.

Someone squeezes my neck hard, and I jump....

I jump out of my sleep forgetting where I am, but he's holding me.

Vincent's holding me. He's here.

It's daylight again, and he's here in my bed.

"Doll... you okay?" he asks, searching my eyes.

I run a hand through my hair and draw in a steady breath. It was just a dream. Or rather a nightmare of a memory.

When he cups my face, his warm fingers make me feel better.

"You're here." He didn't leave like last time. We slept in the same bed together and this is what it would be like to wake up next to him.

"Is that what you wanted?" he asks in a playful manner I haven't seen before.

"Maybe..." I answer, and a little smile tugs at the corner of his mouth.

"Maybe? Remember, I can tell when you're lying. Or even telling half-truths."

A little smile creeps across my lips, and he gives me a curious look.

"Well, hell. She's even prettier when she smiles." He releases my face and crooks his finger, beckoning me to his lips for a kiss. I move forward and plant a little kiss on his lips.

He gets off the bed and drags on his pants and boxers.

"I will see you at eight," he declares.

"Where are you going?"

"Work."

"Do you have to work so hard?" I ask, and the question somehow throws him. He raises a brow at me and gives me a wolfish grin.

I was so mad at this man just days ago, and that smile and his words have charmed me back to him. His ruffled hair is in complete contrast to his usually well-kept suave look and gives him a more youthful appearance. I like both.

"Yes, although you don't eat, the rest of us need food on the table."

"It's Saturday though."

"Bellezza, I have to go... I'll see you at the club later."

My lips part. "The club?"

"Yeah. Wear purple this time." He winks at me before leaving.

I stare at the door and try to take myself out of the trance.

What's happening again?

Or... what's happening now?

That was a good version of us cemented by last night.

I won't forget our arrangement, and I'll continue to hold guard of my heart even when it calls for him, but I have to admit there was something freeing about having him see into the pain that fills my soul.

It's not wise to do that again though. I shouldn't unlock that door to secrets of the past. Although I have no control of my subconscious mind and the nightmares that lurk there, I can control what happens while I'm awake.

It was just yesterday... I couldn't do it yesterday. The faces of ghosts haunted me all day, and I slipped up when Vincent saw deeper than I wanted anybody to see.

I'm glad he didn't ask me more, and I'm glad he just held me.

It's the first nice thing he's done for me since I've been here, although I suppose the joke's really on me because the fact that I'm here and Dad's alive means my arrangement with Vincent is the nicest thing he's done.

God, what am I going to do?

I bring my hands up to my cheeks and sigh. He's allowing me to get my stuff. That's good, but what I want is to have my life back. I don't know what's happening at work, and I've had no contact with anyone for close to three weeks. It's Saturday, and I haven't spoken to Holly or Freddie. What the hell must they think?

The competition ends on Friday. I've already accepted that

all hopes are gone. It upset me a great deal yesterday too when I thought about it, but I had to file it away in the cupboard of lost dreams.

This thing happened with Dad, and maybe it's more punishment for me because I didn't take heed sooner that he was in trouble.

I don't know what Vincent told anybody, and I don't want to ask him just in case I piss him off.

Last night was nice, so was just now... What does it mean though?

It shouldn't mean anything, and I shouldn't see more than there is, but what am I supposed to think when it feels so real to me?

After being in Vincent's castle of a home, my apartment feels small and enclosed. It's also odd to be back.

The place is as tidy as I left it. The only things that look out of place are the newspaper on the coffee table and my food shopping list sitting next to it.

The first thing I do is go to my laptop to check my emails. I just want to see if Freddie might have emailed me.

I have a few hours here to grab what I want. Another person would probably use the leeway to escape. Vincent gave it to me, though, because he knew I wouldn't be going anywhere.

I wish like hell I could see Holly or call her. I wish I could explain what happened and what's happening. I wish I could explain how I'm with a man I'm supposed to be a debt repayment to, and I can't stop myself from feeling for him.

I couldn't tell her any part of it, though, even if I could see or speak to her.

As the emails load, my heart all but soars out of my chest when I see there's a message from Freddie.

It's telling me he understands that Dad needs me, and he got the message from my friend. The friend must be Vincent or one of his men.

Freddie's only instruction to me was to take as much time as I needed and let him know if I needed any help from him.

I sigh with complete relief. It's a relief that I still have the job, and I'm happy for that, although he didn't mention anything about the competition.

There're a few emails from Holly too, checking on me.

It's so nice to see her messages. She's the only person I have in this world to truly talk to. We met in college when the universe shoved us together as roommates, and have been best friends since. She's helped a lot in ways she'd never know. I really do wish I could see her. Just seeing her would give me strength.

I email her and Freddie back, thanking them for their messages and letting them know I'm okay and will be in touch as soon as I can.

I think that's okay and won't get me in trouble. I won't be a fool and assume Vincent won't be doing some shit like monitoring my emails or something like that.

We may be good together when we get physical, but I still need to be careful.

I close the laptop and pack it in my bag.

I head to the bedroom next, which looks even smaller now that I've lived in such a lavish room.

I drop to my knees by my little bed and pull out my keepsake box. There're a lot of things I need to get, but there's something in this box I want to see.

It's the only reminder of Russia I have, and the life I once led. I open the box. There's only one thing in here from that time, and it's preserved in a little cellophane bag.

It's a blue ribbon my mother gave me. It matched my favorite practice dress. The ends are a little scorched from the fire, but the rest is still intact. It looks like a ratty old thing ready to be thrown away. Anyone who sees it would wonder why on earth I kept it.

It's the only thing I'm able to look at and feel the love I had from my mother. I don't even have pictures. I'm sure that demon who took her from me would have destroyed everything. There would have been no trace of us, just known and mourned by the people who knew us, but he would have thrown everything away. Not because he had to. It would have been for spite. He would have burned it to the ground the way the house burned just to be spiteful toward us. His family.

In the end, it was the person who wasn't family who came through for me.

I'm inclined to say it's the Bratva way because of greed, but I don't know that. I think when you're evil, you are just evil. Nothing else explains you.

When you belong to an organization like that, where it's ruthless against the heartless, it facilitates the trait.

That was what that demon was like.

Completely different to my real father. Like the opposite. Papa wasn't evil. He might have ruled with a heavy hand as leader, but there was nothing evil about him. He loved me. My mother and father loved me.

That's what I remember. It's that too that makes me feel the guilt I continue to feel for their deaths.

I put the little ribbon in my pocket. I'll take this to keep her close. Close to my heart.

I take a few more things, and as I leave, I hope that life will get better soon... in whatever way that means.

Marguerite meets me at the door when I get back.

"Buona serata, Signora," she says. "Please, keep an old woman alive by eating something. I worry so much about you."

I smell cookies, and my stomach grumbles with hunger. She hears it and gives me that knowing look with her head tilted to the side.

"Okay, thank you," I answer.

"Thank God. Come." She taps my shoulder, and I follow her

into the kitchen, where I see she's made sandwiches and a host of baked goodies.

Even if I wanted to be stubborn today, I don't think I could be. Everything looks and smells amazing. I dive in straightaway and probably eat a week's worth of food, much to Marguerite's satisfaction.

"Do you want more?" she asks, and I laugh because I'm so full I'll probably burst if I have another bite.

"No, I'm stuffed."

She smiles and sets a glass of orange juice down in front of me on the table. "My dear, you have such a nice laugh. It's nice to hear it."

She takes a seat in the chair opposite me. It's the first we've sat like this, and I don't know what to say to her or talk to her about.

The situation is unconventional, and so am I. I know she reports back to Vincent all that happens during the day, and you can't really trust a person like that, but I don't feel that malicious vibe from her. I never have. If anything, I've felt that motherly warmth I've lacked for the last ten years.

"Did it go okay? Getting your things, I mean?" she asks.

I nod. "I just got a few things. I guess there's clothes here, and they're a lot better than anything I could afford."

Sympathy appears in her warm eyes. "They may be expensive, but your own things mean more to you. It's okay. I understand, and I get it that you can't say much. I can't either. I just do my job. Doesn't mean I am blind to what is happening, or that I agree with it." She makes a point of quirking her brows for those last words.

"You must know why I'm here, then," I say.

"No." She shakes her head. "I never know details."

I don't know how she does it. Just doing her day-to-day work and never knowing what's going on. Add the fact that Vincent is a mobster and most of what he's doing isn't going to be legit. How is she okay with it?

"No one tells you anything?"

"No. It's not for me to know. I can... guess though." She raises her shoulders and gives me a small smile.

Shame fills me when she says that, and my cheeks burn. She knows I'm here for sex. Maybe there were more like me. Foolishly, jealousy takes me. I don't know what the hell's happening to me.

"Has this ever happened before? I mean women here. Like me?" I ask.

She chuckles. "No, Vincent does not have women in his home, and as long as I've known him, he's been the same. The only woman he lived with is his wife."

That surprises me.

"Really?" I ask, and she nods.

I think of Vincent's wife. Sorcha. She seemed so perfect on the video. Then there was what she said. How she loved him.

What happened to her? It's on the tip of my tongue to ask Marguerite, but I hold my tongue as the seconds pass. If she wanted me to know, she'd tell me. So, I can only assume my thoughts are right. *She died.*

"He was different then. The same boss, but his spirit was different. He's not as ... what he might seem. I think you might see that for yourself too." The way she looks at me now tells me she knows what I feel. There's a twinkle in her eyes that's a tell of what she's thinking.

It's almost like I got a part of that someone I was dying to talk to, even if I can't say much.

"Yeah," I agree.

She rises to her feet. "Drink your juice. I won't take up your time. I'll be tending to the baby. Call me if you need to."

I nod.

When she leaves, I take a sip of my drink and a few moments to think. I can tell that Vincent was different when he had his wife. Maybe I get pieces of that man too in the times when I see desire in his eyes for me.

But do I want that?

That's not a question I should entertain. At the same time, I can't stop it from entering my mind.

I'm going to The Dark Odyssey again tonight.

Will we have another fantasy?

If we do, I hope I'll have the strength to leave it because last time was hard.

CHAPTER TWENTY-ONE

A VA

Tony, the same guy from last time, escorts me into the elevator, and we go up to the fourth floor once again.

I don't see the acrobats this time as we go up.

Tony leads me around to the sofa area of the lounge. It's past the bar.

Shock takes me when my gaze lands on a row of cubicles on the opposite side of the hall. Inside are different variations of couples having group sex. This doesn't look that much different from the orgy room and leaves my skin blazing with heat.

"The boss will join you here in a few minutes," Tony says with a curt nod.

I open my mouth to answer but find I can't. He seems to understand my shock and chuckles as he walks away.

Curiosity beckons me to stare and I find myself looking on at the sinful scene before me.

I walk up to the balcony and watch the foursome in my line of sight. Two men and two women. They're each paired together fucking recklessly. The women are on their hands and knees on the padded floor while the men pound into them from behind. All look like they're having the best time of their lives.

My lips part, but my mouth waters with arousal when they stop and move to the sofa area, where one of the guys sits down and the blonde woman straddles him, Then the other guy gets behind her and plunges into her ass. While the two men start fucking her, the dark-haired woman takes her place beside them and moves in to suck the woman's breasts as she waits her turn. There have been many things to shock me this past week. This can go right up there with them.

I'm surprised that I can watch like this and allow myself to give in to the curiosity of sexual distraction. Maybe it was the years of therapy I underwent after Russia that desensitized my mind.

Whatever it was worked in some kind of way because I'm definitely aroused and ... I can understand the fun.

"Have you ever done that before?"

I jump at the sound of his voice so close to my ear. I turn quickly to find Vincent standing behind me. That look of fascination sparks in his eyes. He's had a haircut and looks sharper. It's more like a faux hawk now that accentuates the angles of his high cheekbones.

The corners of his mouth slide into an easy grin. "You gonna continue to ogle me, or you gonna answer the question?" he asks widening his smile.

"What?" I blink, focus, then remember the question. As I do, my cheeks flush. *Have I ever done that before?* "No," I reply quickly and frown like he's just insulted me. My answer makes him laugh. "Have you?"

"Yes."

I swallow hard and am grateful for the subtle light because I'm blushing uncontrollably. I don't know why I'm surprised. This must be normal for him. But what if he brought me here to share me with some man? I wouldn't know what to do.

"I can't. I can't do that," I tell him, and he chuckles.

"Didn't you say you'd do anything, Bellezza?"

Me agreeing to do anything did not extend the invite to be shared. Panic fills me, and I turn to walk away, but he catches my arm and pulls me back.

"Red," I gasp, pulling a word I think he'll understand out of thin air. That makes him laugh even more.

"*Red?*"

"It's a safe word to stop."

"I know what safe words are, baby. I've issued them many times, but you aren't tied to my bed yet, so I don't know what exactly you're safe-wording me for when I haven't done anything." He quirks a brow.

I think past his words and push the image of me being tied to his bed with him fucking me out of my mind.

"I don't want to be shared," I say shaking my head.

"Well... lucky for you, I'm too greedy." His gaze rakes over my body, making every nerve come alive. "I'm definitely having you all to myself."

This feels different. Something feels different. Like I'm not... whatever I am. *His whore*. That word keeps coming back to haunt me because I hate it so much. He's not looking at me like I am. He's looking at me like that first night. With interest.

"That okay?" he asks.

"Yes," I say, and the way his eyes tangle with mine, with such riveted attention, makes me take a moment and wonder if this were another time... or if we'd met under different circumstances, what we'd be.

Like maybe if we met at a bar or somewhere normal to me.

I think it because just now when I answered him, it felt real, like I was really saying yes to him and not our arrangement.

He releases my arm.

"Sit." He points to the sofas next to us.

I walk over to sit, and he sits on the sofa opposite me. There's a bottle of wine and two glasses.

He doesn't take the drink. Instead, he sits back and gives me that look that drinks me in and undresses me with lust filled invisible fingers.

"We're here again," I state, trying to figure out what we're doing tonight. There was no mention of a car taking me back to the house.

"We are." He continues to watch me.

"And we're sitting?"

"And talking."

"What are we talking about?" This feels like a game.

"Stuff. Tell me about your writing. How did it replace your first love?" The question throws me for the fact that it's a question about me and the way he phrased it.

I think about my answer. There's a long version to the truth and a short one. I decide to go with something in between. "I think it's a thing creative people can do. They find a way to express themselves in one way or another."

"You write about other people. Is that what you want to do?"

"I like it." I nod. "Lifestyle writing covers stories about positive and influential people who sometimes change the world in their various pursuits. It gives others hope. It's nice to write about people like that."

"Like how you think Todd Barker is the sexiest man alive?" His lips arch.

My eyes widen. "That was my first article."

"Yes, and it seemed to be your most passionate. I noticed the way you wrote about how younger women will always be attracted to older men. That explains why you like me."

A hot blush creeps over my body. I don't think I've ever met anyone who was so confident and outspoken.

"That doesn't explain why I like you." The words tumble out of my mouth before I realize what I said.

He's listening though and didn't miss a beat.

"Come here," he says. A noticeable sexual tension thickens the air.

I stand and walk over to him. He reaches for me with strong arms, his muscles flexing against his shirt as he pulls me into his lap. I straddle him, and the negligee rides right up my hips. That was probably his intention. A cocky smile fills his deadly handsome face. Beautiful and dangerous, it's a deadly combo.

I press my hands against his chest.

"You're creative... How about you imagine this: pretend we just met here tonight and none of the last two weeks happened. Could you explain then why you like me?"

I consider it and feel the shift in the mood between us. "You wouldn't meet me here."

"Where would I meet you?"

I lift my shoulders into a shrug because I can't imagine where I would meet him, and I'm sure I'd be too nervous to talk to him.

"Somewhere like the coffee shop. You'd find me there."

"Oh yeah?"

"Yes."

"Which one?"

"It's called The Spot. It's on Grand Avenue."

"And... what would happen there?" He runs his hands over the bare skin of my ass and pulls me closer so I can feel the hardness of his cock pressing into me.

The molten-hot desire in his eyes encourages me to continue. To continue to explore this fantasy of an alternate version of us.

"We'd talk, but... I don't know if I could make the first move. I'd probably just stare," I confess with a chuckle. That's the truth, even though it might sound lame.

He smiles. "So, I'd see this doll looking at me, obviously checking me out, and I'd have to make the first move."

I nod and try to bite back a smile.

"Let's say I did," he says with emphasis. His fingers trail up to my waist and linger there, heating my skin where he touched. I watch in anticipation of what he's going to say next. "I walk over to you... and we talk. Then would you tell me why you like me?"

The ball is back in my court. It's just been passed to me, and the intense gaze he gives me pushes desire to the forefront of my mind. It compels me to answer with truth. I've never had a man look at me the way he is. The fact that it's him means more.

"Yes," I hear myself say, and I consider if I really have lost my mind.

He's my enemy. A man who was hellbent on killing my father. A man who has me captive at his home without an end date for my release. A man who owns me and treats me like I belong to him. Like I'm a possession of his.

Something sparks inside my soul when I think that. *A possession of his.*

His...

Like I belonged to him.

We stare at each other, and everything stills. I'm walking a dangerous path here. It would be wise not to confuse this relationship of ours.

It would be wise not to cross the line, but something draws me to him. Something that recognizes truth. He's not looking at me like this is part of our arrangement.

What I see in his eyes is real.

"What would happen next?" he asks, breaking the trance.

What would I do next, or say next in the alternate world?

The question makes me forget who we are and where we are.

I play the game he created, and boldness takes over. As it does, I know what I'd do. I lean forward and brush my lips over his. It's a taste, a mere brush of our lips, but it sends a slither of delight through me.

I want more. The taste makes me crave more, and I cup his face and slant my mouth right over his. When I do, he smooths his hand up my head, holding me to his lips. The notion awakens passion. My lips part from the raw ecstasy, and he takes advantage of that to sweep his hot, wet tongue into my mouth so it can tangle with mine.

He tastes different tonight. Different to the last time we kissed. He tastes like sex and passion rolled into one. Like something you want to relish and savor forever. The thought hits me hard, slamming into my soul, and that awakened feeling expands. It grows and grows, and I feel alive.

The kiss turns from hunger into greed in seconds. Greed consumes me and guides his movements.

He pulls away, and I feel his erection digging into my pussy. He moves me back a little in his lap so he can unzip his pants. I realize what he means to do then, and awareness comes back. I look around me. My gaze lands on the people having sex across from us.

Vincent turns my face back to him.

"It's okay, don't freak." He gives me a devilish grin as he takes out his cock. "Just look into my eyes."

Look into his eyes?

Should I be doing that?

It's always when I look into those magnetic eyes of his that I feel the control I have on my emotions slip away.

I do it though. I focus on him as he moves the thong aside and guides himself into me.

I shuffle over his cock and straddle him properly, gasping as he fills me up and starts moving inside me.

I moan as his movements speed up to a rhythm we both get drawn in. At that moment, I don't even think about the fact that we're having sex in public.

I don't care about that. I just look into his eyes the way he looks into mine.

He gives me a wicked smile filled with temptation, tightens his hold on my ass, and starts fucking me.

The pull of an orgasm comes for me hard and sure with his relentless strokes, but the rawness with which he fucks me has me writhing against him too, worse than ever.

This feels like we should be in a bedroom, but the fact that we're fucking in a sex club, out in the open, drives me wild. I completely shock myself.

He likes it. The wildness in his eyes is accompanied by satisfaction as I move my hips against him, riding his cock as he pounds into me.

He holds me closer and leans into my ear to mutter, "that's right, Bellezza, fuck me baby. Let go and give yourself to me."

I do. That, however, was not something he had to tell me to do.

I was already doing it. Different to my offer.

This is different to giving myself to him that way.

At the same time... maybe it's the same thing. Maybe this is the end result of that. The stimuli and the response. *Cause and effect.*

This could be the end result of the chain reaction I started when I offered myself to him.

What is happening now is, it feels like he's taking more from me than just my body.

His lips return to mine, claiming and possessing me as he pounds harder and faster, fucking me so hard stars spark before my eyes when I close them as we kiss.

His cock strains inside me, and I know that means he's nigh on release. I am too.

He stops the kiss to grab my hips harder. It's painful, but I take it. It feels too good to deny myself of even that.

"Vincent," I call out his name, and a light of raw fascination invades his eyes.

I cry out again, throwing my head back as he hammers into me, splitting me from reality. We cry out together and both come on the wave of a shared release.

We're both left breathless after, and I wonder what will happen next.

This time felt different.

I don't think I'm deluded in thinking it did. It was different because we were different.

Something changed between us, and I don't know what it was or when it happened. He's holding me now like he wants me, and I feel that fear creep into my soul again. It whispers, *would he still want me if he knew what happened to me?*

"I want you," he says into my ear, and my hearts starts beating so fast I think it's going to leap right out of my chest.

It's like he could hear my thoughts.

"I want you," he repeats.

"You want me?" I ask, almost revealing my disbelief.

"I do," he confesses and turns his head to face me. "Come, looks like we're in for another wild fantasy."

He reclaims my lips, kissing me hard, and I resume this fascination even though I know I shouldn't.

I know I'm getting in way over my head with this man.

But... I need him...

CHAPTER TWENTY-TWO

Vincent

Fucking hell, I'm like a man who's lost his mind.

We're in the shower together, fooling around, and only God knows what time it is. I know it's well into the early hours of the morning, but I don't know the specifics.

The only responsible thing I did was to send Marguerite a message letting her know we'd be back tomorrow. I didn't want her worrying, and that also meant I wanted her to stay home and look after Timothy. Something I'd normally be doing most Saturday nights.

I feel like an ass, a slave to selfishness, a fool to passion because I can't get enough of this woman.

I have Ava pressed against the smooth wall of the shower. I already fucked her against it, and my dick's fucking hard again for her, hard just thinking about getting in her tight cunt again.

I want inside her, but I have to leave her lips, and I can't.

I'm fucking crazy. That's what. It's finally happened. I've lost my damn mind from all the shit. All night, I've been trying to get to that point where I rein in control, but the siren has me wrapped around her claws. Delicate fingers that beckon me to keep taking.

I'm in charge here. She's not supposed to want me. She's not supposed to be enjoying this. She's supposed to be debt repayment, but she isn't, and it doesn't feel like that anymore.

It feels real to me. *She* feels real to me, not like she's trying to seduce me to put a hold on my control.

I test it by stopping. I stop kissing her and allow her to kiss me. She doesn't even realize until seconds later, then she stops, and worry settles in her eyes. Worry that I'll tell her the fantasy is over.

It's not, and as she rests back against the wall and the light spray of water from the shower trickles over her, I take the moment to look at her.

Her angelic face, that long brown silky hair soaked with water running down her delicate frame. Petite with the perfect shape to carry those massive tits and her perfect ass.

She looks up at me with her doe eyes searching mine, hungry for me to fuck her again. I'm definitely going to.

I'm going to own that pussy again before the night is over and take her the way a woman should be taken.

I look at her tits, ripe, with the rose-tipped nipples hard, pleading for me to suck them.

I circle my finger around the right one, and she actually looks relieved, and aroused.

"I want these in my mouth," I tell her, fondling both tits, giving them a gentle squeeze before I lower to suck.

I absolutely fucking love the sounds that come out of her. Those moans of pleasure make my dick hard and could keep me going all fucking night.

I work each nipple to life, loving the feel of them pebble harder in my mouth. The hard tip and soft flesh are the perfect combo for me to suck, and they're so big I can't fit the whole breast in my mouth.

It just makes me want more.

And more. I slide my fingers into her wet pussy. Wet from the shower water and what I'm doing to her. She's always so wet for me. Always.

I crouch down as the urge to eat her pussy out comes over me again. I've done it enough times tonight. This here will be the seventh time that my mouth has gotten up close and personal, and my cock is ready to follow suit too.

She gasps and smooths her hand over my hair when I lick over her clit and suck on the juicy nub. What I want is to taste her nectar. I want her pussy juices to gush into my mouth so I can taste her. Taste the want I create in her. This from the woman who fears me as much as she wants me.

Fear...

She should be afraid, but part of me doesn't want that. The part of my mind that tells me I should know better wants this. It wants this version of us where she's giving more than her body to me.

I know she is, and that's why I'm taking. What I don't know is what I'm going to do about it when the sun comes up.

I chance looking up at her as I eat her out, and she looks at me too, her breasts jiggling as I move my tongue in and out of her.

"Vincent... ahhhh..." she moans loud. My name on her lips as she's lost in pleasure is a sight to behold. "I'm coming."

"Come, baby, let me taste you." To pleasure her further, I tweak her nipples. That's all I need to do to push her over the edge.

The gush of her delicious juice flows into my mouth, and I drink her up. I take everything, swallowing and drinking, then licking for more so I can milk her clean. I don't want to waste any. She tastes just like she looks.

Like she wants me.

She's panting, trying to catch her breath when I stand up and take her lips once more. I want her to taste herself on my mouth. I think she does. I feel she does because the moan that resonates from her lips is different to the others.

It's fucking spellbinding, because I want her even more. I didn't think that was possible.

She kisses me back like it's the first time we've kissed, or like we're lovers reunited after not seeing each other for years. It's that intense, and I can't take any more. I need her now.

I move away from her lips and try to reach for her, but she backs away playfully. It's the sexiest thing ever. I almost blow my load and embarrass myself when her fingers flutter over the length of my dick.

Raw primitive need sparks inside me, mixing with the crackle of wild sexual energy as I watch her continue to stroke my length and my cock grows at her touch.

"Can I? Can I taste you too?" she asks.

Nobody ever told me that shyness was sexy. It is.

My gaze rivets to her, locking with her beautiful eyes, and right... just there—here she wouldn't know that she has me right where she wants me. It's fucking dangerous for a man like me. Nobody should have that power over me.

"Yes," I tell her. I can't believe I haven't had that mouth of hers around my cock yet.

The doll drops to her knees and continues to stroke my cock.

She lowers her head, gripping the base of my shaft, and takes me into her mouth. The sight is consuming, and I have to reach out and place my hand on the wall to keep my cool.

She sucks me hard, giving me more of what I crave. Her tongue glides up and down my length as she sucks, and her hot, wet mouth takes me deeper and deeper. She sucks harder, and my balls tighten, then my little bellezza weakens me further when she releases my cock and starts sucking my balls.

Fuck... I can feel my release, and I want to be inside her. I feel like a selfish bastard as I reach for her and pull her to her feet. Like a fucking animal, I turn her to face the wall, grab her ass, and plunge straight into her hot pussy.

I start to fuck her hard and rough, just the way I like it. Her ass jiggles as I pound into her and our bodies slap together with the raw rhythm.

I know I'm too rough, but she takes it, and she loves it. My name is on her gorgeous mouth again. It tangles with her moans of ecstasy, which encourages me to take more and more. I do.

I fuck her until it drains me, and when I blow into her, I am drained. It's like a bit of life force has been taken away, sucked away with the pleasure I sought so greedily to claim.

Her knees wobble as she tries to straighten up, and I catch her, slipping my arm around her midsection to keep her steady.

I know she's tired, but I wonder if like me, she doesn't want the night to end.

I run my hand over her wet hair. It's then I see something I haven't seen before. It's a little scar just behind her ear, in between the top of her earlobe and her hairline. Very small and indented into her skin but there, visible when her hair's wet.

I run my finger over it and lean closer to her ear.

"What happened to you here, baby?"

She pauses for a second, like she's thinking of the right answer, then turns her head and smiles at me.

"Scar from my accident," she replies.

I'd believe her if I weren't who I am. I'd believe her if I didn't know all that came with the darkness of my world.

That's a cigarette burn scar.

I know what it looks like. I've made that mark enough times to know.

In that moment, I know too that someone did that to her.

Who would do that?

Who would hurt her like that?

I remember Mark saying she had a rough life.

Was that part of it?

She looks up at me with her tired eyes. "It was a bad accident. The scar looked worse years ago."

"How long, baby?"

"Ten. I was sixteen." The same sadness I saw earlier this morning and yesterday reappears in her eyes.

I sense that there's something more I'm not privy to, and she was definitely crying for more than Mark.

Feeling her rest against me, I scoop her up and carry her to bed, where she falls asleep in my arms. I look at her cocooned in my arms and try to remember what she's supposed to be to me.

A debt repayment... but she never felt that way to me.

As I watch her in deep slumber again, I wonder what her story is.

Would she tell me?

I sit by the window smoking a cigar, watching the city come alive. The Chicago skyline is right in my line of sight from this side of the building. It shimmers into view with the sun, waking like the rest of the world.

Ava is still asleep.

I look at the beautiful young woman wrapped in my sheets and ask myself for the millionth time what I'm going to do.

She can't stay with me forever, and she's too much of a distraction in a time when I should be more level-headed. I haven't heard anything from Gibbs yet on the Bratva guys. It hasn't been any time for me to form any opinions on what that means, but it does make me doubt myself. Like maybe I am just worried and more wary than I should be.

In terms of Ava though, she has to get back to her life, and I have to give it back to her.

When is the big question.

I think I'm addicted to this fascination I have with her.

Even when I try to keep it at bay, it pushes through. It's going to get me in trouble. It already has.

My phone buzzes next to me. It's a text from Salvatore.

You still here?

I text back:

I am. Come see me in five.

I drag on my pants and take one last glance at Ava before I leave the room.

This suite is one of the guest suites I've claimed for myself. It's like a little apartment, so the bedroom is separate from the kitchen and living room. It's one of the biggest, and since I claimed it, it really is basically mine.

When the boys first set the place up, they were always talking about each of us having a suite.

They do, but Frankie and I were the only ones who didn't follow them. It was strange to them because when we were younger, we were the worst two when it came to sex and getting up to all kinds of shit with women. We couldn't have been more terrible examples and were shocked to shit when the guys set up a sex club.

The biggest reason why we didn't join in the venture was because Pa wanted us to be serious and focus on business. We did just that.

Salvatore gets here in exactly five minutes. He comes in with a smirk on his face he's trying to hide. He saw me last night as I ushered Ava to the room. He was coming out of his room, which is down the hall from here.

He's always here with Mimi, his wife, whether she's pregnant or not. I can imagine them still coming here when they're old. Nick and his wife, Mia, are the same. It's just Gabe and Charlotte who seemed to follow the pattern I had with Sorcha, although they tend to come every so often.

I swear to God I shouldn't know these things, but they tell me.

"Came to check on you," Salvatore says, but his eyes are on the bedroom door. He looks back at me like he has something he wants to ask me but is holding off.

"Did you? Or were you snooping?" I smirk and sit down on the sofa.

"Both." He chuckles and sits opposite me. "Can't blame a concerned brother. Be worried if I don't care, Vin."

"Yeah, I guess."

"I really did come to check on you. We haven't spoken since the other day. I'm sure you could tell I was avoiding talking about business."

"Yeah, I could. I didn't really want to talk business then."

"I was giving you space. This is probably the worst place to talk and bad timing, but Mimi and I are taking Skye on a little road trip to the countryside." He smiles proudly, and I feel proud of the father he is. Skye is his little girl. She looks just like Mimi. Like a little fairy.

"Countryside?"

He chuckles. "That's what she's calling it. It's a clever ruse to get me to drive to this little bakery she heard about in Ohio."

"Christ, Salvatore, *Ohio?*" The man is a badass mobster, but that woman has him wrapped around her finger. There's nothing on this earth he won't do for her.

"Vin, I can't say no to that woman. She drives me crazy, but I fucking love her, and she knows it. And now that we have Skye, it's like I have two little women on my hands. Thank God the next one's a boy. It'll be some balance in my life."

I laugh at him.

"So... my life aside, we'll be away until Tuesday, and as your *consigliere*, I didn't want to go without seeing you first. Didn't want you brewing by your lonesome with shit on your mind."

I take out the humidor and hold it out for him to take a cigar. He does and lights up.

"Pa's furious as fuck that I want time to think about the alliance. To him, I'm pussyfooting and stalling."

"Are you?"

"I don't know. The crap with Mark didn't help one bit, but that's no excuse for me to stall on something that could change our lives."

"Vin, I know you. You don't just stall."

"I know."

"Anything else happen?"

"Dmitri came to see me at the office."

Salvatore raises his brows. "Did he now?"

"To his credit, it was a decent visit. He even suggested coming here for a drink."

Salvatore sighs and bites the inside of his lip. "You still feel the same?"

"Yes," I confess. "I'm still wary."

"Tell you what... Invite them to the fundraiser. That'll smooth things over with Pa."

That's a good idea. Pa's supporting the Children's Society this year and he's holding a party here in a few weeks. It's one of his black tie events he loves hosting. Inviting Dmitri and Yuri to something like that would definitely be to my credit and get Pa off my ass.

"I like that idea, Salvatore."

"It'll work. In the meantime, we'll do some extra digging." He cracks his knuckles.

I feel like I should hold off telling him about Gibbs because I don't want to seem paranoid, but there's little point asking him to be my consigliere if I'm going to keep secrets.

"Salvatore... this is off record, so please don't say anything to Pa yet or anyone else. I got Gibbs checking things out too." I lean forward.

"You have my word, brother." He nods once. "I won't say a damn thing. I think it's good we have a man like that we can call on. At least if he says he can't find anything you'll be more assured that our bratva friends are legit."

"Thank you." I'm grateful for his support and understanding.

The bedroom door opens, and Ava comes out with the sheet wrapped around her. Her eyes grow wide when she sees Salvatore.

"I'm sorry. I didn't realize," she stutters. "I just ... I'll come back later." She backs away, going back into the room, her face flushed with embarrassment.

When I look back to Salvatore, I see he's already looking at me.

"You like her," he states.

"Do I?" I take a draw on my cigar, avoiding his stare.

"You do, and that's a good thing. It's a healing step in the right direction. No matter what happens."

Maybe he's right.

What might not be right, however, is me entertaining what I'm starting to feel for her.

CHAPTER TWENTY-THREE

AVA

We got home later in the day, and I didn't know what was going to happen.

At least I got some form of an answer when we spent the night similar to the way we did the night before.

He came to my bed, and there he stayed until morning. He thought I was asleep when he left the bed.

I wasn't, and now I'm not sure what's weirder. Us like this or the way we were before.

Something has changed between us, but neither of us is acknowledging it. Probably because neither of us *wants* to acknowledge it.

Is it too late for me to repeat that mantra of not wanting this —whatever it is?

I lie in the bed for another hour before I decide to get up. I'm not sure what I'll do today. It's Monday again, and I don't know if I can live another week like the one I just had.

It's just gone seven. Marguerite usually gets here early, but I'm not sure how early. I decide to go downstairs to the kitchen hoping she'll be there, and if she's not, I hope it's okay to make coffee.

She is. She's in there with Lydia, but I can see Vincent in the living room with the baby. They're drawing on some pieces of paper.

He looks up and sees me watching, and it's too late when he does to act like I wasn't.

As he's looking at me, I make my way in there, but I keep a few paces away because I know he's cautious of me around his child. His child, who brightens up the way he did the other week when he first saw me. I haven't seen him since.

Vincent catches him as he tumbles over trying to get to me.

"Easy, tiger," he says, pulling the baby close.

I smile down at them. I noticed there're different versions of him. This is one of them. Watching him with his baby shows a softer side to him that actually makes him more alluring.

He stands up with him and offers me a small smile.

"Good morning," I say. I'm nervous. I'm sure it's evident with the blush I feel creeping into my cheeks.

"Good morning. Sleep well?" He knows I did. He was there. I nod all the same, and the baby giggles.

His sweet little smile has me smiling too. He turns to Vincent and says, "Princess, Papa." He starts pointing at me. "Princess."

Now I can't help but laugh, although part of me notes he wouldn't have been wrong years ago. I was certainly treated like one in another lifetime. I never knew it would be my downfall.

"Yes, baby, she is," Vincent tells him and shakes his head. "He's a little flirt."

"He's sweet," I answer, unsure of what to say.

"His... name's Timothy," Vincent says, looking like he's decided I can know that.

"That's a nice name."

Marguerite comes into the room with a bright smile on her face. "Morning, all. I need that baby now. It's going to take me at least one hour to get him ready for playgroup. He hates that dreadful uniform."

Vincent hands Timothy over to her. "Uniforms are not bad."

"No, if you're in the army, they are okay. No for babies. We won't tell your padre we'll take the cute banana suit today for backup." Marguerite winks at Vincent and shakes her head when he opens his mouth to protest.

She leaves us and takes the lighter atmosphere with her as she goes.

He stares at me, and it's like I'm placed back in my role of being captive.

He reaches forward and touches the underside of my jaw then traces behind my ear, along the scar I was left with as a reminder of Russia. It was a cigarette burn. It was the last one, the deepest one. The one that burnt through my skin. The others faded with time. They faded over the ten-year span.

Vincent brings his hand back to my chin and intensifies his gaze on me.

"I'm changing a few things today," he states, dropping his hand to his side.

"What are you changing?" My breath hitches as I wait for the answer.

"You go to work today," he says, and my heart swells. I'm so happy I think I could burst.

"Really? You'd let me go?"

"Yes, someone will take you there and bring you back when you finish."

"Thank you. I appreciate it. I'm..." I don't know if he cares to hear why I'm so hellbent on going back to work. I'm sure most people, most women, would love to have their bills and everything taken care of. I'm a little different.

"What?"

"I'm working toward something."

"More articles on older men?" He raises a brow, and the tension in the air shifts to the lighter mood we shared at The Dark Odyssey.

I chuckle. "No, I want to be chosen to write the special annual edition of the magazine. This year, it's on someone I really admire."

"Who is it?"

"Coral Winters. She works with charities. I'd love to do the piece on her, and I'll find out if I'm successful on Friday."

"Sounds good."

"Thank you," I bubble.

"You'd... better get dressed."

God, this is something I can hold on to. I won't feel so much like a prisoner now.

I'll have something to keep me sane.

Now, I just need an end date. The day I return to my life.

As I look at him, though, something whispers to me, asking me if I truly want that. To return to my life, a life... without him.

I'd go back to normal.

What if I didn't want that? I've experienced this strong emotional connection I've had with him.

But is it wise for me to go wanting a man like him?

Freddie sits forward in his chair and gives me a look of sympathy.

He's the guy who opened the door to opportunity for me.

He's strict as anything but likes my work ethic. He runs a tight ship and stands for no nonsense but knows when to show compassion.

"How are you?" he asks.

I straighten up and put on my best smile. The smile I've been wearing for the last three days. "I'm okay," I assure him.

He looks happy to hear that. He was glad to see me come

back on Monday, and I was happy things were okay, unaffected with my absence.

The same with Holly. I told them I lost my phone and haven't managed to get another yet. Everyone assumed the reason I was off the last three weeks was because of Dad. Since that wasn't far from the truth, I went with it. Both he and Holly know that Dad has an addiction problem and that he's been in and out of rehab. Both know what we went through when Sasha was killed.

I had to tell them, especially about the times when Dad went to rehab. On the first few instances, I had to take days off here and there. It wasn't that hard, really, to fall in line with their beliefs on this occasion, although this was the worst, and I've never disappeared on everyone before for so long.

"Ava, I have to say I'm concerned about you, and I don't want you to push yourself too hard if your father needs you," Freddie says.

"No, it will be fine. I need to be at work, especially with the opportunity to do the piece on Coral. I want to work hard to be considered."

"You're already being considered. I haven't shared this with Brock, but I will share a few things with you to put your mind at ease." He grins, and I listen on, eager to hear what he has to say. Brock is the competition, and he's not the nicest of guys. If he's not trying to grab my ass at work get-togethers and pretending to be drunk, he's always staring at my breasts. "As you know, the decision will lie with the panel, but they'll be deciding based on five of your articles chosen at random by me. Those were submitted last Friday."

My eyes widen. I didn't know that. We were given a host of things that covered work ethic and our contributions to the magazine over the years. There were originally ten people who were selected for the competition, then last month, that went down to two. Me and Brock. This is the final phase. I worked my ass off with everything, and I pray I do get chosen. Knowing this info about the articles helps ease my mind.

"Thank you. I'm grateful."

"That's my part done. As your manager, though, I want to make sure you take care of yourself. You're a great writer, Ava, and you do good work here, so if you need time with your father, please ask."

I appreciate his words and kindness. "Thanks, I will."

I give him a smile as I leave and head to the coffeehouse where Holly will be already waiting for me.

I have roughly half an hour before I have to meet Pierbo. He's been taking me to work and picking me up. I've met him in the car park of the magazine complex over the last few days, and everything has run smoothly. I do what I'm supposed to, and it's been working.

Holly is sitting in the furthest booth. Today her hair is fiery red. She likes dyeing her hair different colors. Yesterday it was blond.

I see she's already started on drinks without me, and pastries. This is the girl who can eat whatever she wants and never gain an ounce.

She smiles when she sees me and gives me a hug when I get to her.

"Hey, did you have a good meeting with Freddie?" she asks. She's gotten on Freddie's bad side more than once so is cautious of him.

"Yes, it was good. He just wanted to make sure I'm okay."

She nods, and we sit. Worry covers her face when she looks at me from across the table. She's wanted to ask me more since Monday but held off. I feel today I'll get the questions she's been keeping at bay.

The Barista comes over with two steaming mugs of coffee. It's our mixture that we've always ordered. Caramel and hazelnut lattes with a dash of chocolate sprinkled on top.

"I knew you'd be along soon, so I ordered for you." Holly smiles.

"Thanks, I missed this," I answer. Normally, I'd have at least two of these in any day.

"I thought so. It's cheer-up drinks. And I'm possibly trying to create a chilled mood so maybe you'll ease my troubled mind." She gives me a hopeful smile.

"I'm okay, Holly," I tell her. I can't have her worrying about me, and I don't want to add her to my ever-growing list of things I blame myself for.

"You say that, but I sense there's something you aren't telling me. You tell me everything, Ava," she points out.

She's right. I do tell her everything, or at least everything I can. She doesn't know about my past. The everything she's talking about is stuff from the time since she's known me.

I'll bet she'd get a shocker, or her hair might turn white if she ever knew that little old me not only went to The Dark Odyssey, but I had sex in public with a man so sexy you'd drool the minute you look at him.

She'd get more shockers if she knew I'd have sex with the said man like I needed oxygen to breathe. But maybe she'd be more shocked that I offered myself up to him in exchange for the debt Dad owes him.

There's so much to say. So much I would love to get off my chest, but I can't.

I couldn't and end up fucking things up because as wild as Holly is, and as much as she'd think Vincent was hot as sin, she'd tell me to call the police if she knew what happened.

"I'm okay, Holly. Dad's not in a good way." That's truth. I haven't spoken to him again, but I get to see him on Saturday. He's being released from the clinic then.

She seems a little more at ease at my answer. "Is there anything I can do to help?"

"No, there's nothing anyone can do. He says he wants to change, so I'm hoping he will. I'm thinking of either getting a place for the both of us or having him move in with me." If I don't end up staying with Vincent forever.

"Really, Ava?" Her brows knit.

I dip my head, agreeing. "It's best. That way, I can keep an eye on him and he'd have my support."

"What about you? That's beautiful that you want to take such care of him, but what would that do to you? It can be hard facing problems like that every day and not having your own space to get some downtime." She's right, and using the opportunity to home in on her psych degree.

I smile. "Are you practicing on me again?"

"A little." She laughs. Back in college, she wasn't entirely sure what she wanted to do, so she did a joint honors degree of psych and photography because she loved both. It's turned out in the few years we've been in the real world that Holly is a psychologist. My friend wants to be a relationship counselor, but since she's been back in college doing the grad program, she's taking every chance she can get to test out her learning on me. The guinea pig.

"You're right, even if you're testing on me, you are right. I don't want to lose him, Holly," I say, feeling close to tears.

Losing him will be worse than me not having a space for downtime. I came close weeks ago, damn close, and dare I say it, or rather admit it, Dad would have brought it on himself. We've come so far, and this addiction nearly cost him everything.

"Don't worry, Ava. Try to be strong. If moving in together is the answer, then it is. I guess you'll have me for downtime." She nods.

The door to the coffeehouse opens. It's the jingle that always catches my attention. It makes you automatically look up to see who's coming in.

The man coming in doesn't just have my attention, he has the attention of every woman in here with eyes.

Vincent comes in looking sleek in his long black coat. Power and authority ripple off him.

"Damn... that man is gorgeous, and sexy as fuck," Holly mutters under her breath when she sees him. She's right again, and I could tell her that he looks just as gorgeous and sexy as fuck without his clothes too. He looks around and sees me.

I can't be like the others and bask in his presence because I don't know if his presence means I might have done something wrong.

He makes his way over to us, and Holly leans closer. "*Jesus, Ava, do you know him? He's coming over,*" she hisses, eyes wide.

"Um..." is all I can say. I'm not sure what I'm allowed to say.

He gets up to the table and offers up that smile of his that could melt you like hot butter.

"Ladies," he says and looks at Holly, who is almost as red as her hair. "You must be Holly." He puts out his hand to shake hers, She takes it and swallows hard.

"Hi," she answers. "Yes, I'm Holly. Uh-huh."

"Vincent Giordano."

The widening of Holly's eyes confirms she knows his name. "Oh, wow."

Well, at least she's heard good things.

"I'm Ava's friend. I hope you don't mind if I steal Ava away," he says.

"No, not at all..." Holly glares at me, giving me the how could you-keep-this-man-a-secret stare. "I'm sure she'll catch up with me later."

"I'm sure she will," he agrees.

I stand and give her a little apologetic smile, but she's too busy looking at the way Vincent places his hand to the small of my back and ushers me away like we're a couple.

I wait until we get outside before I speak. "I was going back to the parking lot to meet Pierbo. I hope I didn't do anything wrong."

"You didn't," he answers, but he stares ahead while we walk down the street. "I just felt like picking you up myself. You said I could find you at the coffeehouse, so I went there." Now he looks at me, and I can't help but smile.

"Oh," I breathe.

We stop, and he cups my face, guiding me to his lips for a kiss.

It's a kiss that makes me almost believe this is us.

I fool myself into thinking it while he kisses me, although

reality is trying to pull me back. It's trying to keep a rein on my heart.

It's just hard to resist the fantasy when he's the first man to have this effect on me.

He's the first man to make me feel like I could give him everything.

CHAPTER TWENTY-FOUR

Vincent

It's Friday again.

Time is going and I'm getting anxious, but I've managed to smooth things over
with Pa by inviting Dmitri and Yuri to the fundraiser. Pa liked that I did that.

It provided a cushion for the situation while I wait to hear from Gibbs. I'm anxious as fuck, but I'm still holding off doing anything or jumping to conclusions until I hear from him.

I got home early today to work on one of my old cars. While my brothers like bikes, I'm into cars, although I own several bikes as well. I felt like I needed some nonsexual distraction today.

I've been hard at work at changing some of the parts on the engine of my Mustang for the last two hours.

I'm so distracted I don't see Ava walk into the garage. It's her waving her hand at me that gets my attention.

I'm crazy and possibly blind if I can focus on a car when she's standing there in front of me wearing those tight shorts and I didn't see her. My cock hardens just from the sight.

She's got the shorts, and she added a tank top that does the job intended to show off her tits.

"Baby, you didn't go to work dressed like that, did you?" I snap, looking her over.

She raises her brows. "No, I just got back and changed. Are you going to start telling me what I can and can't wear to work?"

"You can't wear that. That sort of getup is for me only. Like fuck am I going to have you parading around Chicago looking like that."

She gives me an incredulous glare, but when her eyes drop to my chest and scan my bare chest, I see the thing that makes me want her. Her own want and desire for me.

"Come here," I demand, and she comes closer. She's obviously out here to see me for something, but I want to be inside her. I slam down the hood of the car, pick her up, and set her on top of it.

"Vincent—" she begins, but I stop her next words with a kiss as I dive headfirst into trouble. Fuck, she tastes so damn good.

She kisses me back, but then she pulls away and slips off the hood before I can get to her.

"What the fuck?"

"Vincent... I need to talk to you," she says with more insistence. There's a tremor of fear in her voice that brings reality back to the forefront of my mind.

"What is it, Bellezza?"

"I got the job," she replies, and I feel like an asshole when that terrified look reaches her eyes, the same as when I first met her.

"That's good."

"Yeah, but it means ..." Her voice trails off.

"What?" I want her to ask me.

"I'd need to leave for Florida in two weeks and stay there for three months. That's what it means. I wondered if maybe ... maybe you could tell me when..." Her voice trails off.

"The debt will be repaid." I say that more as a statement than a question. She nods, and I can see that fear overpowering the want she has. She's scared I'll take away her second love.

"I wondered if maybe you'd let me go, and I could come back after."

I don't think I've ever met anyone like her. So protective of her father that she's willing to do that to make good on the repayment.

I won't be a monster with her. "No," I answer, but it's not what she thinks. The crushed look on her face gets to me though. I reach out and touch her beautiful face and lift her jaw. "Two weeks. You'll stay with me for two more weeks, and that's it."

Her lips part in pure surprise, and she blows out a ragged breath. "Really? It's two million dollars, though."

I don't want to think about that part, and when I think of the situation, I could allow her to go now if I'm allowing her to leave in two weeks.

Part of me can't. The same part that was the stubborn prick that couldn't give her an end date in the first place. I have something I want though. The stubborn side of me wants it. It wants to keep her, keep her for myself and do anything I want to her.

"I know. Two weeks, Ava. That means you are still mine until then."

The blush that flushes down her elegant neck is a tell that she wants me too.

"Thank you."

"I still get to do anything I want to you."

She steps forward and presses her dainty hands to my chest. "We should go upstairs."

"Yeah, we should."

We go upstairs, and this time, I take her to my bed.

"I'm sorry it took me so long," Gibbs says.

He lowers to sit down in the chair opposite my desk.

"No worries. I appreciate your work," I tell him. It's late, really late, bordering midnight. Ava fell asleep long ago.

The thing about the underground is that it never sleeps, and lucky for me, Gibbs is the kind of man to make house calls at any hour. We're in my office at home, and the only people around are the guards.

The fact he's here is not actually that good. He's here about Mark, not the Bratva guys. He hasn't found anything on them yet.

Fucking Mark... I don't want to hear more shit about him, not when I can't wrap my head around what it is I'm feeling for his daughter.

"What have you got for me, Gibbs?"

"I found some very interesting things on this employee of yours. I'm gonna say that when it takes me a long time to find info and I don't find everything, it means there's something well hidden."

Fucking hell. "What do you mean?"

"I mean I found some things, and the things I found suggest there's more. He had the standard access to your business accounts you gave him, but he was also able to hack into your personal securities account in Italy and Switzerland."

My damn mouth drops open. "What the fuck are you saying to me? Mark *hacked?*"

"He hacked but didn't take anything. What stood out though was the way he did it. It's only signature to a few hackers I've heard of. And that's no one in this hemisphere. And in all seriousness, if they are on this side of the planet, they're guarded and kept by the best people."

"Fuck."

"That's not all, boss."

There's more even though he didn't find everything? "What?"

"Mark changed his name ten years ago to what it is now. As

to what it was before, I don't know, and that's enough to make me suspicious. There're not a lot of things that can get a man to change his name in such a fashion. No trace of the past suggests something to definitely hide. In this case, it's who he is. Who he truly is."

"God, this isn't happening."

"It really does seem like he just lost his mind trying to get money to fund his drug habits, and he would have robbed you blind if he wanted to. By doing all that, though, he revealed himself," Gibbs surmises.

"Shit, I always have people checked out before they work for me."

"Vincent, I appreciate that, and I'm sure your checks are thorough, but they're not like mine. I can keep looking if you want. This guy has secrets, mark my word. The question is whether you want to find them out or not."

Secrets...

For some reason, Ava's scar comes to my mind. The cigarette burn scar. I've tried to think it was anything other, but I know what I'm looking at is what I know it to be.

Did Mark hurt her? Was that what he meant by rough life?

No... I don't think he would. The way he bawled his soul out when I took her is not a man who would do that. Then again, how do I know? I've seen this man change like the wind, and he's sneaky too. There is nothing I should trust about him.

He could have been abusive years ago. He could have been something else to the man I've been seeing these last few weeks who was worried sick for his daughter.

I've been protective of her. That thing that changed between us pushed me this way, and I hope like hell he didn't hurt her.

There's something he's hiding, and that means... she could have secrets too. She would if she lied about the cigarette burn.

I want to know what's going on. My plate is full, but I want to know.

"Keep looking. I want you to keep looking." I sure as fuck do because Mark isn't who he says he is.

He wasn't the man he led me to believe he was.
So, who is he?
Or more importantly, what was he?

CHAPTER TWENTY-FIVE

Ava

Dad holds me so tight I'm actually finding it difficult to breathe.

I'm so happy to have his arms around me that I don't care.

I actually don't care.

It feels so good to have his arms around me that all I can think about is this moment we're having.

Me and the man who's been my father for the last ten years. If I'm honest, though, he's been watching over me and loving me my whole life.

I can't help but cry, and he does too. God knows how long we stand by the door in his apartment holding each other and crying.

When we eventually pull apart, he cups my face and looks at me. As he does, I see the man who saved me from the monsters and nursed me back to health.

I can't believe it's been close to four weeks since we stood here together like this. Four weeks since we saw each other.

"My dear Ava, look at you," he beams and plants a kiss on my forehead. "I'm so happy to see you."

"I'm happy to see you too." I nod.

"How long do I have you for?"

"All day..."

"All day?" His face brightens.

"Yes."

Vincent told me to spend the day with him. I couldn't have been more grateful.

I'm more grateful, though, for the fact that Dad looks more like himself.

"Thank God. Let's make the most of it, sweet girl. Come." He smiles wide.

We go into the living room and sit on the sofa. I can't stop looking at him, at how good he looks. He even looks younger.

He looks like he really did try to get better this time.

We spoke last night, and I told him about the job. He was so happy for me.

He sounded like how he did when I first started working. It was like he wanted me to have something I could be proud of and happy doing.

"What's happening now? Did the doctors say we needed to do anything?" I ask.

"There's a lot. And there's no we, Ava."

I shake my head in protest even before he can finish. "Absolutely not. Dad, if this has taught us anything, it's that we need to be there for each other more."

"No... that's not what it teaches us, my dear girl. There was never any lesson for you to learn. Not a damn thing. It was me. This was all me. I did unspeakable things. Stuff I can't even remember. I dragged you into my mess and could have gotten both of us killed. Look how far we've come. All the way from the nightmare of Russia. And I nearly lost it all." He dabs at his eyes.

"You had a problem."

"I had problems, and I just allowed them to fester and grow

into a monstrous entity that took over my life. Never again. Never again will I put you through what I have. I can't express how I felt when you offered yourself to pay my debt." He stills and places a hand to the side of his head.

"I did it because I love you."

"I know, but I know you did it too because you feel you owe me. You did it because you feel... you feel guilt still, and nothing was ever your fault." His gaze clings to mine.

I press my lips together. "I've been okay. It wasn't bad."

It sounds like a lie, but it's truth, and I wouldn't know what to tell him in regard to how I feel about Vincent.

"Did he hurt you?" He keeps asking me that for a reason.

"No... he's never hurt me." Maybe it's the way I say it or what I say, but there's a shift in his expression that takes on a more curious edge. Like he knows how I feel.

"Ava... please be careful. Please. It's danger. Men like me... men like him... it's all danger. I don't want you to get hurt. I know he spared me because of you. I guess that should tell me everything."

He does know.

"There's been ups and downs, but he's taken care of me."

"You... have feelings for him."

My head dips, and I stare at my hands brought together in my lap. I don't know if I can answer that question outside my head. It's been intense with Vincent. In some ways, it feels like I've been with him for months, not weeks.

Dad touches my cheek and lifts my head back to focus on him.

"Ava, you can tell me. It's okay."

"How can it be?"

"Because it is what it is."

"I don't know what it is, Dad. My head is spinning, and I feel like I'm spinning too. I've felt every kind of emotion over the last few weeks, and I didn't know what to do, what to think, how to feel."

"I understand... maybe when you work out what you feel, you'll know. All I'll say is, be careful. I want you to have your dreams. You lost your first love. Ballet was you, and now it's your writing. I couldn't be prouder."

"Thank you. Thanks so much. I'm happy I got the job." I'm still bouncing off the walls with excitement. I can't wait to get started. Of course, that means leaving everything behind. "I'm worried about you here. I'm going to have someone stay with you, and when I get back, we'll get a place together."

He chuckles. "Oh my God, girl. No, you'll do no such thing. I will be okay. I start my outpatient treatment on Monday. I'll be going four times a week to see my therapist, and on Fridays there's a support group. I don't want to go back to the hospital ever again. I don't want to touch any drugs. And I most certainly don't want you to have to shake up your life to take care of me."

"I'll do it. I will." I'm determined to help him where I can and be there for him.

"Ava, how about we see what happens when you get back? Let's do that and go from there."

I think about it and nod. "Okay. We'll do that, but I'm being serious. You know I am."

He taps my cheek. "You are just like her, exactly like her. Your mother would say the same thing."

There was always one thing I wanted to know when he told me the story of how he loved Mom.

"Why didn't you fight more to be with her?" I ask.

"She loved him more. Your father. It was... the story of three best friends who grew up together. One guy rich, the other poor. We both loved her, but only one of us could give her everything she needed. So, I stepped away and watched over you all instead."

I loved my Papa with all my heart, but I love this man before me the same. "Don't you think she wouldn't have cared about wealth?"

"Your grandfather wouldn't have allowed it. It's the bratva

way, my love, and ... deep-rooted family traditions. You don't go against that. *Never go against that.* That's how I was raised. I wish I did though. Maybe things would have been different." He gazes at me and strokes my hair.

I think I must have been twelve when I got the first inclining about what he felt for my mother. I just knew from the way he looked at her. I think Papa knew too. There was no way he didn't.

He paid attention to everything.

Dad was his best friend. That's what I knew him as. But when I looked at him, I saw him as the man who made my mother smile.

Papa was always busy. As the Pakhan of the Ivanezh Bratva, Papa was always working. Always tending to the brotherhood.

Dad was his Sovientrik. His advisor who was an ex-army intelligence analyst.

Even in my younger years, I knew that nobody was more skilled than him. Nobody could protect us better than him, and if he'd been around that day, that awful day, we wouldn't have been ambushed. That's the best way I can describe it.

An ambush.

By the same token, it was only a man like Dad who could rescue me, and he's managed to move me unseen from one country to the next and hide me for the last ten years.

We practically became ghosts. I'm supposed to be one. My biggest enemy thinks I died in the fire, and that is how I pray it will remain forever.

"Sometimes I remember. I've been remembering, and the nightmares are unbearable," I tell him.

"I know. You don't live through the type of horror you did and forget. Please try though. You have your job to look forward to. Your mother would have been proud. You should dance sometimes though, Ava."

I simply smile at him.

He knows why I don't dance anymore.

My love for dance died the day my parents did.

I blamed it for putting us in that position.

If not for me and dancing, I wouldn't have gone to a place that facilitated their assassination.

CHAPTER TWENTY-SIX

VINCENT

Ava just got back from seeing Mark.

I haven't been able to get all that stuff about Mark out of my head since I spoke to Gibbs.

I wondered if she knows what the secrets are, and what hers are too.

This isn't anything to do with me. Digging around like this is the last thing I should be doing.

But if I'm honest, this part—the extra looking around I told Gibbs to do—is mostly because of her. I want to make sure she's safe.

I guess too I want to make sure I cover all bases and make sure Mark didn't have some hidden agenda.

There are so many fucking possibilities. With all the shit that can happen to people like me and my family, I'm surprised I haven't gone crazy with paranoia, believing everyone is against me.

Ava's sitting across from me at the dinner table. She looks

pretty in her little navy summer dress. The chefs have just brought out the food, and once again, they've done a great job.

I wanted to take her to The Dark Odyssey again tonight, but it doesn't feel like the night I wanted it to be with her. We'll go tomorrow.

This news of Mark hasn't changed what I want to do to her.

I'll also be dropping in to see Mark tomorrow. The best way to get answers is to hear it from the horse's mouth. I think I'm entitled to know something since it was me he stole from.

Feeling my gaze on her, she looks my way after the chef pours her a drink and leaves.

"Hey," she says. "What? You're looking at me."

"I'm just thinking. Your father okay?" I ask, and the light leaves her eyes. It's replaced with caution.

"He's okay. He'll be going to counselling starting Monday," she answers.

I narrow my eyes at her and give her a curious stare. "Ava... what did your father do for work before he worked for me?" The question throws her.

She just stares at me and blinks. "He worked at the supermarket."

That's what it says on record. My files say he worked there for over fifteen years, as does the reference, but I think that's a lie.

"Why? What's happened? Has something more happened?"

"No... it's nothing. I'm just curious." I won't tell her about it. This is where I'm drawing the line to exclude her. She would have been eighteen when Mark started working for me. Maybe she didn't know.

Marguerite brings Timothy in. He's fussing. He's had his last tooth come in this week, and he's been miserable.

"I'm sorry to disturb you guys," Marguerite says. "I think I'm going to stay over tonight. I do not have the heart to leave with him so upset."

God, it's times like this when I'm grateful for her. I'm tense and wound up, and not knowing what to do with him would make me feel worse.

"Are you sure, Marguerite?" I ask.

"Yes. I'm just going to get my room ready."

"I'll take him for a few minutes." I reach for him, and she hands him to me.

"I'll be back down in five minutes," she says and saunters away.

Ava watches me with Timothy. I've liked how she looks at us. I know she wants to know what happened to Sorcha. It's understandable that she'd have questions after the incident with the room upstairs and the video.

I think it was obvious that Sorcha died.

Timothy rests his head on my chest and starts mumbling.

"You're so good with him," she states.

"Am I?"

"You are." The question is in her voice. Curiosity over what happened to my child's mother. I'm grateful that she hasn't asked me yet. "You definitely do a good job."

At that compliment, Timothy lifts his head and looks at her. The little tyke starts reaching for her and cries.

Instinct makes her reach back, but then she stops. She looks to me though.

"Vincent, I know you have a thing about me touching your child, but I swear to God I won't hurt him."

"It's not that." It was never that. "You're... the first woman I've been with since ..." God, I can't say it. "Outside family and the people who work for us, you'd be the first to hold him."

"Well, maybe that's no bad thing seeing as how he seems to like me. It's going to be hard to be around a seriously cute baby for the next couple of weeks and not hold him."

She stands up and makes her way over to us, and when she stretches out her hands, I hand Timothy over to her. It feels like a big deal for me. So does watching her hold him. I'm having a hard enough time as it is separating what I feel for this doll, and this just made it worse.

Instantly, he stops crying and takes a lock of her hair.

"You're a little pumpkin belly," Ava coos, fussing over him, and the little devil starts giggling then laughing when she tickles his tummy.

"Jesus, he's actually smiling."

"He is so cute," she bubbles.

Marguerite comes back and seems happy to see Ava holding Timothy. She gives me a look of awe and nods her head.

"That's the first I've seen him smile all week," Marguerite says.

"Well, I hope he continues to smile." Ava hands Timothy to her, and I feel genuine relief when he doesn't start crying.

"Wonderful. Well, it's bedtime. Good night, all," Marguerite says.

"Good night," I reply while Ava smiles wide.

She returns to her chair and looks to me. "See, he was fine."

Maybe... but I'm not.

I rest my elbow on the table and look at her.

"I know you want to ask, so just ask."

"What?"

"You want to know what happened to her. My wife." I make it sound like I'm okay with her asking, but if I were, she would have had the story by now.

"I would never want to pry like that. I know I pried enough that night."

"Why'd you go up there?"

A dimness appears in her eyes that catches my attention. "I wanted... I wanted to see if there was something nicer about you. Something or some part of you that might not think of me as a whore."

I don't think I could possibly feel worse. My shoulders slump. "Ava, you're not a whore."

"No? Wasn't it you I gave myself to? I knew what I was doing when I made the offer. I must have." Her hands start to shake.

"I never thought of you as a whore. That day I got mad, I got worked up like that because I don't want anybody to see that side of me," I confess.

She stares at me for a long time, and I wonder what she's thinking.

"What happened to her, Vincent?"

I glance down at the table and pull in a deep breath. "She... was killed. The same man who killed my eldest brother killed her too."

Her full lips part as sorrow washes over her face. "Oh, Vincent..." she breathes. "I'm so sorry."

"It's okay... um, she was killed, and I wasn't there to save her. I've felt guilt over that, but maybe saving her would have been me leaving her alone in the first place. She was the good girl and shouldn't have been with a criminal like me. Getting married to the mob signed her death certificate. I did." It's coming out now, all that I feel and have felt.

She stands up and comes over to me.

Her beautiful eyes holds mine, and she lowers to sit in my lap, touching my jaw.

"No, you didn't. It's not your fault."

Her telling me that, just like her words that day about the ballerinas, reaches somewhere inside me that wants to believe that. It wants to believe that it wasn't my fault so I can move on.

Selfishness works its way through me, making me want to cling to her words and believe them.

I look at her now and think of the question I teased her with at The Dark Odyssey.

Why does she like me? She does, and I like her too.

It's that fascination over how she makes me feel. I forget everything when she touches me.

As she lowers her mouth to my lips, it feels like we're those people we talked about in the fantasy again, like I really could be that guy. The guy I pretended to be the other day when I went to the coffeehouse.

I slip my hand behind her head, angling her face so I can deepen the kiss and taste her desire for me.

I'm glad the door is closed because I'm taking her right here.

I get up with her and bunch her top so tightly her breasts squeeze together.

"I want you now. Take your clothes off." I can't hold back the need coursing through me.

She takes her clothes off layer by layer until she's naked before me, naked and perfect.

"Is this what you want?"

"You know I do." I've never spoken with such desire for her, never allowed her to see me and see how much I want her.

I indulge myself by reaching to cup her pussy. She's wet and ready to be fucked. I like sliding my fingers into her. I like pulling down that wall she placed up so she wouldn't feel for me.

"You're wet," I say, pulling out of her to lick of her juices coating my fingers.

"Yes." That's the first time she's admitted that.

I turn her around and bend her over the table. While I watch her submit to me and obey me, I think of how I feel. Her body isn't enough anymore.

I look at her and want everything.

But... she leaves in two weeks, and I know when she walks through that door, that will be it.

That will be all.

I don't know what scares the shit out of me more: the fact that she found a way into my cold dead heart, or the fact that I've gone past wanting her.

Mark knows to be wary of me.

I give him credit for it.

I walk into his apartment when he opens the door, and like I own the place, I invite myself into his living room, where I want to talk to him, and sit down.

There're bottles of alcohol on the table. I look from them to him and arch my brows.

"I'm cleaning out the cupboards, getting rid of shit," he explains. "Those were the ones I hid so Ava wouldn't see them when she came around."

I admit that I'm amazed he's so upfront with me. Maybe it's his tactic to soften my heart over the money.

I'm not exactly here about that though.

"I need to talk to you, Mark," I begin, and he nods.

He takes a seat across from me. He looks better than he did the last time we saw each other. His face has filled out a lot more, and it doesn't have that sullen look. What's the same is the caution in his eyes and demeanor.

"Of course. I expected your visit. I... don't remember anything more than I told you last time, Vincent." He shakes his head, and I bite down hard on my back teeth.

I'd preempted this shit. That's why I got Gibbs. I should be somewhat calmer that Gibbs didn't find more than he did in terms of anything that could put the family or business at risk. What grates me is that it feels like Mark hasn't paid for his wrongdoings. That's what I don't like.

He hasn't paid. Ava did. Even if I want her, there will always be the fact that she was a payment for a debt.

He gives me an uneasy look when I don't answer, so I decide to move on to the actual thing I'm here for.

"You know what's amazing, Mark?" I begin.

"What?"

"That you did all you did and managed to hide yourself so well. It's amazing how you could also manage to hack a personal securities account you shouldn't know about, which means you would have had to get into my personal securities file to get access to it. The thing is, the only person who knows the password to all that is me. You gonna tell me that's not amazing?"

The fucker looks like he's been caught in the trap he set for himself.

"I ..." he attempts and stops.

The look he gives me tells all. *Fucker*. This motherfucker is a hundred percent hiding something, and the look of him now, like he's ready to shit his pants, heightens my curiosity.

"You what? I'll tell you what, you certainly have some type of special skills there that could have made you hirable in a lot of places."

"I didn't mean to, Vincent. I don't remember. I don't remember doing any of it. Just what I told you."

I look him over and realize he's telling the truth about not remembering. What I figured is this: the shit made him so high that remnants of a former lifestyle, or something he'd learned, came out to play, and not any old remnants either.

"I'm curious how a guy like you could do all that, yet when I hired you, you'd supposedly worked at a supermarket stacking shelves for a bulk of your life. I took pity on you and gave you a job, got you trained too, but looks like you didn't need it. Or maybe you picked up a few tricks on the way to screw me over."

"No, Vincent. No." He shakes his head.

"No?"

"No, I swear it, on my girl's life, I swear it. She's all I have, and I'd do anything for her. Please believe me when I tell you I didn't set out to screw with you. I messed up and fucked up. I don't even remember doing any of that stuff." He shakes his head rigorously, as if it will make me believe him more. "I didn't know what the hell I was doing at the time. I just needed money."

There's so much shit on the table on this guy, he should be fish food, yet he lives and breathes before me. Christian's right. Ava has done a number on me, worked some whammy to call the hounds off her old man. I'm looking at him now, and once again, the thought of her is holding me back.

I hope this is it, that there's nothing more. Mark was an actual threat to the family that should have been eliminated. It's conflicting for me when I think of her.

I feel for her. I do, but... what happens when duty has to take over? What do I do about the conflict in my heart?

I want to poke and prod. He knows I have more questions. I want to know who he really is. Gibbs' words are playing in my mind. It's unsettling. I hate feeling distrust in any kind of form. I hate it.

"Mark, you better pray there's nothing more. I hope for your sake there's nothing more to find," I say.

His hands tremble, and I almost feel bad for him. It must be some fucked-up shit when you do all he did and can't remember any of it. *Fucking hell.*

"Please, don't take it out on Ava." His eyes plead with me.

"I won't." Even if I wanted to, I couldn't. "She's paid for enough, don't you think?"

I rise to my feet as a tear slides down his cheek.

I leave him. There's nothing more to talk about.

This ends here. I won't come back again.

We're done, unless if I find something that will bring me back here.

I left him alive. It's mercy and compassion.

Even if I don't feel it.

CHAPTER TWENTY-SEVEN

A va

We're here again...

At The Dark Odyssey.

My body comes alive with the anticipation of what we'll be doing tonight. Earlier, Vincent said we'd be doing something adventurous.

We're in his lounge again. I've just arrived, and this time, he was waiting for me. In the periphery of my vision, I can see the couples across from us having sex. However, my focus is on the man before me, who's looking at me like I'm the most beautiful woman in the world.

I believe it when he looks at me like that. It makes me believe he wants me.

Underneath that stare are lust and dark desire that have my head spinning.

Tonight, he wanted me to wear red. Just like that first time, he walks around me, assessing me.

He stops behind me and brings the hem of the slip I'm

wearing up to my waist, exposing my ass. I glance over my shoulder at him, and he gazes back with that wild hold that captures me.

I'm a goner when he runs his fingers over my ass. His touch feels so good I don't quite register or care that he's not the only one who can see my ass. The bartender and the waitress can see too, but I guess for them this is the norm here.

"Your perfect ass looks good in this color," Vincent says and makes his way back in front of me. He's not done, though, with his admiration. Before I can answer, he bends down and rubs his fingers over my pussy lips. "And so does your pussy."

The flame of vibrancy in his eyes leaves me speechless.

"I'm glad I please you."

"You do. Come, let's go play."

Play...

What will we be doing tonight? We actually didn't do that much last time in the way of exploring the club. I did my research. Last night, I looked up the club and learned they have all sorts of things here. From themed rooms you can live out any fantasy in to a sex dungeon.

We're going downstairs in the elevator... Does that mean we're going somewhere dungeon-like?

"What are we doing tonight?" I ask him.

He leans against the wall of the elevator and looks me over. "Something interesting. I'm making the most of my time with you."

I can't believe the days have flown by so quickly.

In twelve days, I'll be in Florida and won't owe him anymore.

How will I forget this?

Forget him?

I've been thinking about it, and I realize there's no way I can, and I don't want to.

"You'll like it," he adds, brushing a soft finger over my cheek.

The doors open, and we walk out onto a stone floor. My heels click against it. It's colder down here.

As we turn the corner, I see two large doors and a couple

come out of them. As they do, I hear the unmistakable sounds of pleasure. I know what I'm hearing, and I imagine it.

Last time, Vincent said I hadn't been tied to his bed yet. It's funny how that didn't freak me out as much as the thought of being shared.

We walk past the doors and head further down an adjacent path that leads out to another set of doors. These are a deep oak Gothic style with wrought iron anvil-shaped handles.

The beauty immediately piques my interest.

They open automatically for us as we approach, and my breath is taken away by more beauty as we walk into a garden surrounded by purple and white orchids with a waterfall flowing into a lily pond.

My lips part in complete surprise. I would never have thought that such a garden would exist here. It feels so out of place for the club, and actually the city. It has an exotic feel to it that makes me think of somewhere in South America or Japan.

It's breathtaking and enhanced by miniature lights that almost look like stage lights spotlighting each area, so it gets your undivided attention.

"You like?" he asks, seeing me openly admiring the place.

"This is amazing," I breathe.

He guides me past the waterfall, and when we turn the corner, two enormous apple trees with bright red apples hanging from it greet us.

At first, I'm amazed. I've never seen apple trees so big. Then I see thick twined ropes draped over one of the sturdy branches. In that instant, a wild, sexy thought comes to me, and I think I might know what we'll be up to tonight.

We stop by the closest tree, and he releases his hold on me.

"This is Eden," he says.

"Like the Garden of Eden?" I surmise. It definitely fits. All except the rope from the tree.

"Yeah." He walks right up to the rope and takes the end. "I want tonight to be a little different."

"Like how?" I ask even though I have a pretty good idea.

"Like last week. I want us to be those two people again who met in the coffee shop, except now you know I like things a little darker than you're used to, and... you're curious."

I stare at him, thinking about what he's saying. Last week, we pretended that we'd just met, and nothing else happened. Nothing with Dad. Since then, it's been like pieces of the fantasy spilled over into reality.

Throughout this whole week, I've had times when I had to remind myself of what's real and that I shouldn't have feelings for this man. I shouldn't do this to myself, especially now knowing that we're supposed to end in less than two weeks.

If we go back to that fantasy again, I don't know if I'd be able to get my mind to leave it and step out of the world of make-believe.

How could I say no, though, when he looks at me the way he is?

"I'm curious." I play along, feeling myself slip into the temptation of him.

He comes back to me. "You are, especially when I bring you here. I have this fantasy of taking complete control over you. You tied to this tree." He leans in close to my ear. "You tied to this tree while I fuck you and take more than just your body. Would that scare you, Ava?"

I turn my face into his, brushing my cheek against the scruff of his jaw.

Holding his gaze, I stare deep into those dark eyes of his, and what I see is something I want.

I admitted it. I want it. I want him.

I'll accept the truth of my insanity for feeling for him. There are worse things in my life that I've had to accept. This is something I'll choose.

"No," I answer, and a sinful smile slides up the corners of his mouth.

"Will you allow me to truly do whatever I want to you?" he asks.

"Yes."

"Yes?"

"I want to."

It's then that the predatory look returns to his eyes. Watching a man like him lust after me makes my damn mouth water and desire pool deep between my thighs.

"Will it hurt?"

"I'd never hurt you," he answers, and I believe him.

I think back to that night again when I begged him to spare Dad's life. I hoped he wouldn't hurt me. He hasn't.

He pushes the straps of my slip down my shoulders. It's loosely fitted, so that's all it takes for it to fall off me, slithering down the length of my body until it gathers at my feet, leaving me in just the thong.

"Your safe word is Red. You can use that now."

I bite back a smile remembering last week when I said it.

"Okay."

"Say it... and I stop." He tugs on the edge of my panties and crouches down to take them off.

He does so slowly, his fingers brushing over my skin, leaving a fiery trail in their wake. He gazes up at me when I step out of the thong and plants a kiss to the smooth skin of my mound.

Rising, he takes my hand and leads me over to the trees. The cool air glides over my back, and I sense that there must be somewhere nearby where there's a more open space, like another door.

The coolness on my skin is perfect in contrast to the heat from him.

He reaches for the first piece of rope and takes my right arm. A closer look at the tree shows some little loopholes drilled into the trunk so the rope can go through easily and stay at that height. That's exactly what happens as he ties the rope around my wrists and secures it. It's when he does my other arm that I feel panic rise in my lungs.

This is different to what we do normally, and nothing in comparison to anything I've ever done. I don't even know why I'm thinking about what I've done.

I've had three boyfriends, none serious, and that was my fault. I didn't want serious, so I picked guys who would never be serious about a relationship.

There was the banker who was always away travelling from one country to the next, the travel writer who wanted to move to Australia, and then the lawyer who was perhaps the closest I got to serious, but he cared more about his career than me.

I felt nothing when we broke up. I felt nothing when we were together.

I felt nothing with any of them.

With Vincent, I've felt everything, and I'm about to feel more.

The rope holds my arms in place. He gets to work on my legs too, and as he ties the last knot, it seals me to him. It's like I've handed myself over to him. At least before, it was just my body. Now, it feels like handing over control has delivered the key to unlock the rest of me.

"Are you okay?" he asks, checking the ropes. "It's not too tight?" He slips a finger between my wrist and the bind to check.

"No, I'm okay," I answer, although there's a slight quiver in my voice.

"Good girl."

It becomes better, and my panic fades when he shrugs out of his shirt and steps out of his pants and boxers.

I could never tire of watching him take his clothes off and seeing him naked.

Since we're pretending we're those people tonight, I allow myself the pleasure of taking in the perfection of him. All lean muscle, sleek and untamed pride.

From head to toe and everything in between, I love roaming over his body and running my gaze from the deep ridge of muscle lining his abs, down to the dark line of his happy trail and on to my favorite part of him. His cock.

He takes hold of it when he sees me looking and runs his fingers along the thick length, then steps closer so he can slide his fingers into my pussy. The warm tickle of his fingers against my clit makes me jump, and I feel the first noticeable thing about being tied up.

I can't move and put my body the way I want to take his thrusts, whether it's with his fingers or with his cock. I'm bound, and his.

A deep chuckle rumbles from his hard chest, and he starts finger-fucking me.

"Does this feel good?" he asks, looming closer. His warm breath tickles my nose, and I moan.

"Yes," I rasp, writhing against the hold of the rope.

He lowers his mouth and starts sucking my right breast.

He's done that so many times to me, but tonight feels different. It feels unreal and insanely better. So good the pull of an orgasm has me squirming against his fingers. I squirm and cry out, wanting so bad to move my arms and legs. At the same time, it feels like the pleasure is being held in place with the restraints. Because of that, it feels a hundred times better.

God... it feels so good, and the luxuriating sensations flows through me sweet, like something I want to feast on forever.

I come hard when he moves to my left breast and starts feasting on that one.

Time freezes, and all I feel is good. The rush of heat from his lips cascades over me, and I want more. I want it all, everything and all that he wants to do to me. I want him inside me, fucking me against the restraint of the ropes.

When he crouches down and nuzzles his face between my thighs, I know then this is just the beginning of his feast on my body.

He pushes his tongue up and starts stroking over my clit.

"Fuck, Ava," he says and stares up at my pleasure-filled face. "Bellezza, I love how soaked you are. Always ready for my tongue or my cock, my fingers, any part of me to be inside you."

He returns to my pussy and takes a long suck on my clit, making me throw my head back and cry out from the overload of pleasure. I sound like a mad woman who's completely lost herself to passion.

Fuck... I'm coming again.

He takes hold of my ass and presses higher up into my pussy, forcing his tongue higher and higher, and I'm there again in the height of pleasure.

"I'm coming," I cry, bucking against his face.

He stops and gives me a conspiratory smile. "No, hold it."

"What?" There's absolutely no way that I can hold this. I shuffle my feet trying to calm myself, and I start panting.

"Hold it right there until I tell you to let it go," he commands.

I start breathing through my mouth and confuse inhales and exhales.

A wicked laugh falls from his lips as he stands and walks over to a bolder, or at least it's what I think is a bolder. It's not. It's a cleverly designed stand with a little drawer that opens.

From inside the drawer, I get a peak of some objects... sex toys. He pulls out a black glossy... *vibrator*.

Jesus, Lord, my mouth falls open.

The vibrator has a sheath on it. Vincent pulls it off and walks back to me studying my expression.

God... I don't even own one of those. Holly does. In fact, she's told me she has a several. She's the kind of girl who goes to lingerie brand parties where the goody bags always include the latest vibrator.

Here's one thing to add to the list of things I could shock her with.

He switches it on, and there's a humming sound.

"Red yet?" he asks.

In the mingle of watching, being restrained, holding my release, and wondering how whatever he plans to do to me will feel, I lose my mind.

I just do.

It slips from me, and I find I can't do anything other than what I've been doing—agreeing.

"I want it," I say.

That smile comes back to his face, wider this time, lifting his high cheekbones.

He moves the vibrator to my pussy, and fuck... fucking hell, I let out a sound, a shrill sound that rises several octaves. It's how pain and pleasure sound.

I'm not sure if calling it pain is the correct term to use for me holding my orgasm, as it's as painful as it is pleasurable.

And... now that I think of it that way, my pussy clenches then pulses, dying to explode against the hum of the vibrator.

"I can't take it!" I wail, thrashing against the hold of the ropes and the vibrator. "I can't... please let me come! Vincent, please. Please, ahhhh...." I wrench and gasp, and groan.

He watches in sheer delight, satisfied with what he's done to me. He smiles, and in it lurks the predator who wants to devour its prey.

"Please..."

It's that last plea that snaps him out of the pleasure-filled trance that's taken him.

His face softens, and he pulls the vibrator away from me.

"Come for me, baby," he commands, and I let go. It actually felt like I was holding the reins of pleasure with my bare hands and allowed it to slip from my grasp. As it does, fire sparks over my skin like someone ignited it with something flammable.

I come hard and fast, the rippling wave of pleasure taking me up into the sky. My head feels light, but it's buzzing with wild energy.

I've never felt this before, so blissful I forget... *everything*. I look at him, and I forget it all. I'm able to push the past out of my mind and think of happiness.

"Feel good?"

"Yes...."

"Do you want more, Bellezza?"

"I do." It's like a drug to me. It feels like some kind of drug that I'm addicted to. Not the pleasure. He does.

With a wide grin, he sets down the vibrator, and I notice he's perfectly erect and ready to fuck me. I'm ready for him too. The need I feel for him drives me insane. I think he can see it.

He walks behind me and takes hold of my hips. Being tied to the tree with his hands on my waist builds the anticipation again, but fuck, it's the epitome of pleasure when he plunges into me. His thick cock slides right into my pussy, showing him how ready I am for him.

Pleasure bursts, pleasure burns, pleasure consumes me along with his thrusts as he ruts into me, fucking me so hard I see stars. It sends an arrow of liquid flame through my soul, and I feel all that he's doing to me in every pore and nerve of my body.

"You're mine, Ava..." he growls, speeding up his pumps as his grip tightens on my waist.

His...

Oh God... his, I feel it, what he was talking about. I never paid attention and truly listened to what he'd said. The words come back to me now, singing in my ear like a choir.

He said he'd take more than just my body.

He has.

My soul... I feel it. It warms to him and glows for him. It calls to him. It's awake for him.

I belong to him...

I know it, and the thought terrifies me because I want it. I want to belong to him, and I shouldn't.

I don't get to worry about the next thought. The next orgasm that crashes over me steals the worries from my mind as we come together.

CHAPTER TWENTY-EIGHT

Vincent

"Don't go to work today," I whisper into her ear.

"I have to," she answers, giving me a little kiss.

I frown when she slips out of the bed, looking for her clothes.

She reaches for one of my dress shirts to cover up her naked perfection. We got back late last night, and we ended up in here in my room.

I like her being in here.

We haven't been able to leave the fantasy just yet. We're still those two people who met at the coffee shop.

"Come back to bed, baby," I beckon. I just want to enjoy today with her. Tomorrow is the damn fundraiser, and I know I'll be on edge all day about it. I've decided to take her.

It'll be different. She'll be going as my date. It was nice watching her get excited about it.

She bends over to pick something off the ground, and I see

her perfect ass. The instant I see it, I lose it. She's not going to work today.

I get off the bed and grab her. She squeals and starts giggling when I pick her up and set her back on the bed

"I want you riding my cock and those tits bouncing in my face," I tell her, flipping her over so she can straddle me.

"Okay," she says with saucy seduction and settles down on my cock.

I get lost in the woman all over again.

I'm lost in her, and I don't want to be found or find any kind of way back to the place I was before she came into my life.

It's one phone call that takes me away from her late in the night.

It's Salvatore.

He found something.

Half an hour later sees me walking across the rooftop of one of the warehouses at the docks.

My three brothers are here. Salvatore, Gabe, and Nick.

They stand by the edge of the roof looking like shadows against the night.

Their faces are stern and crude.

Salvatore said he picked up some suspicious activities here and saw Dmitri with a bunch of guys looking like they were up to some illegal shit. We're always up to some illegal shit, but this is different.

It's dirty, and it's not dirt I know of, but I'm about to fucking find out.

I approach them, and they give me curt nods.

"Anything happen yet?" I ask.

Salvatore shakes his head.

"No. They're waiting for something, though, and that boat there is theirs." He motions down below.

I see Dmitri talking to a guy. In the amber light from the

streetlights and the moonlight, I make out his dark olive skin. He looks Mediterranean.

"Here, get a closer look," Nick says, handing me a pair of binoculars.

I take them and get a closer look alright. I don't see anything much to jump out at me, but what I see is truth. I'm looking at Dmitri, and that mask of playing the nice businessman isn't there anymore.

He stands differently, feet apart and shoulders back. He's smoking, and the look on his face feels like the real him. The real devil. It's cunning and manipulative, that's what it is. Criminalistic and animalistic.

It was the look he was trying to hide.

That fucker. What the fuck are they up to?

"They've been waiting for something or someone," Salvatore adds.

"That guy," Gabe begins and points at the guy. "There's something about him. He was talking to another earlier. A guy called Andreas, who's part of the cartel, wanted by the fucking feds for drug trafficking."

I lower the binoculars and look to Gabe. "You're shitting me."

Gabe shakes his head. "I saw them in a bar. That's what started this."

"Give me more details," I demand.

"I went to check something out at the bar. First, your boy Dmitri was there. When I saw him, I decided to lay low. He didn't look like he was there for a drink, so I didn't want him to get fazed by seeing me. He went out back, and I followed. That's when I saw him link up with Andreas and this guy here." Gabe inclines his head. "I don't know that guy, but if he knows Andreas, then he can't be anybody good."

Shit. This was it. The thing my instincts were warning me about.

We haven't seen much yet, but it's something.

Gibbs hasn't been able to find anything. It suggests one of

two things: that there's nothing to find, or that whatever there is, is well hidden. So hidden it's clean and passes through our checks.

"Maybe this is about drugs. Maybe they want to smuggle drugs. Maybe it's not the fucking diamonds, or *only* the diamonds," I state.

"Whatever the shit is, I don't think we should have anything to do with it," Salvatore says.

"I need something to work with." I take out my phone and zoom in on the guy talking to Dmitri.

We couldn't find shit on Dmitri. Maybe this guy is the fucker who will give me an answer. I take a few pictures of him and message them to Gibbs telling him to look into it.

He messages his acknowledgement straightaway.

I look from Gabe to Salvatore while Nick crouches down and stares on ahead to the road.

"There's a truck coming," Nick says, and we follow his gaze.

An industrial truck comes down the road with a fish logo on the side of it.

The truck stops right by Dmitri and the man, and what I see next gives me everything. My answer to them and to Pa.

My fucking heart freezes in my chest when the back of the truck opens and young girls start pouring out of it, all naked and chained together on one long chain.

There's at least a hundred of them. They have chains around their wrists and ankles, then a chain lining from one to the next.

Fucking hell... what am I actually seeing? They're all young girls of no more than sixteen. In fact, some of them don't even look as old as that.

Dmitri shows his true colors as he takes charge and orders them onto the boat.

My brothers and I watch them pile on.

I have no fucking words. None at all. The man who was talking to Dmitri hands him a briefcase, and the two shake hands. He's the last to get on the boat.

Dmitri lights up again, and a wicked smile spreads across his face.
I see him.
I see who and what he is now.
What he's up to—*sex trafficking*.
It seems like dirty was just the start of my suspicions.

CHAPTER TWENTY-NINE

Ava

"You... you, miss lady, are practically glowing. I don't remember you looking so vibrant," Holly says. She points at me and gives me an accusatory glare.

"It must be that new cream," I lie and swallow hard. She's been trying to ask me about Vincent every chance she gets.

I've been thinking of what to say to her. Somehow, I can't find the words to tell her that he's a mobster, and not just any old mobster. He's a mob boss.

The mafia boss I ...

The mafia boss I think I'm falling for.

Think... Do I just think it? The thought actually frightens me.

He went out last night and came back in the early hours of the morning. I didn't see him though. He left before I got up. He did send me a message, though, about later. He was arranging for Pierbo to get me to the fundraiser party for seven.

Holly snaps her fingers in front of my face and looks on at me with anticipation when I chuckle.

"I'm sorry."

"That's the umpteenth time you've zoned out. Ava, you're seeing that guy, aren't you?" she asks me pointedly with a deadpan expression. "I wasn't born yesterday."

I sigh. "Yes.... I'm seeing him." I can't lie. As to whether telling her that I'm seeing Vincent is the right term to coin it, I don't know. Since it feels like I am and I don't want to get on my best friend's bad side, I'll give her that to ease off the questions.

"And sleeping with him too... a lot."

Yes... a lot.

I've lost of count how many times Vincent and I had sex over the last few days, and I can't believe myself.

Four weeks. It's been just over four weeks, and we're heading into week five. Next week is when I leave him though.

A pinch of sadness that comes naturally ebbs over my heart when I think of leaving and us ending.

We've been on this fast train I remember getting on, and then I'm just going to leave him.

Holly reaches out and touches my shoulder. "You're supposed to tell me these things. It's okay to tell your best friend these sorts of things, Ava. You seem to really like him, but you're not sure about something?" She raises her arched brows.

"Yeah, a little something like that. It's just been... a little wild."

"Wild?" Her eyes sparkle with interests. "From the minute I heard the name Giordano, I thought wild. They own The Dark Odyssey, and the way he looked at you that day, Ava, was just so nice."

That makes me smile.

"Really?" I won't pretend I don't know what she means.

"Yes. I don't remember ever seeing you look like this. What's happening with him? Are you going to stay in touch when you go to Florida?"

Now, that is a question I can't answer. Vincent and I haven't talked about that. I think the reason is obvious. It's already what I've accepted.

The end.

"I think I'll have to see how it all plays out." That's the best answer and

all I can do.

It's complete irony.

I am. I'm ironic to myself.

When we made this arrangement, all I could think of was having my life back, getting the end date and being free.

Now, I don't think it's freedom. Being with Vincent did something to me. It broke down walls I built up over my heart for the last ten years.

For a moment, I allow my mind to drift once more and dabble in waters I shouldn't.

What if I did keep in touch when I went to Florida? What if he did?

What if I came back in three months' time and saw him?

Holly taps the top of my hand and smiles at me with awe.

"I hope it works out. It would be nice."

Maybe it could.

Maybe I could have that.

"Yeah."

My dress is beautiful.

I feel like I'm a princess. Like I just stepped out of a film in this gorgeous gown.

It's a black sleeveless dress with a bodice covered with diamantes and endless length flowing down my legs.

My hair looks beautiful too. Marguerite did it.

It's swooped to the side, so it flows down past my left shoulder and cascades down to my waist.

She did my makeup too. Tonight, she went for a smoky eye effect and a berry-colored lipstick.

It's the first time I've been to The Dark Odyssey and worn so much clothes.

I'm also not wearing a mask.

It's not a masquerade-themed party like the rest of the club. Vincent told me that when they hold fundraisers like these, they try to make them different.

Tony meets me at reception again, and this time, I'm led to a completely different section of the club. We don't walk past the main floor. This seems like a separate route that avoids any contact with the sex and wildness going on in the club.

It makes sense for anyone who's not here for that.

We get out to the courtyard, where I see people dressed in evening gowns and cocktail dresses gathered together drinking wine. Passing waiters hold trays with canapes and more drinks.

This is strange, seeing this too. People out here not in lingerie.

Tony takes me up a set of wide stairs that leads to a hall fit for a wedding reception. It has the Venetian style like the main floor of the club with the gold roof and baroque balconies on each floor.

I'm so amazed at how massive this place is and all the ideas that have been put together to present something spectacular.

It's stunning and breathtaking.

What's more stunning and breathtaking is the man over in the corner who looks straight at me as I enter the building.

There are so many people here, but they all fade out along with the soft jazz music when I see him.

We must be twenty feet away from each other, but the pull of that magnetism is so strong I can barely breathe.

Vincent watches me and starts walking toward us. His eyes on me, only me.

His gaze intensifies and expands when we meet in the middle, and in that moment, I know I've fallen for him.

"Boss," Tony says, breaking the beauty of the trance.

"Thank you, Tony," Vincent says.

I never take my eyes off him. I hear Tony walk away, and that's all I register. Vincent lifts my hand and kisses my knuckles, making me smile and blush at the same time.

"You look beautiful," he says.

"You too," I answer.

"I look beautiful?" He smirks, revealing the dimple in his left cheek.

"Hmmm hmm."

"Come here," he says, beckoning me to his lips.

I move to him, and he slants his lips over mine.

We've kissed in public before, but not like this. Not in front of people who aren't wearing masks and aren't distracted by their fantasies.

These people around will be looking on and watching, knowing who he is and the significance of who he is.

He's kissing me.

When we pull apart, I see I'm right. There are a few women to our left who are openly staring, and they continue to stare when Vincent takes my hand.

We're about to walk away when someone clears their throat, and we turn to see an older man and woman walking toward us.

I know straightaway that they're Vincent's parents. While Vincent looks a lot like his father, there's a stronger resemblance to his mother, who looks my way with a sheen of interest in her eyes.

Vincent releases my hand to shake his father's when they get to us. His mother gets a kiss on both cheeks.

"Ava, these are my parents," he says. I'm surprised he introduced me, considering they must know who I am.

"Good to meet you, Ava," his mother says, putting out her hand for me to shake. "I'm Angela."

I shake her hand. "Nice to meet you."

She seems warm, warmer than her husband, who also shakes my hand.

I notice that Vincent slips his arm around me straight after in a noticeable protective manner.

"Did you just get here?" Vincent asks them.

"We did, as did our very special friends," Vincent's father says. He never told me his name.

I think there was a reason for that too. The way he says *special friends* catches my attention, as does the way Vincent tenses.

"I'll go check in on them, then," Vincent replies with a curt nod.

"Wonderful. Enjoy the evening..." his father says then looks from me to Vincent. "You look good together." His gaze drops to Vincent's arm circling my waist. And he saunters away with his wife.

Vincent presses his lips together in a hard line as we watch them go.

"Is... everything okay?" I ask. It's probably a question I shouldn't ask. He looks back down at me and smiles.

"Yeah. There's one thing I have to do, but don't worry, it won't spoil the night. Tonight isn't business." He gives me a wink.

"Okay."

He strokes the side of my waist and leads me further into the room. We're heading to the archways that goes out onto a terrace.

I glance over to the bar area just before we get there where I see Vincent's brothers. Three of them are there. They all have women with them. All very beautiful. They look like a collection of dolls. One is pregnant but carries off an elegant dress that shows off the rest of her figure. She's standing next to Salvatore. I'm guessing that's his wife. He's whispering something to her, and she's smiling.

Vincent and I go through the archways and into the night again The cool breeze kisses my shoulders, along with the music. There are more people dancing out here than inside. It's nice to watch people having so much fun. It reminds me of the parties my parents used to throw when I was little. The setting and the amount of people here are similar.

We stop, and Vincent looks on ahead. He looks like he's trying to put on a pleasant face, but I can tell something isn't quite right.

I'm so focused on looking at him that I don't see what he's looking at until it's a stone's throw away from us. Away from me.

As I turn and look, I get a shock so powerful it shakes my soul.

The two men who are approaching us are two I never hoped to see again as long as I lived. They exist in my nightmares as shadows. *Monsters.* Monsters who steal all that a person is because when they take, they take it all.

Not just the soul. They steal your hopes and dreams too. They steal your humanity.

Dmitri and Yuri.

The two men who work for my uncle, Ilya Lobonov, the Pakhan of the Ivanezh Brotherhood.

The same man who took everything away from me. They all did.

All thieves.

Murderers.

They killed my parents and stole my innocence.

My lungs are on fire.

Hotter than the fire that consumed the house they think killed me.

CHAPTER THIRTY

AVA

Breathe...
 Breathe...
  Breathe...Ava...
Hot air fills my lungs in a whoosh, and I try not to gasp.

Terror has my insides gripped so tight that my skin wants to flee.

What holds me in place is reality. The past and present combined and those who sacrificed their lives so I could be here.

I have to act normal. *Act natural.* Don't giveaway the secret that I'm alive. If I do, I'm dead, and it will all be for nothing.

I know too much. I know what happened that day. I know the evil that was exacted that day, and that alone is enough to kill me.

"Fantastic setup you guys have here," Dmitri booms with a hearty smile.

It's the same smile he used when he burned me with his cigarettes while he held me down.

"Thank you. I'm glad you like it, but I can't take credit. This is all my brother's doing. He's creative," Vincent answers.

Oh God... he knows them. They know each other.

At this point, I don't know what to think. What to do.

Vincent knows them.

My hands go limp.

Dmitri and Yuri laugh. The laughter comes back to my mind, and my head feels light. My body too, and I'm trying so hard to keep my breathing under control.

The two look at me. I feel exposed.

I look different. My hair was a white blonde back then, like my mother's, and I was ten years younger. I look a lot different, especially with makeup, but there's enough of a resemblance if you get a closer look.

"Vincent, you have a very beautiful creature on your arm," Dmitri says, and my insides tighten up.

He puts out his hand to take mine, and I squeeze Vincent's side, willing him to not let this man touch me.

Please don't let him touch me... not any of them.

I pray in those seconds that if there's any connection between Vincent and I, he won't allow these men to touch me again.

My heart starts beating wildly in my chest when Vincent shuffles, turning me out of Dmitri's reach.

He caresses the side of my waist, an acknowledgment of my silent plea, but doesn't look at me.

"Sorry, I'm Sicilian. I don't let nobody touch my doll," Vincent tells him, and Dmitri backs away, thrown by his remark and the glare he gives him.

I'm so shaken I can't even process that he called me his doll.

"Oh, of course. Apologies, I should have known that."

"Accepted. Why don't you go make yourselves comfortable, and I'll join you when I can."

"Indeed. We'll see you later," Dmitri says.

He glances at me before he goes, and I swear I see some

element of recognition dawn in his eyes. Yuri whispers something to him, and they continue on through the archway.

"Bellezza," Vincent says catching my attention.

When I look at him, he releases me and narrows his eyes while he looks me over.

"Baby, what's the matter? You're completely pale. And shaking." He observes.

I look down at my hand and see that I am indeed shaking. I bring my hands together to try and stop them, but that barely works.

There's so much spinning around in my head, but the one thing that pushes itself to the forefront of my mind is Vincent mustn't know what happened to me. No one must know, and especially not him. He wouldn't want me.

Something registers in his eyes, and he glances to the archway Dmitri and Yuri went through. He stares for a second then looks back to me.

"Ava, do you know those guys?" He narrows his eyes.

"Vincent... can we just go home?" I ask, completely avoiding the question. "Please, can we go home?" It's the first time I've ever referred to his house as home.

If I stay here, I don't know what will happen.

"Of course, baby, come... let's go."

When he slips his arm around me again, I allow myself to feel the safety of him.

Just his touch. His arm around me holding me away from the nightmare.

It's a nightmare spilled over into reality.

———

He kept his eye on me all the way home, glancing between me and the open road. No questions asked.

He looks like he's piecing together things in his mind. I just don't know what. Vincent is not the kind of man to accept nothing as an answer. I'm amazed that he hasn't asked me more.

We get inside, and he takes me right up to his room, where he sits me down.

The look of him suggests it's time for questions, and I don't know what I'm going to say.

I don't want to talk about it ever. I don't want to think about it ever. I have to tell him something though.

I didn't exactly act like nothing happened and I asked if I could go home.

He sits me down on the bed and crouches down in front of me, taking both my hands into his.

"Ava, do you know those men? You look like you know them," he says. I stare into his deep brown eyes wishing I could truly get lost in his stare.

Like I could jump in and hide there forever.

"I, um... I..." I hate lying to him, but I'll have to lie again. I can't tell him any part of the truth. "No... I... don't feel very well. Can I lie down? Please..."

He just stares at me, his eyes searching mine.

"What's wrong with you?"

"My head... hurts. If I lie down, I'll be okay." I nod and reach out to touch his face.

"Okay. You stay here tonight. I'll let you get some rest." He stands up.

"Are you going back out?" I ask.

I'm so scared I can't breathe. I don't want him to leave. What if Dmitri and Yuri truly recognized me and had us followed?

"Want me to stay?" He gives me a little smile.

"Yes."

"Then I'll stay. I have a few calls to make. Sleep, Bellezza." He bends down to kiss me like it's habit then leaves.

The minute the door click's shut, I allow the tears I've been holding back to fall. They fall on a breath I release.

My lungs still feel like they're on fire. My soul still feels like it's aching.

I cry so hard I'm shaking, covering my mouth with my hand to keep the sound in.

How did this happen?

Ten years I've hidden. I've stayed hidden for ten years. Now the monsters are here. Not in Russia where I left them. They're here, and they know Vincent.

Fuck.

It's the first time since I made this bargain that've felt regret to the point where I can't think about what I feel for Vincent.

This isn't just down to coincidence. It's some cruel joke of fate that's come for me. Dad got himself in trouble, and all the pieces on the chessboard were played to put me here, right in the line of danger. Right there in the line of fire where I'm exposed.

What am I going to do?

What the hell am I going to do if they recognized me?

That would mean...

Everyone I know is in danger.

Vincent doesn't know who he's dealing with.

Or does he?

CHAPTER THIRTY-ONE

Vincent

She lied to me.

When you study a person as much as I do her, you know things.

Every time I'm with her, her eyes draw me into her soul, calling to me. That's how I know.

She didn't feel sick. It wasn't that.

Her weirdness at least became noticeable when Dmitri wanted to take her hand.

She gripped on to me in such a way that I just knew she didn't want him to touch her. It was the strangest thing, but I knew it for truth. What I told him was truth too. In Sicily, if a woman belongs to a man, you don't touch her, not even for a fucking handshake, unless you have permission to do so.

I gave the excuse off the top of my head and in the same breath called her mine.

Confirmation to guys that are soon to become my enemies. I

don't think we'll be anything close to friends when I deliver my answer in a few days.

I'm just waiting for Gibbs to get back to me.

As for last night's fiasco, I think I just made some new friends with the feds when I got my guys to send over the details of the boat. I may be a fucking gangster, but I'm not evil. I'm not about to turn a blind eye on a boat carrying a hundred young women— *girls*— to fuck knows where in chains.

Now I seem to have Ava to worry about.

She knew them. I can tell she knew them. Both of them. Dmitri and Yuri.

They didn't act like they knew her though. Not in the least, so that lends to the idea that she recognized them.

Where from though?

What the fuck is it all about?

I give her an hour to herself and call Salvatore to let him know I've left and to keep an eye out.

I decide to go back up to my room and see Ava's fallen asleep in her dress. All around the area where her head touches, the sheets are soaked with tears. Her eyes puffy and red.

I sit in the chair by the bed and watch her.

It's the first time she's looked troubled.

In my experience, there's only a handful of reasons when women behave the way she did tonight, and I don't want to think it could be any of those reasons. I don't even want to entertain the thought.

Not for my girl.

My girl...

Jesus... what the fuck... I'm thinking of her as my girl now?

Mine for how long? Ten more days?

As I watch her, though, she feels like mine. The way Sorcha felt like she belonged to me. It's a massive deal for me to accept that. It's a massive thing for me to acknowledge that.

I knew Sorcha was mine the minute I saw her. We grew up together. Our families were always close. We met when we were ten, and I looked at her and knew she was mine. No matter what

I did to avoid the good girl because of the badass I was, I kept coming back to the same conclusion.

I've known Ava for a day over four weeks, and I feel that same knowing in my heart that she belongs to me.

This woman feels like she belongs to me, and I can't bear the thoughts that come into my head.

Mark saying she had a rough life, the cigarette burn behind her ear, her reaction tonight.

It's all so vague. Too wide apart, but it's all there and feels like the same pain.

It's like I could reach for each piece and bring them together to complete the picture this puzzle is trying to show me.

I don't sleep. I watch over her the whole night. Maybe it would have been better if I slept because as I watch her, I see more revealed to me. There are moments when she's shaking her head and mumbling, then she settles back into her slumber. Then there are moments when she covers her head and cowers like she's trying to shield herself from something.

I don't know what she says when she's talking. It's a mumble, like her lips are sewn together.

She only seems to settle down when morning comes.

It's then I leave her with two things on my mind.

I want to talk to her later, and I think I need to talk to Mark.

Something is going on that I need to know about. Something more involving my new fucking friends.

The fuckers I saw just two nights ago hands down deep and dirty in shit.

What stroke of coincidence this is.

I'm definitely speaking to Mark. Ava wouldn't just know men like Dmitri and Yuri, but he would. After all, he knows me.

I make my way downstairs and find Marguerite tending to Timothy in the kitchen. He's sitting in his little chair and smiles when he sees me.

She takes one look at me and winces.

"Dio mio," she gasps. "What are you doing? Skipping sleep

completely now?" She taps the side of my cheek the way my mother would and frowns.

"Morning, guys." I plant a kiss on Timothy's forehead and turn to face her.

"Morning. There's no way you slept, looking like that." Her brows knit together.

"I didn't." I can't deal with her fussing over me now. "Marguerite, I need to go check some stuff out. I need you to watch Ava a little closer today."

"Is she okay?"

"No... I don't think so."

She eyes me with worry. "What happened? What is happening?"

I never involve Marguerite in anything. That's my rule. I never do. She sees enough and is smart enough to figure things out for herself more often than not. I don't make the mistake of thinking of her as my house attendant and nanny. She's family to me. She's been in my life for long enough to be family, so when she asks a question, I give her an answer. I tell her what I can.

"Something happened last night I'm not sure about, and I have to check it out. Please... keep an eye on her for me."

"You know I will," she promises. "God keep you safe, Vincent."

I smile and leave her. I must have taken one step out of the kitchen when my phone rings.

It's Gibbs.

We meet at Renovata within the hour.

He takes a seat and hands me an envelope that looks heavy.

"Your boys certainly know some interesting people. It explains why they're so clean," he states and raises his brows.

"They're dirty as fuck, aren't they?" I put in.

"Dirty as fuck is just the beginning."

Just the sight of the envelope has me thanking my lucky stars, and I'm glad that while I can hold my own as a leader, I can be friends with a man like Claudius. There are many times when I've had to accept that I needed his help.

This time is no different.

I open the envelope and pull out a wad of paper stapled together. The first few are pictures.

Pictures of Dmitri and the man from last night.

The pictures are old, dated as far back as five years ago. The most recent one was at the start of the year. They look like they're somewhere tropical.

Gibbs is silent for a few seconds, giving me the chance to peruse. I don't get to finish the perusal though. He clears his throat when I get halfway through.

"Where did you get all these?" I ask. I only sent him the few from my phone.

"My resources. Your pictures pointed me in the right direction. That man is Diego Montoro, a known terrorist. He's part of a group called The Ra."

The moment he says the words *terrorist* and *The Ra*, the blood drains from my body and I gaze head-on at him.

The mention of terrorist is bad enough, but The Ra are possibly the worst known terrorist organization known to man. They're anarchists who operate on a global level. What's worse is, you can't stop them. Nobody can stop them because their associates are hidden in governments and the military. It's like a cult of extremists who I know to do all manner of fucked-up shit to accomplish their mission.

"What the fuck are you saying to me?" I seethe.

"The fucker is a terrorist. He belongs to The Ra. I'll take the liberty of assuming that's how your Bratva friends clean up. You seem to be versed in the Ra's activities?" He seems surprised by this.

"I know my enemies." There was an incident a few years

back that involved the Marchesis, one of the crime families in our alliance.

It was in Vegas and never reached Chicago, but we knew enough. Groups like that link up with mafia guys because we can move around and get shit done. We might have something they want or need. They don't care who you are, as long as you can help them get the job done.

"Good, because believe me when I say I don't think you want to have anything to do with these guys. I think you'll want to stay the fuck away."

"Oh, I most assuredly will be staying away." Like fuck am I going to be agreeing to anything. After what I saw the other night, that was decline right there. The party was just to look them in the eye. "What are they up to, Gibbs? What else is there?" I need to hear it.

My fucking instincts were screaming at me not to trust these guys, and now I know why.

We're a breath away from me giving my answer, and the way things were looking, I was going to have to back the fuck down or lose my birthright.

"My guess is that Dmitri and his brotherhood can only be associates. You don't just see a member of the Ra or speak to them the way he is in these pictures. You have to know them. I also found out some more things about your friends," he explains.

"What?"

"My intel has been searching around in Russia amongst those connected to them. They found a host of events that were never accounted for. Assassinations of notable people who no one can link back to them. They did it though. Their Pakhan is one twisted son of a bitch out for conquest."

Conquest? so we'd be little more than pawns on a fucking chessboard.

"This is shit, Gibbs."

"I know."

"I can't believe they cleaned up that well that my people couldn't find shit."

"Boss, with all due respect. If you didn't find shit and still didn't trust them, it's enough to dig around in other areas. Like you did. This is stuff I had to dig deep for. The fact that my only lead was a link with a terrorist tells all."

Jesus... I sigh and nod. "My thanks to you, Gibbs." I sure as fuck know I'll be using this guy a lot more than I have. "I'll deposit a bonus in your account within the hour."

"Thanks, Boss." He smiles and tips his head for a grateful nod.

I'm doubling what I originally paid him. The guy is worth every cent. Now to action this.

Pa stares at me, blank and expressionless, as I finish off showing him what I found. He looks pissed as fuck.

I have no patience for his mood today. Something is going on with Ava, and I want to know what it is. I've given my fair share of time to these motherfuckers, and I want to be done with it.

I was already done from the word *go*.

I didn't trust them from the start, and that was enough for me to say no.

"I'm saying no," I declare. "No to the alliance. We will not work with those people." My tone is harsh, harsher because of Ava.

He doesn't know that part, but he doesn't have to.

All my life, I've shown him respect and done what I'm told. I shouldn't have had to go to Claudius in the first place.

"No, we won't." He sighs.

"Pa, I get what you were trying to do. I see it. Sure, it would have been an opportunity if it worked out, but if you want me to be boss of this family, let me handle the job I've been trained to do. The job *you* trained me to do. You were right. I'm not some fucker who doesn't know his shit. I do."

"And I should have trusted you when you said something looked off." Thank fuck he's in agreement with me. I was gearing up to give him a mouthful.

"Yes, you should have."

"I'm sorry, boy. I guess I was trying to leave my legacy by setting up something big."

"You already have." My shoulders loosen, but only slightly. Now on to the next part of the problem because it looks like we're not done with these guys yet. "Pa, There's more to these guys. Something I have to look into. I need to do it."

"What is it?"

"I'm not sure yet. I'll let you know."

He gives me a nod. "Okay. Vincent... be careful. This is the Bratva we're dealing with. Be careful."

"I plan to."

I leave. As I do, that feeling comes back to me when I remember Ava's reaction. It's dark and ominous. *Evil*.

It's the same vibe I've been getting this whole time.

What is it?

How many times have I wondered what Ava's story was?

How many times have I looked at her and seen pain?

Something happened to her. Something really bad.

I need to get to her.

CHAPTER THIRTY-TWO

AVA

Darkness and shadows fill the area.

It's different today.

It feels more like I'm watching the scene play out, not like usual. Normally, I'm a part of the shadows.

It's gray, then I feel the hard ground and the room comes into view before me.

It's a memory.

There's Papa sitting at the table with the phone in his hands and Ma bringing the food to him.

I try to rush up to him to warn him. He shouldn't have taken that call.

Uncle Ilya is the man who killed those men. It's him, and he's on his way here now. He'll be here any minute.

I try to run. I try to scream.

It's too late. The door to the house bursts open, and in they come. Ilya with the bodyguards who betrayed Papa. They don't want him to be leader either. They're the greedy kind like Ilya who want more wealth the dirty way.

Papa gets up to protest, and Ilya shoots him in his chest.

He falls to his knees. Ma screams.

The blood pours from his chest, and there's so much screaming, so much pain. Hers and mine. It's like an ocean of voices crying out.

Then horror fills me when Ilya pulls out a long knife and cuts Papa's head off. The men cheer as Ilya lifts Papa's head off the ground and holds it up, roaring like a savage. Two men grab my mother, and someone grabs me. I don't know who it is.

They take me and her to the courtyard.

Ilya carries a bucket and throws liquid all over her. The second the smell hits me, I know what it is. *Gasoline.*

I struggle to help her, screaming and crying. Bawling from my soul.

Then I see the fire. Fire that blazes when it touches her skin. She looks to me first, and she speaks, but I never hear her.

I don't know what she wanted to say to me because she's engulfed by flames, and I scream and scream and scream.

Someone is shaking me and calling my name. Calling the name I chose when I left Russia. *Ava.*

The horror fades before me when Vincent's face comes into my view.

He can help me.

I bolt upright into his arms.

"Save her!" I cry, and he holds me.

"Ava... baby," he breathes, holding me close.

I look around the room and realize it's not just him in here. Marguerite's here too.

She looks worried.

I pull back, and a trickle of blood drips onto my wrist. My nose. It's bleeding. Vincent gets up and grabs a tissue from the box on the nightstand. He dabs at my nose and glances back at Marguerite.

"I'll get some warm water," she says and leaves us.

Vincent wipes at my nose, and when Marguerite returns with the warm water and a rag, he cleans my face.

"Marguerite... can you give us a few minutes, please?" Vincent asks her.

"Of course." She leaves us, and he studies me.

I'm giving my secrets away. Putting them on display with my behaviour.

I glance out the window and see it's morning, but I don't know what day it is.

I'm still in his room and am wearing a night shirt I don't remember changing into.

"Ava ... please tell me what's going on with you." Vincent says.

"I had a really bad dream." I'm shaking again.

"You've been asleep since the night before last. Unsettled sleep where you wake in bouts of screams, crying for your mother and father. Speaking Russian. You speak Russian?"

Oh God. This isn't happening.

"I learned it at school. I... speak five languages," I attempt.

He takes my hand and holds it. "Ava... the men at the party, you know them. You recognized them. You looked freaked, baby."

"Vincent, please. I wasn't feeling well." I try to get off the bed, but he reaches for me and holds me in place.

"How do you know them?"

"I don't."

"You're lying."

"I need to go to work. Please let me go to work."

"I'm calling your father."

Christ... this is the last thing I want Dad worrying about. It would send him over the edge.

"No, please, Vincent. Can't you just leave it?"

"Oh, so there is something to leave?"

"Vincent... I get migraines," I lie, and I can see that he knows I'm lying. I just need to let this spell blow over. I can't be around him though. He sees too much when he looks at me. I don't want him to see the truth. "This is what happens. Can I just go to work? I'll be fine."

"I don't know if you should be going to work."

"I missed yesterday, and I have a lot of stuff I have to do." He stares at me for a little while then sighs. "I'll take you."

"Okay." I'll just have to endure a car ride with him and hope that I'll be better later.

I distracted myself with work I didn't need to do. Filing and all kinds of shit the office assistants tend to get done for me.

Freddie took me off a lot of the projects I was scheduled to work on so I could spend this week and next week closing off everything I had outstanding. That was all done by morning, and I'm now here in my office organizing the bookshelf. One more time. This time, I have the reference books on the top shelf and everything else in alphabetical order.

"You know, I don't think those books could be more organized," Freddie says.

I turn to see him standing by my office door looking at the shelf with a bright smile on his face.

"Oh, I just couldn't decide what I wanted to do with everything."

He laughs. "Ava, are you nervous?"

I wish it were just nerves. "Yes, a little. What gave me away?" I smile a smile I don't feel.

"There's nothing to be nervous of. I spoke to Coral yesterday, and she's really excited to meet you. She's got a host of things planned for the two of you to enjoy. I think you're going to have the time of your life."

That sounds amazing, and it gives me hope. "Oh, wow, thanks so much, and thanks again for such a wonderful opportunity. I'm really happy."

Happy? Today I'm far from it. Days ago, I felt the happiness of my stupid imagination and my heart reaching out to love.

Today, I can't even think about that. I'm taking one hour at a time.

"You deserve it, Ava. Nobody works harder than you. And that's why I'm giving you tomorrow off."

"What?" I ask with a quiver in my voice. I should sound happier than that to get such a treat from Freddie. He doesn't offer that to everyone.

"Time off, Ava. A break. That way you can get yourself organized and spend time with your father."

But I'd rather be here. I can't be around anyone right now. Definitely not around anyone like Dad, or Vincent. Not Holly either.

"Oh... thanks so much." I pretend my gratitude. "Are you sure I shouldn't come in and work? There's always so much to be done."

He laughs. "Ava, sweetie. Only you would say such a thing to me. The answer is no. You've done everything, so have some time to yourself. Come in on Monday, and that's it. Spend the rest of the time with your father."

If I press to stay, it's going to look weird. "Thanks, I appreciate it."

"Good, see you in the morning. Don't stay too late."

"I won't." I can't. Vincent will be here in half an hour on the mark.

Freddie leaves, and I turn back to the bookcase deciding to continue where I left off.

I'd just gotten to E. The lady who owned all these books donated them to the office before she left. I found them very useful when I started. There's everything from yoga to understanding plyometrics training. There's a little bit of everything to help us research. It's not massive, but it's quick access.

Footsteps sound against the floor again, and I turn thinking Freddie forgot to tell me something.

It's not Freddie at the door though. It's Dmitri.

The shock from the sight of him makes me drop the book I was holding.

"Oh my, I'm so sorry. I didn't mean to startle you," he says.

Jesus Christ... what is he doing here?

Oh God... why am I even thinking that? He's here because he recognizes me. The same look is in his eyes. The same look from two nights ago.

Fuck.

My heart freezes in my chest when he walks up to me, crouches down, and picks up the book.

He holds it out to me, and I take it. Our fingers brush against each other, and bile rises in my throat.

He touched me. It was the touch I was avoiding. Vincent's not here to save me. He's not here. No one is.

Dmitri smiles that wicked smile I remember. It's so prominent in my mind. Apart from my uncle, this man was the worst.

"I hope you don't mind me dropping by," he states.

"No..." I answer, steadying my voice. I try to push aside terror and reach deep down inside my soul for courage. His very presence is suspicious. I never gave this man my new name. How does he know where I work? "Is there something I can do for you?"

"It's just that... I thought I recognized you."

I play the good actress and narrow my eyes. "I don't think I've ever seen you before. Where might that have been?"

It's not working. A shiver runs down my spine mixed with cold and heat when he looks me over.

"Have you ever been to Russia?" He looks into my eyes. My fucking eyes. The same way he used to when he had me pinned beneath him.

"No... I have not. I've lived here all my life. Is that what you came to ask me?"

"Yes... Ava Knight. My mistake though. I thought you might be someone else."

Ava Knight... I steady my heart.

"Oh, well, if that's all, I'm quite busy. I need to finish my work."

"Of course, you do, dear. Vincent Giordano is quite a good catch. Lucky man too."

"Thank you."

The intense look he gives me as he glares at me freezes my blood. The look doesn't match the fake-as-hell smile he's trying to mask it with.

Or maybe that's his intent.

With a nod of his head, he leaves me.

Leaves me staring after him until I can't see him anymore.

I wouldn't be foolish enough to think I got off free.

No. I didn't

He knows it's me, and if that is so, everyone I know is in danger.

Dad.... Does he know where Dad is? If he found me, then maybe he found Dad too.

What am I going to do?

Then there's Vincent... the only person who might be able to help me.

Why would he though?

This is the Bratva. You go against them, and it's war.

Vincent has a family, and I'm a debt repayment.

My time will be up in eight days.

I have to leave.

I have to get to Dad and leave.

I have a plan.

I sent Dad a message letting him know I needed to see him.

I was discreet, not saying too much because I don't want him to panic.

Vincent gave me my phone back, but I'm careful. He's not here. He left early, which made my plan possible.

I have my passport and clothes that fit in the handbag. It's not enough, but it will do for a few nights.

I've arranged with Pierbo to take me into town. I said I needed to get a few personal things.

We'll be leaving in ten minutes.

I look around the bedroom I've lived in for the last four and a half weeks. I remember that first night when I slept on the floor. I was so scared.

I've lived my life in fear for so long. It's been too long.

Too damn long, so long I can't remember what it's like to just be normal.

There have been glimpses of normal. Glimmers and shimmers of what I could have, and they've all been with Vincent.

Our relationship was so intense, and it still has that same feeling.

I wish for the fantasy. I really do. I wish I could have met him under different circumstances.

The coffee shop fantasy.

It's a good one. One I hold on to and will forever. This is it. It's goodbye. When I saw him this morning, it was the last. His handsome face looking over me with so much worry.

I push it out of my mind and will my tears away.

I leave the room and go downstairs. Marguerite is just walking by with Timothy, who laughs when he sees me. I would have loved to get to know them both a little longer.

"Are you okay, sweet Ava?" Marguerite asks. "Can I get you anything before you go?"

"No, I shouldn't be too long." I hate lying to her.

"You sure Pierbo can't get you what you need? I've been so worried about you." She looks it.

"I need the fresh air. It will be good for my headaches."

"Okay, dear, see you in a little while."

I look at her, and emotion takes me. She was so nice to me when I needed nice. I hug her, placing my arms around her and Timothy, and they both hold me back.

"Princess Ava," Timothy says and starts clapping.

"Thank you, baby." He looks so much like Vincent. I give him a little kiss on his cheek, and he smiles.

When I look back to Marguerite, there's something knowing in the look she gives me. It's like she can tell I mean for this to be goodbye. She doesn't say anything though.

I go through the door never looking back. Pierbo is on the driveaway waiting for me.

"Where to, Ava?" he asks.

"If you head to the mall and park in the parking lot, I'll be able to get to where I want to from there. I should just be about half an hour."

"Okay."

The thing about trust is when it's given freely, it can be broken easily.

All these people around me are trained to know that I can be trusted. I did what I was told, and no one would dare think I'd ever try to escape. And why would I do so when I only have a handful of days left?

So, all Pierbo does is smile as I leave him in the parking lot.

He never questions me, and he probably won't think anything has happened in half an hour when I don't return. Maybe not even forty minutes.

He'll just assume I was delayed. My guess is, I have one hour before he starts panicking.

That's fine. I'm on my way to Dad's. On the subway, it takes a little over an hour from the city center. Then I have to walk to his apartment.

When I get there, I just have to figure out what to do next.

CHAPTER THIRTY-THREE

Vincent

I stare at the picture Gibbs lays before me.

It's of a girl with platinum blonde hair.

She's wearing a ballerina dress and is posing for the camera with a bright smile on her face.

The picture is dated eleven years old and according to the info Gibbs handed me, the girl in the picture is fifteen.

Her name is Juliette Lobonov, the star of the show. The prima ballerina at that young age. This picture of her shows her as Cinderella.

"Is that her?" Salvatore asks.

We're at Renovata sitting around my desk. He's sitting next to Gibbs.

The girl looks different to Ava. Of course, she would be different. It was eleven years ago.

And according to the intel Gibbs gave me, this girl died in a house fire in St. Petersburg ten years ago. She and her family; Ilya Lobonov's brother, and sister-in-law.

"Vincent..." Gibbs says, and I look at him. "It's her, isn't it?"

It is.

It's Ava.

My version of her may have dark brown hair, and she might be eleven years older than she was in this picture, but I can see it's her.

She's a child, and her face has changed into the beautiful woman she is now.

But I can definitely see it's her.

What's the same is her eyes. The girl in the picture doesn't emanate the pain yet, but there's the spark that I see whenever she talks about her dreams. This is a picture of her in her element. In her first love. Ballet.

The pride and happiness is practically leaping off the picture.

It's a happy picture. What I've learned though is sadness.

It's her so that means Ava is Ilya's niece. So she more than knows Dmitri and Yuri.

"It's her," I confirm. "How did you come by these?" I ask Gibbs. I know has his ways that are probably his trade secrets, but I still want to know. This is the third time he's come to see me.

Last night, I told him to extend the search on Mark to include her. I knew I wasn't getting shit from her, and the same way I knew something was off with Dmitri, I knew the same rang true here too.

"The name change office. I worked my way from there. The files are stored at the highest level of security because most often, people in the witness protection programs have to get their names changed. Mark's couldn't be found. So, I figured since our guy was so tech savvy, he must have had some influence. Friends in high places who could turn a blind eye. But I have higher friends who can look a little deeper and find something hidden. It took some hard work but they found he didn't just change his name but the girl he was looking after as well, and his son's."

I've just gotten over the fact that the girl in the picture is Ava. What does Gibbs mean by the girl Mark was looking after?

"His daughter?" I fill in, and both Salvatore and I look at each other when he shakes his head.

"No, she isn't his daughter. If you are telling me that this girl is Ava, then Mark's not her father. He's not Ilya Lobonov's brother."

"So, who the hell is he?" Salvatore asks.

"It's a good thing you people keep me in business. It certainly balances out my high blood pressure. Mark, whose real name is Alessandro, was Sovientrik to his best friend, Roberto Lobonov, Pakhan of the Ivanezh Bratva. I'll add here that Mark was a high tech ex-military intelligence analyst who worked as a link to government intel, hence his hacking abilities. If that girl is your girl, then her real father was Roberto Lobonov. She was somewhat of a princess. Her family were treated like royalty. They all supposedly died in the fire, but Alessandro and his sons went missing. One of the sons is the guy who died six years ago. As to the other, I don't know."

Holy fuck.

What the fucking hell?

I just stare at Gibbs and allow the shock to take me.

What the fuck does all that mean? It's clear that something is more than amiss.

They died in a fire in Russia, but they're here in the States under fake names?

And Marks' not her father.

I blink several times trying to process everything and think back to the night I first met Ava. I think of the way she sacrificed herself for Mark.

My stomach churns. The secrets are spilling before my feet, and I'm seeing the truth unfold itself. What will it reveal?

Ava acted like someone who'd been through shit. Like someone who'd been abused, and I don't want to say that out loud because if I do, it will make my worries real.

"Thank you, Gibbs," I tell him.

"I think that might be all, Boss. The rest is on you. But if I can do anything else, let me know," he offers.

I nod my appreciation, and he leaves us.

I turn my attention to Salvatore. "What am I doing, Salvatore? What am I digging for? She leaves in a few days, and then I won't see her again. We all go back to our lives, and it will be like we never met."

He gives me a long stare. "You love her."

I open my mouth to protest, but I find I can't. The last time we spoke about Ava, he told me I liked her. Now it's gone to *love*. He's jumped from A to Z, and I can't protest and tell him he's wrong.

I stand up and walk over to the long French windows.

"Vincent... it's okay to love her."

"No," I answer, turning back to face him. "I can't. I can't go down that road with anybody. I know I can't even use the excuse of it being too soon after Sorcha anymore because it's not. That's bullshit, and I won't sell it to you. I just can't love anyone like that ever again. Our lives are dangerous."

"What about me? You telling me I can't love my wife, or the other guys can't love their dolls?" he asks.

"It's different."

"How?" he barks, raising his voice. He looks furious with me, and he has every right to be.

"You never lost your babygirl, Salvatore." He'll know what I mean. The same way Sorcha and I met as children, he met Mimi the same. In fact, they've known each other longer. She met him when she was four. She was always his. "You didn't have to hold her cold dead body in your arms and accept there was nothing you could do to bring her back. You didn't have to do that. None of you have gone through that, and I don't want you to. I can't bring someone else into my world and have the same thing happen. I can't do it. And not to Ava."

He gets up and walks over to me. "Brother... I hear you. I hear you loud and clear, but you can't tell me it's right to end it just like that. You're digging because you want to know what happened to her, and you got a piece of the puzzle. People who move like that carry secrets. Deep, dark ones. I won't tell you what to do. Only your heart can do that. Just know that I'm here for you when you need me."

My phone buzzes in my back pocket, and I reach for it. It's Pierbo.

"Yes," I say into the phone.

"Boss, I... I lost Ava."

CHAPTER THIRTY-FOUR

Ava

I can't believe I made it this far.

Good. I can do this.

I can.

So far, it's been fine. Although I've just been on the subway.

Nothing would have happened to me there. I would have been ahead of the game, and no one would have been able to track me down. If they were tracking, they would have come to a dead end because I threw my phone away when I entered the subway station.

That doesn't mean people won't be able to find me.

Vincent, or Dmitri, or whoever from the Bratva they send for me.

Now that I'm above ground, I'm weary and walking like it too. I don't care though. I just have to get to Dad, and then we'll know what to do and where to go when we put our heads together.

It was all on him the last time we had to make a grand

escape. I was a mess, and I wouldn't have known what the hell to do. Back then, he had Sasha. Now, it's just me, and we'll make this happen.

I walk faster, passing a man carrying balloons when I see Dad's apartment block come into view. There's another guy at the corner with more balloons. People are always selling things on this road. They're not allowed to do it, but they still do it, until the cops catch them. I know that some pretend to sell what they're selling, but really it's an elaborate setup to sell drugs. I used to wonder if that was how Dad got hooked.

It was always strange to me that he would turn to them when it was the thing that helped take Sasha's life. I've never had the curiosity take me to try it. Not once. There was a time back in college when it was offered to me, and I refused.

I go into the building and head to the elevator. The doors open. A woman and five small boisterous children with their faces painted pile out. It takes her a minute to get them under control and away from the entrance before I can get in. She offers an apologetic smile, and I return it.

I always pray that one day, when I'm not so screwed up, maybe I might think of having a family. I'd want kids, and I'd hope to happen on kind strangers if they got out of control the way those little ones were.

I shake my head at myself. That life is for someone else. I have to make it to the next minute and hope I can take care of Dad too.

As for Florida and my piece on Coral... well, that was always a dream and clearly not meant to be. I can't do it. There's no way I can do it. It's far too risky.

I was thinking Dad and I could leave the city tonight. We could take the bus across the country. Maybe toward somewhere like Arizona, and then we could leave the country from there.

It's going to be hard to stay on track and be ahead of people like the guys we're dealing with.

They're always one step ahead. *Always.* The only way we escaped last time was because they thought we were dead. That's how. While my father was Pakhan, I didn't really know anything about the business. Women are always kept out of business. It was Dad who taught me all I needed to know when we left Russia. Just so I could keep safe. Our brotherhood had access to so much. So damn much. They were like an army. You don't mess with people like that.

The elevator doors open, and I rush out, grateful to see Dad's apartment door. I can't wait to see him. I can't wait to tell him what's happened. He's the only person who's been able to take care of me and calm me down.

I never had to give him details of the horror I went through. He just knew. He knew and healed me.

I rush up to the door but stop in my tracks when I see it's open. The door is slightly ajar. Dad never leaves the door like that. There's never a reason to. He lives on the third floor so wouldn't keep it open like the people on the first floor who might be unloading groceries from their cars.

A slither of panic crawls down my spine, and I swallow hard.

I open my mouth to call out to him, but I think better of it. *Never do that, Ava. No.*

My lungs constrict when I push the door open slowly. My nerves are tingling on high alert.

There's an ominous presence about the place, and cigar smoke.

Cubans with apple smoked wood. It's a specific smell. A smell I came to associate with Dmitri.

My hands start to shake at the thought, my soul quivers, and the icy tendrils of fear work its way through my body.

I take one step and another. The hallway is clear, but the smell... that smell gets stronger. *Is Dmitri here?*

Jesus, is he here? If he found me at *Escada*, then what was to stop him from finding Dad?

Ava Knight
Mark Knight.

If Ava Knight could be found, then people would know that

her father is listed as Mark Knight, and they'd be able to find out where he lived. It's not like we lived in secret.

I take another step, and another, following the pungency of the cigar smoke. It leads me to the living room and to my biggest nightmare.

A scream rips from my throat before my brain processes what I'm seeing before me.

Dad...

He's hanging from the beam on the ceiling with his eyes gouged out and the words:

We know

written on a note on his chest.

I scream and scream, tears flowing from my soul, pouring from my eyes.

There's so much blood everywhere.

He's covered in it. He's soaked, and it drips from his body to the floor.

I scream so much I feel I might die from the terror, die from the pain, die from the loss of another father.

Arms grasp hold of me from behind, holding me in place as I scream. I dare not look to see who it is. I can't. I know it's one of them. It's probably Dmitri or another henchman here to kill me too.

I cry waiting to feel it. The press of a gun to my head, or hands around my throat ready to snap my neck, or maybe they'll slash my throat, cutting me open.

"Ava," the voice says in my ear, a hand now stroking my head. "Baby..."

It's only when he says that, that I turn my head to look at him.

Vincent.

He came. He's here. Sad eyes look down at me and back to Dad. Sad, heavy eyes that look so unlike the man he was when he was ready to kill weeks ago.

He shakes his head, and pure compassion fills his features when he stares back at me. I'm still bawling my eyes out so much I can't catch my breath.

He loosens his grip on me, and I sink to the floor allowing the weakness to take me.

He lowers too and holds me close.

"Baby, please. Come, let's go home. Come home," he says against my hair.

Home... I gaze up at him, and my mind scatters. I can't think straight. I certainly can't talk.

His next words are stolen with a ticking sound.

It's a distinct ticking sound that just comes on. I don't know where it's coming from, but it's there. *Tick. Tick. Tick.*

Vincent grabs me. He just grabs me and throws me over his shoulder.

He runs to the window with me. That same window I used to escape with Dad weeks ago.

We don't get to open it. An explosion rips through the fabric of reality, and then we're smashing through the glass of the window. I see fire billowing forward, then I'm flipped around and cocooned against Vincent's hard chest.

We're falling, falling amongst shards of glass, smoke, fire, and my screams. Still he holds me.

My body jerks hard when he reaches for something to hold on to. I glance at the railing of the fire escape. The explosion weakened it, and we continue falling until we smash into the ground.

I swear he's dead. He took a hit, and our weights combined hitting the ground together must have had an impact.

Blood pours down the side of his face, and his eyes flutter open as he winces in pain.

"Vincent," I wail. I can't believe he's alive.

"Doll, are you okay?" he asks through gritted teeth.

"I'm not hurt," I answer quickly.

Ahead are people who heard and saw the explosion. Fire

rages from Dad's apartment so high up it's taken out the whole section.

That was supposed to kill me.

It's the least of my worries though. Tires screech on the road ahead, and a motorcyclist tears down the corner. He pulls a gun from his back and aims it at us.

Another comes.

Vincent leaps into action, shoves me behind him, and pulls two guns from his back pocket. Two shots are fired, and the first cyclist is dead before he can pull his trigger. The next doesn't make it to us. Their bikes crash into the wall.

Vincent takes my hand and runs with me down the road. We get to a midnight black Kawasaki, and he hands me the helmet that was hooked to the handlebar.

He takes my shoulders and holds them firm.

"Do not let go of me. You fucking hold on and don't let go. Do you hear me?" he warns.

I stare at him, my eyes so wide they're dry and hurt. His eyes bore into me with that mixture of what I always see, but deep within them, I see for the first time how much he cares about me.

"I hear you," I answer and put the helmet on.

He gets on the bike, and I get on behind him, slipping my arms around him tightly. I hold him and press my face into his back as I will the sounds around me away from my mind, and the images of Dad.

I will them all away because it's all I can do.

The nightmare world has spilled over into reality indeed, and it's brought hell with it.

We are being followed, chased.

Vincent speeds down the road as two motorcyclists follow us. I chance looking to my left and see them. Two are on that side. Another on the right I can hear.

They try to shoot at us but miss.

Vincent leads them to Main Street, where the roads get bigger. That's when I see six mean-looking motorcycles leap down from the car park complex. I recognize those moves. One of the bikers I know is Salvatore, although he's wearing a helmet. There's another guy without a helmet that has long black hair billowing out in the wind and a cross tattooed on his cheek. He and Salvatore take out the two bikers chasing us, and Vincent speeds along with me down the road.

More bikes come, and cars come from the corners while bullets fly all around me.

I hold on tight. Holding on so tight it's like I'm holding on to him and holding on to life.

The noises lessen, and I assume we've lost them, then a car pulls out from the road up ahead and stops.

It stops in our path.

I gaze on and see the people in the car.

Dmitri is the driver, and Yuri is sitting next to him. In the back is the devil. My uncle Ilya.

"Hold on tight, doll! Hold on!" Vincent shouts and pushes past the speed barrier. These bikes were designed to go lightning fast. It does.

They thought he was going to stop. The other cars that pulled out to join them thought the same, so did I. The only thing you can do in a standoff like this is stop.

But Vincent doesn't. He goes faster, and it's too late for anybody to scatter when he drives the bike right up onto the car with Dmitri, Yuri, and Ilya and practically leaps over it.

Shock flies through me at the formidable force he is and his determination to protect me.

More bullets echo behind us, but they fade. Then I hear them no more.

All there is in my ear is the hum of the engine and the hammering of my heart.

The tears never stopped falling.

They continue as we ride on and ride hard.

CHAPTER THIRTY-FIVE

Vincent

"You alright?" Claudius asks me as I take off the bandage off my arm the doc put on it. I can't deal with things like that. They get in the way.

"Jesus, Claudius, I don't know how to answer that question. I guess I can say I'm alive."

He laughs.

The guys are all here. My brothers and their crew. They're outside the office. I came in here when the doctor arrived. He thinks I have a broken rib, and he's shocked I'm not dead.

Pa is on his way here. My mother was here already. She has Timothy while Marguerite is tending to Ava

"Well, at least you finally got to do a daredevil stunt and didn't end up in the hospital," Claudius says, tilting his head to the side.

I won't even think about that. The last time I tried anything like what I did with Ava—*fucking jumping bikes over cars*—I was nineteen. I busted my ass and ended up missing the first month of college. I'd entered a dare with this devil in front of me.

"I did."

"That's why we're friends. You're the only guy outside my pack who's as badass as me. Your brother comes close though, so watch it." He smiles, but then seriousness enters his eyes. "What do you need, Vincent? Looks like we're at war again."

I blow out a ragged breath and think of all that happened in just a handful of hours.

They killed Mark, and they wanted to kill Ava too.

The whole fucking thing was set up so it would take them both out. She hasn't stopped crying.

"I know," I agree.

"You didn't tell me there was a doll worth all this."

I stare back at him, not knowing what to say. "It's complicated."

He smiles. "Gangsters and dolls. It's always complicated. I look forward to hearing the details. I'm gonna go check a few things out. You call when you need me."

He puts out his hand to shake mine, a symbol of our friendship and alliance.

"Thank you, old friend."

He dips his head for a nod and leaves.

When he does, my brothers come in.

It was an all-star cast out on the streets today. Anybody could have gotten killed.

The plan was they'd cover me while I got Ava out.

It was the secret squad who tracked her down, but they saw Mark dead in his apartment before she got there. We had a handful of minutes to concoct the plan we managed to pull off. It's just luck that we were able to get everyone there who could help.

"You guys alright?" I ask.

"Vin, you're asking us that? You look like shit," Salvatore says, taking a seat in the armchair.

Gabe shakes his head at him while Nick nods.

"Vincent, you do look like shit. Why don't you rest while we go out on the street?" Nick offers.

"I can't rest. There's too much to figure out. Too much to go through in my head," I reply.

I look to Salvatore, who sits forward.

"Vin, they wanted her dead. So, they're going to still want her dead, and I'm guessing anyone else helping her stay alive. That's the first part we need to think about."

I stare at him. It's an extension of the conversation we were having earlier. The question of why I'm doing this. Why I'm digging.

That was hours ago. That was before I knew she was in so much danger. Before she tried to escape.

When Pierbo called me and told me he lost her, I could have just let her go. After all, with a handful of days left in my care, so to speak, what was the big deal in her leaving early? It could have been goodbye. Except for the worry in my heart.

It's still there. Had I not gone after her and got the secret squad to look for her, she'd be dead. They would have killed her.

So... now I'm involved, the question is, do I want to be? Do I want to save her?

"I can't let them kill her," I answer.

Salvatore looks to Gabe, who stands, and Nick cracks his knuckles.

"We can't either," Salvatore answers. "And, we always have your back." Nothing is truer than that.

"I don't want to get you guys involved in this. It's not right to. Fuck knows what the fuck I stirred up today with the Bratva."

"Doesn't matter. We're here," Gabe says.

I look at the faces of my brothers, from one to the next, and feel in complete awe at their support and love for me.

"Thank you. I thank you. I am grateful." I bring my hand to my head. It hurts like a mutha, but I've got to figure things out. "There's a reason they want her dead. I need to know what that is. I need to know what that is before we do anything else."

I haven't had the chance to bring everyone else up to speed on what Gibbs found yet, but Salvatore knows.

"The details on her past are off... completely off," Salvatore points out. "And it doesn't exactly tell us much. Not to mention the fact that we saw Uncle Dearest today, and he looked like he definitely put the show together."

I never missed that part at all. Ilya was in the back of the car I drove on. I saw his face. Hard and horrible. Now I really wonder why it is he wants his niece dead.

"She must know something. She has information," I say, and he nods. "Salvatore, please show Nick and Gabe the stuff Gibbs found. I–"

The phone rings. The phone on my desk.

It never rings because I don't give out the number to people. I just have it for the sake of it.

When strange things like my phone that never rings, rings, I can only jump to the conclusion it points to.

I answer it and am surprised by the deep Russian accent that answers me.

"Ilya Lobonov here, Vincent Giordano."

We've never spoken before. He sounds exactly the way I expected him to sound. Like a fucking prick.

"Well, hello there. I'm so glad I had this opportunity to tell you, you can go fuck yourself. Clearly, we aren't agreeing to any kind of alliance with you." Tomorrow was the meeting. It feels so liberating to tell his ass no.

He chuckles. "You're turning us down? Really? Like we'd want to sign up with you after the shit from this week. First you ruin my virgin market, now this," he growls.

Fuck. Virgin market. I've heard it all now. "How do you know that was me you ruined your market?"

"I fucking know, boy. You do not know who and what you're messing with. You don't know, so don't try to think you and I are the same. We aren't. Give me the girl, and we will spare your lives." This fucker is the kind that loves the sound of his voice. I have news for him.

"No... there will be no such deal." I look at my brothers, who now look tense. They must have figured out who I'm talking to.

"This situation does not involve you. There is no reason for you to get involved and piss on us more than you have. Our business deal was actually legit. We just needed to make arrangements for our shipments. That was all you were supposed to be in this."

"Then things changed," I fill in with a sing-song voice.

"Give me the girl, Vincent. That is my final warning, or you will not like what happens next."

Threats... I know they're not empty.

I know enough, and I'm entering dangerous territory to protect a woman who reached somewhere inside me I thought was dead.

Is that enough?

Is love worth this?

I look over the faces of my brothers willing to go into battle with me. I have my friends who will walk by my side into the valley of the shadow of death. I have my son to think about.

The last part of Sorcha. My son is the love of my life now.

I think of all those people as I contemplate my next words.

Salvatore is my consigliere. He can't hear what's being said, but no one has to guess as to whether this conversation is good or bad. I focus on him, and he nods his head.

People used to think it was scary how we all seemed to be able to communicate with each other without speaking. We're doing it now because as he does it, Gabe and Nick do too, reinforcing their former promises to have my back.

I can't be with Ava. That's a whole separate issue that's on me. It's separate and different to this... but I can't allow them to kill her either. I won't.

That's the answer and how we will proceed.

"No," I answer. "Fuck no."

"Very well, Vincent Giordano. I hope you know you just signed your death warrant. You do not mess with the Ivanezh brotherhood and expect us to lie down and take it."

"You heard me."

"And you heard me. Fool, you would sacrifice your people for a piece of ass. For pussy."

I bite down hard on my back teeth. "Ilya Lobonov, be grateful we are not standing face to face right now. I'd rip your face off with a knife and snap your fucking neck. This conversation is over."

I slam down the phone, disconnecting him.

The question of what next hangs in the air like it always does.

Fuck, what next though? What will they do next?

"I'm going to talk to her. I'm gonna see what I can get out of her." I leave them and make my way up the stairs.

Marguerite's in my room with her. Ava's still crying, and I don't expect her to stop. It's the worst time ever to badger her for answers, but I need to.

Time is of the essence now. I can't allow her the time she needs to grieve.

I can't allow her the time she should have to process Mark's death.

I can't allow her the time she needs to trust me. I hope that she will trust me enough to tell me what I need to know.

Mark's dead, but right now, I'm a dead man walking with a target on my back. At war with the Bratva.

Maybe this is what happened to the other family in the past. If it is, I can't allow these people to kill mine.

So, I have to make her tell me what I need to know.

CHAPTER THIRTY-SIX

Ava

Marguerite leaves with one last look over her shoulder, and I find the strength I need to stand as Vincent comes into the room.

He closes the door and takes in the mess I am.

I won't lie there in my grief and not find whatever strength I need to thank him.

Dad is dead... and there's no reason to keep me here.

I'm supposed to leave in a few days. We're supposed to end, yet there was no part of today that felt like that. He came for me and saved me.

He's injured. I can see it on his face. There's a massive bruise on the side of his cheek and a cut by the corner of his eye. He's wearing a T-shirt, and all along the side of his arm is battered with bruises so deep it distorts his tattoos.

I suck in a sharp breath, holding the tears back as he walks up to me.

Vincent takes me into his arms. I sink into the warmth of the embrace. He rests his chin on top of my head while I hold him too.

"I can't thank you enough," I whisper. My voice sounds hoarse and raspy.

He runs his hand over my head and cups the back while he looks down at me.

"You're mine... remember? I take care of my things. No need to thank me." He seems to be trying for lighthearted. I wish I could try too, but I can't. There are too many dead faces in my head. "I'm sorry about your father, Bellezza."

I start shaking again as another bout of tears takes me. "They killed him, Vincent. They killed him... because of me."

"No... please don't say that. How can it be?"

If I answer that question, I'm going to have to tell him more. I don't have the strength for that.

I don't have the strength for anything.

"Ava... it wasn't your fault. That's the first thing you need to know. I'll be straight up with you because if you want to cast blame, then it's my fault too. I took you to the party. That's where you saw them. I accepted your offer and brought you into my world, where you don't belong."

I clutch his shirt and wish his words away. We might have started out the way we did, but I never felt like I didn't belong with him when I was with him.

"Please don't say that to me," I answer.

"It's true, Ava. A better man than me would have let you go."

"Look what you did for me today..." I say, trying to get the words out. "I don't have anybody who would have done what you did for me today."

When I think of the elaborate setup to save me and the way everyone moved around to clear the way for Vincent to get me out of danger, it was amazing.

He was amazing and pushed the limits. My God, did he ever push the limits. I would have been dead in that apartment. I wouldn't have stood a chance. I wouldn't have gotten out.

"Well... maybe I can remember that as something good.

Ava... we don't have time for guilt and blame. I am going to be straight with you, and I hope that you can trust me." He takes a breath and continues. "We were approached by the Ivanezh Bratva a few weeks back to form an alliance. The last few weeks has seen me battling in my head the question on whether or not to do it. That's how I came to know them."

I listen, taking his words in, knowing what he's expecting me to do next if he's talking business with me.

He's a mafia boss. He's not supposed to be talking business with me, not like this.

"It was weeks ago?" My voice shakes.

"Yes. It was complete coincidence. It all just happened. I didn't trust them from the outset, and I was going to say no to any business relationship with them." He cups my face. "I had no idea they knew you, or... had any kind of link to you. I would never put you in danger. Not ever. I need you to believe me when I say that. There's no way I would have taken you to that party if I had any idea who they were to you."

His words...

He's talking like he knows something. He's talking like someone's filled in the blanks and pieced together some parts of the puzzle.

"Vincent... I ..." I begin.

"Ava... I understand you're scared. These are dangerous men. So, I understand why you didn't want to talk to me about it. What I need to know is why... why do they want you dead?"

I shake harder hearing that. I shake so much my thoughts rattle in my mind. He's holding me, and I can't bare it. I can't breathe.

They want me dead. They've always wanted me dead. But first, they wanted to make sure they played with me and messed up my mind. Tortured me. Torture me and make me worry if I just had hours to live, *minutes, seconds.*

It's not just what I know. It's what they did to me.

I back away from Vincent, out of his grasp, and shake my head.

"Ava, tell me what happened to you. What did they do to you?"

"I can't... I can't talk about it. I can't say it outside my head." I never have.

I never needed to tell Dad. He knew. He knew what men like them did to girls like me. He didn't need to be told.

I had to have therapy for three years just to get me back on track to some level of normalcy. All the while I spoke to my psychiatrist, I never gave details. I never said the words. Said the names I was supposed to, to acknowledge what happened to me.

I think if Ilya didn't hate Ma as much as he did, she would have suffered the same fate.

Sometimes, I wished they had just burned me alive the way they killed her.

Throw gasoline on my skin and set me on fire. It would have been over quickly. I wish they'd done that because what they did was so much worse.

"Ava... to help me fight these guys, I need to know. I need to know what happened," Vincent says.

"I can't," I cry. Feeling trapped suddenly, I rush over to the window. He comes up to me and reaches for my arm. "I can't, Vincent... Please don't make me." I try to pry the window open, but either it's stuck or my hands are shaking so damn much that I can't grip the latch to open it.

He tightens his grip on my arm.

"Juliette," he says, and I stop. I just stop.

I stop, and my lips part. Hearing that name, being called that name, reaches me deep inside. It reaches that girl I used to be. I might be here, but she's still locked away in that room with the monsters. She's still watching for the shadows. She's still hiding.

But that can't be me.

Such a terrible thing couldn't have happened to me.

"Is that your name?" Vincent asks, and I turn to face him. "*Juliette?*"

Hearing it again makes something snap in my brain. Something cracks around the edges, and I start shaking my head.

"No... that can't be me. I can't be that girl, Vincent." I shake my head harder. "She is not me. I can't be that girl who watched her uncle cut off her father's head and burn her mother alive. I can't be her. That couldn't have happened. It wasn't me. I can't be that girl who was raped by her uncle over and over again." *Rape...* I said it. I actually said it. His eyes bore into me like daggers. I'm on a roll, and now that the secrets are starting to spill out, I might as well drop them all. He won't want me now. "I can't be her... I can't be that girl who was raped by all her uncle's men. They raped and tortured me. Burned me when I tried to fight back. Why didn't they just kill me then?"

When his hand drops to his side, I fall to the ground and scream. I scream the way I did back then, scream all the pain from my being. I unleash it and let it out, feeling like surely this must be it. I'm going to die from this.

Those arms that surrounded me earlier when I found Dad surround me now. They take me now and hold me.

Through the blindness of tears that blur my vision, I see tears stream down Vincent's cheeks too.

He scoops me up and holds me to him, holding me as close as he can, and I let him.

"I got you," he whispers. "I got you."

I continue to cry, letting the pain drain from my body while his words soothe me, like balm on my weary soul.

CHAPTER THIRTY-SEVEN

Ava

My eyes flutter open, and I stir.

I stir awake from a deep slumber, but I see it's dark outside. A hand caresses the flat of my stomach, and I tilt my head up to see Vincent watching me.

He's lying on his side, and I'm cocooned in his arms.

I can't remember us going to bed. I can't remember falling asleep either.

I hate crying myself to sleep.

He eases himself up onto his elbow and looks at me. He's taken off his shirt, and there's a bandage going around his waist.

"Oh my God..." I gasp when I see it.

He looks down at himself and shakes his head. "It looks worse than it feels. I'm wearing it for Marguerite's benefit. She insisted. It'll be gone by morning." He gives me a little smile.

"Did you break something when we fell?"

"Maybe."

"We should go to the hospital."

He reaches for my face. "Bellezza, I don't do hospitals. I hate them, and I avoid them if I can. My philosophy is, if I can move, then I can move. I'm fine. Stupid question, but I'm gonna ask it all the same. Are you okay?"

I shake my head. "No... I don't think so, Vincent."

"Talk to me, baby."

"No. You shouldn't be... you shouldn't be next to me." He knows my secrets now.

"I don't want to be anywhere else than next to you," he says, stroking the edge of my jaw.

"Even after what—" He doesn't let me finish. He moves forward and kisses me.

He kisses me in such a sensual way that it fades the worries from my mind, just like always and so much more in this moment.

I kiss him back as he holds me.

"We're those people from the coffee shop again, Ava. Baby...none of the things that happened today happened. We're in bed, and we're that couple. That's what this is. We don't need to be at The Dark Odyssey to live the fantasy. We're here. Will you come with me?" He speaks against my lips, and my soul vibrates with the luxuriated sensation of him.

I imagine it. In that version of us, I'm happy and he's holding me. We're here, and I couldn't love him any more than I do right now.

Love... yes. I do. I truly do love him. I fell hard and sure for him. Right now it's the thing that's keeping me alive.

"Yes..." I whisper.

"What should we do? What to do you want me to do, Bellezza?" he asks.

I pull back slightly and run my fingers over his jaw, holding his gaze so I don't break the fantasy and slip back into the darkness of the real world.

"Tell me, baby. I see it in your eyes."

"Make love to me, Vincent."

"Make love? Now, that's another fantasy I have, Ava... where you give me your heart and soul. Is that what you want?"

"You have them, Vincent. You have me. My heart, body, and soul are all yours."

As he comes to my lips once more, I melt. I dissolve and soften at the feel of his hard lips on mine.

His mouth on mine speaks to me without words that we were so much more than what I thought we were, and I'm pulled into the fantasy of those two people who met at the coffee shop.

He kisses away my fears and nightmares. All of it goes, including my grief. It's just like magic. Soothing, to pacify the pain. The more he touches me, the more it fades, and soon it's gone completely from my mind.

I feel his touch and his lips, and that is all that exists in my world. Him.

I'm swept away as the kiss intensifies, becoming brazen. The kind that holds nothing back. It fills me with that wild need for him again. Wild need mixed with that transcendental desire for each other. We tear at each other's clothes until we're both naked, his lips barely leaving mine.

When passion takes us, it sets my soul on fire and my body comes alive with the energy that pulses from it.

Each touch, each kiss, each whisper of desire sings through my soul and seals me to him.

When his ruthless cock plunges into me, it strips away everything but my need for him, possessing me so I know he's taking the last things I have left. Heart and soul.

I already gave him my body, and as I give it to him again, I hope he knows what he means to me. I tried so hard not to fall for him, and I couldn't stop. Now that I'm so wounded, I need his touch to make me whole. To fix me.

Fix me....

The thought brings the image of that girl who was locked away and pushes through the darkness. My dark knight is light in the darkness, so dark that darkness fears him. He cracks away the shadows surrounding me and her.

And then it happens. Something light drifts in. At first it drifts, then it flows. It's hope, hope that I grab by the reins and allow to take me away from the shadows the monsters created.

We move together as one molded by passion's call to make love.

Then, together, we surrender, and I feel the culmination of ultimate pleasure claim me and heal me. A million glowing stars swirl through me all at once, and love flows through me like liquid fire.

Love I never expected to feel with anyone. Love I never dreamt of feeling with anyone.

I could only feel like this with him. I could only give myself to him.

Only he could break down the barriers I set up, because only he could see how broken I was.

As our breathing stills, he holds me, and I feel loved. I feel it all around me, and I know he feels it too.

He looks at me with it but dips his head, almost avoiding my gaze.

"Please... look at me," I plead.

He does, and his eyes search mine. "I...." He doesn't finish. He doesn't need to. I felt the rest of the words.

I felt the affection in my heart, and I understand why he can't finish.

But I'll absorb the warmth he gives me as he holds me.

For just a little longer, I stay in the fantasy and imagine us as those people.

I know we aren't, and I know I have to leave this world we created entirely.

I'll hold on for as long as I can though. I don't want to leave just yet.

CHAPTER THIRTY-EIGHT

Vincent

The gentle breeze lifts the ends of her hair.

The sunlight beaming down on her face makes her look younger than she is. I keep seeing her as a kid in that picture. That picture was taken a year before all the evil was done to her.

I look at her and wonder how anyone could hurt her.

We're sitting by the river that flows through the grounds of my home. I haven't been out here in months, but I thought today would be good for both Ava and me to go out for a walk and talk.

It's good for my rage.

I've been trying... trying not to lose my head.

The beast inside me went mad with a thirst for blood when she told me what was done to her. As she spoke yesterday and I processed what she was saying, I had a hard time convincing myself to calm the fuck down and not go out on the streets and kill every motherfucker who called themselves Bratva.

I mean it. All of them, starting with her fucking uncle. The only thing that stopped me was her.

She needed me more. She needed to know that I was with her, and I needed to support her. That's what I'm doing now while the boys check things out and come up with a plan. The plan, which is to kill, kill, kill. *Fucking kill.*

They will all pay. I will see to that.

"It's beautiful out here," Ava says.

Ava... the name Juliette suits her. Ava does too, but I wonder if she'll ever use her real name again.

"You like it?" I ask with a little smile, and she smiles back.

"I do. I imagine it in the winter as well. I love winter. In... Russia, it snows all the time. It's freezing, but it... it's nice."

Russia. If she's talking to me about Russia, that means I've helped her in some way. Last night helped.

I made love to her. I felt when she gave herself to me. I don't know if she knew I gave myself to her too. A thing I never thought I'd be able to do again. Not ever.

"Snow's a rare thing in Sicily. In fact, I don't think I've ever seen it. I'm more of a tropical person. Russia's cold, Sicily's hot. Cold and hot just like you and me, right?" I smile.

She nods when she pulls in a breath. I know she's gearing up to talk to me. "My father... well, Mark. I mean Mark. I guess you know a lot about me now to know he wasn't my real father."

"Yeah. I know."

"How'd you know?"

"The same way I found you. I have friends who can do a lot of different things. I could sense that something bad happened to you, Ava, but honestly, I was checking things out with your father from a few weeks back because he couldn't remember what he did. It was then that I found out he changed his name, and that let us to you too when it came down to it."

"He was my parents' best friend. But he was in love with my mother. They grew up together, and she chose to marry my real father. Mark watched over us and would do anything for any of us. He was the brother my father wished he had." She tenses up, and I know it's hard for her to talk about. I reach across and take her hand.

"Baby, I don't want you to go down that road again. I'm guessing the reason why your uncle wants you dead is because you know the truth. You guys didn't die in a fire. He killed your parents."

She nods. "Yeah. He killed my parents, but the thing is, if anyone in Russia knew the truth, he'd lose everything. My father had dealings with the president. He worked for the Russian president. That's how it was set up. I don't know much, but my uncle wanted the power and the wealth. He was the eldest and was furious that my grandfather wanted my father to take over leadership of the brotherhood. Mark told me that years passed, and he was always trying to infiltrate. I didn't know he was so evil."

Fuck. This guy really is a nasty piece of work.

"My parents were always heavily guarded when they travelled. We went to visit my aunts in France, and our flight got cancelled. I had a ballet performance and told them I'd die if I missed it. My father found a way to get us to St. Petersburg, but we didn't have guards. They were supposed to meet us there, link up with us in a few days. We were at a house that belonged to my grandfather. We got there, and I did my performance, but everything changed before the sun went down. The guards never got the message, and Mark and his sons were away on business. My father's bodyguard double-crossed him and saw it as a way to get to us. No guards, which meant we were left open to attack."

Her hands start shaking. But she continues talking. "No one knew where we were. No one knew where we'd gone, and it was a month before Mark and his sons found me. They came and found me locked up in the basement. It was one of Dmitri's cigars that started a fire. Mark came with men, and my uncle's men killed them all. The fire made it difficult. We got trapped in the basement. That's where Mark's eldest son; Maksim, died. Between him and Sasha, they got me out after my uncle and his men left. We knew it was a lucky break, so we left the country. We knew what it meant if any of us were found. Death. So much death, all because of a ballet performance I could have missed."

"Ava...is this the accident that stopped you from dancing?" I ask, understanding the story as it continues to piece together.

"Yes... I always wondered, what if I'd just missed that one performance? None of it would have happened. We would have stayed in France and left when the storm blew over. We would have made it back, and all I would have lost would have been a performance."

"Ava, I've learned that we can't think like that. There's no way you could have possibly known that." I home in on Salvatore's words to me the other week. "It seems to me that your uncle would have found a way to do whatever he had planned. No matter where you were. That was just one opportunity. That's all it was. These things happen when you're dealing with people like that. There's nothing you can do about it."

"I appreciate you saying that. It's hard not to blame myself. For years, I felt I owed Mark my life. Now he's dead."

That's why she offered herself to me. She sacrificed herself, putting herself right back in a similar position she was previously in.

I'm not like those men. I'm ashamed of the way I behaved most times. I hope she never thought of me like that. *Like them.*

"Now you know... That's the story. That's the reason for everything. That's why they want to kill me. They stand to lose billions and their lives, Vincent. It's not like I'm just some person. I'm Roberto Lobonov's daughter. People will know me the minute I dye my hair back the color it used to be. It's a strong testament of what happened if I give it."

"Have you ever thought of going back to do just that?" I'm just curious.

She's shaking her head before I can even finish.

"No. I can't. I'm not strong like that. Do I want revenge for my parents' death? Yes, of course, I do. Every day, I avenge them in my mind in some ways. Sometimes I even save them. Sometimes it all feels like a bad dream that just came to screw with me. Then I remember it's real and my uncle is a man of serious power. Mark was so distraught from the loss of Maksim, that I think part of him died in the fire too. Then, when Sasha died, it was like he was gone. Part of me hoped he would get strong and avenge my parents' death and overthrow my uncle. The more he deteriorated, the more I realized that was never going to happen."

I give her hands a gentle squeeze.

It must have been so hard for her.

"I'm going to fix things, Ava. I'll get you your vengeance," I promise.

Her gaze clings to mine. "Vincent... I'm scared because I don't want you to get hurt. You've lost so much. You have a son to worry about, and you can't worry about me."

"It's not up for discussion, doll. I'm just telling you. I can't let them take you, and I can't let them get away with what they did to you. It's not in my nature to let a thing like that slide."

Maybe I let love in and it made me crazy. Pa hasn't called me crazy yet, and I've seen him twice today. Both times, he fell in line helping out. The same as everyone else. We're doing what we always do when we have situations like this.

I'm just waiting on a location, and then I'm gone. I don't plan to wait for the enemy to strike.

She throws her arms around me and hugs me hard. "Thank you. Please... be safe, Vincent. Please be safe. I don't know what I'd do if something happened to you."

I hold her close to me and think of that too.

Yesterday was close for me. That bomb could have taken me out. It nearly did.

We stand, and I slip my arm around her as we start heading back to the house.

As we get to the concrete path, I hear a helicopter. Then I see it coming in the distance, and two more.

It's very uncommon to see helicopters in these parts, and since I'm on high alert, everything is suspicious to me.

"Ava, get in the house! Go to Nick. He'll take you down to the basement," I shout, and she runs into the house.

I'm glad she does because as the helicopters get close, I realize I was right to be suspicious. I run toward the house too and signal everyone. All my guards are spread out with guns at the ready while the helicopters lower and men with gas masks start jumping down. They look like army guys. Bullets start flying, and I run inside to make sure Timothy, my mother, and Marguerite are safe.

Everyone has a task. Nick is to take Ava to the safe room down in the cellars. Gabe and Salvatore are muscle. Pa is to contact Claudius. There's about fifty men on the grounds that are skilled to deal with these guys, but not if we're vastly outnumbered. And we are.

Fuck... there are too many of them, and they're all coming in the house. I shield myself behind a pillar to dodge the bullets that fly my way and fire back when I can. Timothy was upstairs with Marguerite.

These fuckers. They've attacked my home.

In the height of everything, I see a haze of green gas filling the room. Tony drops down first like a rag doll, then a few others follow.

When I see that, I run, covering my mouth and nose so I don't inhale the gas.

I have to get to my boy.

I leap up the stairs, taking them two at a time, and run into his room. He's not there.

Shit... Fuck. God, please tell me they got to the safe room. I don't know where they were in the house. Marguerite and Ma know the doors that open up to it. I had them installed to mirror the setup at my parents' house.

"Vinny!" Pa calls out. He's to my left coming out of the library. He collapses, and a trail of green smoke follows through the door.

I run across the platform to the other side of the house. That's where I find Salvatore on the ground and Gabe trying to revive him. He's barely able to shake him before the gas gets him too.

It must be some kind of knockout gas.

It swirls over me, tickling my nose. There's no way that I can avoid being affected by it. The men had on gas masks.

Clever.

That bastard. I give him credit. Ilya had to basically tie us up to beat us. Couldn't fight like a real man. At the end of the day, though, what does it matter? The end result is the result you want, and that's what he's getting.

He did say I wouldn't like it if I pissed him off. He wasn't joking. I dash back to the second floor in an attempt to get to the entrance to the safe room by the bookshelf. Then I hear it. The sound of my little boy's cry.

I look through the window in an instant as his cries gets louder. It's a loud screech like he's in pain. My heart shatters when I see Dmitri carrying him. The men file back into the helicopters.

Dmitri gets in with my boy.

"Noooooooo!" I wail.

I hoist myself up through the window and jump down onto the roof.

Adrenaline fuels my moves, but everything is a hazy blur.

The green gas must have got me too.

"Timothy! No... bring him back!" My lips are moving, but I don't know what I'm saying. I lift my arm to do something, but it drops heavily to my side, and I drop to my knees, sliding down into the crevice of the rooftop as the helicopters take off.

"No!... No."

Darkness swallows me, taking me whole.

Dark like the deepest part of a nightmare where I just lost my child.

CHAPTER THIRTY-NINE

Vincent

I'm standing at the door again.

The door to the old house.

So, this must be a dream. No... it's that nightmare, and I don't want to go inside the house.

I know what's waiting for me inside.

I know she's waiting for me.

I can't do it. I can't keep doing this to myself. I can't keep holding on to this memory of death, trapped in limbo like a spirit chained to a plane of torture.

My hands move to the door handle, and I turn it against my will. Against the fact that I don't want to go inside this house ever again.

The door clicks as I push it open. Taking a step inside, I see it's different. The men aren't there on the ground with bullet holes in their bodies. There's no one here. There are no bullet holes in the wall, and someone's in the kitchen.

The radio is playing like it usually is when I get home. Sorcha likes that love song channel. That's what it's on now, and there's humming. It sounds like her, but I dare not believe it could be.

I walk right up to the kitchen door and stop before I get there, worried that this is a new kind of crazy. Like it really happened this time, and I lost my mind.

I can hear, though, and something inside me wants to see.

I push the door open, and there she is making coffee.

Sorcha's wearing the little shirt dress I got her for Christmas, and her hair looks like she's just had it done at the salon. As always, she smiles when she sees me.

"Vinny, look at you. You look tired," Sorcha says and comes up to me. She stands on the tips of her toes and gives me a kiss.

"Babe, you..."

She saunters back over to the coffee machine and looks over in anticipation. I don't know what I'm going to say though.

"What?"

"You died," I whisper.

For a moment, I wish with everything inside me that this could be real. That she didn't die. That all that horror that happened was the nightmare I just woke from. But when she smiles and looks away, I know this can't be real.

"I still think the kitchen needs to be redone. Something more earthy. I like neutral colors. It calms the soul."

"Sorcha..."

She comes back over to me and reaches up to touch my face. "I meant what I said that day."

"Which day?"

"When we first brought Timothy home and you did that video. You are the love of my life and I love you."

"I love you too."

"I know. That's why I need you to wake up. Timothy needs you. They all need you. Vincent, please wake up."

Wake up...

Her smile fades, then she fades before me as my eyes flutter open.

I take a deep breath and find myself staring up at the ceiling.

"Vincent." Ava grasps my hand as I stir, but then she pulls away. Tears stream down her cheeks.

"Hey, you're awake," Salvatore says. He walks up to me with caution in his expression.

One look at the two of them, and I remember.

"Timothy," I gasp and bolt upright, nearly falling over. This shit they gassed us up with is still in my system. Salvatore catches me as I stumble over. "Fuck. They have my son."

"Sit down, Vincent," Salvatore says, pushing me back down to sit. "He's okay. Ilya wants you to call. He left a message to call him when you wake up."

Ava starts crying harder. I look to her knowing she blames herself. It's not her fault though. It's mine. What the fuck am I going to do? What the motherfucking hell am I really going to do?

"Get me a phone," I demand.

Salvatore takes out his phone and gives me a piece of paper with a phone number on it.

I dial the number, and Ilya answers on the first ring.

Fucker.

"Wonderful, looks like you're ready to take me seriously," he says.

"You give me my boy back, you motherfucker. I'll fucking hack off your head if you don't give him back."

"And I'll kill him if you don't give me the girl. Looks like we both have requests. You're just being greedy by wanting them both."

I look at Ava and can't believe it's come to this. A matter of choice. This bastard is making me choose between my son and my girl. *My girl.* There I go again making mistakes.

What am I doing though?

"You fucker, you know this is all wrong. How the fuck can you take him? He's a baby!" I roar.

I don't know why I bother. The fucking words fall on deaf ears when it comes to men like him. Look at what he did to Ava. He is truly evil, and this bastard has my son.

"There's always a way to get what you want, Vincent Giordano. I'll tell you what. Looks like you need to sleep on it a little more. I'll call in the morning. You can tell me what your decision is then. Nine o'clock."

It's him who hangs up on me this time.

When he does, Ava walks out, and I try to rush to her.

I may be wobbling, but I'm still faster than her. I grab her arm before she gets to the door.

"I'm going to get him," Ava cries. "Don't you dare stop me. They want me. Let me go."

"Stop it. I'll find a way." I'm talking out of my ass, pulling words from the air because I don't have the answer. I don't know what way I'll find, but I know I have to find one. Men like him don't trade. They make their mark by teaching a lesson. If she goes, I lose them both.

"What way? What can you do? Vincent, you know there's no way around this. He wants me," she says with a firmness I've never seen in her before.

I shake my head free of the daze from whatever shit they knocked us out with and pull her upstairs.

Thank fuck she comes because I don't want a scene. The fucking shit has already hit the fan, and I need clarity to figure things out. I can't have the others looking at me. Guilt like never before is already weighing on my soul. My boy is the last thing I have left in this world to live for, and he's not here.

The fucking enemy has him, and I know they won't hesitate to kill him.

I take her to my room and practically throw her on the bed.

"Stay there. You stay there and do not move," I tell her.

"Vincent… you know this is wrong. You can't keep me in here when I could be the only thing to save him. They want me. Let me go. Just let me go," she pleads.

"I can't," I answer, and it feels like it comes straight from my heart. There has to be a way.

I leave her in there, locking the door. It's the first time I've ever locked her in.

I rest against the wall and bring my hand to my head. What am I going to do?

They have my son. They took my son.

I can't allow them to kill my son. I can't let that happen to him. I just can't.

If I do... I'm dead.

CHAPTER FORTY

AVA

He's locked the door.

I'm locked in here, and I can't stand it. I can't stand knowing that I could be trying to do something, yet I'm just here.

I'm the answer to this mess, yet I've been locked in here for the last couple of hours watching day turn to night. Not doing anything, just sitting on the bed watching and waiting.

Blaming myself as usual.

It's all my fault again.

The events of the past were things I blamed myself for, and they weren't exactly a direct result of me. They were all occurrences that happened indirectly. This is different.

This is completely direct.

Ilya wants me. He wants me dead, and he's taken Timothy to force us into making that happen.

Do I trust him? Never. Do I believe he'll just hand over the baby in exchange for me? No.

But I think anything is worth a try. Timothy is just a baby.

Tears roll down my cheeks as I think of how terrified the poor baby must be. I've come into this home and caused a complete upheaval. There was already loss in their lives, and I came along causing a stir.

The phone next to me on the nightstand starts ringing, startling me. It's been silent in here with only the sounds of my cries within these walls.

The phone rings out and starts again.

I'm surprised no one answered it, given the situation.

It does the same thing, and I answer just so I don't miss something that might be important.

"Hello," I say, steadying my voice.

"Hello, my niece," comes the voice that fills my nightmares.

I always hear the other men laughing and see their movements. Him, though, I hear his voice the same as I am now.

"Give the baby back, you bastard!" I cry.

"Shhh shhhhh. There, there, pet, I'm offering you the chance to do something with your worthless life. If you come to me now, you might be able to save this poor child." He chuckles, and I can just imagine his wicked face. I saw enough of it yesterday. He looked older with his silver hair and more evil.

"How will I get to you?" I ask. I don't bother to contemplate the fact that Vincent told me he'd find a way. He's used to criminals, but he doesn't know my uncle. He doesn't know that this man is the essence of evil and won't think twice about killing a child.

The sooner anyone can get Timothy back, the better.

"There's a door through the closet just to your left," he answers. A chill runs down my spine. Fuck... fucking hell, he can see inside the house. How? When would they have been able to put cameras in?

Maybe it's not that though. Maybe they're just using what's already here. Shit. That means they can see and hear what everyone else is doing, what they're planning.

"Juliette..." he seethes and says my real name. It's the third time now that I've heard it in ten years. This time, though, doesn't have that dreadful effect it had yesterday. I feel empowered and ready to face him. "I can see you. I can see your mind as you realize that I can see you. Don't you fucking dare try anything, or that's it. This is a chance I won't offer again."

"I'm listening," I say. I school my face and push my shoulders back. He's not going to faze me. I won't allow him to. This man took so much away from me. I can't allow him to add more guilt to my heart.

"There's a door through the closet. It's open. It leads to the safe room. Just before you get to the safe room is another door that leads out to the back of the house. Go there and head into the woods. We'll be there waiting by the gates for you. Go through them. We've disabled the cameras there."

Oh God... I can do this. I can.

"You will give the baby back when I get to you? I won't go anywhere until you tell me you will. He has nothing to do with this."

"I will give him back," he says, and I pray. I pray that this one time he might have some heart, something human to keep his end of the deal.

That's all I want. He can do whatever he wants with me after. I was a ghost anyway.

I died a long time ago. I've been a ghost in a shell of a body I called Ava Knight.

"I'm on my way."

As I walk through the woods, I keep thinking what will happen when Vincent discovers I left.

I keep wondering what he'll think... how I knew about the entrance to the safe passage through his room.

I hope he'll understand why I did it. I'm sure he'd do the same thing for Timothy if he could. Somehow, I think of his mother; Sorcha, and what she must have gone through when she died. I think she would like that I tried to get him back. Once again, it's the only thing I can do.

I think it's the only thing anyone can do.

I just wish it didn't feel like I was spitting in the faces of all the people who've tried to help me prevent this very thing I'm walking to.

Death.

As I walk, my legs heavy, my heart heavier, I feel like such a disappointment to them all.

Dad, Maksim, Sasha... Vincent.

They all tried to save me. As I walk to what I know will result in my death, voices of the dead call to me to run away. *Turn back and run away*, they all say.

My heart drives me forward in hopes of saving a little boy.

I see the gate ahead, and as I approach, a bright light goes on. A car light.

I can see it now. It's a black Sedan.

A shadowy figure moves against the dark. When I get closer, I see it's Dmitri. Yuri is driving the car.

I unlock the gate and walk through, not bothering to acknowledge Dmitri. I no longer care for myself. Fear is so embedded in me that I just want this to be over quickly.

"I thought that was you, Juliette Lobonov," the asshole says, but I still don't look at him. I still ignore him.

He opens the door to the back of the car, and I slide in next to the devil, my uncle, who's smiling at me.

"Very good, so glad to have your cooperation," Ilya says. The asshole and animal he is reaches across and runs his hand over my thigh. "I think we'll have more fun with you this time before we kill you."

Bile rises in my throat, and my skin blazes with that heat and cold mixed together as he continues to touch me.

"I will kill you myself this time," he adds.

"The baby. When will you call them to make the exchange?" That's all I care about.

"Juliette, you never were that bright, were you?" He chuckles and gives me a wide, wicked grin that makes me glower at him.

"What do you mean? What are you going to do?" Even now, the voices of the dead scream to me.

"I'm going to do the thing you knew I was going to do, which is nothing."

My breath hitches, and tears pour from my eyes. I ball my fists and punch him. I try to open the door, but Ilya is fast and strong. He grabs me and hits me with the back of his gun, making me see stars. I slump down against the door, holding my head and feeling the wetness of blood.

"Stupid bitch, that's the last time you try something like that. I will give that baby back after I teach Vincent Giordano a lesson he'll never forget because all three of you will be dead before the next moon rises."

He hits me again, and I black out in an instant.

CHAPTER FORTY-ONE

Vincent

She's gone. She's actually fucking gone...

Christian walks over to the security panel on the CCTV and switches everything off.

We watched it. Watched her get the phone call and watched her walk through my closet and into the passage that led to the safe room.

I watched as far as her going outside, out through the side door and into the woods, then we lost her.

"They won't be able to see now," Christian says.

I pick up a glass paperweight from the desk and launch it at the fucking wall. It smashes, and the glass goes everywhere.

They all look at me.

Christian, my brothers, Claudius, and Pa.

"This is fucking shit!" I shout.

"You wouldn't have known, Vincent," Christian imparts. I look at him, and he holds my gaze.

He figured straightaway that my CCTV was being hacked.

That and the fucking phones in the house. Those fuckers snuck her out right from under my nose, and they took my boy too. What the fuck was the point of me setting up this fortress of a place with all the security in the world only to have this shit happen to me?

I reach for my phone and call the fucker again.

This is my hundredth call since we discovered Ava was gone. He's not answering, though, and I don't know what the fuck's going to happen now because I've practically lost any leverage I had over Ilya.

"Vincent, you have to calm down," Pa says. He comes closer to me and places his hands on my shoulders. "We'll figure it out. We'll figure out something. I've got the secret squad trying to locate them and all the boys on the street doing the same. Everyone's doing their best."

I nod and look at the solemn faces surrounding me.

Things are bad, and they know it. I know it.

I don't think I'm going to see my boy alive again, and as for Ava... she's dead.

There was never a question about what would happen if Ilya got his hands on her. Death.

What must he be doing to her?

She's been gone for hours, and Timothy the whole day. He could be dead too.

I blow out a ragged breath and move out of Pa's grasp.

I can't deal with this.

I walk out and head outside, where the cold night air stings my cheeks. I lean against the wall feeling the weight of the world on my shoulders.

I don't move until a hand rests on my back, and I turn to see Salvatore.

"Vin..." he says.

"I don't know what to do. It's death again, isn't it...?"

"Let's try not to think like that." He nods. I lower to the ground with my back against the wall, and he sits next to me.

We stay like that all night. No one comes out to us because

there's nothing to tell us. No updates, no news, and in this instance, no news isn't good news. It's all bad.

As the clock strikes nine, I ring that bastard's phone again.

When he answers, I'm not sure what emotion I should feel. Happy that he answered, furious as fuck that he didn't answer before, or furious as fuck about the whole situation. I feel all of it at once.

"You motherfucker!" I shout into the phone.

I have the same faces glaring at me as last night. They've all been here offering their support in whatever way they can.

"Do calm yourself. I have no reason to speak to you now. I'm doing you a favor."

Prick... he's fucking playing with me.

"I want my son back, and I want Ava."

"I will allow you to try to get your son back. You pissed on us, and this is us shitting on you. It will be a pleasure to watch you try to save your boy. Didn't think of him, did you, when you thought you could be all high and mighty taking charge?"

"Where?" I demand. There's no point entertaining any conversation with this asshole.

"Peyton Prison. Get there for midday on the mark, and we'll tell you what to do. I don't have to tell you to come alone, and no funny business. You won't like what will happen if you try to screw with us."

Once again, he hangs up, cutting me off before I can say another word.

I slam the phone down on the table and look back to everyone.

"I have to go to Peyton Prison at noon. This fucker wants to kill me too." Obviously, it's that because I can bet my ass whatever plan he has in store for me won't include me coming out and getting my boy back alive. He didn't even mention Ava.

Claudius steps forward. "I know that place. We could work that to our advantage," he says.

"I'm supposed to come alone. He'll fucking know if we try any shit he won't like."

"If I'm right, the oldest section of the prison has no surveillance. We can go through there and meet you in the middle. I know the way."

"I can tap into their surveillance the same way they used ours here," Christian says. "I can do it. I just need another pair of eyes to get set up."

"Me," Salvatore says. He and Christian are the two tech geniuses in the family.

"Looks like we have a plan," Pa says.

I want to hope, but I don't know if I can. I certainly won't give up, though, before I've even began if I have a shot.

"Okay, let's do this."

It will be on me when I get in. Everything will be on me once I step inside the building. That's the part I worry about.

What will happen?

What has this bastard got planned for me?

Another day, another enemy ready to kill and take from me.

It's the story of my fucking life.

CHAPTER FORTY-TWO

Ava

"Hello, sleepyhead. Boy, you sure love to sleep. Thought you were dead." Ilya laughs.

I wake to the horrible face of my uncle looming before me.

He reveals crooked teeth that make me cringe, and his eyes crinkle with deep crow's feet.

I look around. I'm outside in an old courtyard with overgrown vines and a field of unkempt grass. I don't know where the hell I am, though, in terms of location.

It looks like an abandoned school, or... a prison. The building before me has windows with bars on them. Most of the glass in some of the windows without the bars are broken.

My location is the least of my worries as I look down and realize I'm tied to a pole. There's rope wrapped tightly around me, starting at the top of my shoulders and running down my body. I'm well and truly screwed.

"Where am I?" I seethe.

"That's none of your concern," he says, stepping away from me.

I start panting. It's difficult to breathe against the ropes though. What is he going to do to me?

What has he already done to me?

I've been asleep since I got in that car. Whatever he gave me knocked me out good. It was night; now it's day. Seems like it's late morning.

What did they do to me during the night? It's awkward to feel between my thighs. I don't feel sore, but that doesn't mean they didn't touch me.

"Did you touch me?" I ask the words. Bile rises in my throat at the same time, churning my stomach.

Ilya laughs that horrible laugh and runs a hand through his gray head of hair.

"I didn't. Much as I wanted to, it's no fun if you're asleep. You can't scream then. I can't take pleasure in your cries for help, knowing that no one will save you. I can't take satisfaction in fucking your brains out knowing it will damage you."

What a sick bastard. What a fucking sick bastard.

"Why are you so evil? You're supposed to be my uncle." My breath hitches, and the words tumble out on a splutter.

"I don't care about family relations. I do what I want to do and take what I want. Dole out punishment the way I want. You and your worthless mother were thorns in my side. My idiot brother wanted to be good for her. Imagine it: a good criminal? Unheard of. He wanted to be a slave to the president, do as he says and do it when he's told. Jump and ask how high. And he wanted me to do the same fucking thing."

"We had enough wealth," I spit back. We had so much, and so did he, but he wanted to be in charge. God knows how wealthy he must be now.

"My dear Juliette, the thing about power is what you do with it. You never settle for less than what you can achieve. Never be under anyone's thumb. Your idiot father was happy to take orders. It was enough for him. I ended that shit show as soon as I could. Nothing will ever make me happier than the way I hacked off his head that day and burned your bitch mother."

Tears threaten to fall as I remember it all. I've been in so much pain since, and he's taken so much pleasure in their deaths. I hang my head, but he catches my face and lifts it back up.

"Today is another joyous day. I took pride in cutting out Alessandro's eyes and hanging his ass myself for his treachery," he taunts.

It was him who killed Dad. The tears fall now. I can imagine how he must have suffered. It must have been so awful and painful. Oh God. I should have told him to hide when I sent the messages. I was just being so careful I didn't think. I certainly never thought they'd find Dad that quickly. It all happened so fast.

"You animal. You fucking animal!"

"Yes, I am a fucking animal. You people seriously had me fooled. All these long years you were here and not dead. Things have a way of working out in the criminal world, no matter where you are on this planet." He laughs a crude, sardonic laugh and tightens his fingers on my jaw, digging his nails into the skin. "Whether you're in Russia or on the arm of a crime boss."

He's talking about Vincent. I think of Timothy then and start to cry harder.

"What did you do with the baby?"

"Don't worry about him, Juliette. His father will get the chance to save him while you can watch. I wonder if he knew what kind of whore you were," he jeers with that laugh again. It pains me to my soul, and I try to look away. "Awww, look at this... The look of love. You little whore. I forgot how much you like older men. If I didn't want you dead so badly, I'd give you another round in the sac."

He lets go of my face and smiles.

"Your death will finally set me free. I'll watch you burn like your useless mother."

Burn...
That's what he's going to do to me.
Burn me alive, just like Ma.
I start sobbing, and he laughs harder.

CHAPTER FORTY-THREE

Vincent

Peyton Prison was said to house some of the most dangerous and psychotic prisoners in the State of Illinois.

The official reason for closure was down to lack of funding. The unofficial was actually because of the unsavory practices that went on within the walls. Lobotomies were just the start of the type of things doctors would do to prisoners who displayed any form of mental health condition. In the end I imagined that the doctors were the psychos looking for any excuse to carry out their experiments.

The shutdown of this joint opened up the door for other types of psychos like Ilya.

It's not the first time I've heard of the place being used by criminals of the underground. It certainly won't be the last.

As I walk through the rusty front gates with my heart beating so wildly in my chest and my nerves on end, I pray for the first time that Marguerite's pleas to the Lord will help me.

It's the first time I've turned my sights that way because I get the feeling that I'm going to need miracles in abundance.

Two guards come through the large wooden doors that would have been the entrance to the main reception.

Two more come out carrying guns. They aim them at me, then Dmitri steps out with a smug-as-fuck expression. *Asshole.* I hope I put a fucking bullet in his head before the day is out.

Fucker... look at him. He's got a bright smile on his face and is looking at me like he has me right where he wants. I hope I'll get a minute with him, any of them. They all hurt Ava. Him though... it was him she looked at the most on the night of the party. She glanced at Yuri, but Dmitri terrified her.

"Hello, *Boss*," he mocks.

I'm not going to entertain his conversation with any kind of pleasantries.

"Cut the shit. Take me to Ilya," I tell him.

"Wow, testy, testy. You really are a prick."

"Yes, I am." It's important I stop talking to him now. I don't want to lose my shit and blow my chances. That rage inside me, though, is hard to calm in this shit storm.

"Search him," Dmitri orders, and the guards start searching me with a pat down on my sides to make sure I'm not carrying any weapons. As if I would be that stupid.

I don't know who would be. When we enter shit situations like this, the enemy's weapons are what we look to take the first chance we get.

My weapons are going to literally be whatever I can get my hands on when the fights starts and the bullets fly.

That's when the guys—my backup—will come.

That's what I hope for, anyhow.

I don't actually know how it will all go down. Or if I'll make it out with Timothy and Ava.

Satisfied that I'm not a prick with any weapon concealed up my ass, Dmitri calls off his dogs and they nudge me forward to go inside the building.

It smells old and unused. It has been decommissioned for the last twenty years or so.

These guys look comfortable, though, like they've been here

awhile. It's not uncommon to use a place like this that's supposed to be derelict for other purposes if you want to do things under wraps.

I just pray that the surveillance is as we think it is.

I left Christian and Georgiou on it. Christian assured me that the place is as Claudius said it was. The older section of the building has no surveillance, so that's we're my guys will be coming up. The section with the surveillance is where Christian will be hacking into and should be in there now.

"Vincent," he says in the earpiece I'm wearing. I at least have that to take some comfort in. I walk on like I can't hear him. "Brace yourself. What you're about to see is not good."

Holy shit. Fuck... I wish he would tell me more than that.

"The guys are on the way, Vincent," Christian says in my ear. "They're in the building making their way to you. Hang tight."

Hang tight? My thoughts of where they are, are stolen away. I'm not left wondering for too long about what shit I'll have to face.

I'm led into a massive courtyard, and my stomach twists into knots when my gaze lands on the horror ahead of me. Off in the distance in the field are Timothy and Ava, about thirty feet apart.

Timothy is in a glass tank. He's standing on a stump and tied up to a pole. Water starts to fill the tank. He's crying and screaming.

Ava is tied to a pole. I can't quite figure out what it is they're doing with her. She sees me. Her gaze lands on me, and even from here I notice the sadness in her eyes.

I ball my fists, seething at the sight.

"See what I got for you?" booms a voice. It's Ilya.

I turn my head to the left and see him on the stone platform the guards would have used back in the day to watch over the prisoners.

He walks down the wide steps with a bright smile on his face. This is the first time we've met in person.

The last glimpse of him was just that.

The fucker looks just as twisted as he did in the back of that car.

"I want them back!" I shout, and he laughs.

"You Italians are all the same. So strong-willed and of the belief that you're above everything and everyone else. Not so. You're part of my game now. I'm calling the shots. Not you." He chuckles and tilts his head to the side.

"You son of a bitch. How can you do that to a child?" I don't know why I bother to ask. It's a very foolish question.

Out the corner of my eye I keep an eye out on the tank. It's filling up. It's big and could take a little time, but it doesn't take much for a child to drown.

"Do I actually look like I care? This is a game to me. You are the joke of it. The toy. This is what we do to fuckers who think they can screw with us," he declares and presses the button of some device I'm just noticing in his hands.

As he does, a little wall of fire shoots up from the ground about six feet away from Ava then starts spreading over the grass like dominoes falling, setting alight the ground as it moves. It looks like they've poured something flammable on the ground for the direction and pattern it moves. It's too uniform for it not to be.

Ava screams, and my heart stops beating. They want to burn her and drown Timothy.

"I thought I'd make it interesting since you want to save her so badly. I wonder if you'll try to save them both. Or will you save the girl and leave your son to drown?" Ilya taunts. "First, though, you got to fight. We're Russians. We love a good fight." He laughs.

The crackle of glass turns me around as a guy with a tub full of broken glass approaches us. He sets the tub on the bench table nearby. Another guy follows with another tub. This one has some white sticky solution in it.

Dmitri smiles wider, devilish, and starts wrapping his wrists with a white hemp cloth and knotting it in a manner I've seen common to Muay Thai fighters.

He walks over to the bench and dips his hands in the solution, which I'm sure now is glue, and then he dips his hands in the glass and laughs.

I remember my first thoughts when I met him. I thought he looked like a cage fighter.

I know what sort of fighting we'll be doing.

The dirty kind. And it seems that I'll be using my bare hands.

CHAPTER FORTY-FOUR

Vincent

"Can't talk big now, can you, *Boss*?" Dmitri laughs and throws a punch my way.

I dodge it and back away.

We're down in the clearing at the bottom of the steps. The men have formed a ring around us, and Ilya is still at the top of the steps, watching.

Dmitri comes for me again with a one-two punch that I dodge one more time.

I don't fight back yet because I'm analyzing his moves and seeing how good he is. My guess so far is that he's done this a lot before.

"Come on, you pussy, fight me!" he roars.

"You calling me a pussy? I'll fuck you up with my bare hands. Look what you have to do to try and beat me, motherfucker," I spit back.

He doesn't like that and comes for me again with a jab, leaving himself open, wide open.

I take the chance to land my knee in his chest and extend my leg to his face. It happens so quickly that it catches him off guard, shocking him, and he stumbles.

Now he knows I have skill too.

I can give as much as I get in a fight. It's always harder, though, when I fight someone with pro skills. They're good, definitely better than those without, but what makes them a match for me is resilience.

What gives me some edge, however, is that I don't play by any rules or expectations. I fight raw from the streets, meaning I can be dirty too.

I can be. It's just better when I'm not distracted. Ava and Timothy are across the clearing from me and these bastards can do anything. Ilya could decide to set Ava ablaze and that would be it, or he could flood the fucking tank with my baby.

Or, one of them could shoot me dead now.

I need the guys to get here. I have no idea where they are. They set out two hours earlier than me, but taking into account as to where they had to enter the area unseen, it took them longer to get here. Then there was the whole aspect of coming up with some kind of plan and hacking the fuck out of the systems.

I watch for my face when Dmitri launches at me. I'm sure he won't hesitate to mess me up. He'll fucking do it and probably use the same glass to cut my throat.

He kicks me, getting me hard in my stomach, and I stagger backwards. I have to jump out of the way to avoid the punch he was about to land in my throat. That would have killed me.

Fuck.

Like an animal, he rushes me with his teeth bared, and I send a roundhouse kick to his midsection. The combo of his forward speed and my own has more effect. It knocks him back. Then a side sweep sends him to the ground.

This is it, my opening. I just needed a way. I jump on him and land one fist after another in his face. I manage to stun him enough to immobilize him.

Earlier, I spotted a knife in his pocket. I allow him to punch me and take the blow of the glass on his wrists but only so I can grab his knife.

The fucker doesn't see my next move until it's too late. Way too late.

He only catches a glimpse of the knife. It flickers in the sunlight, the metal shimmering as I slice his throat open. Blood gushes out in abundance. It's not enough though. This man is one evil motherfucker.

"This is for Ava," I tell him and stab him straight in his heart.

The minute I do, his eyes bulge wide and the light leaves them as he dies.

Normally, I don't like looking at that. I don't like seeing that last spark of life go. I'm not a sick fuck like most who enjoy killing. On this occasion, however, I will take the accomplishment.

Just as I preempted, the men around attempt to come for me, so I grab Dmitri's gun and end a few. There are too many of them though.

"You fucker!" Ilya wails. He pulls out his own gun to shoot me, but the gun flies out of his hand as he cocks it.

I look to the right and see Salvatore and some of the others coming through like the cavalry coming to my rescue, guns blazing.

I don't waste time. I can't. Timothy and Ava need me. I run like my feet are attached to lightning bolts.

I run with everything inside me watching the horrific nightmare scene ahead.

Ava to my left, Timothy to my right.

I get an ounce of relief when I see Pa and Nick jump over the wall across the field. They're closer to Timothy than I am now, but I'm still bounding toward him like a mad man.

I'm forced to stop in my tracks when the wall of fire surrounding Ava shoots up, rising well over twenty feet into the air.

That sick bastard. That's Ilya's doing. Fucking with me to make sure I'm more fucked than I already am.

"Papa!" my boy cries, snapping me out of the panic that's taken me and I look to his tank and see Nick trying to get him out.

The combination of Ava's screams and Timothy's wails pierces through my soul. My parental instincts are calling to me to get my boy out of danger while my love for this woman is imploring me to do the same for her.

"Vinny, get Ava!" Pa shouts. The urgency in his voice cuts through the haze of contemplation. "We'll get Timothy. Get her. She's going to die."

Die...

I look back to her at the same time her screams stop. That's what moves my feet and I continue my pursuit to her, hoping like fuck Pa and Nick can get my baby out of danger.

The fire wall surrounding Ava is even bigger now, and dense. That fucker must have used gasoline or some sort of powder. It's so hot my throat is dry and my skin burns. I'll have to jump through to save her. It's the only way.

I whip off my jacket, cover my head, backpedal a few paces then leap into the wall of fire.

When I go through I see Ava slumped lifeless against the pole and I pray she's still alive. The fire hasn't reached her yet, but being enclosed in the infernal heat is enough. I race to her and thank my lucky stars when she lifts her head and looks at me.

When I get to her, her lips part and she shakes her head.

"Save the baby... leave me. Please...." she mutters, once again thinking of herself last.

I don't answer. There's no time. I get to work on the knots on the rope tying her up and loosen them. As I do, she crumples in my arms, and I pick her up. She can barely stand. The fire is too hot now. My lungs are tight, burning, and I'm weak myself.

"Vincent... save Timothy. Leave me."

"Come on Ava. Let's go," I answer and turn my attention back to the wall of fire.

I'll have to go in the way I came. Jump through it.

My jacket is already burned and damaged from my entry. I pick her up, holding her close, and cover our heads. Then I run faster than the last time. Adrenaline pumping through my body and Timothy on my mind.

One leap through the fire, and we make it. *Barely.*

My clothes catch fire. I drop Ava and roll on the ground.

"Vincent!" It's Gabe. He sprays me with a liquid that puts the fire out.

I'm alive. Jesus, I'm alive. I get up and look over to the tank. To my horror, it's more than half full now, and Timothy's head is just above the water. Nick and Pa are trying to open the tank to get him out, but they can't.

"Gabe, take her to safety," I tell Gabe, who picks up Ava and runs with her.

Panic moves me again in a frantic haste and I rush to the tank.

"I can't get it open!" Nick yells as I reach him. He and Pa are trying to yank open the top.

I growl as terror truly takes me. The top of the tank is sealed shut. That is indeed the opening, but I think it's one of those that are activated remotely. That means I was never going to be able to get him out with my bare hands, and they won't be able to either.

The fucking tank is filling up faster. The water is coming from below through some kind of tap, and this tank structure looks like one of the evil devices they used on the prisoners who got the death penalty. They used to do all manner of shit to people. Drowning was just one thing.

I see Nick's gun in his back pocket and climb up and grab it. He jumps down, and so does Pa.

"Boy, that's dangerous," Pa yells.

"It's the only way," I answer and fire the bullet at the base of the tank. A hole pierces through, allowing some of the water to spill out.

Pa takes out his gun too, and we both shoot the same spot until the glass cracks open. The water gushes out in a heavy flood, and my baby screams and screams so hard it shakes my soul.

I run to him and undo his ropes.

When I get him down from the platform, I hug him so hard, and fuck, I don't care that fucking tears roll down my cheeks. I got him, and I'm happy.

What makes me happier is turning back to the platform behind me and seeing Salvatore and Claudius pointing their guns at Ilya. He's on the ground kneeling with his hands behind his head.

Fucker. He'll get his.

It's over.

CHAPTER FORTY-FIVE

Ava

Yuri is lying on the ground near the ivy bush.

His eyes are a cold vacant stare, a horrifying image of the dead. Bullet wounds riddle his body, and his face is as white as a sheet. *Dead.*

On my way up the stairs with Gabe, I saw Dmitri dead too, eyes open just like Yuri.

The same vacant stare, the same pale white of death.

They deserved it, and I'm glad they got it. Part of the wall that enclosed my soul inside me crumbled.

I'm weak from the fire, so weak I just want to lie down. But I can't miss this. This event of vengeance. This event that should have been my death turned into vengeance.

Most of the men are dead. It's just a few here and there who are left.

Ilya is on his knees before Vincent.

I'm standing between two of his brothers—Gabe and Salvatore. Both protected me fiercely.

I'm standing in the gathering of the men who came to make this rescue possible, and I'm watching the moment I've only ever dreamed about.

My uncle brought down to justice and given a taste of his own medicine.

It's just a taste, however, because none of this is enough to make up for what he did.

It's something though. A massive, momentous something that I'm processing. I can't believe it's real.

Ilya has been brought to his knees like the dog he is.

Vincent hands Timothy to his father, who takes him away. I watch him go through the door and soothe his grandson, who's started to cry for Vincent. It's heartbreaking. All of it is. He should never have been dragged into this mess. I will always feel guilty for that.

My gaze returns to Vincent. He's still holding the gun he used to shoot the tank. God... the baby nearly drowned. It was all set up to make certain he would. I was to burn to death and Timothy to drown.

I can't conceive the evil in this mess. I can't begin to accept that evil way of thinking. Heartless and soulless. That is what my uncle is. He and his men, from one to the next. There's no difference. They're all the fucking same.

As I look at him now, I know in my soul that he deserves death too.

Vincent gives Ilya a kick in his face that sends him to the ground, flat on his back, blood spurting from his nose.

"Motherfucking dog! You fucking piece of shit," Vincent snarls and points the gun at him. He pulls the trigger back. *Click-clack*, that's all I hear ring through my ears.

He's ready to shoot him, and I watch. I watch in anticipation of the end.

Then Vincent stops mid-motion, like he just remembered something.

He turns to me.

"Come here," he says.

I take my steps as strongly and confidently as I can. My eyes never leaving Ilya, who has now clocked on to me.

Confidence ripples through me in abundance, filling every pore of my being as I finally face my biggest fears, my biggest secrets, my greatest nightmare.

I stare at Ilya on the ground and want nothing more than to kill him.

"What should I do with him?" Vincent asks, breaking my stare.

I turn to him appreciating the control he's passed to me. It's on the tip of my tongue to tell him I want his death because that is exactly what I want. I want death for him. I want my uncle to suffer death the way he made my parents suffer, all of them.

But... just shooting him here feels like he got off easy.

I look back at my uncle and think long and hard about what I want. If we kill him here, no one will truly know all that he did, and he won't get the full blow he deserves.

The answer comes to me in a spark of thought that feels right.

"Russia should deal with him," I say. As the words fall from my lips, Ilya's eyes go wide with terror. He knows what I mean by that. He damn well knows. He knows I mean the truth. When the brotherhood learns the truth of what he did, how he killed my father, that will be his death and utter humiliation. That will kill him. *They* will kill him.

"I will take him there myself. Hand deliver him to my people. My face will be enough to sentence him," I add. I sound stronger. I don't sound like me.

This is what I became after the storm.

I look back at Vincent. He nods his agreement.

I'm so tired.

Four days have passed since the showdown at the prison, and much has happened in the space of that time.

I went to Russia, returning to my homeland, and I did exactly what I said I would do. Hand delivered my uncle to my people. Vincent made the arrangements. He contacted the president, and then everything fell into place the way it was supposed to. Easy because of who my real father was.

Ilya was shamed and executed sometime yesterday.

I don't know the time, only that it happened. I only went to do my part.

Which was to show my face as who I was. So, I showed my real face. The real me. I died my hair back blonde and looked the way I should look. Like my mother.

Amazing what hair color can do. I looked just like her and like the older version of myself. The former ballerina who was on her way to fame.

I was evidence and testament enough of the truth.

I landed at O'Hare International two hours ago, and as I did, I felt I could put the past behind me for the first time and close the door on that chapter.

I'm on my way back to Vincent's house now, although I know I don't have to be. Tomorrow is supposed to be my last day with him.

This morning, when I checked my account, there was two million dollars in there.

The same two million dollars Dad stole from him.

Its' a fortune to take care of me for the rest of my life, which is just the thing that got to me.

It's a goodbye present, a very expensive goodbye present, one that has significant meaning though.

I don't know anyone who wouldn't be screaming with joy and happiness to wake to such a gift. I can't do that though, because Vincent meant more to me than that.

The car pulls up on the drive, and I get out.

I walk into the house, and Vincent steps out of the living room, caution in his eyes.

He still has bruises on his face from what happened to him.

He looks me over. It's the first time he's seeing me with my hair this color. It must be odd. It was odd to me too to see myself like that. I liked it, so I decided to keep it as it is.

"Hello," he says first and walks up to me.

"Hi." Tears pull at the backs of my eyes, but I smile when he takes a lock of my hair and allows the ends to curl about his thumb.

"You look beautiful. You look like you should." The corners of his lips tip up into a small smile.

"Thank you. How's Timothy?"

"He's okay. He's back to being my little tyke." He grins.

That makes me smile. "I'm glad he's okay."

"He is. Come," he says and puts out his hand for me to take.

I take it and follow him into the living room. He sits me down on the sofa then settles in next to me and faces me.

"Did it all go okay?" he asks.

"It did. I didn't stay for the execution. I didn't need to."

"I understand. I hoped you wouldn't. You shouldn't see a thing like that, no matter how evil the person is," he states with a nod, and I agree.

"Thank you for giving me the power to do that."

"Did it help you?"

"Yes." It helped in a way I can't fully express to anyone. I became the holder of Ilya's fate, the way he was over me. "I feel like I can move past it now. The whole situation and everything helped me to move past my fears."

He touches my hair again. "I'm sorry. I'm sorry any of it happened to you. I feel like I didn't do enough to make them pay."

"Vincent, there's no more you could have done for me to make them pay. The people who hurt me most are dead." There are more guys, more of them who worked for my uncle who hurt me, but I couldn't face them. "There's a new leader being called for the brotherhood. He'll be dealing with the others in Russia who worked for my uncle. I know they'll mete out justice, but I'm done there. I don't know when I'll go back, if ever. This trip felt like a mission of sorts."

"Time will heal you properly now, baby. It will heal you in a different way," he assures me. "When it does, you'll know how you feel about Russia. Until then, focus on you." He gives my hand a gentle squeeze.

"Thank you. Thank you for everything. Absolutely everything. Thank you for saving me." I wipe away a tear.

"You are more than welcome."

"I'm not taking the money though." I shake my head.

He raises his brows. "Why the hell not?" he asks in a lighter tone.

"You gave me two million dollars, Vincent. That's an awful lot of money," I breathe.

"Don't you try to give it back. It's a gift I want you to have."

"I can't take it."

He chuckles. "Ava, I don't know anyone who would turn away money like that. It's in your account, and it's staying there. You will have it. I am sorry about your father, Mark. This all started with him and that two million. You have it. See if you can achieve a dream or two with it. Maybe it may take you back to your first love. Dancing."

Seriousness washes over his face, and the humor fades.

"Can't I just... have you?" That's what I want. It's something I know I won't get, though, from the somber look in his eyes. "Can't I just be with you?"

He shakes his head, and his eyes become glassy. "No."

"Why?"

His gaze clings to mine. "You can't be with me, Ava. You don't belong in my world, and I can't run away from who I am. It will follow me wherever I go. I'll still be the beast. I'll still be the monster in the darkness. When you kiss me, I won't turn into a prince."

Tears runs down my cheeks. "I know what your life involves. I know all too well what can happen, but I still want to be with you."

"I know better than to drag you into a life full of danger when I can put a stop to it now. I can't sit here and pretend that

I will always be there to protect you. I can't. I can't put you in a position where I could lose you and there'd be nothing I'd be able to do about it."

"That's not fair."

"It is."

"Vincent—"

"No, Ava... no."

"Vincent—"

"I love you..." His words cut off mine.

Love me... His words imprint to my soul and are the last things to break down that wall. Love. Love from a man I love too. Love from a man who knows my past, knows what happened to me, and still loves me.

"Ava... I love you enough to let you go, and let you live," he adds, and my being shivers. I don't want him to let me go.

"I love you too, Vincent." I've never said those words to anyone except my parents. I've always dreamed of saying them to the right person, and I am. I'm telling the person who should hear them, but he's telling me he can't be with me.

"Then allow me to do this for you. Allow me to take care of you and do the right thing. You're free now. Free to go and... free of me." He blows out a ragged breath, leans forward, and plants a chaste kiss on my forehead.

When he lets go of my hand, my heart breaks in two.

One last look, and he walks away. I watch him walk out the door and turn the corner. I don't see him anymore.

The tears fall now like pieces of my soul weeping.

CHAPTER FORTY-SIX

Vincent

Two months later...

Pa sits at the head of the table. We're at the family home, and everyone is here.

All the men and their wives.

My father sits with my mother, then there are all my uncles with their wives to his left, and at the right of the table it curves to seat Georgiou and his wife. I look at my brothers for a moment, just to focus and think about how far they've all come.

Nick and Mia, Gabe and Charlotte, Salvatore and Mimi.

My brothers have been men for a very long time now, but it's now that they look all grown up to me. We're here, and they look happy. They look happy with their dolls, as they should be.

Christian is sitting next to me and sees me looking. It's probably clear what I'm thinking about. He gives me a curt nod, and I do the same. We're the only single guys at the table.

This is a rare day to get everyone together like this. The last time it happened in a similar fashion was when Pa announced the restructure. That was the meeting room. We're in the dining room now, sharing one last meal with my parents before they leave tomorrow.

It's been a good day, and I'm still trying to keep the mask on that I'm fine.

I'm ready now to take over. I got myself there, to that point where I can look at the big picture and know I can do it. It's a job, and I'll give it my all to be in charge of the family and the business.

My heart's not here though.

It's somewhere else. It's stuck on the last time I saw Ava. It's stuck at the place where I told her I loved her then let her go.

I'm stuck there like I'm in limbo, my thoughts still with the girl, the second woman in my life to have my heart, mind, body, and soul. She owns them all, and now she exists in my mind. In my memories. Like Sorcha.

I've stayed out of her life since that night, becoming a ghost. It was exactly like we never happened, except she's always on my mind.

Me and her. I have that fantasy of us being those people who meet at the coffee shop, and sometimes I allow myself to think about what would have happened to them next.

She'll still be in Florida working with one month left to go. I hope she's happy. That's what I hope. I hope she gets to live her dreams and be safe.

I hope she forgets me.

Pa stands up and raises his glass of wine. I focus my attention on him, just like the others.

He looks around the table at everyone. "It's time. It's been a great day. It's been great having everyone here," Pa says. It's the most emotion I've ever seen him show. "Even better to be in good spirits. Angela and I fly back to Sicily in the morning. We're going to miss you all a great deal. I know you are in good hands though. Very good hands."

His gaze turns to me, and his smile widens.

"Thank you, Pa," I say. "I'll try to be half the man you are."

"My boy, you'll be more than the man I am. You will not be half or any part of me. You'll just be you, and it will be more than enough. I can rest in our homeland knowing you're all safe and well taken care of."

I stare at him, lost for words. That's the best thing he's ever said about me.

He reaches out his hand to mine, and I stand, but I don't shake his hand. I hug him, and he chuckles.

"Thank you, Pa," I breathe. It's strange. I feel like a boy again. Like that boy I was when I knew I would have to take charge one day.

"You are more than welcome."

When we pull apart, he holds up his hand for everyone to see the ring my grandfather gave to him when he became boss of the family. He takes it off and holds it out to me.

"For you, *Capo Familia*," he says as I take it.

I place it on my finger, and everyone claps.

Pa places a hand on my shoulder and nods his final approval.

I smile back feeling the accomplishment.

I stare at the display of ballerinas in the case in the room I devoted to Sorcha. They are the last to be packed away.

All the other trinkets have been boxed up and the photos placed in albums. The painting has been wrapped up too. That was the hardest thing to take down.

As I did, however, something lifted from my shoulders. The weight of guilt freed itself from me. It was as if the memory of Sorcha sealed to my heart instead of the visual reminder of the painting I wanted to see every day.

I arranged a nice area in the attic for her things. All that's left in the room now is this case with the ballerinas.

Yesterday, when I went to see her at the cemetery, I got

the strong impression that I should do this. Like she wanted me to do it. Pack her things away and keep her in my heart instead.

When I got back, I started packing up.

I stopped here because it reminded me of Ava. Not so much of that night when she came up here and was looking around. The ballerinas just reminded me of her in general.

The little ballerinas all look so delicate and pure. Unbroken and angelic. Just like her.

She'll be back in Chicago next week. Back to her life as it was before me.

She's been out of my life for the last three months, and I'm sure she's... moved on. I want her to. I want her to have met someone else, and I hope whoever it is will treat her right. Treat her the way she deserves.

Footsteps sound behind me, and I turn to see Marguerite coming in.

When I came back yesterday, she saw me up here but didn't say anything.

I think it was because she probably wanted me to do this a long time ago.

"Are you okay, Vinny?" she asks, crossing the distance between us.

"No," I answer with the truth, and she taps my cheeks in that habitual way.

"You did a lot in here, Boss," she muses, looking around the room.

"Yeah. It's just these to go. But ...I... I don't know..."

"Do they remind you of someone else?" she asks, giving me a knowing look.

"Yeah.... Um... Ava. She liked them."

"You know you don't have to get rid of everything, but if it helps, it helps. If you're having trouble letting it go, maybe it's okay to keep them, since they both liked the dancers." She nods her head.

"I don't know, Marguerite. I feel like I need to get rid of all of it. Get them both out of my head. Out of my mind. You know, out of sight, out of mind."

"Will it help? Will it get them out of your head?" she asks with a pensive stare.

I shake my head and draw in a breath. Focusing on her, I try to guess what she's thinking.

She hasn't said anything about Ava, but I know she has an opinion on what's happened. Apart from that day months ago when she told me I needed to move on, she hasn't given me her opinion since.

"What?" I ask because I can see a million things racing through that very wise head of hers.

"Do you really want to know?"

I dip my head, gearing myself up to hear it. "I want to know, Marguerite. What are you thinking?"

"I think you loved Ava, and you were lucky to have love twice. I think that she loved you too, and I know the real reason you aren't with her is because you're afraid."

I press my lips together and rivet my gaze to hers. There's little point in trying to tell her she's wrong when she's right.

"Don't you think it's wise for me to be afraid? It's dangerous. My world is dangerous, Marguerite."

"Vincent Giordano, you are the boss of this family. You stare danger in the face and laugh. It is not danger you are worried about. If it were, you'd send your boy away to live in some kind of high security fortress with metal around it. He is still here with you because you know that the best person to protect him is you. You're not worried about danger. Your fear is to do with your heart. You're scared to have it broken again the way it did when you found Sorcha dead."

I hang my head down, holding it there as truth molds to my heart. My cold, dead heart, which only started beating again when I was with Ava.

Marguerite struck a nerve deep inside me. One I never knew anyone could see. She saw straight through me, saw straight through the mask I wore and showed to others.

She lifts my head and cups my face with a smile.

"You shouldn't be afraid of heartbreak. Not in the way you are." Her smile widens, and she looks at me with warmth emitting from her eyes.

"I can't help it."

"You can. It's far better to have loved and lost than never to have loved at all. It's better to love and not allow fear to rule your heart. It's better to live your life in love and love each other than be without it. Danger is everywhere, Vincent. It's everywhere. People can drop dead from anything. You can die from anything. Do not hide behind that excuse." She releases me and nods.

"I don't know what to do."

"Do what your heart tells you. Whatever that is will be the right thing to do."

She bows her head with reverence and takes her leave.

She walks out of the room, but her words stick in my mind.

Do what my heart tells me...

My heart has been screaming at me. It's so loud it's deafening.

I already know what it wants me to do.

The question is, can I do it?

Can I move past the fear in my soul and do what my heart needs me to do?

I wish I could.

CHAPTER FORTY-SEVEN

Ava

"You must be so happy. It's such a massive accomplishment, Ava," Holly bubbles.

She throws herself down on the sofa and grabs a handful of sweets from the bowl I've set on the table.

"It was fantastic."

"That's the word I'd describe for the issue. The way you wrote the article was just fantastic. I bet you get a Reader's Choice Award for it or something." She laughs.

I smile. Such a thing would be nice.

I got back last night and spent the day unpacking and resting. And ...*thinking*.

I'm smiling like I have been for the last three months I've been in Florida, but I'm still thinking about him. *Vincent*.

I don't know how I'm supposed to forget him. I don't know how I'm supposed to fall so hard for a man like him and then just un-love him. I was with him in a very unconventional taboo relationship for a handful of weeks, and I know I'll never feel the way I did about him with anyone else.

"Ava... you okay?" Holly asks, waving her hand in front of my face. "You're miles away."

"I'm sorry."

"Mind still in Florida?" she smiles.

"Not so much. I loved being out there, but I'm happy to be back. I... want to organize a memorial for my father."

Her face falls and fills with sadness. "Oh God," Holly winces. "I'm sorry. It was bad of me to forget. I mean... I didn't forget. I did remember. I was just excited about Florida."

"I know, and I didn't think badly of you," I assure her.

"What's going to happen?"

"I'll organize a small memorial and invite a few people who knew him. Then I guess that will be it."

There was so much to sort out after I left, so much I had to leave behind. Once the police did what they needed to in the little that remained of Dad's apartment, I hired someone to salvage what they could from the remains. They didn't find much, just random things here and there. They're things I can remember him by though.

"Ava, I'm so sorry. I'm still in shock."

She thinks it was an explosion. Nobody knows the truth. No one but Vincent and his family knows the horror of what I went through that day when I found Dad dead. Killed with a message for me.

I've had to file it all to the back of my mind.

"You'll get through this, Ava." Holly nods her head. "I'm here if you need me."

"I know. You've been there for me more than anyone else. It's more than I can ask for. I'm grateful for you."

"We're friends. Of course, I'm going to be there for you."

I had to leave so quickly after the whole ordeal. Freddie wanted me to take care of myself and forget the trip. I didn't think that would have been healthy for me to do. Instead, I postponed it for a week.

That was after I last saw Vincent. That week was spent tying up loose ends, speaking with the police, and preparing to leave. The police knew the explosion was caused by an actual bomb, but because the CCTV was down that day in the apartment complex, they don't know who did it. That also meant they didn't see me going inside the building that day or what happened after.

"Have you heard from Vincent?" she asks tentatively. We haven't spoken about him much. Every time she tries to ask I side step her questions.

I shake my head. "No. It didn't work out." It didn't, and it's wise for me to forget about him. It's going to take me a long time to do that. It may take forever, but it's what I have to do.

"Didn't he ever message at all?"

"No, it's just one of those things, I guess, that you think may work but they don't. I'll be okay." I want to change the subject. I need to. No one will ever know what happened to me during that phase of my life, and it's best that I move on.

Holly takes the hint that I don't want to talk about him anymore.

"Tell me about Florida," she says with a smile.

That I can do. We spoke on the phone every chance we got, but I was really busy. Coral had me doing all kinds of things. It was great to get to know her, and she even got me involved in the charity work she was doing too.

I start talking about my adventure in Florida. It's a distraction.

When I get like that, it feels like my mind splits in two. Part of me can be on autopilot while the other can work through the issues on my mind, and my heart.

I thought a trip to the coffee shop was in order before work.

I got here about twenty minutes ago and ordered a latte. I sat in the little booth I always sit in when I'm here alone.

Usually I'm here with Holly, but sometimes, I just like to come by myself.

It's a great place to think when you need to take stock of your life.

I have much to think about. I still have two million dollars sitting in my bank account that I haven't touched. I haven't needed to because my job in Florida was an all-expenses-paid trip paid for by the company, and my salary covered my bills here.

Now I'm back. I feel like if I touch it, I've accepted that it's goodbye.

I'm still holding on, *foolishly*, and I need to let go.

I take a sip of my drink and remember that night at The Dark Odyssey when Vincent and I created that fantasy about what we would be if we'd met under different circumstances.

The couple in the coffee shop.

Just the thought of the fantasy brings tears to my eyes, and one tracks down my cheek.

I'm so stupid.

I shouldn't do this to myself. I reach forward to grab a napkin to dry my tears. I hate crying in public.

I dab my cheeks and glance over to the counter where the Barista is serving a customer. That's when I see him.

Just like always when I look at him, my breath is stolen away.

Vincent Giordano is standing by the counter, his eyes fixed on me, piercing and vibrant. He's just as handsome as I remember.

My lips part, and I can't move. I can barely breathe. I can only stare like I did in that fantasy we conjured up.

When he takes a step forward, my heart stops.

The air thickens around me with anticipation, and I watch him stride to me with confidence and grace. It's not until he gets to me that I rise to my feet.

He stops a breath away and looks me over.

"Hi... I'm... Vincent Giordano. I noticed you sitting here, so I thought I'd come over and say hello," he says in that deep baritone timbre that fills my fantasies and dreams.

Hot tears of joy blind my eyes, choking my voice, then slide down my cheeks.

I swallow hard, thinking of the fantasy. It's here. He's here. It's happening.

As elevation lifts my soul, I throw my arms around him. I can't speak, so I show him how I feel and hug him like I never want to let him go. He holds me too, cupping my head, and I feel like I'm whole.

I can't believe a simple touch from him can make me feel so whole.

"Hello," I answer, and he holds me closer, close to his heart.

It's a place where I finally feel like I belong.

EPILOGUE

Ava

Eight months later...

"You're going to spoil that boy rotten," Marguerite says, looking down at Timothy curled up in my lap.

He looks so small when he's sleeping. I love when he falls asleep on my lap after I've read him a bedtime story. It's our thing we do in the evenings before Vincent gets home.

"I think I will. Is that bad to set out to spoil your kids?" I chuckle. I call him mine, because he is. He became mine the day I stepped back into this house, and I will look after him as such for as long as I live.

Marguerite laughs. "Maybe it's okay to spoil them with love. Not too much spoilage though. Too much of anything is never good."

"What are we talking about here?" Vincent says, coming through the door.

Marguerite and I both look at him at the same time.

"Spoilage. I think I may be guilty of spoiling my son rotten. I can't resist though." I laugh and gently ease him onto his pillow. He stirs but then settles back into his slumber.

"Then don't," Vincent says and reaches out his hand to me.

I go to him, slipping into his embrace, and he gives me a brief kiss. Marguerite watches us with awe, and I smile back at her.

"We'll try not to be too late," Vincent tells her.

"Take your time," she bubbles, then my wonderful husband ushers me out the door.

We've been married for five months, and our lives have been filled with happiness. We spend our evenings together either having one wild adventure after another at The Dark Odyssey or having a quiet night like tonight when we head to the ballet.

The ballet was his idea a few months back. Just us going together, and I loved it. Watching has never been the same as doing it, but watching it with him is a different magical experience altogether.

"So, I'm looking forward to tonight," he says as we walk down the stairs.

"Watching the ballet?" I smile. I know it's not his thing. It's nice that he does it for me though.

"No, watching you watch it," he answers with that smile that always melts my heart.

I stop and gaze up at him. "Thank you."

"What for, baby?"

"Everything. I love you so much."

He presses his head to mine and kisses the top of my nose.

"I love you too, Bellezza."

Every time he tells me that, I feel it all over. Inside me and all over.

I realized that the people in the coffee shop weren't a fantasy.

They were always us, and every day that we're together is another fantasy waiting to happen.

My dark knight in shining armor made me whole again.

Vincent

I stand back and watch her in the garden with Timothy.

She's playing with him in the little sand pit and they're making a castle.

The both of them get the biggest smiles on their faces when they see me.

What's even better than their smiles is them rushing up to me.

It's the best thing about coming home every day.

This part when I hold them and I know they're mine.

My boy and my girl, my wife.

Timothy squirms out of my arms and rushes back over to play in the sand pit. The sun picks out the lighter parts of his hair.

I continue to hold Ava and beam down at her in my arms.

"I love when you get home early," she says standing on the tips of her toes to give me a kiss.

"You love when I come home early because it means more bed room time for us."

"Busted, can you blame a girl? It's no bad thing to fit in as much bedroom time as possible." She giggles.

"No it's not."

"Besides, how else are we going to fit in the other two children you want?"

I smile wide and crouch down to kiss her stomach. She's only a few weeks pregnant and we've both been obsessed with the news.

I hold her out looking at her tiny frame and think of how she healed me.

"I'm not complaining," I answer standing up. I cup her face and pull her in for a kiss.

As she kisses me I feel like the prince.
She really was the princess who tamed the beast inside me.
She was solace for my soul and I love her.
Following my heart was one of the best decisions I ever made.

THANK YOU SO MUCH FOR READING.
I HOPE YOU ENJOYED READING ABOUT MY TRULY SEXY ITALIAN STALLION, VINCENT GIORDANO AND AVA, THE SASSY HEROINE WHO STOLE HIS HEART.
IF YOU DID I CAN'T WAIT TO SHARE CHRISTIAN AND LILLY'S STORY WITH YOU IN TAKE ME.

ACKNOWLEDGMENTS

For my readers.
Always for you.
Thank you for reading my stories.
I hope you continue to enjoy my wild adventures xx

ABOUT THE AUTHOR

Faith Summers is the Dark Contemporary Romance pen name of USA Today Bestselling Author, Khardine Gray.

Warning!! Expect wild romance stories of the scorching hot variety and deliciously dark romance with the kind of alpha male bad boys best reserved for your fantasies.

Come to the dark side and follow her here:
★Reader Group- The Dark Odyssey - https://www.facebook.com/groups/462522887995800/
★ mailing list – https://www.subscribepage.com/faithsummersreadergroup
★ Amazon https://www.amazon.com/author/faithsummers

Made in the USA
Columbia, SC
04 November 2021